The DESIRE

KAREN DEEN

Contact

For all the news on upcoming books,
visit Karen at:
www.karendeen.com.au
contact@karendeen.com.au
Facebook: Karen Deen Author
Instagram: karendeen_author
TikTok: karendeenauthor

Dedication

To every person who has ever doubted where they fit in this world, we see you and adore you.
There is always a place for you to just be yourself.
If you can't find it, then make it.
Nobody gets to define who you are, except you.

THE DESIRE

KAREN DEEN

Prologue

REMINGTON

"Merry Christmas," Nic announces as we all sit around the table in his suite at his hotel in Rome.

This time last year I was off in the Bahamas, but instead, Nic insisted that Flynn, Forrest, and I spend Christmas with him and his family. It's different than spending it on my own, but I couldn't say no to him when he needed us. Since my mum and dad started traveling to Inverness in Scotland every year to be with my sister and her family, I try to find an excuse to be anywhere but there with them.

Kids, a cramped house full of noise, people, and of course, the cold that seeps right into your bones and brings bucketloads of snow that can leave us all snowed in together. All things that don't rate high on my list of fun experiences at the best of times, but especially the kids part; not my scene at all. I always make sure I see my parents before they leave and give them presents to take up to my sister's for the rest of my family. And then I plan my escape vacation, or I blame work. We are, after all, in the hospitality industry, and it's a busy time of the year. I make out how important I am, and that I can't be far from the office, in case we have a major problem.

This trip counts as work, especially since I'm currently dining and staying in one of the Darby Hotels which is who I work for. The only thing I hate is seeing the disappointment on my mother's face every year, but I'm sure as soon as she is with her grandchildren, she forgets all about me.

Raising our glasses with Nic's toast, I look around, and I can see on everyone's face that we're all glad he finally went after Tori. This woman had him twisted inside out, and it wasn't fun to be around him while it all fell apart. He was a freaking nightmare the whole three months she was away, but it did make him wake the hell up—his words, not mine, although we were all thinking it.

Nic drove me, especially, fucking crazy the whole time! Wanting updates almost hourly it felt like, on where she was, was she okay, did she need him, was she seeing anyone else? The last question almost killed him waiting for my answer.

I wanted to say, "*No, you dickhead, why would she do that? She is so desperately in love with you, but she's just off doing what women do—which is making you pay for hurting her.*"

Better him than me. I'm not the settling down kind of man.

There's too much to do in life, and being committed to anyone will just slow me down. Work is restrictive enough, but I love my job, so it doesn't worry me. Being head of security and IT intelligence for Nicholas Darby and The Darby Hotel chain is like my dream job. Working alongside three men who have become my best friends and in a job that has me traveling all over Europe, I couldn't have landed a more perfect role for me.

Life changed a few years ago when Nic took over the family business, and once the four of us connected, we had the dream team. He's the boss but never treats us like that. We work on the basis of mutual respect and brotherhood. You have my back and I'll have yours. It's as simple as that.

Before I started working here, I had been wandering from job to job over the years, which has helped me gain valuable experience in my career field. But it also allowed me to see amazing things, have adventures, and chase the adrenaline rush, which is what I crave the most.

I almost killed my mother with worry when I was growing up. I was the stereotypical kid with no fear, jumping off roofs, riding bikes like a maniac, sitting on the handlebars while friends were steering. But as I got older and turned eighteen, not needing her permission for anything, the daredevil stunts just got more intense. The first time I told her I was going bungee jumping, she threw her hands in the air and declared, "*I give up. I don't want to know anymore until after you have done whatever crazy-ass thing you are going to do and that you have survived.*"

Life just got more exciting from that moment on. The thrill I've felt in every single danger I faced is the best rush. Sure, sex is up there but in a different way. They say variety is the spice of life, and believe me, I have had plenty of spice. I slept my way around the world— in a respectful way, of course. I've met a lot of beautiful women who have turned my head but none of this love at first sight that people talk about. Lust is a powerful thing, and I think people confuse that with love in that first initial interaction. It makes for great sex, but then real life comes into it, and that lust can very quickly turn into a drag of trying to mix your life with someone else's wants and needs.

I'm a selfish bastard, and I'll freely admit to it!

Flynn's voice jolts me out of my thoughts. "Yes, Nic, finally you are merry, and the grumpy jerk has left the building," he declares as we all clink glasses to celebrate the happy season.

"If there weren't parents in the room then I would reply to that comment, but I'll refrain right now." Nic smirks at Flynn and the rest of us, including Nic and Tori's parents, who are just laughing at them both, knowing that Flynn is right.

Dinner was perfect, as expected. Nic would not settle for anything less, and you'd have to be a ballsy chef to serve anything less than the best quality to the four top executives of the whole company.

Time has gotten away from us, and the parents left a few hours ago, leaving us four men, Nic's girlfriend Tori, and her best friend Elouise.

"This was nice, but it's time for you all to fuck off now." Nic stands and motions to the door.

"Nicholas, you can't say that." Tori jumps up, but she's wobbling a little on her feet, and he wraps his arms around her protectively.

"You bet I can. I only have an hour left to play Santa Claus with you before the day is over." Nic's glare tells us all what that means. And I'm not waiting around to witness any more of this over-the-top loving between these two.

"That's my cue to leave," Forrest declares, standing up from his place on the couch, while the rest of us follow. The table is scattered with wine and champagne glasses, evidence of the great night of laughs and fun we had.

"Did you FaceTime Mum and Dad yet?" Flynn asks Forrest as they head toward the suite door. For two brothers, they couldn't be any different if they tried. Although they have similar looks, personality wise, it's like chalk and cheese.

"No. Come back to my room and we can do it at the same time. That way we can support each other to get through the crying and constant talking over each other that we are going to get. She has already thanked me twenty times for sending them to New York for a holiday. You know this call is going to painful." Forrest, for once, is a bit more relaxed than normal. He is the serious one in the group, and it makes sense because he is the chief financial officer, a job that would bore the shit out of me, but he loves it.

"Ugh, if I have to," Flynn complains.

"You do, so move your ass." Forrest rolls his eyes at his younger brother as they leave.

To be honest, we are all very relaxed after good food, beautiful wine, and great company all night. No one is drunk, but you can tell the defenses are down, and it's nice for a change.

"Rem, can you see Lou to her room, please?" Nic asks, his hand landing on my shoulder, squeezing it in appreciation.

"It's okay, I'm only a few floors below you," Lou says in her sweet little voice as she comes up beside us.

"Not a chance. I don't care if you are next door, we don't let a female friend walk on her own, at night, after a few drinks," Nic replies in his deep voice as Tori looks up at him in admiration for looking after her friend.

I have only met Elouise a few times. She's beautiful and she will turn any man's eye, including mine each time I see her, but personality wise she's so not my type. Quiet, reserved, and conservative at times, all the things I'm not. Although, when she's with Tori, she lightens up, and with a few drinks in her can match wit with the best of us. For some reason Flynn seems to think she is his type, but he's definitely dreaming. She could never keep up with him.

Both Tori and Elouise are thirteen years younger than Nic but only ten years younger than me. I'm the baby of our group, being thirty-six, while they are all around forty or over. The girls might be younger and have no real worldly experience, but they fit in with our group perfectly. Elouise might be the quieter one when we're around, yet from what I've seen, Tori is a fiery one, and she can hold her own, that's for sure. She has proven that already. Anyone who gets Nicholas Darby to settle down has tenacity way above her age and life experience.

"What he said," I reply and point my thumb over my shoulder toward where Nic is now standing, then I take her hand and link it through my arm. It's warm, but so tiny as her little fingers wrap around my bicep. I pat her hand to reassure her.

"I don't want to bother you, Remington." The squeak in her voice makes me look down at her. Oh yeah, there is no way she would cope with Flynn, although he hasn't given up trying.

"No chance of that. We're on the same floor. Now stop worrying and let's get out of here before we see something neither of us want to be witness to." Her giggle tells me she knows exactly what I mean.

The door of the suite closes behind us, and our footsteps are hardly noticeable on the expensive Italian wool carpet in the corridor. Silence falls effortlessly between us, and the trip in the elevator is not long, but I can tell I make her nervous. It's not intentional, but the way she's looking at the floor and scuffing her feet is a dead give-away. The ding of the elevator doors opening has her looking up, and as we step out, I turn to the right, heading to her room.

"How do you know which room I'm in?" Her legs are moving fast, trying to keep up with my stride.

"Head of security, remember? I know everything about everyone in our little circle." I chuckle at her shocked look. Reaching her door, I use my card that opens all the rooms belonging to our group. It is for safety only, and I would never use it unless there was imminent danger.

"What… how did you do that? That's…"

I stand to the side and push the door open for her to enter. "Creepy, weird, yeah, I know, but it's for your own safety. I need to be able to get to you in a hurry if there is ever a problem. But rest assured, I would never use it for any other reason. Your personal space is just that, unless I need to protect you."

Surprisingly she accepts that and just steps past me into her room, turning to look me directly in the eye. "You really are the eternal tough guy, aren't you?"

I can't hold in the laughter at her seriousness. "Yes, Elouise, I'm your private bodyguard whether you like it or not. It comes with the territory now that you're close to the boss man."

"But I'm just a little nobody." Again, her eyes drop to the ground. Oh, this woman really needs a good dose of self-confidence.

"Wrong, you are Elouise Patterson, teacher and tamer of the little people with snotty noses who can't tie their shoelaces. Award winner of best teacher in your county last year, and from what I hear, a very well-respected staff member at your school. Daughter to Jan and Bob Patterson and sister to Robert, Neil, and Arthur who are all older than you. You are the only one in your family to have attended university, and also, impressively passing with honors. I'm sure all of that makes you an important someone to a lot of people." I didn't mean to spew out all my intel on her, but I have a photographic memory for the fine details, and once I recall information, it just all comes rushing back into my brain.

"Oh my…" Her hands come up on to her cheeks that are now blushing at how much I know about her. "Do you know what size underwear I wear too?"

"Do I need to answer that?" I say, chuckling at her comment.

She shakes her head at me with a smile that tells me she is impressed with her witty reply.

"Now, is there anything else you need help with? I trust your room is to your liking." I'm trying to keep the conversation going with her to stop her from being so embarrassed.

"Um, yes, it's so posh. I've never stayed anywhere like this," she says, turning her back to me and waving her arm around the room. She is not in a suite but one of our best king-sized rooms in the hotel.

"We aim to please. Well, I will let you settle in for the night. I'm sure you would love to climb into the deep spa bath and finish the night off with some relaxation to send you to sleep." My hand is still on the door handle, not stepping into the room uninvited.

"If I knew how to work it then I might have, but I'll just take a shower instead." She slowly turns to me with a look of disappointment on her face that she is trying to hide but not very well. I have a feeling she couldn't get away with lying even if she tried.

"Why didn't you call the concierge or one of us and we could have shown you?" I can feel the sternness on my face. "That's what we're here for. Damn, surely we aren't that scary." I know I can be at times when I'm in strict work mode, but I would hope she isn't that worried about me.

"I didn't want to make a fuss." The look she gives me, I feel like there is more to it than that.

Shit!

It dawns on me now. She's embarrassed and doesn't want to say anything. Nic mentioned that she hasn't traveled at all, and staying here must be like going from eating two-minute noodles to caviar in one swift jump.

I need to make her feel more comfortable here.

"Can I come in and show you? I know they are hard to work

out. Took me a few tries before I got the hang of it." Waiting for her to acknowledge, I start walking straight into the bathroom.

Everything is so tidy, and it's like nothing has been touched. Hopefully the more she travels with us, she will become more comfortable in her room. I make a note to talk to Nic about it so he can get Tori to have a little chat with her. Elouise never has to worry about cost when she is with us. Nic has more money than he will ever know what to do with, and it's my job to protect him and his fortune.

Turning the taps and adjusting the temperature to nice and warm, I reach for the bubble bath on the vanity to make it perfect.

"No, wait! I'm, um… allergic, yes, that's it, allergic to bubbles." The nervous look on her face tells me it's a lie, but I'll run with it.

"Shame, nothing sexier than a beautiful woman in a bath full of bubbles. The sense of mystery is fucking hot. Leaves a man wondering what's beneath the surface."

Her head whips up, and she stares at me so hard I swear she can see straight through me.

Fuck, why did I say that? I shouldn't embarrass her.

But what I wasn't expecting was the visceral reaction to the vision that is now in my head.

Both of us stand frozen, just looking at each other.

Think, fucker, say something.

"I'll get you the other bubbles then. They will look just as good on you in the bath." I charge past her out of the bathroom and straight to the bar fridge. Grabbing the bottle of champagne, I crack the seal and start to pour it into a glass before she comes up behind me.

"No, why did you do that? I don't want to waste Nic's money." Now there is a bit more oomph in her voice. She knows how to stand her ground when she needs to.

"I can assure you, he can afford to treat you to a champagne or two." Turning, I push the glass into her hand. "Drink up, we don't want to waste it." And I need a moment.

Marching back into the bathroom, I turn off the water and start the spa bath motor, and the water starts bubbling away nicely.

I push my palm into my hard cock, willing it to go down. I count to one hundred and think of all the grossest things I can imagine—and I've seen a few in my travels. Bull eyeballs, fried monkey balls, fresh brains with the blood still coating it. Why the hell isn't any of that working?

I'm not sure how long I've been standing in here, but music starts wafting in from the bedroom.

What is she doing?

I stand in the doorway and lean against the door jamb just looking at her. She has kicked off her shoes, the champagne glass is empty, and she is swinging to the music with the bottle in her hand.

How long was I in the bathroom after I turned off the water?

The song "Sexual Healing" by Marvin Gaye is floating out from her phone. Her hips are swaying, eyes closed, and hand waving over her head in time with the music. The red fitted shirt hugs her boobs as it crosses over them, leaving her cleavage now visible, and the bottom of the top creeps up her stomach, leaving her bare skin on show.

Pale and flawless, every bad thought I tried to conjure up in the bathroom is now long gone. Shit, is that a bellybutton piercing? The tiniest sparkle catches the light as she moves.

Holy. Fucking. Shit.

I would never have expected that. Maybe there is more to this little mouse than she has shown us. What else is she hiding under those clothes?

Oh no, do not go there. Shut that thought down right now.

My cock is throbbing, and it's wrong, so fucking wrong!

Fuck the bubble bath, she looks fucking enticing just like this!

My feet are moving across the room against my brain's instructions, but I just want a touch. Nothing more, just one dance.

Elouise's eyes are still closed, but she knows I'm behind her. I can tell the way her hips are now moving in more a circular motion, trying to entice me to take that last step.

I wish I had more restraint, but I'm fighting a losing battle when the words are whispered from her lips. "Dance with me, Rem."

The innocence is gone, and the champagne courage has taken over. How can I deny such a sweet request?

"Just one dance." The rasp in my voice already tells me I won't be stopping at one, but I'm trying.

"Mm-hm." Her voice is smooth and rolls off her tongue with so much sexual tension as I step in behind her, and my cock is wedged hard in her ass crack, so there is no way she can't feel what she's doing to me. I wrap my right hand around her waist and land straight on her piercing, and I'm unable to hold back the growl that leaves my mouth. At the same time, I run my left hand down the side of her thigh and rub up and down on her white skirt.

"You're quite the little Christmas decoration tonight, aren't you, but far from the fucking sacred angel you portray to the world."

She wraps her arm around the back of my neck, with those long red nails with the Christmas pictures on them scratching my skin and making every muscle in my body hard.

"I'm a good girl." Her breathy voice signals that her body is as on fire as mine is. The way she is rubbing her ass against my cock, she is far from a good girl.

"Maybe outside this room, but right here, right now, you want to be my bad girl, don't you?" I whisper, running my nose up her neck and hovering just beside her ear. Every sexual pheromone in her body is lighting me up.

"Yes, fuck yessss." She moans like she is already close to coming just from her seductive dance.

"This is a bad idea. I don't do relationships." I bite down on her neck and then lick the sweat off her.

"Good. I don't want to date you, I just want to fuck you." Who is this little vixen in my arms? Because she isn't the woman I just sat next to at dinner.

"You say that now." I should be pulling away, but her hand grasps tighter, the nails digging into my skin, and it feels fucking awesome.

"I've never had a one-night stand. Just once I want to do something reckless, want to stop being the perfectly boring teacher that everyone sees." She turns in my arms to face me so quickly that the bottle of champagne drops to the floor. Thank God it's empty and only a small one.

"I trust you, Rem, be my one-night stand. But you can't tell anyone. It'll be our secret." Both her hands now running over my chest, and I can't deny her, but I need to be sure.

"Are you drunk?" I ask, trying to keep my hands off her for a moment until I'm sure.

"No, just so horny. Alcohol makes me super horny, and I'm sick of using my vibrator to fix it."

And that's where my restraint snaps.

"Merry. Fucking. Christmas." I slam my mouth down on hers and taste the lips that have been taunting me since I walked in from the bathroom.

This is a big mistake, so if I'm going to do something stupid, I may as well make it worth the risk.

The hint of champagne is still in her mouth as my tongue dominates her. I'm not holding back. She is begging for me to help her let loose, and that is exactly what I'm going to do. If she wants to be a bad girl, then I'm happy to take it all.

My hands are on both sides of her skirt that was knee-length at dinner, but now I've got it hiked up to the crease of her ass cheeks. Which means everything is nice and available to me to take.

As I lift her onto the coffee table, her little squeal and giggle is like an aphrodisiac.

"Dance for me, naughty girl, and show me how that hot little body looks… naked. Strip for me. Show me how bad you can be."

She wants to feel sexy. Her cheeks are pink, blushing at the thought of it, but I'm going to help her.

Her phone switches to the next song, "Temperature Rising" by Tory Lanez, and it's perfect.

I sit down on the couch in front of her. She's still swaying, but her confidence is slipping.

"Dance for me, and I'll make it worth your while," I demand. Pulling my shirt from my pants, I start to unbutton it slowly. "You strip, and I'll follow you," I suggest, giving her the incentive she needs. Spreading my legs wide, I palm my cock that is clearly visible how hard it is.

Biting her bottom lip, I know where she wants to place that cock. And that red lipstick she's wearing is going look perfect on my skin when I give it to her.

"If you want this, you need to earn it. I want to see you wet and desperate."

Her hands are now moving, and the look in her eyes has changed. There is no innocence left.

Oh yes, baby, show me what you're hiding.

The skirt I pushed up is already showing me the white lace of her panties and her bare fucking pussy, one I'm going to take great pleasure in running my tongue through as soon as she's naked. She unbuttons her white skirt, sliding the zipper down, until it's hanging loose on her waist. She doesn't waste any time letting it fall down her legs, and she kicks it to the side with a flick of her foot. She is really in the moment now.

My shirt is completely unbuttoned, open with my chest on show, and I can see she's turned on by what she sees. That makes two of us, baby!

"Show me those tits, now." Watching her run her hands over them isn't enough. I want to see them, nipples rock hard and ready for me to bite while she is screaming my name.

"Only if you show me your cock." Well, look at that. The bad girl is now in the room.

"Do you deserve it?" Undoing my belt, I slide it through the loops in my pants. Popping the button as she starts teasing me with the bottom of her red shirt, pulling it up and showing me part of her breasts.

"Show me and I'll prove I do."

Flipping her shirt over her luscious tits, she pushes her breasts together so they stand out, ready for me to devour them.

I can't get the zipper down quick enough, and there is nothing holding my cock back. Already the tip of it is sticking out from the top of my briefs and leaking pre-come everywhere. I need relief. Pushing my pants and briefs down, I let my cock bounce free and stand straight up on my abs. I can't help taking it in my hand and squeezing hard just above my balls. I must slow this down. She is taking all my control away from me, and that has never happened before.

"Prove it!" I can barely voice in more than a sexual growl.

I want her, and I want her bad.

I was wrong about her not being my type, because sexually, that body is on the top of my Christmas list this year.

Her top hits the floor, and her tits are bouncing as she closes her eyes, hands in the air and her hips lost in the movement in the music. This is the most sensual thing I've witnessed.

Before I can say the words, it's like she can read my mind. Her arms dropping, her left hand settles on her breast and squeezes to give her some relief, and then what I'm not expecting.

She slides her right hand under the white lace panties, and I can see her rubbing her own clit. The moans coming from her as she is lost in the moment are so sinful. I want to watch her get herself off, but my cock has other ideas. I promised her better than making herself come.

"Stop!" My hoarse voice stills her body, eyes flashing open with a small sense of panic.

"I'm the one who is going to make you fucking come like you've never come before." Standing, I drop the rest of my clothes. Her body is shivering from her heightened awareness of my naked body so close to her.

"Perfect." I take one of her nipples into my mouth and suck while I run my hands over her body covered in a fine sheen of sweat. Her body is practically on fire from her dance performance that was just for me. Already I'm feeling greedy, and I never want to think of her giving that pleasure to any other man. She's not mine and never will be, but it doesn't mean I can't feel possessive of her.

"Remmmm…" Her body becomes weak in my arms as I continue to bite and tease her supple tits.

From the time I felt the first twitch in my cock as a teenager, when the testosterone was kicking in growing up, the rush always came from looking at a set of nice, plump tits. It's my thing, and I fucking love to feel them, taste them, and slide my cock between them, the head of my cock reaching in and out of many a woman's wet mouth as I fuck my way home. I love to coat her face in come as I shoot it into her mouth and watch her lick it off her lips. A satisfying good time before I escort her out the door.

But tonight, I want to feast on all of her, to show Elouise what it's like to be devoured by a man. Setting the bar so high she will never settle for anything less, or if she does, then she will always remember this Christmas night.

Her breast pops from my mouth, my lips still tingling at the sensation of her hard tantalizing nipple. I drop to my knees, my hands pushing her panties down past her thighs and letting them fall the rest of the way. With our height difference with her still on the table, her sex is at a perfect level for me as I dive in and start to swipe my tongue through her bare pussy.

Fuck, I'm in heaven!

"I can't stand…" Her voice is weak, telling me if I want her shattering on my cock, I need to move now.

I stand up, and her panting is music to my ears. Wrapping my arms around her waist, I pick her up off the table she's still standing on and carry her straight to the bed and lay her out. I push her legs apart, crawling over her, and see panic on her face.

"Condom?" She sounds scared that I'll get angry, but little does she know it's normally me who insists. There are very few times I have been without one. Usually because I've been too drunk. But tonight is different, I'm completely lost in Elouise's body, which has never happened before.

"Shit, yep." Pushing back off the bed, I grab my wallet out of my pants pocket, taking one from there. I'm suited up, back between her legs before she has time to lose that high she's riding.

"Better." A smile of relief on her face turns into to an open mouth, a loud moan escaping as I pound straight into her.

She's so fucking tight, fits me like a glove. Her body arches off the bed as I push hard, losing all restraint. We both want this, and I want to make sure she remembers the first one-night stand she had.

My balls are tight and drawing higher. I need to finish this, and as I watch her tits bouncing below me with every thrust, they are calling me.

Dropping my head, I take her nipple between my teeth and bite down hard. Pleasure races through my cock as I bury myself deep inside her, and her pussy shatters, her come exploding all over me.

"Remington!" Her scream is all I need to start unloading inside her. My cock is still pulsing as I ride out the orgasm for both of us.

Rolling off her, I lie on the bed beside her, and it hits me what a huge mistake I've just made. The reasons start rattling through my head with speed.

Cutting one of my best friend's grass, which is not cool and breaking the bro code. No matter if she is right for Flynn or not, he is still trying to get her attention.

Having a one-night stand with a woman I will see all the time, which is a big no-no.

And the worst part is she was the best fuck of my life.

What the hell have I done!

"That changes nothing, right? We act normal." Elouise can't even look at me, staring at the ceiling.

"Exactly." Thank God she's not acting clingy, no cuddling.

"Our secret, never breathe a word." There is determination in her voice.

"I'm taking it to the grave. But tell me one thing." I have to know.

"Sure," she answers as I lean up on my elbow to look down on her.

"Did I tick your one-night stand off the bucket list?"

"More like you burst it off the page." The smirk on her face tells me all I wanted to know. I blew her mind like she just blew mine.

Not that it means anything, because we both know we can't go there. It's a one-and-done thing.

We aren't each other's type, and I don't do relationships!

Chapter One

ELOUISE

"I can't believe you are getting married to Mr. Rich Hottie, and I'm going to be left the old spinster schoolteacher that lives with ten cats for the rest of my life." Hands on my hips, I watch my best friend Tori being measured for the wedding dress of the century.

It's what happens when you're marrying a guy where money is no object. I'm still shaking my head trying to process what the last twelve months have been. Tori falling in love, though with a few bumps along the way, before ending up with the love of her life and now planning a wedding in Australia. They only got engaged a month ago, but Nic doesn't want to wait forever, so the planning has begun for a summer wedding in Australia early next year.

Like, what the actual hell is her life.

The only reason I have ever managed to leave the country is because her husband-to-be flew me to Rome as a Christmas surprise for her. And now I get to fly to Australia to be her bridesmaid.

We were just two twenty-six-year-old women living our middle-class existence. Maybe I should have dreamed bigger, like Tori did. Her dreams of traveling the world had the universe delivering an extremely sexy older man right into her lap, who just happens to own one of the biggest hotel chains in Europe. I don't think traveling will be a problem going forward.

Am I happy for her? Absolutely, but there is always a nagging tinge of jealousy there, and it has nothing to do with Nic's money, but just having a man to share her life with.

Instead, stupid me is still sitting here single, living in my same little house, working my same day job in a small district school, teaching little kids the same things, year in year out.

But to be honest, I do love my job. Working with five-year-olds who are just discovering the world of learning is so uplifting some days. When they finally manage to read a whole book on their own and are almost bursting with excitement, it rubs off on me too. Most of the kids come from homes where both parents are working, so they don't have a lot of time to read with them. Teaching them to do it on their own is the first big hurdle in life that will allow them to work toward their dreams.

To be honest, this is probably where I will remain for the rest of my life. Watching Tori living some luxurious life, while I will be just as happy living in the suburbs, married to some quiet man who works a stable job, with two children and maybe a cat. It's what I imagined as a girl growing up, and I'm not one to step out of my comfort zone.

Well, except just that once, and it will haunt me forever.

I can't even look Remington in the eye anymore. Sure, we chat and are friends, but this guy has not only seen me naked, but witnessed me acting like a total horny whorebag who used him for sex.

He acts like that night never happened, which I'm thankful for, but also a little disappointed at the same time. I relive it every single night in my dreams, which is all types of wrong, especially six months later.

I have worn out two vibrators and tried various other toys, but nothing gets even close to making me come like he did.

"Lou! Hello, earth to Elouise. Were you even listening?" Tori yells at me as I'm chastising myself for even thinking about him.

"Shit, sorry. Yep, I was totally listening."

"You can't lie to me, remember, I can see right through you. You're blushing, so whatever you were thinking about, you can tell me later." She winks at me, so I know I must be pink on my cheeks, as I was heating up slightly at my fiery daydream. The seamstress is trying not to get involved, but you can tell she is intrigued too, looking at me all flustered.

Why am I so predictable?

The worse thing is I can't tell Tori one single tiny detail of what I was thinking about.

Ughhh, why was I so stupid?

"Yeah, yeah. Now what was the question?" I ask, trying to divert my thoughts and her from looking at me like I'm hiding something, which I totally am. I've never kept anything from my best friend before, and it is so hard.

"Do you think I should have a shawl made in case it gets cool at night? Surely, it's not always hot in Australia." Tori is looking at herself in the mirror in the mockup dress they have made from cotton to get the fit right.

"That's a good idea. Not that I would know about the temperature. Maybe ask Nic, isn't he chief wedding planner?" Both of us look at each other and burst into a fit of laughter. For a man who happily told everyone he was never falling in love or getting married, here he is buried so deep in planning, trying to make it perfect, that he is unbearable some days—or so I hear from the boys when they complain to me about what he's like when I'm not there.

"It would be fine if he would let me help with some of it, but instead, we just argue about it. Come to think of it, that is probably his plan all along. He loves to argue because it always ends up with me naked." She rolls her eyes at me, both of us knowing full well what happens every time they argue. "But the dress is the only thing I have control over—oh, and your dress, which we totally need to get started on."

It's something I've been trying to avoid so I can try to lose some weight. Nobody wants to look overweight in the photos. Especially next to the gorgeous bridal couple.

"I can't wait to see the real dress." I know she will be the most beautiful bride ever. Her striking red hair against the cream of the dress, I can't think of anything more stunning.

Watching Tori slip behind the curtain to get changed, I wish I had even a small part of her confidence. She doesn't care what other people think, but for me, I can't seem to shake the worry of other people's impressions. I've tried so hard to wipe the guy I was with briefly before college, my ex, Keith, out of my memories, but I can't get his words out of my brain. He knew I didn't belong in this world too, and it feels like those hurtful words are constantly hanging over me like a shadow, reminding me of how the world sees me. People don't understand how words can be so cruel.

"Okay, let's go eat now. Thank God I don't have to suck my gut in any longer," Tori announces as she exits from behind the velvet curtain. Back dressed in her blue jeans, white shirt, and a navy blazer, she is really rocking the part of the high-flying executive now that she works for Nic and The Darby Hotels. I'm so damn proud of her.

"How can you be hungry? It's only ten am, surely breakfast wasn't that long ago." Standing and picking up my bag off the floor, I catch a glimpse of myself in the mirror. My brown hair really needs some urgent help. It's so lackluster and drab.

"I didn't get breakfast, we got out of bed late…"

"Don't want to hear anymore," I say, cutting her off and trying to straighten my hair out so it looks like I care. "And why do you always look so hot, and I'm like the old schoolmarm? I seriously need to get my shit together. I hope you have a hessian bag ready for my head in your wedding photos."

"Elouise Doris Patterson, I don't want to hear another word out of your mouth like that. You are beautiful inside and out. No, that's too sweet, you are one good-looking, sexy chick who obviously needs to get some action so all that crap you just said gets totally forgotten. Take it from me, the right man is good for the ego!"

"Bitch, really, using my whole name, you sound like my mother. Come on, we need to feed you so you stop acting so prim and proper. The second description of me was more up your alley."

Linking arms with Tori, I lead her toward the door where her driver is waiting.

"Now this part of our friendship I can really get used to. Morning, Wallace." I love the old man who is the driver for both Nic and Tori.

"Good morning, Miss Elouise." He holds the back door open for both of us.

"Doesn't she look beautiful this morning?" Tori asks him as she slides in first, looking back at me.

"Of course, she does," Wallace replies as I start climbing into the car, and I slap Tori on the leg for embarrassing me.

"You pay him to say nice things." I roll my eyes at her.

Suddenly Wallace's face appears in the door opening. "Ah yes, but they don't pay me to tell lies. I never lie about a woman's beauty." Such a warming smile lights up his face and makes me feel all soft on the inside, before he closes the door.

"I love Wallace," I say, looking at Tori who is also smiling at me.

"Well, he's not wrong. But yeah, I love him too, he's like an adopted grandfather." Both of us giggle as he hops into the driver's seat, not wanting to embarrass him.

"Where to, my ladies?" His warm older gentleman eyes are reflected at us in the rear-view mirror, and I can see the smile just from his eyes.

"Ole Teatime," we both proclaim at the same time, perfectly in sync. It's our favorite café that Tori discovered around the corner from her new office in The Darby Hotel headquarters.

"Of course, why did I bother asking?" His chuckle is dimmed by the sound of the car starting, and we slip into the busy London traffic.

"I'm going to have the biggest stack of pancakes with strawberries, I'm that hungry." Tori looks like she is dreaming about the food already.

"Thank God the wedding is still a few months away, otherwise all you would be getting would be lettuce leaves with a side dish of celery."

"Not happening. You know me, I love my food, and when you

have a fiancée who used to be a top chef, there is no chance I'll be starving myself."

That's what I love about Tori. She is so down to earth and doesn't care about any of society's expectations. On the outside I'm good at doing that, but on the inside, I'm always in a world of self-doubt. Tori knows me and what I'm like, and thankfully loves me anyway. It's funny how in our friendship we balance each other out. I'm the calm to her feistiness, and she is the risk taker to my conservative. So, we work perfectly in some weird way.

She's the yin to my yang.

Waving the last little goodbye on the last day of the school year is exciting, but I have no energy to go out and celebrate. The summer school break is like heaven. But for the few weeks leading up to it, I'm dragging my feet to work every morning, hoping that at least I will make it through the day without wanting to tape the mouth shut on at least one of the kids for being so painful.

It only takes one of the kids to start irritating another, and then next thing you know, you have a room full of chaos. It's not their fault entirely. It's the end of the year, and they are just as tired as I am.

"Keep smiling until the bus turns the corner," I say. Peter, my teaching buddy, is beside me as we both smile so hard it hurts, waving like mad until the lights of the bus disappear around the corner. Flopping forward, with my hands on my knees, I let out the biggest sigh, and I can hear him doing the same beside me.

"Tonight, I need to go out and get really drunk, drown out the last few days and remember that I know how to have an adult conversation." Peter sounds as drained as I am.

"Is it just me or are the kids getting harder to handle each year? I swear when I started here four years ago, they were angels, and today it felt like there were definitely a few demons in my room." We reach the doors side by side for our classrooms where we have decided we have the hardest jobs in the school. Teaching the youngest kids in the school is funny and challenging at the same time.

"I hear you, sister. This year's cohort was crazy, but there were some cuties too. You get the good and the bad, I guess. So, are you coming out with us tonight?" A lot of the staff head out for drinks on the last day of the year to the pub down the road from the school.

"Not this time. I have a function with Tori and Nic that they have invited me to. Not that I feel like going, I'd just as soon curl up on the couch at home tonight with a cheese toastie and a big, and I mean really big, actually *huge*, glass of red wine. But I promised Tori last Saturday when we were at the wedding dress boutique that I'd go. You know what she's like, hard to say no to, so I'm heading home to get dressed up and look like I have way more money than I do and act more sophisticated than I am." Rolling my eyes, I walk into my classroom, thinking, "*What the fuck am I going to wear?*"

"You will have fun, you always do with Tori. You two are bad news when you're together. Just because she is marrying some rich guy doesn't mean she's not the same old Tori we know and love. Give her a hug from me and tell her I still think she picked the wrong guy. I was a far better option. Her loss!" he yells from the room next door as we both get into cleaning up our rooms for the last time this school year and packing everything away for six weeks.

School is out, thank God!

Standing in front of my bedroom closet, I look at the sad state of affairs. There are six cocktail dresses, and I'm sure I have worn them all multiple times. Prior to Tori meeting Nic, I only owned two, and the rest I have picked up at thrift stores. Tori wants to take me shopping, but I have so far refused. I don't want to be her charity case. Not that she has ever made me feel that way, but I never want our friendship to change. I have some money, but I'm saving it to purchase my own place. I love my little rental home, but I want something to call my own. But I might have to dip into my savings and add a few more dresses into the rotation.

Okay, the little black one it is then. You can never go wrong with that. Next, I take my silver heels and bag out of their boxes and lay it all on the bed. Now the big decision, hair up or down?

Up, I think, it's quicker, and I don't need to wash it. I still haven't had time to do anything with the color. Maybe over the holidays I can finally have a pamper day and visit the hairdresser.

As I'm pulling out my shapewear underwear, my phone flashes on the bed with a message.

Tori: Change of plans. We are doing drinks at Rem's place before the fundraiser.

Tori: Wallace will pick you up in thirty minutes and then pick us up on the way back into the city.

"Fuck," I mumble. This is the problem with living out of the city and Tori now in the center of London. Besides missing her terribly, there is always lost travel time when we're going out.

Elouise: Bitch, a bit more notice would have been nice. You know it takes me forever to hide the dowdy teacher and turn into the night goddess.

Tori: I know! I'm always waiting on you.

Elouise: Fuck off! It's you every single time.

Tori: Stop bitching, the clock is ticking. Get moving.

Elouise: I hate you right now.

Tori: Yeah, yeah, see you soon. You love me.

Elouise: Hmmm, maybe. *tongue poking out emoji*

"Shit." I look at my watch; she's right, the clock is ticking. Grabbing my underwear, I run for the bathroom, and I'm about to have the quickest shower ever. A splash-and-dash and then on to the transformation.

Standing in front of the mirror doing my makeup, all I can think of is Remington.

There is something about him that has me infatuated with this man. I mean, besides the memory of the night he fucked me into a sexual coma for days, but we aren't talking about that. I've been trying to wipe that from my brain since that night, but my body won't let me. It is constantly chasing the high that I have never experienced before.

Damn it, now I'm getting all tingly again.

It's hard enough to be around him, but now being in his home is going to be torture. The last couple of times they met at his place I have managed to avoid it, but there is no backing out now.

Touching up the last of my lipstick, the front door buzzer rings. Wallace is letting me know he's here and will be waiting by my front door to escort me the whole ten steps to the car. Bless him.

"Okay, Elouise, you've got this. Time to pretend to be rich." The woman in the mirror looks tired, but she will have to do. I don't like to keep Wallace waiting.

The ride into the city isn't too bad tonight, not as much traffic as I was expecting. Pulling up at Nic and Tori's apartment complex, I can see them waiting at the front door. Tori is on Nic's arm as they make their way to the car, looking like the perfect power couple. I wonder if that's what I would look like on Remington's arm.

Shaking my head, I need to stop this. *He is way out of your league, so get over it and move on.*

Friend zone, that's where we both sit and will stay going forward.

The same place I have been trying to convince Flynn he needs to be too.

Christ, what is it with these men? The one who is chasing me I don't want, and the one I want is not interested in any way. Maybe I should go for quiet, stable Forrest. The one I have no connection with at all. Wouldn't that put a cat among the pigeons.

Wallace opens my door, and Nic helps Tori slide in beside me.

"Evening, Lou." His deep timbre echoes in the car, but his eyes never leave Tori as he makes sure she is in and seated safely.

"Hi, babe, I love that dress. Looking hot, as per usual." Tori smooths her gun-metal-gray satin dress on her lap so it's not creasing and then leans over and air-kisses me on the cheek.

"You look stunning too," I say, smiling at her. She is still my real Tori under all the glamor, I remind myself, seeing her fidgeting with the dress. We both grew up in jeans and the occasional skirt and dress. Now our lives are full of ballgowns and high heels. One day maybe we will get used to it, but right now, we are newbies at all this.

"What about me?" Nic's chuckle comes from the front seat. "It's always about the women."

"Oh, sorry, yes, very handsome, Nic. Because it's not strange that I am admiring how my best friend's fiancée looks. You weirdo." I love the relationship that has grown between me and Nic. I don't need another pseudo brother, Lord knows I have enough of my own, but he is a guy friend that is nice to have. He is as protective of me as he is of Tori, telling me when they got together that he knew how important I am to Tori, so that makes me important to him too. Such a big softie underneath the big gruff exterior.

He needs to be a special kind of man to cope with the firecracker that is Tori some days.

We fall into conversation about our days and what the weekend plans are, and before I know it, we have pulled up to the curb outside an old English two-story home. It's funny, I would have pictured Rem living in some super-modern apartment. But instead, it looks like a piece of history, albeit a very expensive piece. There is a wrought-iron fence, and looking through it, I can see his work car, a standard black Range Rover that all the boys seem to drive, with the darkest tinted windows. Beside it sits his baby, the black Porsche that he loves. Fast cars go with his dare-devil attitude in life.

He really is a contradiction.

Remington loves risk and will seek out the most extreme things around the world to do, yet his job is all about keeping people safe from danger. I swear I should have studied psychology at university instead of teaching. People intrigue me.

Walking the path to the door, like the third wheel next to Tori and Nic, I can feel my stomach doing somersaults. It always happens when I get together with all the guys, but then within five minutes I feel at home. It's just that initial few moments when I feel like a fraud around them. They have never done anything to make me feel like that, this is all on me. Like I said, humans are complex, and I wish I knew more about how the brain works. Come to think of it, perhaps I don't need to know what goes on in my head sometimes.

The heavy wooden front door opens and the noise drifting out tells me that everyone else is already here.

"About time. You're one beer behind," Rem declares to Nic, standing on the edge of the step.

"Well, some of us work harder than others." Tori laughs at Nic's reply and steps inside past Rem. Nic moves to the side so I can follow her.

"Ladies, looking beautiful as always," Rem says, motioning with his arm for me to enter too.

"Thank you," is all I can manage to say as we are ushered into what looks like a large sitting room where Forrest and Flynn are already seated. Not surprisingly Flynn's here with a date who looks all classy and refined, less trashy than his usual girls. Both of the guys stand and kiss Tori first and then me. I'm part of the inner circle, and Flynn's date doesn't like it. She looks down her nose at me, like she can see right through me.

Don't look at me like that, you snotty-nosed bitch. I could take him from you in a second by just saying the word. So, you might think you are better than me, but you are just the consolation prize, baby.

Too busy staring down the society snob, I didn't hear Rem come up behind me. As he invades my personal bubble, I inhale his rugged scent. It's like a woodsy aroma and reminds him of being out in the fresh air. For me, the whiff of it overtakes my senses and makes me want to gasp for air, but not in a bad way. The kind of feeling that sets your body on fire, and with him being so near me now, it's like he is stealing all the oxygen from my lungs.

The moment his hand touches my lower back, and he leans forward to talk quietly in my ear, a full-body shiver is happening and the hairs on my arms stand on end.

"What can I get you to drink? You look like you could use one." As he steps to my side, I get the up-close view of him in his expensive-looking black suit, white shirt, and black bow tie. The black beard is like a frame for his strong square jaw, neatly trimmed, and the memory of it between my legs has me blushing. His black hair is not as neatly trimmed as his beard, instead a little wilder, and it suits him. I love the rugged look on him, it's sexy as hell. His deep brown eyes are always full of mischief, and tonight is no different.

"A glass of bubbles for you?" he asks, winking at me, and I just want to run away before I embarrass myself.

"No, something stronger. A margarita or maybe a straight shot of tequila." I refuse to cower away; I can't let him have the upper hand all night. Friend zone, remember? "Anything that will make your company more bearable tonight." I step another foot away to give me some more breathing room.

"What, me? I'm the perfect gentleman." He fakes a look of shock and then starts to laugh. "Okay, fair call. Margarita coming right up. Tori, the usual gin and tonic?" he calls to her as he walks from me to his drinks cabinet that's set up in the corner of the room. Very dark wood, but it fits the room's décor.

This house is not what I would have pictured for Rem, but surprisingly, he fits it perfectly, playing the host with power. It's something about the way he portrays himself that exudes the dominance a man in his position holds.

I look around the room. The leather couches are black with a gray throw over the back of the one opposite the open fire that is lying dormant during the summer, and a few patterned throw cushions compliment the gray. Behind the couch are the front windows that have thick dark gray curtains that look like they are there to help shield his privacy. But in true Remington style, there are two layers to shut the world out, because from the outside, all you can see in the dark is the plantation shutters that are all closed. They are great to channel the light in during the day but the need for netting and curtains over the top so no one can see in this room is something he would insist on. The floor is a dark wood, almost black, with a dark charcoal patterned rug. The walls are an off-white color so as not to distract the eye from the scattered photos of landscapes that can only be described as breathtaking. The angles are artistic, and whoever the photographer is has real talent.

The whole house is old but with a stylish modern feel. I can see how it portrays strength and confidence in its dark manly colors. A reflection of the owner who you can tell has no woman in his life to add those slight feminine touches, which is just the way he wants it. Which is why I try to remind myself every time my thoughts wander to him, he doesn't do relationships, and the reason is he doesn't *want* a relationship. It's a choice for him, not like me who just can't find the right guy.

"What do you think of my home?" His voice is back beside me as he passes me my drink. I wonder if he will suspect something's wrong if I drink it down in one go.

"Lovely, just not what I was expecting." Shit, I shouldn't have said that.

"What did you expect?" He smiles as he answers for me. "A slick modern bachelor pad, full of technological gadgets."

"Mm-hmm," I answer between sips of my drink that I'm drinking way too fast on an empty stomach.

"You aren't the only one who is full of little surprises, Elouise. You'd be surprised what I'm hiding under this suit." Running his hand through his hair almost has me salivating. Down, girl! You might know exactly what he is packing in those pants, but I'm not sure that was entirely what he meant.

Who am I kidding, that's exactly what he was hinting at with his double entendre. He might pretend ninety-nine percent of the time that nothing happened between us, but that one percent of the time just slipped through.

"Where's my drink, Mr. Host?" Tori saves me with her complaint that her drink isn't in her hands yet.

"Coming, coming. So impatient, just like in the office." Chuckling, he heads back to the drink cabinet, giving me the reprieve I need. I quickly scurry to sit down next to Tori, who is trying to start a conversation with Flynn's date, but she has the face of a dead fish and isn't saying much.

As I sit, Tori looks to me, facing away from the fish woman. Rolling her eyes at me, she tries to convey without words that it's going to be a long night if we are expected to be all buddy-buddy with her.

The boys are all now standing in front of the drink cabinet, laughing over something and getting a little louder, which is normal. They might work together every day, but when they clock off, they let their guards down and try to relax, most of the time with no work talk.

"Are they always this rowdy?" Fish-face asks. Shit, I don't even know her name yet. Not that it matters, she doesn't want anything to do with me.

Tori and I look at each other and just start laughing.

"This is just normal conversation. You should see them after a few more drinks." Tori is trying to be nice, but the scowl on woman's face tells her story. She likes a quiet reserved man who takes her on his arm, helps her be seen at all the right functions, and then if she's really lucky, takes her home and fucks her missionary style in her perfect little bed.

"Ugh, how unsophisticated. Can you tell me where the powder room is?" She stands, and Tori points her in the right direction.

Once she's out of earshot, we both burst out laughing.

"What the fuck, Flynn misfired with his pick for tonight's date. Not his type at all," I can't help but saying.

"She is like a wet fish," Tori says, taking a sip of her G&T.

"That's what I thought too." Clinking our glasses together, I feel so much better, finally settling into the room and part of the group. Thank goodness the boys aren't like that woman who obviously has money like they do. They act like they did before they found their wealth, or so Forrest tells me, and he's probably the only one I would believe.

A ringing like from an old bell sound comes from the foyer. I'm guessing it's the doorbell.

Rem walks across the room, looking confused. "Who the hell is that? I'm not expecting anyone else. The security gate's closed, they needed the code." His tone of voice is one I have heard a few times when he's in work mode. Full of suspicion.

I hear the door open, and Rem sounds surprised to see Wallace our driver at the door, talking so softly that we can't hear what he's saying.

But it is followed by the slight voice of a woman with a very broad French accent talking in broken English.

"Pardon me, monsieur. You are Mr. Remington Elders?"

"Yes, and who are you?" The apprehension in his voice tells me that something is wrong.

Nic must have sensed the same thing, heading toward the foyer with a serious face.

The whole room is silent as we wait to see what is about to unfold.

Chapter Two

REMINGTON

Not having my phone in my hand is not normal for me, having just passed it to Flynn to show the guys one of the videos of the next thing I'm thinking of doing, rally driving in Australia when we visit for the wedding.

But the problem is that I couldn't check the security feed on my phone to see who is at the door until I get to the security panel on the wall near the front door.

I'm confused by the sight of Wallace and a shadow of someone behind him as I pull the door open. The vision before me is definitely not what I was expecting, and to be honest, I'm totally confused by it. I only open the door because it's Wallace, Nic's driver, who I trust with my life, standing there looking very anxious.

Next to him is a smallish woman with dark brown hair, long and in a braid, with an old-looking bag on the step beside her and a little boy fast asleep on her shoulder. Her back must be screaming in pain, holding him. He is not a baby by any means, and there is nothing to her either.

There is a fear in her eyes as she looks up at me.

Wallace steps forward and whispers in my ear. "Sorry to bother you, sir, but she is very insistent that she has information you need to hear. I tend to agree." He steps back and walks back down the path, showing respect to not be around for the discussion, which leaves me looking down on her and wondering, *What the fuck is going on?*

"Pardon me, monsieur. You are Mr. Remington Elders?" Her French accent is very thick, and you can tell that her English is not strong. The hair on my neck stands up, and an awful feeling runs down my spine that she knows my name.

Swallowing the lump in my throat, I ask, "Yes, and who are you?" The uncertainty as to what is going on is in my voice as I'm speaking.

"My name is Adeline Dupont, and this is your son, Blaise Elders."

My heart has hit my chest and stopped beating. The rushing noise in my ears drowns out everything around me.

The hand that lands on my shoulder is enough to get me to try and regain my voice, but I can't figure out what to say.

Nic pulls me back inside the foyer, and I can hear him talking, but it doesn't compute. It's like I'm standing on the outside of a situation looking in.

He directs her into the study which is just inside the door on the opposite side of the hallway from the sitting room.

"Rem, I'll get rid of everyone else and get the girls to sort out some food and water. This is going to be a long night." He pushes me to sit in the seat across from them.

Son? I don't have a son. This has to be a mistake.

That's it, a mistaken identity, I don't know this woman. Never seen her before, let alone fucked her. There might have been many women, but I don't forget a face with my photographic memory.

You hear of it happening, people with money get targeted. Well, I'm smarter than that. Surely, she knows that DNA is easy to prove.

Yep, DNA, that's what I'll do. First thing tomorrow.

I can hear people moving around, but the only person that seems to be leaving is Flynn with that weird woman he brought with him.

"I'll be back." His voice is behind me from the doorway of the study, and then the door is partly closed again.

This woman and I are just staring at each other, no words are being shared.

The little boy who is now sitting on her lap, face still in her shoulder, starts stirring. Not waking up fully from his sleep, but enough that he shifts position, and his face turns to the side on her chest and he looks straight toward me.

All I see looking back at me is the same face in every picture of me on my parents' walls of when I was his age.

Fuck!

The house has gone quiet. Too quiet so that I can hear every slightest noise. The creaks in the floorboards in the kitchen, the whispers that are barely there but enough to know my friends are here somewhere and I'm not alone.

"You see it, yes?" the French woman whispers to me in her broken English.

Don't answer her. Don't say anything that can be used against you.

"I have never seen you before." I have been looking at her so intently, but her face is definitely drawing a blank. I know I don't remember all the names of the women over the years, plenty of times we never even exchanged them, but I know she isn't one of them.

She nods and tells me I'm right as she is frantically rummaging in her pocket looking for something.

She pulls a crumpled envelope from her pocket and thrusts it toward my hands. Reaching forward, I take it from her and look at the little boy who is peacefully asleep. My hand is visibly shaking, and I know it's because the moment I open this and read it, I have a feeling my life is about to change forever, and I'm not prepared to let that happen. But whether I like it or not, life has a way of changing, and you can't do a thing to stop it.

"Read, *s'il te plait*… um, please." She motions to the letter.

Slowly opening the envelope, I slide the letter out and flatten it to make it easier. There is a page of beautifully written words, thankfully in English.

Dear Remington,

Please excuse my English is not perfect.

This letter is because something has happened to me. Adeline has our son Blaise for you to take care of.

I am Camille Roux. We met in the mountain in France when you lost from hike Mt. Blanc. I took you to my place, lots of cheese, bread, and wine. You slept in my house, with me. A night of nice sex. The day after you leave, I find your wallet. You are long gone. I kept it safe, in case you come back.

When I find out I with baby, I asked Adeline my friend to use money in wallet to take the child to you if anything ever happen to me.

I'm sorry for not telling you. You are rich and I a poor goat herder. I couldn't bear to lose Blaise. But I always told him about you, show him your picture on plastic card.

I know you shocked and you be angry at me. I was selfish, but mothers love couldn't let him go. Sadly, though now I am gone, and he needs you.

He is a good boy, likes to play in the fields, kick a ball and draw. Please be kind to him and give him good home with lots of love.

I thought of you often and knew deep down you were a good man. My heart could tell.
Tell Blaise I love him every day.

Thank you for giving me Blaise for the time I had him. I will always be grateful for the gift.

Camille

My eyes go to Blaise, picturing his mother that day on the

mountain. Then back to the top of the page and rereading to try to get it to make sense.

I can't deny the story because I was there, and I did sleep with Camille. We had many bottles of unlabeled wine which was potent in strength, and I remember waking with a hell of a hangover. I doubt I would have had a condom with me, but to be honest, that part is hazy. Probably one of those rare drunk times I would have skipped that part of the process even if I did have one.

Engrossed in the memory of what happened, looking up now, I see the room filled with my friends. The guys who will always have my back.

Nic sits beside me and motions to the letter. Handing it over to him, I flop back into the couch and push my hands up over my face and into my hair. I'm always the man who takes control of every situation, yet right now, I'm useless.

"Adeline, thank you for being patient. As you can see this is a big shock to Remington." Nic's calm voice is welcome next to me. "Can we offer you some water and food?"

"*Merci.*" Adeline looks around like a scared animal at all the people as she leans forward to take the water that Tori is offering.

"Do you speak much English?" Elouise asks from beside me, making me jump a little. I didn't realize she was sitting on the arm of the couch next to me.

"A little," Adeline replies with her hand in the air, tipping it from side to side signaling that she does, but it isn't great.

"*Serait-ce plus facile si je vous parlais en français et traduisais pour vous?*" Elouise shocks us all with the most beautiful French coming from her.

"*Oui, s'il vous plaît, ce serait tellement plus facile pour moi d'expliquer pourquoi je suis ici.*" A smile of relief comes across Adeline's face at being able to speak easily to Elouise in French.

"I just asked her if she would like me to translate to make it easier for her. Which she said yes, if I could. I'm sure she has a lot to say, and it will be hard for her in English. Are you okay with that?" There's kindness in her voice as she looks down at me. I couldn't be more thankful for her friendship than I am right this moment.

"Yes, please. The letter said something has happened to his mother. Can you ask her about that? I'm afraid of the answer." It's quite clear from the letter she has died, but I need to know how.

Sitting waiting as the question is asked and Adeline replies with tears running down her face is awful. Before she worries about explaining anything, Elouise is up and walking to Adeline, sitting down beside her and giving her a hug. Comforting her from having to retell a story about a friend she was obviously very close to if Camille trusted her with Blaise. The gentle sobs on Elouise's shoulder start to subside, and slowly Adeline's head rises up, and she wipes her tears off her face.

"Camille, Blaise's mother, was out in the pasture bringing the goats in for milking when they think she fell and hit her head on a rock. Blaise was with her, and sadly, Adeline found them both the next day when she went to visit. She found Blaise curled up on the ground with his mother, hugging her and singing to her."

My heart hurts for Camille and for the little boy. What a traumatic time for everyone. Even Elouise has had to stop to compose herself, and I can hear Tori crying too. I only knew Camille for one night, but I can feel her loss deeply, and that surprises me.

"When Adeline checked Camille, she was near death, and by the time they got the doctor from the village up there to her, she had passed. They believe the cause of death was a brain bleed from the blow to the back of her head." Elouise's arm is around Adeline's shoulder and slowly rubbing up and down the top of her arm in comfort. I can't believe how strong she is being and taking charge of the room. It should have been me, but I have been stripped raw, and everything that made sense before seems so far from my grasp at the moment.

"Shit, how fucking awful," I hear Flynn mumble under his breath. He obviously just left long enough to put his date in the car with Wallace and send her home, then came straight back inside to us.

"How did she know where to find Rem?" Nic asks, and Elouise relays the message. Adeline starts reaching inside her jacket to a concealed pocket, then holds out to me a weathered brown leather wallet. One that my father had given me on my birthday one year, and it has my initials embossed on the front corner. I was annoyed I lost it that trip, but to be honest, I didn't know where on the journey it had disappeared. I hadn't needed it for days while hiking, so it truly could have been anywhere.

The cards that are in it have been long cancelled, and the cash, I'd assumed would have been taken by whoever found it.

Taking the wallet in my hand and running my thumb over the front of it seems so strange, like a piece of my past. Opening it up, I find everything is still exactly where I had them. My driver's license at the front, credit cards in the slot behind it. And there is still cash in the long back pocket.

Adeline starts talking very fast and frantically to Elouise in what sounds like the same sentence over and over again, to which Elouise tries to calm her down, talking to her and what looks like reassuring her all is okay.

This is so fucking frustrating. I'm kicking myself so hard now for not paying more attention in school when we were offered language classes. I was too busy with my head stuck in a computer or clowning around with my friends. I remember we did a bit of French and Spanish, but I couldn't hold a conversation in either language these days. When I'm traveling, most of the places I visit the people speak limited English, so I've gotten by, or used my phone to translate which doesn't always go well either.

"She is trying to tell you that she only took money to get on the train to find you. She promises she never took anything else. She is scared, Rem, terrified of what is going to happen now that she's here. She has never been out of France, and I doubt she has visited a big city often."

"Oh God, please tell her it's okay. I believe her, and I'm grateful for what she is doing for this little boy." I can't let the words *my son* pass my lips until I know for sure. Even then this will take some getting used to. But if he is my son, then I will protect him like I protect everyone else in this room.

Quickly relaying my words, Adeline's shoulders drop, and the tension in her body seems to settle.

It's like seeing her so scared has jerked me back to reality. *Get control of this situation, you idiot.*

"Right, we need to get things sorted. Elouise, please tell Adeline she will stay here tonight in the guest room with Blaise. I know I'm asking a lot, but can you possibly stay as well so she feels comfortable about being in a house with a strange man? Flynn, can you find someone to do a DNA test first thing tomorrow morning, and we will want the results expedited. Nic, can you and Tori organize some food that a child might eat, I have no idea. Forrest, can you get in touch with Ian and tell him I am offline and on leave; he is in charge until he hears from me."

This is what I need to take control of things, divert my attention from how my life is about to explode. I hate when there are elements out of my control, unless it is when I'm about to do something that will scare the hell out of me. It's the one reason I will give up control of everything just to get the adrenaline high. Because I know it will only be momentary, and the rest of the time I want to be in complete control.

"Whoa, buddy, slow down there. We are here to help you, and we don't need to rush anything. Forrest, can you contact our lawyer and have him on standby for anything we might need help with tomorrow?" Nic, being the boss, is now taking over and trying to be a good friend, but I need to be running the show.

"Yes, that's a good idea." Just nodding, I try to think of what else might be needed to be done.

"Hang on, guys, don't you think you need to actually ask Adeline if she is okay with staying?" Elouise asks. "You can't just order her to do what you think is best. Plus, until we know what is happening with Blaise, you need to give her the consideration and respect that she deserves as his carer at the moment. Don't take that away from her until she is ready to step back. Camille gave her a dying wish that she is trying to fulfill. It's important to her." Elouise sits up straighter, and the strength in her voice is not something I've heard before. I've never seen her in her work environment, but I can see that this is her in her teacher role of protecting a child and the vulnerable.

I want to scream at Elouise and say if she turns up on my doorstep with a child, claiming it's mine, then I will damn well do what I want. This is my house. But the cold stare that is coming from Elouise makes me back down slightly and listen to what she is saying.

"Okay," I grunt at her, with a nod for her to ask the question.

"Adeline is very appreciative of a place to stay tonight. She doesn't have any money for accommodation, so she has offered to cook or clean for you to pay for her stay. I told her that she is a guest and there is no need, she is safe here, and that I will be here with her." Elouise's voice is a little gentler this time, knowing that she has things sorted the way she thought it should be.

Tori stands up. "Right, now you men have voiced your opinions. Here is what's actually going to happen. I will get Wallace to take me back to your place, Lou, and grab some clothes for you for a few days just in case. Forrest, you can do the work things that Rem mentioned. Flynn and Nic, can you go to the shops and get some toys, food for kids, but not junk food, and a baby monitor so we can hear Blaise when he wakes. Lou, just call us if you think of anything else, and Rem, my friend, you need to just take a breath. We will get this sorted, and once we know more, then we will worry about the next steps you need to make. But whatever it is, we've got you." Tori walks toward me, and I know she is about to put her arms out to me. She is a hugger. Standing and letting her embrace me, I won't deny it feels good to be comforted.

"Thanks, Tori, but don't worry about the baby monitor. I'm a security man, remember? I'll just set up a camera with the feed to my system, and I can get alerts on my phone and watch. And what was wrong with my plans?" Having pulled back, I look down at her, watching as she starts to laugh.

"That you expect Elouise to sleep in a cocktail dress and wear it for the next few days, and that's just for starters. Pfft, men..." She walks over to Nic and reaches up to give him a kiss, then hugs Elouise, and the both of them start whispering to each other. "Now feed this poor woman, and I will be back in an hour or so."

"So, bossy." Flynn smirks, his comment directed at Tori.

"Too right, and you would all be lost without me. Now get moving, people, chop, chop." Tori points her finger at us like school kids, but it's what we needed to break the moment.

Forrest stands and takes his phone from his pocket, looking at Nic. "She does know we are grown men, right? Who ran a hugely successful business before she arrived. Man, you do realize what you are getting yourself in for marrying her."

"Absolutely! Wouldn't have it any other way. And she just thinks she's in charge, but we all know who wears the pants around here. Where's the Range Rover keys, Rem?" He's moving toward the door of the study, with Flynn following him and Forrest already talking on his phone as he leaves the room.

"And yet you are all doing exactly as she said. You're delusional." Elouise finds herself amusing and turns to Adeline to offer her some food, which she happily accepts. Then Elouise turns back to me. "Don't you have a camera to set up?"

I'm moving before I realize what I'm doing but then laugh to myself as I walk down the hallway. Just like that, I'm doing what I was told too.

These two fucking women have some voodoo hold over us.

Satisfied that I will be able to hear and see if Blaise wakes, Elouise and Adeline head upstairs to the guest room that I showed them, to settle them both in for the night. Although it's not late, only just after eight pm, Adeline has been traveling all day, so she is exhausted and I'm sure appreciates time to rest. Every guest room has a bathroom attached, so I assure her that I haven't put any cameras in there and she should get changed in there. I'm not sure that she really understands the security system, but Elouise has assured her it is for their safety and so we can help her with Blaise if she needs it.

Forrest has gone home to make sure everything is in place for tomorrow. Nic and Flynn have been back and delivered everything Tori told them to get, and I have sent them home too. I know they want to help, but I just need some space right now. Tori just left after dropping Elouise's bag to her and spending a few minutes with her in the other guest room that is next to mine, where Elouise will sleep. Tori didn't want to leave, but Elouise also assured her that it will be better for Blaise if he wakes that there aren't too many people here initially.

Tori hugged me tightly again as she left and assured me that everything will be okay. I'm not sure she's right, but let's go with that for now.

Standing in the kitchen and looking out into the dark of the night, all I can think about is poor Camille. She was a gentle soul and loved her simple life in the mountains. What an awful thing to happen and for poor Blaise to lose his mother so young. I remember her laugh was so happy and bright. She didn't seem to see any bad in the world. I don't even know much about her family, but I assume if she has sent Blaise to me then there is no one else she trusts to take care of him. Or maybe she wanted more for him. She knew I lived in London and traveled the world looking for adventures. To a goat herder from the mountains of France, maybe that seemed like a dream she would like to see her son experiencing too. I guess we will never know. Fuck, I wish I knew French. If he is my son, how the hell am I going to communicate with him?

A wave of grief washes over me, and I know I can't ignore it.

"Camille, if you can hear me. Even if he isn't mine, I will make sure he is okay. I will watch over him until he can navigate this world on his own. I promise I will fulfill your wish. He will be safe." Closing my eyes, I let that settle over me.

I might not want kids, but I could never stand by and let one struggle through life on his own when I have the means to make sure he's okay. That would just be cruel and that's one thing I'm not. I might be arrogant, self-centered, and an asshole most of the time, but I will never watch someone struggle when they don't deserve it.

Hearing her gentle footsteps on the floorboards, I know Elouise is behind me.

And as much as I have distanced myself from her, I could really use her comfort tonight. Just the softness of holding her in my arms would be calming, but I'm trying not to admit I'm actually craving more.

ELOUISE

Hearing Rem talking about the poor woman he met years ago almost breaks my heart.

We all picture him as the muscle in the group, our protector. But who is going to protect him now from his own emotional turmoil? As much as I hate being in the friend zone with him, he needs me, and I can't turn my back on him. Even if he tries to push me away like he did everyone else tonight, I won't let him. He is just as vulnerable as Blaise is now. Men are great at putting walls up, but I see through that and won't let him drown in his own panic. Because that is what he is doing on the inside, I'm sure. His distancing is a perfect indicator.

Standing behind him now in my comfy jeans, top, and bare feet, my hair hanging down, I feel more myself. I'm not wearing the mask of the socialite that I put on to pretend when we are out together or at the big functions Tori constantly invites me to.

Turning to face me, he is still in his suit pants, but the jacket is long gone, along with the tie, discarded when he was installing the camera. His shirt is partly undone and the sleeves rolled up. His bare feet are doing something weird to my brain and are just the perfect final detail of making him look irresistible. For God's sake, they're just feet, but there is something about arriving home and kicking off your shoes that makes you relax; I know because I'm the same. It's grounding.

Leaning back against the sink, he rests his hands on the edge of the counter.

"Are they settled okay up there? Do they need anything else?" He's talking but isn't really with me.

"Yes, they are both snoring comfortably in the bed. Adeline kept telling me how grateful she is for the help." As I walk a few steps closer, he doesn't move, just keeps looking at me, bewildered.

"Are you okay?" A few more steps and I'm in front of him. Toe to toe.

"No," he whispers, and at least he's being honest.

Wrapping my arms around his waist and laying my head on his chest, I hold him as tight as I can. His body is rigid, his hands still not moving, knuckles whitening as he holds onto the counter tighter.

"Let it out, Rem, it will help, I promise. It's just us, and you know it'll stay between us." The thought of the secret we're already keeping is the triggering moment for him.

He stands up straighter, taking my body with him. His arms enclose me, his head dropping into the curve of my neck, and I can feel him breathing fast. I just run my hands up and down his back to let him know that I'm here and I won't let him go. If it were me, I would be releasing a bucketful of tears, but being the strong man he's trying to be, instead he is battling to breathe through his emotions.

After a few minutes, he finally lifts his head and rests his forehead on mine.

"What if he is my son?" Six words of utter fear come from his lips, but I know deep down he thinks he is. And God, you only need to take one look at Blaise to see he is a mini Remington.

"Worse, what if he's not? Because your heart has already been sending out feelings that first moment you looked at him." I think he would be a little broken, although he doesn't realize it yet, if the DNA test came back that he is not the father.

Our hearts and minds work in ways we don't understand and can't control at times, and this is certainly one of them.

"What the fuck am I going to do, El? I don't know how to be a father." That's the first time he has ever called me El, and I have to admit, I kind of like it. It's just ours, no one else's, just Rem and me.

"No one does when they first begin. But just think of the upside. You don't have to do shitty nappies and middle-of-the-night feeds," I say, trying to break the seriousness of his fear now that he has let it out.

A small, very small chuckle releases from him, and then the biggest sigh.

"Thank you for staying. I need you." I know he doesn't mean that the way I want him to, but I'll take it anyway. To be honest, it would be the worst time to take this out of the friend zone. I would never know if it was because he wanted more or just because he needed me to hold him up through this.

"You don't need me. I know you would work it out if I weren't here, but I'm happy to help." I step back a little from him, because I think distance would be a good thing right now.

His hands move to my shoulders.

"You speaking in French like that is sexy as fuck. You could talk dirty like that to me anytime." The darkness in his eyes is not a good sign. I need to shut this down right now.

"How would you know I wasn't telling you that you had the smallest cock I'd ever seen and that you were shit in bed." Smiling at him, I take a few steps away out of his reach.

"We both know you can't lie, and we both know that neither of those are true. My big cock fucking rocked your world, and you can't deny that."

"Keep dreaming. Now, where is the food? I'm starving." I look around the kitchen for what the boys left for us.

"Yeah, me too… starving." His deep tone is one I know, and I need to ignore it.

Don't look, focus on the food.

As much as I've wanted to be back in his arms since that first night, I know I can't do that tonight. In my head, I'm telling myself to push all those thoughts away.

Because no one wants to be the comfort fuck.

I'm better than that, and if Rem was thinking clearer, he would never treat me like that either.

Time to eat and then get into bed… alone.

That's my plan, food and sleep.

Stick to the plan.

Chapter Three

ELOUISE

"Oh my God, this is the best pizza I've had in a long time. It's the different combination of toppings. I've never had pumpkin, spinach, feta, and sundried tomatoes before, but man, it's good." I'm so full, and Rem has hardly eaten anything. Well, by his standards anyway.

I've been trying to fill the silence and talking between mouthfuls, just useless information and stories about my week at school. I even resorted to the first-date style questions—tell me about your family, what music do you like etc.

He answered, but they weren't long answers. I offered him a drink to calm his nerves and to help him sleep, but he declined, telling me he wanted to be alert in case he was needed. And he doesn't think he would make a good father. This guy is so protective of anyone in his circle that poor Blaise will be complaining as a teenager that he can't move a muscle in any direction without Rem knowing.

I know we don't know yet, but in my mind, I'm already convinced they are father and son.

Exhausted from the night's turmoil, I've packed away all the garbage and cleaned up from earlier, while Rem sat staring out into nowhere.

"I think it's time for us to go to bed." And as soon as the words are out of my mouth, his reaction is instant, standing and moving toward me.

Before I can move or say another word, his hands are taking mine. "Together, let's go to bed together." He leans forward to kiss me, but I turn my head to the side before he has a chance to catch my lips and instead lands on my cheek.

"That's not a good idea, Rem." Pulling back, we look intensely at each other.

"I disagree. I think it will help us both sleep." His voice is all rugged but not like that voice I remember when he was inside me. He has the deepest sex voice I've ever heard, full of lust when we were in that moment, but this is nothing like that. He is almost begging, just like I was to him that night he made my wish come true.

"You will regret it tomorrow." In my head, I know I will too.

"You're wrong." He sounds frustrated.

"I can't be your quick fuck to drown the anxiety you're feeling." My words cut him deep.

"I would never use you like that." His words are like a knife because he can't see that he just did.

"Then listen to me and go to bed alone. That's what you need more than you need me." I pull my hands from his grasp and turn to walk away.

"Fucking women, they always think they know what's best," he calls after me.

"Because we usually do. Good night, Remington." I walk quickly down the hallway and up the stairs, knowing I need to put as much distance between us as possible before I do something more stupid than Christmas night. If I give in to him, I will end up hating us both for the pain I will feel tomorrow when we slip back into that friend zone that I already know is an awful place to be.

Closing the door to the bedroom I'm staying in and sitting on the big bed, it reminds me of how different our lives are. The whole bottom floor of my house could fit in this one room.

Oh, how I'd love to pick up my phone and call Tori, pouring my heart out and her giving me the advice that I'm doing the right thing. But instead, I'm here, on my own, wanting to scream that I just turned down another night with the man who has turned my world upside down.

Contemplating my decision, I hear Rem walking down the hallway, the floorboards creaking as his feet stop outside Blaise's door momentarily and then my door. Please keep walking, I'm not sure I'm strong enough to say no a second time. It feels like forever before I hear him move again, continuing to his room and then his door closing.

Good, another barrier between us.

I take my time washing off my makeup and getting into my pajamas, and by the time I lie down in this huge bed that feels like sleeping on a cloud, I thought I would be ready to fall fast asleep. But over and over again, I picture little Blaise lying in the field with his mother for all that time until Adeline found them. Was he cold and hungry? How scared and confused must he have been? I can't help shedding a few tears for Camille but more for the little boy who will still be so traumatized and now in a country where he has no idea what people are saying or what is going on.

A world of strangers and strange places.

Eventually I can't hold my eyes open any longer, and I can feel sleep coming. I have no idea what time it is, but I drift off seeing Rem's eyes full of despair from tonight, and I know sleep won't be peaceful while I worry about them both.

REMINGTON

There have been plenty of nights I have survived on limited sleep, but nothing a coffee wouldn't cure. But I'm already two strong coffees down and I still feel like I've been run over by a truck, then it stopped, reversed, and ran over me again.

It's not stopping me, though. I've been up since four am working. I couldn't sleep any longer, and there was no point lying there tossing and turning. I did a quick scan through the security footage of Blaise and Adeline sleeping, not expecting anything, but I just wanted to make sure they were okay. Then I went online to see if I could find anything on Camille or Blaise. It's not really ethical the way I'm searching, but in my job, sometimes you just need to be able find out things through other channels because there is no time to do it the legal way. The only thing that showed up was Blaise's birth certificate that listed me as the father, and she gave him her surname Roux as his middle name and my surname as his last name. She didn't have to list me or give him my name, but part of me is thankful she thought enough of me after our brief encounter to do that.

I didn't expect much to show up in my search due to her living such a simple life in the mountains. The same with Adeline. Which in a way is satisfying that they aren't trying to scam me. Again, another thing that helps convince me that Blaise is my son, but I can't do anything until I know for sure.

Spending the last few hours focusing on what needs to happen, I have my plan and will put it into action once everyone is awake, which also includes learning French on the app I have downloaded already. Nic messaged me and will be here with breakfast by eight o'clock. Tori suggested they get some French pastries and fresh baguettes to make Blaise and Adeline feel at home.

Forrest has already delivered the DNA kit from the lawyer to Nic so he can bring it to me. They have organized for a rush on the results, so we should know in twenty-four to forty-eight hours. We discussed last night that we don't want everyone here at the moment until Blaise has had time to get used to where he is and not be so frightened, so Nic will just drop everything off to me and leave.

Last night I couldn't even bear to say his name, but by the time I woke this morning and saw him sleeping so peacefully, there is no denying how much he looks like me. I have to accept the inevitable and let it sink in, that overnight, I've become a father whether I like it or not.

My life is not set up for a child, and to be honest, I'm not ready to change anything.

I love my job, and I don't want to give it up. Plus, I can't expect Nic to bend my role in the company for me. If there is one role you don't want compromised in the company, that is the head of security. Yes, he is my friend and will try to help, but I would never take advantage of that. There is a line I don't want to cross and that's Nic being my boss when we are working and a friend when we walk away from that position each day. I know there are times that the line blurs, but I don't want that to be all the time. I respect Nic enough not to put him in that position.

As soon as everyone is awake, I will put my plan into action, get the DNA test underway, and hopefully everything will be sorted by the end of the weekend.

I'm a details man. It's what I do. I plan things, solve problems, and mitigate risk. And I'm fucking good at it!

My phone and watch both buzz at the same time, letting me know there's movement and voices in Blaise and Adeline's room. Nic's quick breakfast delivery to me a few moments ago has been just in time, and hopefully that will satisfy their hunger, and then we can get on with the day.

I push back my chair from the desk in my office where I had just resettled after talking to Nic at the door and shut down my computers. I need to go and face my responsibilities.

Locking down any emotion that goes with it, I just need to treat all this like a work issue. Identify the problem and solve it.

I'm standing in the kitchen and preparing more coffee, ready for when Adeline and Blaise finally come downstairs. I can hear footsteps coming down the stairs, and I know it's not them. Instead, they are a set of footsteps that I have memorized since she first stepped into my house last night.

Elouise is awake, and I feel a weight lifting off my shoulders. She is the bridge between me and them.

I'm leaning against the kitchen counter, my third coffee for the morning in my hand, when she walks into the room looking just as tired as I am. Sleep must not have been her friend either.

"Good morning." Picking up the coffee I made for her off the counter, I hold it out toward her which brings a big smile to her face.

"You're an angel! Seriously, this is just what I need to wake me." I can tell she is still reluctant to come too close to me after what I said last night, and I don't blame her. I'm surprisingly thankful, like she said I would be, that she didn't give in to me last night. I was so off kilter that I wanted something to ground me, or some*one* really. It's my go-to when I want to drown out anything that has made me feel out of control. It doesn't happen often, but when it does, I usually bury myself in a hot sexy woman and forget about the world while we enjoy the high that a hardcore fucking gives you.

"How did you sleep?" Elouise asks me as she takes the first sip of her coffee, and her eyes almost roll back in her head in pleasure.

"I didn't. Well, not more than a few twenty-minute naps, but I don't constitute that as sleep." I open the app on my phone again to check the security camera and see that Adeline and Blaise are still in bed but sitting up and talking. I'm sure she has a lot to explain to him. But it lets me know I still have time to talk to Elouise like I need to.

"Ughh, me too. I tried hard but kept thinking about everything that happened last night. Especially what happened with poor Camille and Blaise. I can't even imagine that poor little boy—"

I put my hand up to stop her. I don't want to picture it, I can't. There is no time for me to dwell on that. We need to move forward, and the last thing Blaise needs is us taking him back to that awful time.

"What?" There's confusion in her eyes as she looks at me.

"We have more important things to talk about right now. I think we both know what the DNA test result is going to say." She nods as she sips more coffee, trying to get her brain to comprehend what I'm saying. "I have a proposal for you which I think makes sense. You speak fluent French, and I don't speak more than a few words. Blaise is going to need someone to help him, plus teach him English so he can assimilate into living here and get ready to go to school. I have searched his records, and he is four years old, so we have a bit of time."

"Wait, what are you saying?" I can see the coffee is starting to take hold as she stands up straighter, paying attention to my words.

"Don't interrupt, I'm getting to that." I can't help my abruptness this morning.

"I never realized how bossy you can be." The smirk on her face is not doing anything for me.

"You are about to find out." I push up from my lean on the counter and place my cup in the sink then turn back to her.

"I've decided you should come and work for me. Be my translator and English teacher, as well as Blaise's nanny. I don't know how to care for a child, and to be honest, I don't have the time. You will move in with us, care for him, integrate him into this life, and travel with me if needed at any time. I will pay you far more than you currently receive. We will start moving your things in on Monday…" I pick up my phone and push send on the email of the employment letter of offer I drafted early this morning.

"What the hell are you talking about? I'm not moving anywhere, and I have a job that might not pay well but that I love. And besides that, what makes you think I would want to work for someone so arrogant!" Slamming her coffee cup on the counter, she storms toward me, poking her finger into my chest over and over. "*You've* decided? Who the hell do you think you are? I'm the only one who decides what I do in my life, asshole."

Both of us freeze at the sound of a little boy's voice in the distance. Her eyes dart to the door entering the kitchen and back to me. "This discussion isn't over," she hisses in an agitated whisper, stepping back from me.

"Open the email I just sent to you, and you'll see that it is actually over. It's an offer you can't refuse," I say, forcing the point that I won't take no for an answer on this.

I need her here, end of story!

Both of us move apart and face the doorway, and Adeline enters sheepishly, holding the little boy's hand in hers, but he's hiding behind her legs. All I can see is the mop of black curls starting to peek around the side of her and one little eye trying to assess his surroundings.

"*Bonjour, Adeline. Bonjour, Blaise.*" Elouise's voice is her normal soft caring voice she used last night when around Adeline. I've got to hand it to her, she turned off the attitude she was about to unleash on me like the flick of switch.

"*Bonjour, Monsieur Elders, Mademoiselle Elouise,*" Adeline timidly replies, but her eyes keep flitting between us, trying to work out what she should do next.

"Please tell her to call me Remington, and she doesn't need to be scared of me," I say, looking at Elouise who glares back.

"Debatable," she mumbles under her breath, before she translates my wishes to Adeline.

"*Merci, Remington.*" Adeline smiles slightly for the first time as she replies to me.

"*Bonjour,* Adeline and Blaise," I say. Hearing his name from me has his little head popping out from behind her legs and his eyes opening wide.

"*Papa.*" He gasps, and that one word I never thought I would hear referring to me falls from his lips. The hairs on the back of my neck stand up but not in a good way. From sheer fear. This is my worst nightmare standing in front of me.

If I have learned one thing over the years it is never show your fear. Don't give it any power over you. Push through it. It's the only way to get to the other side. Take the emotion out of the situation. If I can jump from a plane from ten thousand feet, then I can talk to a four-year-old.

The problem is that he isn't just any four-year-old, he's *my* four-year-old.

Fuck!

Once again Elouise takes the reins and walks forward, creeping down to talk to Blaise at his eye level. I can tell he is listening to her, but his eyes haven't left mine. It's like looking at my younger self, and it feels weird, like an alternate universe.

Hearing Elouise's voice in English brings me out of my daze.

"I have explained that you are happy to meet him and that you are glad he is here to stay with you. He is also hungry, so I told him his papa would get some yummy food for him." Standing from where she was crouching with Blaise, she takes his hand slowly from Adeline, leading him to the stool at the kitchen counter.

"Rem, food?" she snarks in her not-so-sweet tone. Oh yeah, she's still pissed at me.

Moving to place the platter of pastries and bottles of juice on the counter where I already had plates and glasses set up, Elouise puts an apple pastry on the plate for Blaise and the innocence of a little boy who is hungry overrides his fear of me.

Taking his first bite, I can see him starting to look around my kitchen which is probably like nothing he has ever seen before. Unless things had changed, Camille didn't have any television in the mountain cabin, and there is no internet service that far up, so it's not likely he would have seen anything more than the homes in his village and maybe the occasional trip to Paris, but that is doubtful. And even if he did, then he wouldn't have visited anything like this place.

Adeline and Elouise are chatting between them, and I've had enough of being left out. As I found out last night, Blaise doesn't speak English, but Adeline does, so she will talk to me even if it is difficult.

"What are you talking about? I'm in this room too and not just a fu…dgsicle statue on the wall." For fuck's sake, I can't even swear in my own home anymore. Seriously!

The giggle that Elouise is trying to keep in just makes me more agitated.

"Don't you laugh at me. This is not funny." Pointing my finger at her, my annoyance comes out in my voice when I see Blaise wince. Shit, now I've scared him.

"Oh, but if you could see yourself, Rem, the master of control and a man who loves to drop a few swear words, then you would know how funny this is and will continue to be. Should I start the swear jar now?" I want to tell her to fuck off, but I can't as she continues to laugh but out loud now. Adeline looks between us, so confused.

"Enough!" I growl but in a whisper so as not to put any more tension in the room. Finally stopping her, I turn my attention back to Adeline.

I lower my voice and try to lose the annoyance that is biting at me below the surface. This is my damn house, and I will be the one in control of what happens here. Not be dictated to by a woman that is currently driving me crazy.

"I know English is hard for you, Adeline, but please try. I would like to be able to talk to you and be part of the conversation too," I say, glaring at Elouise so she understands how pissed I am with her and the whole situation.

"Yes, Monsieur Remington, I try." She's still looking at me with that gravity of fear in her eyes. She is so far out of her depth that I'm pretty sure she will say yes to anything I ask. But that's not the point.

"Thank you. I appreciate it, and please call me just Remington, no need for monsieur, okay?" I feel the tension in my shoulders finally start to ease, being able to speak and join the conversation.

"Okay." She nods her head.

"Would you like a coffee, Adeline?" I ask, knowing how much she is probably in the desperate need of some morning caffeine. It's been an intense few days, I'm sure.

"*Merci.*" Finally, she takes one of the pastries too.

Moving back to the coffee machine, my back to them all, I take a few deep breaths so I can settle them both in, especially Blaise. I'm not ready to be a father, but I also don't want his first impression and memory of me to be of someone he fears. I love my father and can't ever imagine being afraid of him.

Oh shit, Mum and Dad. That's a conversation I'm not looking forward to. They will be so excited and want to be involved, which will just make things worse at the moment. I know it's wrong, but I'm going to keep this from them until I have a handle on it all or can at least communicate a little with Blaise.

I place the coffee down in front of Adeline with the sugar if she needs it and start with the first question I have.

"How long are you staying here in London, with Blaise?" I would never ask her to leave, but I need to know so I can plan.

"Leave, um… tomorrow, yes, Sunday." She just freely replies like it's no problem.

"Wait, what? You can't leave that quickly." I look at Elouise in desperation. "Tell her, Elouise. That's ridiculous to just dump Blaise here and leave him alone with a complete stranger."

"Oh, look, already he is giving in. I thought you didn't need me to translate anymore." The sarcasm in her voice makes me want to push this point about how I told her this morning about how I needed her, but she didn't want to hear it.

"Not stranger… you Papa. I need to go home to my kids." At this point I'm not even sure she is talking about her own children or the goats.

For fuck's sake, this is a complete shit show, and it hasn't even been a day yet. How the hell am I supposed to look after a boy who is scared out of his brains and deal with little miss pain in the ass Elouise next to me, looking so pleased with herself as she watches me struggling.

"You will stay a week," I tell her before I even have a chance to stop the words from coming out my mouth.

"Rem, stop. You can't tell her what to do. Don't be so rude." Elouise is up, with her hands on her hips. What the hell was I thinking that having this woman in my house would make my life easier?

"The poor kid will be so scared if she just dumps him and runs. What sort of person does that?" I know if we were on our own, Elouise and I would be yelling at each other by now, but both of us are trying to keep the tone of our voice on an even level.

"I am sorry, I cannot stay. Camille say you look after him. Not my son," Adeline interjects with a little more force into the conversation.

"That would be great if I even knew I had a son, or time to prepare to look after him." My mind is racing at how I'm going to do this.

Remember – face your fear and then run straight through it.

"Welcome to parenthood, idiot, you have to learn on the run, adapt and change. So, get ready to start sprinting, and for God's sake, show both Adeline some respect and Blaise some kindness. I mean, she has been through a lot to bring him to you. She could have just dumped him in an orphanage in France or even raised him as her own." Elouise is trying to appeal to my heart. She hasn't realized yet I don't have one.

I know I shouldn't have even let the thought enter my head, but Adeline raising Blaise would have been a perfect solution for everyone.

"Don't you dare even contemplate that, I can see it written all over your face. Man up!" Looking into Elouise's eyes is like waving the red flag in front of a bull.

How dare she question me like that.

"Fine. Do the test. Once we get the results Adeline can leave, but not until then. What if he's not mine?" I say, standing my ground with both of them.

The women look at each other and then at Blaise who is just quietly eating and confused by all the talking, and then they look back at me.

"See him." Adeline points at Blaise, and they both start laughing.

"She's right, just look at him, Rem. If he's not yours, I will eat my hat." She sits herself back down at the counter while they both continue to giggle at me.

I want to argue with her, but I can't.

The DNA test is really only for my peace of mind and the lawyers. I know he's mine.

"Now sit down and eat, and if it's at all humanly possible, maybe try to make friends with your son. You have a long road ahead of you, and it starts today."

I'm too wound up to say anything else, so I find myself sitting on the stool next to Blaise and taking an apple pastry the same as his, shoving it in my mouth before I can get myself in any more trouble.

Looking straight ahead at the window that faces the back

garden, I'm hoping the sight of the sun will bring some sort of calming feeling washing over me.

Not happening.

My blood is pumping loudly in my ears from the frustration.

The kitchen is filled with silence as the conversation stops, and the only sound I can hear is the chewing of breakfast and the slurping of coffee.

Then the softest voice breaks the silence with a few little French words.

"*Papa, où est ma maman?*" Blaise reaches out and touches my arm, and the warmth I feel shocks me.

Looking into his eyes, I can tell he already trusts me, and he doesn't even know me.

Elouise's voice is almost a sniffle when she repeats for me, "Papa, where is my mama?"

Oh, Blaise, I don't know how I'll help you get through this, but I promise to try.

And in this moment, I can feel him start to chip away at my heart to let him in.

If only it were that easy, buddy. I just don't know if I have it in me.

Chapter Four

ELOUISE

My heart is breaking for this little boy.

Losing a mother at such a young age is tragic enough, but then to have so much upheaval in the days following must be so confusing.

I don't know how to answer his question, so I'm sure the emotionally stunted man sitting next to him has no idea. So, when the words come from his lips, it surprises me.

"Safe up with the stars." The tenderness of Rem's reply has the tears that I was trying to hold back now trickling down my face. Rem set his large hand softly on the top of Blaise's that is still resting on Rem's arm. I wish I could capture this moment with a photo, but it is too precious to intrude on. That first connection between the two of them you can never replace.

Instead, I softly repeat Rem's words in French so Blaise understands. "*En sécurité avec les étoiles.*"

Blaise nods at Rem and gives the first true smile I have seen from him since he arrived on the doorstep. And although he likely doesn't realize he is doing it, Rem gives him a small reassuring smile in return.

Shocking us all, he does his best to repeat my French words, which brings a little giggle from Blaise, as his pronunciation is terrible, but at least he is finally trying to reach out to him.

For someone who was adamant he never wanted a child, he is doing okay with his first attempt of reassurance.

The morning slipped away quickly as we went through the process of the DNA swab and having Wallace pick it up and take it straight to the lab. I sat with Blaise and played with some of the toys the guys got last night. I didn't give them all to him, as it would have overwhelmed him. Just a few little cars, some Lego, and two soft teddy bears. I did have to laugh at the teddy bears that are exactly the same, just one bigger and one smaller. Maybe they were thinking it would help with being like father like son, but it just made me smile that these big tough guys even thought of it.

All the playing and overstimulation from the day is catching up with Blaise. Adeline suggests she take him upstairs for a nap, and I'm betting that as soon as his little head hits the pillow he will be out like a light.

Rem was in his office while we played, I think it was all too much for him.

Now sitting here alone in the living room, the last twenty-four hours are all running through my head. One minute I was at school, then the next minute I was here for a completely different reason than I thought. I should go and let Rem know that they are having a sleep, but I doubt I need to. He probably already knows because of the security system.

Stacking up the toys in a neat pile at the corner of the rug, the tiredness that I was feeling yesterday starts to come over me again.

I just need a moment to decompress and breathe, to just be alone. Not with a child near me or trying to be the calming translator for everyone, and especially nowhere near the grumpy man who has me constantly back-flipping who I thought he was. This morning, I was about to tell him where he could jam his coffee, being the arrogant jerk he was, demanding I do what he needs me to, already having an email ready to go before we discussed anything.

Shit, the email!

Reaching for my phone and opening the email, my eyes nearly pop out of my head. This man is crazy, there is no other word to describe him.

Employment Letter of Offer
Elouise Patterson

Dear Elouise,

Please find your offer of employment from Elders Enterprises in the job description of a teacher/nanny for Blaise Elders.

The job will entail living on site in the residence of Remington and Blaise Elders on a full-time basis. You will be responsible for Blaise Elders at all times, with personal leave being approved ahead of time on an as-needed basis.

This will be a twelve-month contract that will be reviewed in six months' time, depending on the progress of Blaise Elders with integrating into an English daycare and school environment and social situations.

The job will also involve traveling with Remington and Blaise Elders when needed, and all costs to be covered by Elders Enterprises.

The salary for a twelve-month period will be one hundred thousand pounds, plus an expense allowance to cover all needs for both you and Blaise Elders while in your care.

You will be allocated an assigned driver and car to be used at any time.

The rent on your current home for the next twelve months will be paid to hold the property, as well as a cleaner/caretaker to service it during your time away from home.

Elders Enterprises will also help to negotiate with your current employer, if needed, to hold your position for twelve months while you are working in this role.

Once we are advised of your acceptance of this offer, the employment contract will be forwarded to you to review and sign. Elders Enterprises will also pay for external legal advice with a firm of your choice to review the contract for you before you sign it.

We expect that this offer will be finalized in forty-eight hours from the date of this letter.

Yours sincerely,
Remington Elders

What. The. Actual. Fuck!

This man is certifiably insane.

Actually, no, it's worse than that. He is a completely arrogant douchebag.

Jumping to my feet and marching to his office, I can feel my temper raging, and he is about to have it unleashed on him.

Not even knocking I'm so angry, I throw open the door, coming to a stop in front of his desk. His head whips up at the intrusion.

"Elouise, what's wrong?" He jumps to his feet in a panic.

"You high-handed prick. I'm not some little pushover you can order to be at your beck and call. Take your job and shove it where the sun doesn't shine. I won't take orders from you!" If I was outside on a cold day, you would literally see the steam coming out of me.

"Whoa, whoa, whoa, calm the fuck down. I see you have read my email and it's not to your liking." His voice where it had compassion to it when he was concerned for my safety a moment ago is now long gone, and it's replaced with a calm controlled voice I haven't heard before. This must be his boardroom voice where he uses it to get what he wants. Well, it's not going to work with me.

I might lack confidence around these big business tycoons and know that I don't fit in, but I do have self-respect, and that's more important.

"To my liking, are you serious! Yes, Rem, the money is a ridiculous amount that would be three years' wages for me. Who pays someone that sort of money? Oh, that's right, you do, so I can be your private beck-and-call girl. Someone who can take care of your problem upstairs. I get it, kids weren't ever on your agenda, but guess what, shit happens! And you need to learn to deal with it, because you can't just throw money at a problem and hope to solve it." My hands are on my hips, and I have been giving it to him with all the attitude I can muster.

"Are you finished your rant?" He sits back in his chair like he doesn't give a crap what I just said.

"God, why did I even think that I was attracted to you in any way?" Huffing, I throw my arms in the air.

"You weren't, remember? You told me you just wanted me to fuck you, that's it. There didn't need to be any attraction there. A one-night stand that was better than your fucking vibrator. I believe I executed your wishes to your liking, end of story, moving on." He places his hands on the desk, clasped together, trying to show no emotion.

"This has nothing to do with that night!" My frustration turns to anger now. "But while we're at it, you were the one that wanted to be in my bed last night, so you can't tell me there was no attraction." I stare at him with eyes that I hope convey the disgust I'm feeling toward him as I say the words that hurt me on the inside. "Or was I just the body that was here, ready to be used to fuck away the panic you were feeling?"

My breathing gets faster as I continue to rant. "Someone you could control, oh yes, just like the letter of offer. You can't leave the house unless I say so, you will do as I tell you so I can still live my playboy life with no responsibility for my son. Yeah, nah, not happening, asshole." Turning, I'm ready to walk away.

"Elouise." His voice is not as raised now. I want to keep walking, but something holds me back. I'm standing there just breathing, albeit rapid, but breathing still, and I try to slow it down. I'm not ready to turn and face him yet, because I know I will explode again.

"Can we start over and talk about this calmly?"

Hearing him moving from his chair, I don't know what to do. Am I capable of a calm conversation right now?

Before I have time to contemplate it much more, his hand rests on my shoulder as he steps in closely behind me.

"El, please. I'm sorry, it's not how this conversation was supposed to go." His words are soft enough to caress me if I weren't so angry, although I can feel the warmth of his hand, and as always, it's doing something to me that I try to shut down every time. It makes me think about something I can't have, and after this morning, I'm not sure I would even want it.

"Come on, El, please, just sit down and let's talk this through." He pulls on my shoulder to turn me to face him.

His body's too close to me, so the only solution is to step away and sit on the chair. Damn it, he got me to do what he wanted anyway.

Sitting with a huff, I cross my arms and face him. I'm not the one who needs to be talking and explaining anything.

"Okay… I see it's up to me to explain." A small smirk appears on his face, which is kinda cute, not that I would admit that to him. It's a smile that tells me he is humoring me but is happy to do it.

"You think?" I roll my eyes at him, waiting for him to start.

"I'm sorry I treated this like a business deal, it's not what I meant, but I wanted for you to understand that I would never use you or take you for granted. I find if everything is in writing then there are no misconceptions down the track. I need your help, El, I think that's obvious."

Well, I'll give him points for not being stubborn enough to deny that.

"Go on." I want to hear what else he has to say before I tell him my thoughts on everything.

"I know I'm asking a lot, and I understand if you say no, although I'll admit I'll be pissed, but that won't be at you..."

"What you are asking isn't just a lot, it's huge! You want me to put my life on hold for you."

"No, not for me... for Blaise." His eyes drop from focusing on me, shielding any emotion that may be showing in his eyes that he doesn't want to give away.

Bastard. He knows how to hit me in the heart. Sure, use the cute little lost boy against me. Using my weakness to get what he wants.

Ughhh.

"That's not fair." I look at him, waiting for his eyes to come back to me.

"Maybe so, but it's true." Now his eyes are almost pleading with me. "He needs you more than I do. I don't know how to help him if I can't communicate with him." This man is such a contradiction.

One moment he is the sexiest man I've ever seen, the next he's the asshole who was just in the room before, and now we have the compassionate guy who is almost desperate to work out a way forward.

My neck is sore from the whiplash.

"Look, I know this is a lot to take in, and everything in the letter is negotiable. It's just a starting point. Is the money not enough? Is that what you were upset about?"

"You have no idea anymore how the normal people of this world live these days, do you? That is three times my yearly salary. Which to you might be pittance, but it's a job I love, and it's enough for me to get by. So, no, it's not the money." Relaxing my body language, I drop my hands into my lap. I still want to be angry with him, but I just can't seem to stop myself from letting it go.

"It's just a lot. Sure, I know how to look after kids, but I'm not a parent either, Rem. I don't know how to raise a child. I know how to teach them, and I can help him with his English so the two of you can communicate, but you can't just pay me to become his mother while you don't change any part of your life."

I can see he is getting agitated. "That's not what I'm asking you to do!" he huffs at me.

"I beg to differ." My voice holds a little too much sarcasm in it.

"I gave you time off. I know I will have to find a professional nanny for those limited times, and when they aren't here, who do you think will look after him when neither of you are here?" He jabs his thumb into his chest indignantly that he is taking some responsibility.

"Oh, how kind of you, giving me the clause that tells me I have to work twenty-four hours a day, seven days a week, but oh, lucky me, I can have time off when I notify you in advance. Are you fucking kidding me, Rem? I doubt that would even be legal in any job."

"That's not what I meant, and you know it." Standing now, he starts to walk around the room in frustration.

"Why don't you just hire one of those professional nannies then?" It would make more sense.

"Because they're not you." His low grumble that I could only just make out tells me more than he knows. He wants me here, but he doesn't know how to handle that emotion, and to be honest, neither do I.

"Hmmm," is all I can say as I let him walk until he is ready to tell me what's in his head.

Finally, he stops at his desk in front of me, leans back against it, ankles crossed and hands on either side of him, grasping the desk, hard enough his knuckles are turning white.

"Can you just think about it and stay with me for a few days until you have made a decision? By then we will have the DNA results and Adeline will have left. I can't imagine that is going to be easy on Blaise, and he is going to need you to help with that."

How does he do that so easily, pull at my heart strings? I hope it's not intentional, but then I have a feeling he's a man who is used to getting what he wants in life and knows how to get it.

My mind is racing, and I have no idea how to even comprehend everything that is happening around me. I know what I need to do.

"Okay," I reply gingerly.

"Okay, you'll do it?" A look of hope washes over his face.

"Steady on there, boy. Okay, I will think about it. I need some air. I'm going for a walk." Standing, I start to leave the room and the panic hits him.

"Don't be long!" comes from him with too much demand in his order for my liking.

"Rem…" I drawl, turning back to look at him.

He swallows hard, his Adam's apple moving, and I can't help being transfixed on it.

"Please don't be too long, it's turning cool outside." His voice is less bossy this time, although his face still shows panic, even though he's trying to hide it.

"Then I better get my coat, the English weather is unpredictable." I walk from the room with a smile on my face, chalking one point to me in the battle that I can see is far from over yet.

Walking back from my room and past Blaise and Adeline's room, I quietly open the door and see them both still fast asleep. Good, I have time for a quick walk.

Just walking from the house and down the road a little, I realize I have no idea where I am, and I'm hopeless, with no sense of direction. Okay, I need to mark down this address before I get lost. What a great look that would be.

While I pin my position on Google maps, I see that down the road and around the corner there looks to be a park which is perfect. I don't need to walk, I just need fresh air away from Rem who makes me feel like I can't breathe every time he gets too close to me.

It's not a huge park, just big enough to have some nicely manicured gardens with beautiful box hedging around the edges. A few trees for shade in the summer, a pretty little gazebo on one side with children's play equipment and a swing set. This will be a perfect place to bring Blaise.

I'm so glad it's empty at the moment because I just need space.

Sitting on the bench in the gazebo, I can hear the slight rustle of the leaves in the trees. The breeze is picking up a little. I hate to admit it, but Rem was right. There is a little chill in the air this afternoon.

My phone in my hand, I push Tori's name which is the real reason I wanted to leave the house. I need to talk to her but don't trust that Rem wouldn't be listening to me ranting like a crazy woman. Not that I would be saying anything I wouldn't be happy to say to his face.

Still, I need to talk to the only person I know I can word vomit to about men who have no freaking idea about the real world.

"Lou, what the hell is going on over there? Nic is on the phone to Rem, and I can hear a lot of yelling."

Just the sound of Tori's voice has the tears starting to fall, and I can't tell her why.

"That would be the arrogant asshole Remington complaining that I didn't just fall at his feet and do as he commanded me to." I try not to sniffle so she doesn't know I'm crying, using my shirt to wipe the tears from my face.

"Do I need to come over there and sort the idiot out? What the hell happened?" This is why I love my best friend. She has no idea what happened but is on my side anyway.

"Oh, where do I start?" Dropping my head back, I close my eyes, take a deep breath, and just try to get myself a little calmer.

Rattling off everything that has happened to Tori, including reading her the contract Rem sent me, is exhausting. Meanwhile, she is constantly talking over the top of me with outrage at his stupidity.

"I'm so fucking frustrated and confused as to what to do," I tell Tori as I sigh, getting to the end of everything. I needed to vent to her, and Tori's voice comes screaming through my ear as she yells across the room to Nic.

"You can tell Remington that he is the biggest dickhead I know. An absolute twat!" She is just as mad at him as I was when I first read it.

"Right," I agree with her comments.

"This is what you are going to do. Of course, I want you take the job for so many reasons. Number one is because you will be closer to me, less than ten minutes away at all times, and I miss you like crazy. Secondly, I know you, and there is no way you will leave poor little Blaise to battle through the next few months trying to find his place in this world. You are what he needs. Thirdly, because you can travel with us whenever we are on work trips, and Lord knows there is way too much testosterone on the plane on most trips. And lastly, the money will help you finally buy that house you have so desperately been saving for. But don't you worry, Rem is going to pay for being so stupid. You tell him, if he wants you that desperately—which being a man who we both know is in complete free fall that he not only wants you but needs you—that you want double that amount. It's two hundred thousand pounds or it's no deal."

"Tori! I can't rip him off." I scream so loud that if anyone was in the park, I'm sure they would have jumped with fright.

"You aren't. Take it from me, he can afford it. That way when you walk away after twelve months, you can buy a home closer to the city and of far better quality than either of us ever dreamed of. I know it will be a hard year, especially living with an arrogant boss-hole. But we both know you can put him in his place, and it will be worth it in the long run."

"But what about my job? I doubt they will say, 'Sure, take a year off so you can go live a life of luxury. We will keep your job open.' No one is that important." Picturing that conversation with my school principal in my head, I'm already dreading it.

"Lou, you have been around these guys long enough to know what happens. When they want something, they make it happen. That is the least of your problems. The only question you need to answer is, can you live with Remington for a year?" Tori doesn't even understand the half of what she is asking me.

That's my biggest worry.

How the hell am I going to live in the house with a man that, every time I see him, makes my heart skip a beat? I can't breathe when he is too close to me and his cologne is wrapping around me.

And him being the same man I lie in bed at night and masturbate to my memories of the night he fucked me into absolute sexual bliss.

I close my eyes and drop my head. What the hell am I going to do?

I whisper into the phone, "I don't know, Tori, I just don't know." There is no confidence in my voice at all.

"Do you need me to come over? I can be there in a few minutes."

I know the boys always talk about the brotherhood of male friends and having each other's backs. Well, I can tell you that has nothing on a woman who feels she needs to protect her best friend. As angry as I am at Rem right now, and totally confused about my decision, I won't inflict on him a full Tori rage.

"No… I'm okay. I've just got some thinking to do…" Lifting my head, I open my eyes and realize the sun is starting to lose its strength, and the cold air now registers with me since I have stopped ranting.

"I'm here if you need me. Just remember, you aren't doing it for Rem if you choose to do this, it's for Blaise and for you. Rem can go fuck himself." With determination like that in her voice, I now understand why she has fit perfectly into their corporate world. I can just imagine her in a boardroom getting her point across. Pity I'm not even one tenth as strong as she is.

"Thanks, hun, but can you do me a favor?" And this is where we differ.

"Sure, anything."

"Don't talk to Rem about this. He has enough on his plate, and he doesn't need Tornado Tori descending on him. I need to handle this one on my own. Okay?"

"Ughh, you are too kind. I'll try, but I'm not promising anything. If he brings it up with me, it's game on, asshole."

"Tori."

"Okay, my lips are sealed. But that doesn't mean my hand won't punch him in the arm the next time I see him."

"Oh God." I can't help but laugh at the image of Tori facing up to Rem who is a full head taller than her. But then again, I wouldn't put it past her.

"Now you need to get back to the house. It's getting later, and Nic just showed me a text message from Rem. He's worried about you."

"No, he's not, he's just worried Blaise will wake up and I won't be there." I start to walk a few steps before realizing I'm going in the wrong direction. Turning around, I walk back toward Rem's house, feeling a little self-conscious of being on my own in a place I don't know.

"He's already awake and asking for you. Now just get back there and sleep on it tonight. Call me if you need me, otherwise I'll be there in the morning whether Rem likes it or not."

Tori's words are like a virtual hug, knowing that she is so close and if I called her, she would be here as fast as humanly possible.

"Thanks, hun. I'm okay. I'll message later tonight. Bye."

"Talk later." Her voice is gone, and there's silence in my head again.

Turning the corner of his street, I can see his house in the distance, and I know I'm so far out of my depth.

I don't belong here in this world.

But can I manage to survive it for a year and blend in? Or more to the point, be confident enough to be more than the hired help, which is what I will be. When we are out somewhere, how will he introduce me? As Blaise's nanny, someone who works for him?

How did I go from his one-night stand to the friend zone and now the hired help? I've gone the opposite direction of every fairy-tale romance ever told. I guess I'm no Cinderella who went from the maid to the princess.

I push the button on the gate, and it opens automatically; he has obviously been waiting for me.

Seeing Rem standing at the open door and the warm lighting of his home behind him, I know what I need to do.

"El, are you okay?" He steps back so I can pass by him at the front door.

"I will be. We need to talk," I say with determination in my voice that I'm not feeling deep down inside.

But isn't that what they say? Fake it till you make it.

Well, this is me faking it. When really, I want to crawl into a ball in my own bed and forget this all happened.

Suck it up, Elouise, and show this man that you can play in his world too.

Or at least try to.

Chapter Five

REMINGTON

Where the hell is she!

She's out there wandering around in a foreign place, talking to Tori. I knew that's what she would do. Just like I called Nic to let off some steam about how goddamn frustrating women are, to which he laughed hard at me, and I didn't appreciate it. He totally understands what I mean, having Tori. She drives him crazy every day, but somehow, he loves her for it.

Beats me how.

It's one of the things I love about being single. When a woman annoys me, I can simply walk away. Except this time, I need Elouise, so that's not possible. It's going to be a long year with her living under my roof, but I have no other choice. And to be honest, I don't know what I will do once that year is over. I will still have to hire a nanny to care for Blaise when I'm not here, which does grate on me slightly. I grew up with my mother a stay-at-home mum, which meant she was there in the morning before school, and when I came home, she was there to greet me and my sister with open arms and usually some homemade afternoon tea.

I haven't thought about that for years. It's funny how you take for granted the things your parents did for you, until one day, something triggers you to look back and understand how hard they worked to make your life so easy.

Blaise and Adeline woke up, and I managed to communicate with her that there are some snacks in the kitchen for them and that Elouise is out taking a walk. Adeline mentioned that as soon as Blaise woke up, he was asking for the pretty lady and where she is. I felt like answering, "Yes, I'd like to know that too."

I messaged Nic to find out if Tori was still on the phone with her. At least that way I knew she was still safe and hasn't done a runner on me. Not that I think she would, and I know it's the sense of panic I'm still feeling, which is so uncomfortable and not something I'm used to.

I hate not feeling in complete control!

Sitting in my office, watching the security cameras, I see her a few houses down the street walking slowly back toward my home. Head down, shoulders slumped, her body language tells me that she is struggling. After walking to the front door, I continue watching the security screen so I can see her approaching the gate. Stopping for a minute, she seems to contemplate coming in but finally reaches for the buzzer, and I'm already opening the gate.

As I open the door and watch her walk toward me, I feel an overwhelming sense of relief which is unexpected, but one that I shake off as just relating it to my Blaise anxiety that I can't seem to settle.

"El, are you okay?" That's not what I thought I was about to say, but the words overtook my original thought of telling her that she should have been back before now.

Fuck, thank God I didn't say that. I'm not her father, and she's a grown fucking woman. That would have just started the screaming match again, and that is not what either of us need.

"I will be. We need to talk." Not even making eye contact with me, she walks straight toward my office and doesn't stop to see Blaise and Adeline, who both look a little worried.

"She rattles off something in French to Adeline, which I interpret to be something about being back in a minute, before I storm down the hallway after her.

If there is one thing already pissing me off about having her in my home, it's that she seems to think she is the one who is running this show.

Not fucking happening!

My house, I'm the one who is in control.

Damn women are hard fucking work!

Walking into my office, I close the door behind me with a little more force than I should have, and it has her turning and glaring at me.

Count to ten, Rem, don't fire her up before she even starts talking.

I can't sit behind my desk this time. Pointing her to the couch that is set to the side, she just nods and takes a seat as I drag one of the chairs from the desk to be in front of her, trying to keep a casual feel to this talk.

"The floor is yours, Elouise," I say, inviting her to get out every concern that she has bottled up, and I'm sure Tori has had a hand in planting more thoughts too.

"I want to help Blaise, and as much as Tori will yell at me for saying this, I want to help you too, but…"

My heart started to slow until she ended the sentence with a but.

"But what?" Christ, woman, now is not the time to leave me hanging.

"We need to set some rules, and that letter you sent me needs some serious tweaking. Christ, I hope you have someone vet your other contracts before you send them, because that really pissed me off. To be honest, you are lucky I'm here." The way she glares at me, she reminds me of Tori in the office some days, and I can see why they are such good friends. What the hell am I getting myself into?

Ignoring her dig at my letter, I just brush over it and want to get her to continue. "I can do that. Just name it, we'll change it." I'm finally able to relax back into my chair a little, knowing deep down it will be okay.

"You don't know what I'm going to say yet you are already agreeing. Maybe I should just ask for the ridiculous amount of a two-hundred-thousand-pound salary like Tori said." Her little giggle has that calming feeling you get when that first mouthful of a really smooth whiskey is sliding down your throat.

"Done." I don't care what she wants to be paid, I'll pay it.

"Wait, what!" she shrieks and sits up tall like she is about to jump out of her seat. "I was joking, that's just highway robbery, I couldn't do that to you. Just forget I said that." She wrings her hands nervously, thinking she has done something wrong.

"El, let's get something straight right now." Leaning forward, I take her hands in mine. "I would pay you whatever you asked me to for one simple reason… I trust you. I will be able to walk out that door every day to do my job of keeping everyone in our team safe, knowing that my son is safe with you." Her hands are so cold that I start rubbing mine over the top and stroking with my thumb to help warm them. "I know I could hire an agency nanny and then bring in a tutor, but this is not just a normal situation. Blaise has been through hell, and I don't want to put him through any more trauma. He is already attaching to you as someone he likes and trusts, like we all did when Tori first introduced you to us. That's what's important to me." I should be letting her hands go, but they feel so comfortable in mine.

"But I have no idea what I'm doing. What if I make mistakes and make it harder for him? I would never forgive myself." And this is why she is the perfect person. She cares more for that little boy than she does about herself. It's not about how I'm asking her to put her life on hold for a year, move into my house, or be stuck running my household. She is worried about Blaise.

"Have more faith in yourself, El; they didn't give you a teaching award for being useless. You know what you are doing, just go with your gut when you're unsure. I've done it most of my life and it's never steered me wrong. Including now, asking you to help me. We will make a good team, and before you know it, we will be through the year, he will be ready to head off to school, and you will be begging me to continue working for me," I say, trying to make her smile, but instead, it brings a shiver up her arms, and she pulls her hands away from me.

"That won't happen. Before the year is up, we will both be counting down the days to be rid of each other." A small quaver in her voice has me wondering what she is worrying about, but I don't have the energy to think about it much more.

"So, we can go through and work out all the other problems, but is it a yes?" I just want to lock this in.

"Before I say yes, these are my non-negotiable items. I need to be able to take time off without explaining why. We will need to interview for a babysitter for when I want to go out or just need time on my own. It would be nice to still go out with Tori when she asks me, and let's be honest, most of the time you're there too, so we need to have arrangements in place."

"Makes sense, what else?" She's right, I don't want to stop her from having fun with us all.

"At night when you are home, Blaise is your responsibility unless you need to work." She points her finger at me. "Which can't be every night. You need to learn how to juggle work and being a father. I'll help translate, but you will both need to find a way of communicating until we can get his English stronger and..."

"Yes, yes, I've already downloaded an app to start learning French." I roll my eyes at her, because for a moment, I felt like it was a teacher talking to her student. That better not become a thing.

"Good. But I have one more thing." Now the confidence drops from her voice, and I can tell it's something personal. Shit, I didn't ask if she had a boyfriend or someone I didn't know about. No, that's not it, my security team would have told me, or Tori would have dropped that in conversation, especially after a few drinks.

I nod for her to continue.

She waves her hand between us. "Nothing like last night can happen again. It was a one-and-done thing at Christmas, and we both agreed to that. Friends, that's all we can ever be. I can't be the hired help and be here for relief when you need it."

"What the fuck, is that what you think of me? Jesus, El. I'm not hiring you to be my prostitute!" I burst out, standing and running my hand through my hair. She must think I'm such a dick to ever treat her like that.

"That didn't come out right. I didn't mean that, no, sorry. I never meant that. God, I'm so bad at this."

"Well, let me help you. You are not the hired fucking help, you are a friend who I'm paying to help me with my totally fucked-up life. And I would never ever treat you like that, damn it. I don't use women like that, and I would hope you think more of me than that, otherwise maybe this is a mistake." I feel like I've been kicked in the gut. It's like the memories of my ex, Shannon, from years ago are flooding back into my head. Accusations being thrown around about me that were far from the truth.

"No, Rem, please, I'm sorry. I just meant like last night you needed comfort, and I get that, but it can't be me. It's too hard. Plus, it will confuse Blaise."

Taking a deep breath, I can see how upset she is, and her cheeks are flushed from embarrassment. Well, at least that's what I think it's from.

"Look, El, I told you that night, I don't do relationships in any shape or form," I say, trying to make sure she understands that I was serious about that. It's been over ten years since I tried a relationship, and I'm never going there again. It's just not worth it.

"And I don't do friends with benefits, so we are on the same page. Let's leave it at that and move on."

I want to say more, but she's right, we need to move on.

There is silence for a moment while we both digest what was said, and then she says in her soft voice, the one that does something to me that it shouldn't, what I have been desperately waiting to hear.

"Now we agree on all that, then yes, I'll help you, but only for a year, and then I go back to my old life, and you will continue confidently on with your life with Blaise. Deal?" She stands in front of me with her hand outstretched for me to take in mine.

I'm still rocked by what she said, but I'm desperate to finally sort this out.

Taking her hand which is much warmer now, I say, "Deal, and El…" I can feel a sense of warmth through my body as the panic that has been filling me since yesterday is finally settling somewhat.

"Yes?"

"I can never thank you enough for this. I'm truly grateful." I know it's the wrong thing to do, but the sheer relief has me pulling her into my arms and hugging her tightly. There is no one else I would want to struggle through this shit show with, and I want her to know that.

Feeling her trying to pull back a little, changing the subject seems like the right thing to do.

"Now, let's eat. I'm famished, and I think there is a little boy out there that was looking for you earlier." Stepping back, it feels right to put the respectful distance between us that friends would have.

If there is one thing I'm good at, it's compartmentalizing and keeping things in the right boundaries. So being just friends means that that is the last time I will have El in my arms.

"Sounds like a plan." She gazes at me with a look that is almost one of longing, then she shakes her head a little and walks from the room.

My eyes drop to her cute ass that her jeans fit snuggly.

Fuck, don't start that shit!

Friends.

Line drawn.

Don't step over it.

After finally sorting out the contracts last night with El and sending them off to my lawyer, he then turned up at the house this morning with the final copy for her to sign and the package that we have all been waiting for. The one that feels like it is a bomb encased in an envelope.

I told him I would open it later. I just wanted all the papers with El signed, and the rest, I'm already certain I know the answer.

But now I'm sitting here, watching Blaise playing with Adeline on the floor and staring down at the envelope in my hand. Even though I'm certain of the answer inside, I can't seem to open it. I don't know why.

Feeling the couch beside me dip, I turn to El as she sits next to me and places her hand on my thigh.

"It's okay, no matter what it says, I'm here for you."

I stare straight ahead at Blaise. "But what if he's not mine?" I whisper, and my real fear is coming out. I didn't want kids, but the shock is that now I'm not ready to let him go. How did that even happen?

"Then we work it out. Either way he needs you to be his father, biologically or not. Camille wanted you to raise him. We will make sure that happens." How is El so smart and practical, and here I am, a complete mess.

Dropping my head slightly, I close my eyes and take that deep breath before I finally rip the top of the envelope open and pull the letter out.

Ninety-nine-point-nine percent probability I am his father, and I've never been more relieved of anything in my life.

The fear I thought would be rushing through my body doesn't come, but instead, a sensation that is like nothing I've ever felt. Attachment to another human being, other than my parents and sister. I know what it's like with the guys too, we are so close and it's more than just friends, but this is so different. The responsibility and feeling of love for a tiny human that I never imagined I would get to experience. Can I say I love my son yet? Yes, but not in a way that I would say is a father-son love that can never be broken, but I'm sure it's something that will grow over time. We are strangers, yet strangely, I feel him imprinted on my soul already, and I know that no matter what happens in life, I will always protect and care for him until my dying days.

"You look relieved, Rem, but at the same time I can see your brain racing." El's hand is still sitting gently on my thigh, and it's comforting.

"If you'd asked me two days ago, I would have told you I could never be a father, but now I have no choice. It's time to work out how I do that." I gently slide the letter back in its envelope, ready to place it in the safe with all my important documents. One day I will look back at it and wonder how I ever doubted Blaise was mine.

"The same way that Blaise will learn how to be your son, you will both work it out together. No parent is an expert the moment the baby is born. You will make mistakes, that's normal. But no matter what happens, just remember to always tell him how much you love him and want him here with you, reassuring him that he is safe, and the rest will fall into place." There is something about El that naturally soothes me, even if I'm not asking for it. She knows what to say and when to say it. A quality that I'm sure makes her a wonderful teacher.

"I couldn't do this without you, you know that, right?" I say, placing my hand on top of hers.

"That's what friends do." She smiles at me like we are sharing a hidden joke.

"So you say. Speaking of friends, I have been ignoring messages all morning that I really should reply to. Flynn has been painful. We all know he is like an excitable puppy who wants to play with the new toy." I laugh a little and El joins in because we both know that is the most accurate description of Flynn.

"Why don't you spend a bit of time with Blaise first. They can wait a little longer. It won't kill them."

"A woman who is not afraid to stand up to Flynn, this is going to be fun."

"I think he has learnt by now that no amount of his charm is going to make me pay attention to him," she teases. Winking at me, she stands and walks toward Adeline and Blaise.

She underestimates Flynn, but then again, if he was truly interested in her as the love of his life, he wouldn't have backed away as easily as he has. He's just playing his cards and seeing how they fall.

El is talking to Adeline in French, and Adeline now stands up from the floor where she was playing with Blaise.

"We are heading into the kitchen to go and make some lunch, and we'll leave you two boys to it. Remember, he doesn't bite." Her joke is not funny. What does she mean she is leaving me alone with Blaise? I don't speak French.

Before I have time to object, they have left the room, and Blaise and I are left looking at each other with the same bewildered look. The only difference is that his only lasts a split second and then he is back playing with his cars. Okay, how hard can this be?

Sitting down on the rug with him, I try to fold my legs under me which is no easy feat when you are a six-foot-three man with long legs. Blaise just peeks at me up from under his head of black curls that fall over his eyes when he is looking down. Poor kid can't even see properly. We need to get him a haircut, but not just yet. I don't want to scare him.

Without even asking, he picks up a car, handing it to me so we can play.

"*Voiture, Papa*?" Hearing him say Papa now that I know there is no mistake has a cuteness to it but is going take a bit to get used to.

"*Merci, Blaise*." I drive it with him for a few seconds, then I decide he needs a track to drive around.

Taking some of the blocks, I get busy building a road for him to drive on, and before I know it, we have been playing for a while driving our cars on the block roads and occasionally crashing into each other. That brings a laugh from Blaise that gives me a sense of relief knowing he is happy here—well, at least for the moment. But the next big challenge in his life is about to happen, and it's going to be hard on him.

Once I tell Adeline the DNA results are here, then she will be packing to leave. How can she even do that to him? I could've been a serial killer, and she was just prepared to turn up and dump Blaise with me and leave. It's really grating on me. I only met Camille for one day, and yes, we had fun, but she didn't really know me either. The more I think about it the more it annoys me how trusting these women are. Part of me is glad Blaise is now here with me instead of Adeline, because I know he is safe.

His little voice drags me back from heading off on a tangent.

"*J'ai faim, Papa*." He looks at me like I know what the hell he just said. Think, Rem, you are going to need to learn how to work this shit out.

What could a little boy need?

A drink? Okay, I make a motion with my hand of holding a glass and drinking from it, to which he just waves back at me. What the hell, I wasn't waving.

Food maybe? I pretend to pick up a sandwich and take a bite and chew it, then make the noise of when it's something tasty. Pointing to him and then back to eating my imaginary food, he starts nodding very slowly, not entirely sure we are talking about the same thing.

My phone, idiot, why didn't I go to that straight away? I type the word *food* into it and have it repeat it back to me in French, and it makes Blaise's face light up, and he starts nodding faster with a big smile on his face.

"Yes?" I ask him if that's what he was asking for.

"*Oui, merci.*" Jumping up from the floor, he holds out his hand for me. This is the first time he has wanted to do this. I haven't instigated it either. I think we were both scared to let our guards down, and here the four-year-old is showing me up by being the first to move forward. I really need to take control of what is happening here. To be an adult, the person who drives the narrative.

Pushing up off the floor, I'm not as quick as his little body just springing onto his feet. I'm a man who takes pride in how fit and flexible I am, but I can see keeping up with a four-year-old will test that in a new kind of way. There is no slacking off at the gym now.

Holding my hand out and taking his tiny one in mine is a new feeling for me, and although it doesn't feel natural, it's not terrible either.

Walking into the kitchen, Adeline and Elouise are at the counter, sitting and chatting. The food is laid out ready, but they are just talking to each other and didn't bother coming to get us.

I have a feeling that El deliberately left me alone so that I would start to make some sort of connection. Not that I need her pushing me to do something. I'm a grown man and can figure this out for myself.

The smirk on her face when she sees we are walking hand in hand tells me I'm right on the money. I don't know what I was thinking that night in Rome, that she was shy and lacked self-confidence, because all I see in front of me is a woman who is already managing to manipulate me without me realizing it. I need to be careful of Elouise, she has more power than I was expecting. This is going to be interesting.

After lunch, the conversation with Adeline that I knew was coming was brief and straight to the point. She wanted to go home and has decided to leave tomorrow. I still don't understand how she can just walk away so easily, but I need to move on from that. Nothing is going to change.

Picking up my phone, I know I can't put it off for much longer. I mean, if it was one of the other guys, I would be pissed at being shut out like I have done to them, but I just couldn't process everything and I needed space to do that.

I open the group text message thread. My fingers move across the screen and then hit send, and I knew my message will have them all diving for their phones.

Rem: Congratulations to me. Seems I gave birth to a 40-pound four-year-old boy on Friday night.

Forrest: Like it was ever in doubt. Congrats... I suppose. Is that what I'm supposed to say?

Flynn: Shit, I know what I'm saying. Sorry, buddy, but I'm just glad it wasn't me.

Nic: Let's be honest, Flynn, there's probably a dozen or more of your kids running around this world, and that is scary as fuck.

Nic: Rem, I know you think it's terrible news, but I think he is great. Welcome Blaise to the brotherhood.

Rem: It's growing on me. Not that I have a choice.

Flynn: Fuck off, Nic. I'm careful. Always followed my mother's advice.

Rem: Oh God, do we want to hear this?

Forrest: Doubt it. Because let's be honest, it's too late now for you!

Rem: Not funny...

Flynn: Wise woman, our mum. Her words of wisdom: 'If it's not on, it's not on!'

Nic: Ughhh! We are forty-year-old men, why are we talking about condoms? Seriously!

Flynn: Some of us don't have the luxury of ignoring them like you do with your little cock tamer, and this text message is the perfect reminder.

Nic: Watch it! You're lucky you aren't in the same room as me right now!

Flynn: Yeah, yeah, Mr. Tough Guy. You know Tori would laugh and agree with me.

Rem: He's right.

Nic: I liked it when she wasn't so comfortable around you all. Then she was off limits to your bullshit.

Forrest: You're kidding yourself if you think she was ever off limits to Flynn.

Nic: True.

Flynn: See, he gets it. You are all fair game in my world. How else am I supposed to keep myself amused and you fuckers from taking life too seriously?

Nic: As per usual this conversation has turned around to be about Flynn. Back to Rem. What do you need from us, buddy?

Rem: We need a meeting, the four of us. I have no fucking idea what this means going forward, and we need to work that out.

Flynn: Nothing changes except we all get to call you Daddy now.

Rem: I will end you if those words ever come out of your mouth.

Nic: Flynn, for fuck's sake, be serious.

Forrest: I agree, we need to talk.

Nic: Rem, your job is safe, and we will work this out. When do you want the meeting and where?

Rem: Tonight, in the office. Adeline is leaving tomorrow, so I need a plan of action.

Nic: Done. 7pm.

Flynn: I had a date to get my cock sucked, but sure, I can change that for you.

Rem: Oh, don't change it on my account. You go right ahead, you will only be five minutes late. That's all you need, right?

Forrest: That's generous, I would've said three minutes.

Flynn: Fucking hahaha.

Nic: Okay, you need anything else today, Rem?

I'm not sure I'm ready for this, but it feels right.

Rem: Yeah, I want you all to come and meet my son.

My finger hovers over the send button, but then I just do it. I can't hide away from them forever, and I'm going to need their help, that is a guarantee.

Flynn: Fuck yeah, I'm on my way. Plus, I get to see the hottie living in your house now. Might have to move in with you too. Then she couldn't ignore me so easily.

Forrest: She ignores you because she is not interested. Christ, when are you going to get it? Rem, it would be a pleasure.

Flynn: What, no one is going to acknowledge how lucky Rem is right now? I'm picturing those mornings in the kitchen in her little PJs, hair messed up, and she is looking all soft and supple.

Nic: I swear to God, if you ever touch her, not only will I end you, but I won't hold Tori back when she absolutely tears you to shreds. She is 100% off limits. I've told you before. DO. YOU. UNDERSTAND. DICKHEAD?

Fuck! Sweat breaks out across my brow at Nic's words. They can't ever find out what I did. And what makes me feel even worse and like a piece of shit is where I thought Elouise was just a passing infatuation of Flynn's, maybe I was wrong. Damn it, I knew that night I was making a mistake, and having her here is probably going to be just as big a mistake. Thank goodness El is stronger than I am and stopped anything further from happening. Because I know without any hesitation, I would have fucked her the night Blaise arrived here. With no regrets, I would've taken what I wanted from her—sexual gratification.

Flynn: Whoa, okay, boss man. Geez. It was a joke.

Nic: Don't care. Rem, are you sure you want us all there at once?

Rem: No, but come anyway. Maybe before we head to the office. Tori can then stay with Elouise. I'm sure she could use her friend. I've totally blindsided her.

Nic: I'll try to control Tori when we get there.

Laughing to myself, I know what I'm about to cop from her. If there is one thing I've learned about Tori, it's that she has trouble keeping her feelings about something contained. So, I'm totally expecting it.

Rem: May as well rip the band-aid off now.

Forrest: Was thinking the same thing. See you at 5?

Rem: 5 is good.

Nic: See you then.

Flynn: What, nobody is going to address the fact that 2 out of 3 of you have threatened to end me in this message? Remind me why we're friends.

Forrest: Probably would have been 3 out of 3 but Mum would kill me for saying that to her golden boy, little brother.

Flynn: Ughhh, you are all assholes.

Rem: Yep!

Nic: And finally, he gets it.

Forrest: He is a bit slow but got there in the end.

Flynn: You can fuck off.

Rem: Done.

Nic: I'm out too.

Forrest: Already gone.

Flynn: All so fucking funny.

Sitting back in my office chair, I smile at the banter. It's totally what I needed to break the seriousness of this situation. This meeting tonight won't be easy, but I'm an action man. I need to get things happening straight away. No wasting time. Once I get into the office tonight, I can start moving forward and get everything in place.

But for now, I need to just take a moment before I go back out and let them all know everyone is coming over later and have Elouise explain to Blaise what is happening. All that keeps repeating over and over in my head are Nic's words to Flynn.

"If you ever touch her, I will end you!"

If he ever finds out what I did, I'm screwed.

Especially if he finds out it was a one-night stand, in one of his hotels, when she had been drinking and he gave me the job of getting her back to her room safely.

Oh, she was safe alright, no one could get to her when she was under me.

Flashbacks of that night play in front of my eyes like a movie reel.

Nope, stop thinking about her perfect body writhing while I pounded into her. The way she screamed for more.

"Down, boy," I mumble quietly to myself as I push my hardening cock back down. "We can't ever go there again." I shake my head at the fact that I even have to say it to myself.

Pushing up from my chair and standing, I readjust my jeans and remind myself why it can't happen.

I love my job, my friends, and my life. No way I'm risking all that. Besides the fact I'm not made to settle down.

Except the little dark-haired boy in the other room has just changed that statement whether I like it or not.

I need to plan my next adventure. An adrenaline rush is what I need to clear my head. Works every time.

The image of El performing her strip tease flashes in front of me.

Not that type of adrenaline rush, idiot! Something dangerous, like swimming in boiling lava… Oh, that's right, I already am!

Chapter Six

ELOUISE

Watching the way Tori marched into the room and walked straight up to Rem, slugging him in the arm, made me laugh probably more than it should have. She waved her finger at him and gave him her thoughts on the whole situation in a whisper, but that didn't stop her from giving it the same emphasis that she would have if she was screaming. I couldn't hear a word she said, and although I made her promise me not to say anything, I knew there was not a chance in hell she would be keeping that promise. All I was hoping to achieve was to save Rem a little and hope she wouldn't go full ham on him… not sure it worked, but at least I tried.

I have been watching Blaise all afternoon. It's been a big day for him, telling him Adeline is leaving and now meeting everyone, and with the increased noise in the room when we are all together. I wanted to tell Rem it was too soon, but I'll have to learn it's not my decision to make. I can't tell him he has to be the father and be involved, then criticize the first decisions he makes.

Flynn is on the floor playing with Blaise and has him laughing even though Blaise has no idea what he is saying. This week I need to help him understand a few basic English words so he can start to not feel so confused in a crowd.

The guys are standing around watching and laughing at how ridiculous Flynn looks when he is pulling faces at Blaise. I don't know why I'm not attracted to him. As someone who wants kids and spends every day with them, coming home to Flynn would be just more of the same. Ahhh, yes, that's it in a nutshell. I don't want to marry a kid when I put up with them all day long.

It's time for us to feed Blaise some dinner and for the guys to head to the office for their meeting. They have ordered some takeout to pick up on the way there, and Tori and I will order something for ourselves later. To be honest, we will be starting with a drink before that because I can't wait for the guys to get out the door. I desperately need girl time with Tori. I had already discussed with Adeline earlier that I think it's a good idea for her to spend some one-on-one time with Blaise tonight before she leaves in the morning, which she was actually thankful for. But deep down, part of it was me being selfish, wanting time on my own with Tori before my life changes tomorrow, when I have a four-year-old glued to my side every moment of the day initially.

After dinner, it didn't take much convincing for Blaise to want an early bath and story time with Adeline. He was tired from such a busy day.

Walking back into the kitchen after getting them settled upstairs, I stop momentarily, looking at Tori. She opens her arms wide, and I walk into the biggest hug from my best friend.

Standing there for a few minutes, I just take the strength she is offering, but finally, we pull apart.

"How are you holding up?" she asks, pouring the first glass of wine and pushing it toward me. Tori looks concerned for me.

"I'm okay, it's just a lot to take in. Friday night I was exhausted, school was done for the year, I was all dressed up for your dinner, and then I had plans of doing nothing but lying on my couch for at least a week, reading and bingeing on Netflix. Then boom, and here I am about to move in with Rem for a year and be a nanny. This is just ridiculous, and what is even more crazy is the obscene amount of money that he is paying me to do it." I take the first sip of my wine, when I really want to down it in one go. But the responsible person in me tells me to pace myself. I might be needed by Blaise, and right now, he is the most important person in this house.

"Don't do that. You are worth every penny he's paying you. And if he wants to have you work day and night, then he can pay for it. But enough about that. Let's talk about the best part of this arrangement. I get my bestie back close to me, plus when we travel as a group, you will be with me too!" She claps her hands together as she settles next to me on the stool at the kitchen counter.

"Hold your horses, missy. You travel for business, and Rem is not going to want Blaise there when he is working. Plus, you are paying him to be on the ball to keep you all safe, so you don't want him distracted," I remind her, trying to pull Tori back before she makes too many plans in her head. Truth be known, I'm probably too late.

"Pfft, he has people to do that work for him. I'm sure that's what Nic is telling him right now. It's not like they aren't going to make changes in his role to make his life easier and more flexible." Tori thinks she's telling me good news, but I know that's exactly what Rem doesn't want. I can read him like a book. He thinks that with me here he can continue to work the same as before Blaise arrived. He's delusional, but I haven't bothered to voice my opinion on that.

"I'm sure they have a lot to work out," is all I can reply, my mind picturing Rem in the boardroom arguing with them all about how he thinks this is going to go down.

"You haven't seen these guys in action in meetings. They will have a plan sorted quickly, there will be arguing and smartass comments flying across the room, and then in the end, Nic will put his foot down and it will be decided. The rest of the night will be used to eat and have a few drinks while they all joke about how the one man in the room who never wanted to have children is now a father. Poor Rem, I can just imagine how he will be coping tonight." Tori laughs to herself as she is picturing it in her mind.

"I'm pretty sure Rem can handle it. He never seems short of an answer for anything." I think back to the conversations we had over the last few days. Every time I brought up a problem, he would have an answer to the issue that usually just involved throwing money at it in some way.

I can already tell that will be a problem between us going forward, but it's early days yet.

"You seem to be becoming friends quite easily. I mean, I know you have known him for a few months now but nothing more than a group friendship. But for him to trust you with his son is huge." Tori looks at me, questioning how friendly we are. Shit, does she suspect something or is she just fishing? I need to make sure I don't show anything on my face because this woman knows how to see right through me and read me like a book. I need to deflect as best I can.

"Do you think, or am I just the solution to a problem? He has no idea about communicating with a child, let alone one who doesn't speak any English. The moment I opened my mouth and French words came spilling out, I became the answer to his situation. Sure, we get on just fine, otherwise I never would have taken the job. But I have a feeling it will be a long year."

"I've known you most of my life, and if anyone can handle an arrogant man who has no clue, it's you. Just kill him with kindness. Not like me, I would put him in his place with a mouthful of words, telling him exactly what my opinion is and where he could shove his wrong opinion."

"We all know I'm not like you, Tori. Plus, he isn't your boss. I need to tread carefully," I say, giving her a nudge with my elbow.

"Yeah, yeah, I'm sleeping with the boss, but that doesn't mean I can get away with being a bitch. Nic is the first one to tell me to shut up and get back in my place. But I still tell them what I think regardless of that, and the guys are used to it by now. And surprisingly, sometimes they even listen." We look at each other and start laughing, knowing that what Tori just said is funny. Not sure they listen to her or just humor her to shut her up half the time. Either way, I could never stand up to them like she does, but I guess I'm going to have to learn with Rem. It's going to be a balancing act of trying to help him settle into his new role as father, trying to cope with him being my boss, and keeping him in the friend zone like we promised each other when I agreed to do this.

I haven't even realized that I polished off the first glass of wine before Tori is topping my glass back up.

"Well, here's to your last night of freedom for a while. Let's get smashed!" Holding her glass up to mine, we clink them together and giggle.

"We both know I can't do that." I take the next sip of wine and am already feeling more relaxed than I did before Tori got here.

"Bullshit, I already told the boys that's what's going to happen and that Rem can deal with Blaise and Adeline when he gets home. You aren't on the clock yet. She's still here and speaks some English. Rem needs to stop being a big wuss and step up. So tonight, we are free to do what we like."

"I don't think that is a good idea. I mean, Adeline is still here tonight, but what about in the morning? Trust me, hangovers and little kids don't work well together." I remember one of the nights I agreed to go to a mid-week charity dinner with Tori and we had a few too many drinks and not enough food. Oh man, the next day in class was hell.

"Oh, stop being a party pooper. Toughen up, girlfriend, we are only twenty-six, not forty-six. Plus, he is only one child and seems pretty quiet. You can handle one kid with a sore head, I have faith in you."

"Good for you, I don't. But you're right, I'm not sure when we are going to do this again for a while. So, bottoms up, baby." Gulping down the wine, I place the glass on the counter for another refill, knowing this is a big mistake but to hell with it anyway.

"What do you mean you told Tori they could drink as much as they liked tonight?" I hear Rem's voice coming in the front door and Nic's deep laugh after him.

"Give her a break, man. You kind of dumped this on her with

no warning. She deserves one night to break free a little from your cage you are about to put her in."

Hearing Nic's comment makes Tori and I both start to giggle again. There has been a lot of that tonight, and I don't even know what time it is. We set ourselves up on the floor in Rem's front lounge with the bar, built a nest of all the pillows and blankets we could find, and just drank, talked, and laughed like old times. It feels like forever that we have just had a girls night in. Well, not really in, because we aren't at home. Well, technically, I suppose this is now my home for the next year, so yeah, a girls night in. Except this time, instead of Tori just crashing on my spare bed, Nic will take her home, and I will sleep off this spinning head upstairs in the fluffy cloud bed.

"Don't let him put you in a cage… that sounds kinky as fuck." Tori is lying with her head on the pillow next to me, both of us giggling at her comment and then we turn and look toward the two men standing in the doorway of the room staring down at us.

"Victoria." The sound of Nic's deep growl fills the room and bounces off the walls.

"Uh-oh, I'm in trouble. Maybe I'll get a spanking when I get home." Tori laughs at herself as she says it.

"Ughhh," Nic groans.

"Still think letting them get smashed was a good idea?" Rem slaps Nic on his shoulder, but his eyes are almost piercing through me the way he is staring at me, making me hot all over. Down, girl, he is officially off limits to you, he is now my boss man.

"Time to go, I think you are done here." Nic leans down to help Tori to her feet. I should get up and hug her goodbye, but I decide I like it down here more. Plus, I don't want Rem to see how drunk I really am. I wish I could handle my alcohol better, but I just can't. It gives me way more confidence than I have normally, but it's the head spins that are the danger.

"You too, Elouise." Rem holds his hand out to me.

"Nope, I'm good… comfy right here. I'll head to bed a bit later." Truth be known, I'll probably just nap here and sleep it off.

Tori giggles because she knows exactly what I'm doing.

"Not happening. I'll be back for you." Rem looks down at me, and I can't tell if I'm turning him on or disgusting him at how drunk I am.

He turns and walks away from me toward the front door, with Nic attempting to get Tori to follow him, hooking his arm around her waist and pulling her close.

As she is stumbling with him, she looks back over her shoulder and mouths, "Sorry I made your daddy mad," pointing toward Rem, to which I can't help but burst out laughing. Oh yeah, he can be my hot daddy anytime.

"Love you, Lou," she calls from the front door, only to have both Rem and Nic shushing her so they don't wake up Blaise.

Ughhh, that reminds me I can't be thinking about him as a sexy daddy to me when he is a real papa to Blaise.

What the hell was I thinking saying yes to this job?

Closing my eyes, I can feel myself wanting to drift off to sleep to the sound of the boys' quiet murmurs at the door. But the sound of the solid wood door closing has them popping open wide, knowing it means he is on his way back to me.

Shit, deep breath, you can do this.

As I try to push up to a sitting position before he arrives, it already sends the room spinning around me, and my stomach feels funny and it's not in a good way. The rolling tells me that I need to get to my bathroom sooner than later. I'm not sure I really ate tonight, and that's coming back to bite me on the ass now.

"So, drunk El, we meet again." He's wearing the smuggest look all over his face as he stands in the doorway with his hands in his trouser pockets.

"Nope, we agreed, we aren't meeting like that again, ah-ah, not happening. Bed, yep, going to bed, my bed, the fluffy one, lonely." I slap my forehead. "I mean alone, not lonely." Finally I manage to stand, but only with the help of the couch where I am hanging onto it like it is going to save my life. I'm leaning my body weight to the side so my leg is resting on the arm of the couch.

"Let me help you." Rem now moves toward me, and I panic that if he touches me, I might do something stupid. I start stumbling backward to get away, but instead, I just make a total fool of myself. My feet get all caught up in each other, and the next thing I know, I'm falling and sprawled out along the couch. I hear Rem laughing with the deepest belly laugh.

"Very elegant." Now standing over me, I can picture him just lying down on top of me and pounding me into the couch, and it would be magnificent.

"Now, don't try to move because we both know that would be a big mistake. Let me get you up." Before I can even say a word, his arms are under me, and he lifts me much easier than I was expecting, but of course, the movement has my stomach rolling again.

"I can walk," I protest as we start toward the hallway that leads to the stairs.

"I beg to differ, El. I think this is a far safer option, don't you?" That stern voice is back, like he doesn't need me to answer because it wouldn't matter what I said anyway. He would ignore it.

My body was rigid against his, but to be honest, after his words, I just give in and snuggle into him. Oh, he smells so good. What is it about men's cologne? It's like a spell being cast over you as soon as it hits your senses. Well, not every guy, but whatever it is that Rem is wearing has me wanting to lick up his neck and nibble on his ear, tangling my hand in his hair, then letting him kiss the hell out of me. Then his mouth would start sliding down my body and devouring me in all the best ways.

My eyes close as I start living my fantasy, hearing my name on his lips, and I want to let out a moan, telling him to keep going.

"El… Elouise, are you still with me?"

Shit, it's not in my fantasy.

Trying to push my eyes open, his are staring straight back at mine with such power behind them.

"Mhmm," is all I can manage.

"Are you sleeping in your clothes or am I helping you undress?"

"Clothes, all clothes, lots of clothes." I stumble over the words that are pouring out of me while my body shivers at the thought of him stripping me naked.

Fuck my life!

This is going to be torture on a daily basis, and no amount of money will be worth it.

I wonder if he will be angry if I change my mind.

I feel my body being lowered, then the comfort of the mattress under me, and thankfully Rem starts putting distance between us. Sleep starts to claim me, or the alcohol is taking over my body, one or the other.

The blanket from the end of my bed is tucked in around me, and all I can hear as I drift off is Rem's voice.

"Trouble, fucking trouble."

Same, Rem, same.

This morning was a lot.

My head was pounding, and I wasn't letting on to anyone. Rem kept checking, but I refused to admit to him that my hangover was as bad as it was.

I sent a message to Tori telling her how much I hated her, but it just came back with several laughing emoji and the words that she hated me too. She was struggling through Monday-morning meetings, but at least I got to be here.

But then we had to go through Adeline leaving and Blaise crying. Although he handled it better than I was expecting, but then again, it is probably a novelty at the moment, meeting his papa and all the toys and flashy things. When the reality that she isn't coming back sinks in, then I expect things to get harder.

He has just woken up from a nap, and now Rem has sprung on me that we are taking him to see a pediatrician this afternoon to get a checkup. Which I would have waited a few days to do, but of course, I shut my mouth and just agreed. He is only four years old, not an adult, and too much in one day is overwhelming. I guess that will be my problem later when he starts acting up because he is grumpy and tired.

Sitting in the back seat with Blaise, we pull into an underground parking garage not far from the Darby Hotels office. The building looks posh, and knowing Rem, the doctor is probably the best that money can buy. Probably how he got an appointment so quickly.

Getting Blaise out of the car and taking his hand, he looks a little frightened. The parking area is dark and I think very daunting to him.

"This way." Rem points, not aware of the anxiety that Blaise is feeling, and starts to walk beside us. His long legs take big strides, and Blaise's little ones are struggling to keep up. In the end, it was easier to pick him up and walk with him on my hip. He snuggles his head into my shoulder, and then I feel him relaxing a little with the comfort of being so close to me.

I start talking in a whisper to Blaise in French, explaining to him what is happening and trying to put him at ease. Rem just looks at me, and I can see him getting frustrated that he isn't part of the conversation, but I don't care now. My job is to look after Blaise, and that's what I'm doing.

The ride in the elevator is silent, and to be honest, my head still hurts too much to use the energy to fill the void with useless chatting.

Walking through the glass doors, the waiting room looks bright and cheerful, just like you would imagine a pediatrician's office would look. The walls are painted like a forest, with of course animals, fairies, and elves. Blaise finally lifts his head off my shoulder and looks all around him. I take him to the corner of the room where there are toys, a small table with coloring set up, and books to read. I can hear Rem talking to the receptionist behind me, but I'm too busy helping Blaise choose a picture for us to color together.

We were still busy trying to stay in the lines in our picture when I hear a male voice calling us.

"Blaise Elders."

Picking up Blaise into my arms again, I turn, and Rem is standing with his hand outstretched to the doctor.

"Dr. Keats, I'm Remington Elders, and this is my son Blaise." What is with all the hot-looking men in this town, seriously.

"Nice to meet you." His voice seems kind, which I suppose goes with the job.

Before Rem even has time to strike up a conversation, Doctor Keats turns to me and talks to Blaise.

"Hi, Blaise, I'm Dr. Keats, but you can call me Dr. Drew." He smiles softly at Blaise then lifts his eyes back up to me. "And you must be Mrs. Elders?" He holds out his hand to me, and I almost choke on my spit.

"No, sorry, no, I'm just the nanny," I say, fumbling over my words, and I'm already annoyed at myself for saying it, although to be honest, it's what I am, and I need to get over that and move on.

Rem breaks the awkward moment as he steps closer to me. He sets his hand on my back, and I'm not sure if it's for comfort to stop my embarrassment or to stake some weird claim on me.

"My apologies, this is Elouise Patterson, a good friend of mine who is helping me with Blaise until he gets settled in. Did your secretary pass on the details?" I can tell in his voice that Rem is a little frustrated.

"I have been fully booked all day, sorry. All I know is that you have just taken custody of Blaise, but I have a feeling you are about to tell me there is more to it than that." He turns to his side and directs us with his arm toward the door he came from. "Please, come in and we can chat."

I'm waiting for Rem to start walking, planning to follow him, but his hand doesn't drop from my back, and instead the slight pressure is telling me to go first. Different to when we were in the parking garage, where he just walked solo to the side of us.

Following Dr. Keats into the room, it is again a very calming place, with a mural behind his desk with stars and rainbows and cartoon animals all dressed as doctors and nurses. This guy cares about his patients, and you can tell that he wants them to feel at ease in a scary room.

Rem pulls the two chairs closer to each other and takes my forearm, helping me sit down with Blaise now in my lap.

"Okay, let's get to know each other," Dr. Keats says while

looking straight at me, with eyes that shouldn't be that suggestive in an appointment with a child.

I swear I hear Rem growl under his breath, but I'm sure I'm wrong.

But one thing I do know is that today can't end soon enough.

I can't handle the situation I'm in, so what makes this guy think I can handle him too? I mean, who hits on a patient's nanny!

Even if he is super-hot, and in another life, I'd be down to play doctors and nurses. But right now, I just need to learn how to play the nanny for my boss.

Fuck, what is wrong with me! My life sounds like the kind of train wreck you'd see on a damn rom-com.

I didn't think I'd be saying this today, but someone bring me more alcohol, and make it snappy.

Chapter Seven

REMINGTON

They tell me he's the best pediatrician in London, and he'd better be with the price he's charging me for the after-hours appointment.

He might be the best doctor for kids, but the way he is staring at Elouise like he wants to examine her instead of Blaise, then this might be the only visit we have here.

"So, tell me Blaise's story and what resulted in the change of circumstances of you gaining custody." Dr. Keats glances only briefly toward me, his concentration still on Elouise and Blaise. For his sake, I hope he is centered on my son, which is the reason we are here.

"His mother died, and I only found out he existed when he arrived on my doorstep on Friday night." Surely that's all he needs to know. Because to be honest, there isn't much more to tell him.

I can tell he is waiting for more, looking back toward me. "Oh, and he was with her when it happened," I add.

"Was it traumatic for him?" Finally, he is interacting with us both, looking between me and Elouise.

"I don't know, I haven't spoken to him about it." The look of disgust on his face that I haven't tried to reach out to my son makes me want to get up, take Blaise and Elouise, and storm out of here.

Pompous prick!

Before I can even answer, Elouise has my back and jumps in.

"Which isn't Remington's fault. Blaise only speaks French. I am doing the translating until Rem can get his French up to speed. So, we are doing the best we can in hard circumstances." Looking across to me, she gives me the reassuring smile that she wasn't about to let me look like an asshole.

"I see. I'm sure it's been a difficult few days then." Finally, a look of respect toward me from Dr. Douche. "May I ask for you to help me with talking to Blaise then too? Not sure my French will be good enough, and I want him to feel comfortable with me."

I sit back and watch him go through everything with Blaise, from all the physical examination, to testing his hearing, eyesight, and a gentle conversation about what happened with his mum. I have to hand it to him, his thoroughness makes me think he is worth the small fortune I'm paying him.

"Blaise seems to be a healthy little boy with just a few little things I would like to keep an eye on, nothing serious, but I think it would be worth monitoring. He has a little heart murmur I can hear, and although it is probably nothing, as we have no prior history on it, I would like to check on it later just to be sure it's normal. Many children have them and grow out of them." I'm not about to tell him I had the same issue when I was younger because I don't want him dismissing it in case it gets worse.

"I will have my secretary set up some appointments for you and be in touch. Who should I tell her to contact?" I want to tell him me, but I know it will be Elouise who takes on that role because I can't be here all the time, it's a fact of life.

"Please have her speak to Elouise, but I would like to be emailed as well and with the reports each time you see him if I'm not here. So, I can keep a file on his medical history too." I look into Elouise's eyes, trying to make her understand it's not that I don't trust her but more that I'm a details man. I want to know everything.

Her nod is enough to tell me she realizes what I'm like.

Driving home after the appointment, the car is silent. I didn't know what to say, and obviously neither does Elouise except for the occasional giggle with Blaise in the back seat. He's been talking to himself, well, actually I think he was singing a song that sounds happy, so at least he wasn't too traumatized by the doctor. Not sure I can say the same.

It's a strange feeling to say I trust him with my son, but I just don't trust him with my nanny. Ughh, I hate that word, but I suppose I need to accept that's what she is at the moment.

Driving up my street, I'm reminded that I love my house, but there's one thing that still annoys me to this day about it, that I don't have a garage to drive straight into. Especially now that I have Blaise, it would be nice to be able to get him out of the weather. Summer isn't too bad, but winter and the rain is going to be painful going forward. I drive in through the security gates and park at the front door, and before I even have a chance to get out of the driver's seat, Elouise is out of the car and coming around to get Blaise out.

"I'll take him." My tone is short with her. It shouldn't be, but I'm still feeling agitated at the way Dr. Douche looked at her.

She might not be mine, but she's not going to be his either. She deserves better than a man who is trying to hit on her in the middle of an appointment.

It's surprising how quickly Blaise feels comfortable with me, and I know he doesn't really know me, but there is something between us that I can't explain. I just want to protect him, and he trusts me to take care of him. I know we have a long way to go, but it's a good start.

The day was long, and I let Elouise take control once we got inside. It didn't take her long to feed, bathe, and get him into bed. Listening to her talking to him, I might not be able to understand what she is saying, but what I can tell is how gentle she is with him. His little laugh coming from the bathroom when he was playing in the bath made me smile. Although he has had a difficult time lately, he is still happy, and that makes me feel content that we are doing the right thing so far. It's the moment he goes quiet that I'll be worried, because one thing I have learned from my niece and nephew is they never shut up. Every time my sister is FaceTiming me, I can hardly hear her. She tunes them out, but I don't seem to have that skill obviously.

Standing in the kitchen, I have two glasses of red wine poured, waiting for Elouise when she is finished upstairs. But very quickly, I'm dismissed when she only comes down to tell me she's going to bed. The problem is that she has already changed and is in silk pajama shorts and a singlet that hugs every curve in her body. Her ass cheeks peek out the bottom of the shorts as she turns and walks back toward the stairs.

My brain takes me back to a place I promised myself I had moved on from, and the tingle in my hands reminds me of what it felt like to have that ass gripped tightly as I took her hard.

Fuck, this is going to be a long twelve months.

The first glass of red on the counter, I down in one go, the second following straight after, and then I pour a strong scotch to take my mind off her as I open my computer and throw myself into work. I might not be in the office at the moment, but it doesn't stop me from overseeing everything. I have Ian, my second-in-charge, standing in for me, but I can't completely walk away. It's what calms me. Being in control is what I need to settle the craziness that lives in my head on a daily basis. My mom called me hyperactive as a child, and I don't know if I was or wasn't, you didn't get things diagnosed back then, but all I know is I have a lot of energy that I need to work off daily. Otherwise, if I can't either physically or mentally put my body to work in some way, then I feel this rush that I can't keep calm. It's why I love to do dangerous things that take my body to the extreme and push the adrenaline over the edge.

Because when I'm done, the peace that comes is actually what I crave.

No one knows that. They just think I'm an adrenaline junkie, but it's more than that.

I'm chasing the calm that I can't ever seem to find.

I hope that Blaise hasn't inherited the same trait, because two of us in the same house isn't going to work. For the short time I spent with his mother, she seemed relaxed and lived a calm life. Fingers crossed that Blaise is more his mother than me.

For all our sakes.

"Flynn, I don't give a flying fuck if you think you can handle it, I've heard that before. Let Ian do his job, and you don't respond to that email until we know more. Got it?"

His mumble in my ear that I'm being a prick is a standard answer.

"Tell me something new. Now message me once it's sorted." I hang up on Flynn before I lose my shit with him.

I can't believe Flynn was stupid enough to get caught on film having sex with the daughter of one of our biggest competitors, and the video has ended up in the hands of someone who is claiming to be a wannabe Insta influencer. Who is now trying to blackmail him and the Darby Hotel company to stop them from posting it online. Ian is busy getting everything on the background of this woman, as well as talking to Felisha Kentwall and her father, who have received the same threats and want it shut down just as quickly as we do.

Broderick has also been called back from Australia where he is visiting with his girlfriend who is also Nic's mother. If anyone can get behind the scenes and dig up information, it's Nic's private investigator. I wish we didn't have a need for him in our business, but things keep cropping up that call for his expertise, which is the type we deliberately don't ask too many questions about.

Although the Kentwall family want everything buried quickly too, I don't trust them. I mean, how the hell did the video get leaked in the first place, and who set up the camera in her hotel room? There is more to this than what is showing on the surface, that I'm certain of. It is way too convenient to be happening with one of our competitors.

Fucking Flynn! I suppose I should be grateful it hasn't happened before now.

This morning has been what I needed, a crisis that I can jump on to, to help Ian sort out. I hardly got any sleep last night because I couldn't stop thinking about Elouise and the way Dr. Douche was looking at her; it lit me on fire, and I wanted to claim her again, which is all kinds of dangerous. And even after wanking myself off to get the image of her perfect little ass in those silk shorts out of my head, I still couldn't shake it. So now I'm cranky and pissed off at both this situation Flynn has put us in and myself for not being able to clear Elouise from my wank bank. This never happens to me. I have many hot bodies I have slept with, and yet I can't picture a single one, and the only image that keeps going through my brain on repeat is my nanny.

"Thought you were on leave." Her soft voice coming from the door has me looking up.

"I am, this is what leave looks like," I snap at her a little too quickly. The truth is I'm never fully on leave.

"Okay then… well, sorry to disturb you, but Blaise is going to need more clothes and ones that fit him. I've looked at what he arrived with, and it's not much."

Why is she bothering me with this? That's what I'm paying her a heinous amount of money for.

"I'll give you my personal shopper's details," I say before looking back at the screen with the problem that Flynn created and Ian is trying to sort out. A video I don't want to have to sit through again, of that I'm certain.

"Oh my God, you are such an ass. He is four, he doesn't need a damn suit. He needs play clothes." Hearing her feet getting closer to my desk, I look up at a woman who is about to let loose with some rant that I'm not in the mood for today.

"Elouise, sort it out. It's what I pay you for." Standing abruptly, my chair rolls back quickly, slamming into the wall.

"Don't you dare speak to me in that tone. I'm not your punching bag when you are stressed. Now here is your first father duty. Get your keys, you are taking us shopping. To a normal store that sells clothes that will make *your son* comfortable to be able to play like a regular little boy." She glares at me, hands on her hips.

I may as well be fucking her because she is annoying enough to be my girlfriend. Another reason why I choose not to be in a relationship, if this is what living with a woman is like.

"Watch it, Elouise, today is not the day to pick a battle. As I said, I don't shop for clothes." I'm waiting for her to back down, but she is only getting more fire in her eyes. It should piss me off, but instead, it's only fueling the fire in me. This is not ideal.

"Oh, it's not a battle, it's more of an order, isn't it. You pay me money, so it gives you the right to order me around, apparently. Well, I have news for you. Paying me doesn't absolve you from your duties as a father. This little boy is scared. He might not be showing it, but who do you think he would rather be in a change room with to try on clothes… Yes, I can see it finally registering in that stupid male brain of yours. He looks up to you, Rem, give the kid a break and at least spend a few days with him before you go back to work."

I want to tell her to get fucked, but part of me knows she's right, and I hate that.

"Are you done?" I can't turn off the hate dripping in my words.

"Are you taking us shopping?" I had no idea that Elouise had this much confidence buried deep down in her.

"Fine, give me ten minutes." I pull my chair back from behind me and drop into it, already typing an email as she replies.

"Then to answer you, yes, I'm done." Turning to leave my office, she speaks sternly as she is exiting. "And make sure you leave the asshole attitude in this room. Blaise doesn't deserve a sulking father because he was guilted into spending time with him."

My fingers tense into fists above my keyboard as I try to stop from answering her the way I want to.

I might be in a bad mood, but what is up her ass this morning? I might not have spent much time with her when we were out in a group, but still, I never would have guessed her to be so moody.

Ughh, this is going to be the shopping trip from hell.

There is a reason I don't shop, because I hate it and it's a waste of my time. But now it will be twice as bad with a woman in a foul mood and a little boy who will be overwhelmed with all the people, lights, sounds, and visual stimulation.

Sitting into my chair and laying my head back against it, it dawns on me why she wants me there. Why didn't she just come out and say that when she asked me? Blaise needs me there to feel protected in a world that he doesn't yet understand. So, while she will be looking for clothes and making sure he has what he needs, my job is to be his rock. The place he can cling on to in the stormy and turbulent waters.

Damn, women are hard to understand. Someone needs to write the road map. Mission impossible, now that I think about it, because they are all different. But it would be handy if they came with a manual.

I finish the email to Ian with the extra input that I need to contribute, and I have to trust that between him and Broderick, they will be all over this without me being there. Ian is good at his job, otherwise he wouldn't be working with me. But the truth of the matter is this is why I didn't ever want kids.

My job is my life.

It isn't a typical nine-to-five, five-days-a-week deal. My role in the company is twenty-four hours a day, seven days a week, three hundred and sixty-five days a year. We never know when a threat will come, and it's my job to make sure we have mitigated as many of the risks as possible before they even occur, or when things come out of left field, I need to drop everything to make sure it's stopped before it even gets started. Nic and the guys learned early on that I only go to them with things they need to know about. The day-to-day security issues that my team deals with are not something they need to be worrying about. The same as I don't need to know about the finances of the company. I trust that Forrest has that under control and that when I spend the money, the bills get paid.

So instead of me being in the office, like I normally would have been right now, probably yelling at my team or being debriefed at what they were turning up, I will be shopping.

For fuck's sake, someone help me!

Taking a deep breath, I pick up my phone and walk out, and all I can think about is how this will be worse than having my eyes scratched out by a cat, my least favorite animal.

The trip in the car is calm, and I can tell Elouise is trying as hard as I am to put on a happy front for Blaise. We are a united team when it comes to him, and regardless of what's happening, it will always be the truth. For all the ways we irritate each other already, there is one thing we agree on, and that's Blaise's welfare. I might be new at this and am obviously struggling with having someone depending on me, but I'm trying.

"I still can't believe you wouldn't let me take you to Harrods," I can't help mumbling as I'm walking around the back of the Range Rover to help Blaise out of his car seat.

"You're ridiculous, Rem." And for the first time today she is actually laughing. It's a nice change to the stress of the morning and her yelling at me.

"What? It's a one-stop shop and would have had all the best labels." A perfectly good reason to me.

"Oh, and you forgot to mention the personal shopper that you would have enlisted the help of too. There will be plenty of time when he hits teenage years where he will be happy to max out your platinum credit card with all the latest fashion, I'm sure. Take the win now that he knows no difference and that I'm a practical person. These clothes will get paint on them, holes in the knees from playing football, and rips in the sleeves from climbing trees or jumping off fences."

I fall into step next to her, with Blaise between us and each of us holding one of his hands. "What makes you think he will be climbing trees and fences?" I smile as the words leave my lips.

"Because he's your son, I thought that would be a given."

Now it's me letting the rumble of laughter escape me. "Fair point." Looking down at Blaise, I wonder what he is going to put me through as he gets older. Damn, this could be a bumpy road.

Walking into the Marks and Spencer store, I'm taken back to my childhood, when my mother would drag me in here to get my new shoes for school every year and twice a year for clothes, the start of spring and autumn. Mainly to check on what size clothes I was. I never thought I would be back here buying clothes for my own son. I know Elouise is trying to do the right thing by me, but I'm not sure she understands how much money I have. I could buy a wardrobe full of Ralph Lauren clothes for Blaise and wouldn't blink an eye if he put a hole in them the first day he wears them. I'm humoring her today, but once I know what size he is, I will have clothes delivered to the house and she will do it my way going forward. My son deserves the best I can give him, and this certainly isn't it.

Stopping just inside the door, I can feel the hairs on my body start twitching at the number of people and the noise. I know I love action-packed activities, but this is different. Not that there is any threat to either Blaise or Elouise, I just don't like being places where I have no control over what is going on around me. I take calculated risks, but to me this is just one big mosh pit of people and racks of clothes.

As Elouise starts to venture into the mosh pit with a shopping cart, I can feel Blaise edging closer to my leg, and it occurs to me that from his height all he can see is a lot of legs, shopping bags, and people's backsides or crotches. Instantly I lean down and lift him up into my arms. I can feel the nervousness in him as his body is rigid.

I know he can't understand me, but still, I offer my words of reassurance.

"You're okay, little man. I've got you." Maybe it's just the tone I'm using, but it's working as he settles a little more relaxed into me and starts to look around to see what is going on.

Things like this will get easier for him, but today, it's overwhelming.

"You've got ten minutes, Elouise. Blaise doesn't like it." Walking up behind her, she doesn't even flinch or acknowledge me.

Still flicking through the racks of boy's clothes, she pulls things out and lays them over the side of the cart.

Fuck this, she can look for clothes, I'm taking him somewhere that looks like more fun.

I walk out of the aisle and toward the sign that's hanging from the ceiling, crooked, but obviously no one around here cares.

Toys.

If us boys have to suffer shopping, we both need a reward.

"Okay, little man, let's find something that takes away the pain of this place." Pointing to things, I watch Blaise's reactions, trying to work out what interests him. "What sort of toys do little boys like? You know I'm new to this. You need to help me." I head into the section where there is a train set, and on the other side of the aisle are farm sets. His little feet start to kick back and forth, letting me know he wants out of my arms.

Crouching down and resting him on the ground, he reaches out for the farm set. A barn with what looks like a variety of animals, cow, horse, chicken, and goat. Of course, he'd be drawn to something that reminds him of home.

"You like that?" His face lit up like a Christmas tree tells me the answer.

"What an adorable little boy you have." A super-sweet, almost too sweet voice comes from behind me as I turn to see a woman with a shopping basket hooked over her arm. She's wearing tight jeans with black knee-length boots over top. A tight black shirt tucked into her jeans, with her breasts spilling out the top of it and fake blonde hair that is pulled up in a messy bun. Bright red lipstick and way too much makeup for a trip to the department store.

"Thank you," I reply bluntly and turn back to Blaise who is my main focus.

"How old is he? Let me guess, five. He looks big and strong. I'm good with kids, they seem to gravitate to me." Her voice is already grating on me, and I just want to walk away, but my mother taught me manners.

I don't trust easily, so when a stranger shows interest in my son, there is no way she is getting one piece of information about him.

"That's nice," is all I reply as I stand and try to look over the top of the shelves to see where Elouise is. Still digging around in the clothes racks and completely oblivious to the fact that I need her.

"It's so lovely you are shopping with your son. Where is his mother?"

I shouldn't have answered like I did, but I was hoping it would shut her up. "She's dead." The aggressive tone I used didn't even make her bat an eyelid.

"Oh, I'm sorry, so you are a single parent like me? It can be so hard and lonely. Maybe we should exchange details and we can meet up to chat about it." Who the hell is this woman and where the hell did she come from? Do I have sucker written on my forehead or am I giving off some rich bachelor vibes?

Looks like I need to get myself out of this, because if the dead comment didn't give her the hint, then nothing will.

Right, let's just get the farm and get out of here.

I try to take Blaise's hand, but instead of clinging to me like he was less than ten minutes ago, he drops to his knees to look at more toys on the bottom shelf, pulling another farm off the shelf that looks different to the first one he picked up. Of course, he starts wrapping his arms around this box too. I'm trying not to make a fuss, and I can hear this woman still talking next to me, but I've blocked out what she is saying.

Not wanting her to hear me say his name and getting frustrated because I know that no matter what I say, he won't understand me anyway, I don't know how I'm going to get him up without just pulling strongly on his arm.

Crouching back down, I grab the box out of his arms, pick up the other farm that he picked first, and also grab the third farm that he hasn't even seen yet. The look on his face is one of confusion, but as he starts to stand up, my spare hand clasps down onto his shoulder and I start steering him out of the aisle in the direction I last saw Elouise. I can still hear the voice behind me of the damn woman who obviously thinks, for God knows what reason, that I want to talk to her. She is following me, and I can't seem to get Blaise's little legs to move quick enough.

Finally, Elouise comes into view and looks up from the mountain of clothes she has in her cart, and her facial expression looks confused.

"Rem, what's wrong?" As I get closer, Blaise starts talking to her in French, and I don't have time to explain, so I do the only thing that makes sense to me.

"Let's go, you have plenty, we'll just buy them all," I bark at her and just march past her and grab the cart from her on our way to the cash register.

"Rem, wait!" she calls after me, but I'm not stopping. Thankfully

I find a cash register that is free, where I dump the boxes on the counter, and as Elouise catches up to me, I grab all the clothes out of the cart and throw them down too.

The crazy clinger woman is still standing in the line behind Elouise, smiling at me like we have some weird connection. There is only one way to get rid of her.

Tapping my credit card on the machine and ushering both Blaise and Elouise past me to head to the car, I turn to the woman who is now calling me by name since she must have heard Elouise use it, asking for my phone number.

I answer it in a final statement that will hopefully sink in. "Nice to meet you, sorry, I need to catch up to my wife and son."

Stomping behind Blaise and Elouise out the door, all I can hear is El laughing and mumbling under her breath, "Did the nice lady scare the big tough security man, flashing her big titties at him and batting her eyelashes."

"El!" I growl as I open the back hatch and throw all the bags in.

Storming around the car and lifting Blaise into his seat, I strap him in, and like a hammer hitting me in the chest, I see the look he is giving me… I've scared him!

Great, just great.

This is why I hate fucking shopping! Next time we do it my way.

Jumping into the front seat, I turn to El. "Time for ice cream, and I don't want to hear a word from you."

Still laughing at me, she pretends to zip her lips, but the giggle still escapes. Which has me just rolling my eyes at her and hoping Blaise will love me again after a double scoop of rainbow ice cream.

Am I buying my son's love? Absolutely! Because I seem to be failing at this parenting gig, and I don't know how to fix it.

Not the best way to start, but it will do for now.

Maybe I don't just need French lessons but should enroll in parenting 101 too. I can run a whole division of a huge multinational company, yet I don't know how to father a four-year-old.

I'm quickly learning which job is harder.

Chapter Eight

ELOUISE

"It was the funniest thing I have ever seen, Tori." I'm lying on my bed, FaceTiming with her after I got Blaise to sleep.

I don't have to worry that Nic is in the background listening to us because the boys are on a Zoom call, and Rem and I agreed to have a late dinner together after they've finished.

Today's little adventure—or misadventure for Rem—was probably the best thing that could have happened to us. We ended up laughing at each other in the car and could both see the funny side of Rem's fear of the brazen lady who was trying to hit on him. I mean, seriously, he is a big tough-looking guy, but he just crumbled in the shop. I think it shocked him because I'm not sure it's ever happened to him before. I didn't say anything, but it definitely had to do with him being with Blaise, and instead of thinking about himself, his protective nature clicked in straight away and he was thinking about a potential danger to his son by this unknown woman. I'm sure he will work that out for himself soon enough, but for now, it's my little secret.

"This woman must have thought she hooked herself a meal ticket. I mean, he did stand out, in his perfectly cut jeans, RM Williams boots, a white business shirt with a navy sports jacket that you can just tell is high quality and not something you would buy in a shop like that. And he had a cute kid with him, hot daddy bingo!"

"Oh my God, I can see it now. Maybe we could go and ask for the security footage from the store. It would make for a great video to post in the group chat." Tori's suggestion has us both laughing so hard that the tears start to run down my cheeks.

"Poor Rem, he was so out of his comfort zone that his only way to shake her off was to call me his wife. I mean, we all know that could never be the case." In the back of my mind for a fleeting second it sounded great coming off his lips today, but it won't happen, so I dismissed it with a laugh straight away.

"Absolutely not. Flynn would kill him for taking his girl, even though I would kill you if you ever became Flynn's girl, so there's that too. Safe to say, we need to find you a better candidate so my guys don't kill each other over you. Plus, who'd want to be the person responsible for breaking up the dynamics of our friend group? The guys all love you like a little sister, which is kinda cute, don't you think?" Tori has no idea the more she talks, the more depressed I feel. Yeah, yeah, I get it, he will never be mine. That's why today was a good day. For the first time since I got here, I feel like we are slipping into the friend zone, finally.

"Oh yeah, adorable to have four successful, uber rich and protective men who see me as a little sister. Because that's going to make finding a boyfriend so easy. I think it would be better if they didn't care." It's okay for Tori, she already has her man.

"You are looking at this the wrong way. Think of all the friends that they can introduce to you. It will save you stalking men in Marks and Spencer like that poor woman today. I mean, the only bonus points I'll give her is that it's slightly better than trying to pick up in the vegetable aisle at the green grocers. I mean, it's just pathetic to be looking for a guy while you are holding a very large… purple… aubergine. Nothing smells more desperate than that."

"Far out, Tori, where do you come up with this shit? Seriously, our mothers raised us to be ladies… well, maybe… okay, let's just say they tried." I can only imagine what she would think if she knew that I was as far from a lady as possible on Christmas night, when I danced like a pole dancer on stage in a strip joint, just for Rem.

"Oh, please, I am such a lady, just ask Nicholas."

I hear him walking up beside her where she is sitting on the couch. "I call bullshit. You are talking to the two people in this world who know you the best. There is not one part of an English lady in that body of yours, and I wouldn't want it any other way." His deep voice breaks the conversation, and I see him lean down and kiss the top of her head, and it tells me it's time to end the call and go back downstairs for dinner with Rem.

"Ahh." Tori's gasp at his comment has us all laughing. "Lou, tell him he's wrong."

"Tapping out here, not getting in the middle of this argument."

"Only because you know I'm right," Nic's voice booms through the speakers on my phone.

"Good night, my friends, enjoy the fight and what comes after that," I say, knowing that these two fight then fuck. They can't deny it, we've all been witness to the yelling, and then that look Nic gives her, and we all clear the room. I'm not as volatile as Tori, but God, I wish I had a guy that looked at me like he wants to pin me up against the wall right in that moment because he can't wait.

"Well, it better be me that comes after." Tori's smile and answer just confirms my thoughts. These two are ridiculously in love, and she can't hide that. It's written all over her face as we end the call.

I need to stop thinking about Nic and Tori because nobody wants to be visualizing their best friend having sex. Ugh, my life sucks if that's the closest I'm getting to sex these days.

Checking in on Blaise as I walk quietly past his room, I slowly make my way down the stairs when I hear Rem singing to himself over top of the noise of him making dinner.

Holy shit! This man can sing. Like, really sing. Not just an okay karaoke-grade voice but the smooth tones of a sensual ballad. Oh, that's just not fair. I don't need another reason to be fixating on this man. Standing just back from the door so he can't see me, I let it wash over me, and it vibrates all the way into my loins and does things I have been desperately trying to turn off in my body.

Wrapping my arms around my body and closing my eyes, I picture dancing with Rem while his voice wraps around me, seducing me and doing things to my body that I have dreamed about for a long time. Like the way he could make me feel sexy and wanted just the way I am. I want it all, the romance of the moment, him showing the world that someone like me could be loved by someone like him. But that's not all I want, I have never said it out loud, but I want more. Hot, steamy seduction to the point I'm begging for things I don't even know exist yet, and then giving in to be completely dominated by this man. His power is something that I want to experience in all the best ways. I honestly didn't know that desire was deep inside me until I got a taste of it with Rem. He is the only man I would ever trust to do those kinds of things to me. I grew up conservative and have never strayed too far from the edge, including my sex life, but with Rem, I want to jump off the edge of the highest cliff and let him make me scream… very, very loudly.

I don't realize that the feel of his hands in my fantasy, moving up and down my body, are mine in reality as I snap my eyes open to the sound of Rem calling out to me.

"You don't have to stand out there to listen." His voice breaks from the song just long enough to call me out for being a weirdo and hiding in the hallway. If only he knew I was feeling myself up while his words were like sex on his lips. I take a quick deep breath to stop me from looking like I was panting and hope like hell I'm not flushed, but I doubt it.

His voice then continues with the song that is playing in through the speakers in the kitchen. One thing about this house, it looks like it's old, but it has every bit of modern technology integrated into it.

I feel stupid, but I might as well just own it, now that he knows I'm here.

"Well, aren't you full of hidden surprises?" I tease, taking my place on the stool at the kitchen counter. I watch him from behind, dressed in a pair of gray sweatpants and a tight, white t-shirt that is hugging his arm muscles just perfectly. What is it with guys and the gray sweatpants? I mean, seriously, they know the way we react to them. If he is trying to keep me in the friend zone, those sweatpants should be banned in this house. My brain almost slaps itself for thinking such a stupid thing. Of course, I still want Rem wearing them. If I can't touch it, at least I can look at it and dream of what might have been.

That's until he turns around, and yep, the gray sweatpants can definitely stay.

"Not really. I like to sing when I cook, it's relaxing." He leans against the counter next to the stove while something is frying away in a pot.

"Oh yeah, I like to sing in the shower, while I do housework, but that doesn't mean it's worthy of anyone else listening. Whereas you, my friend, could be on stage with that voice." I'm not just saying it to make him feel good, it's the truth.

"No, not my thing. Don't like to stand out. I'm happy just to blend in. It's why I love my job so much. I'm not the face of the business, just the one behind the scenes doing everything needed, but nobody really knows who I am." Rem turns back to the stove, attending to whatever he is cooking which smells divine.

"Well, I'll happily listen to you cook every night if it comes with a serenade. But I didn't take you to be a Michael Bublé fan. 'Always on my Mind' is one of my mum's favorite songs, but I haven't heard him sing it. Her version is some old country star." I watch him smile at me, totally gobsmacked at his little secret. "But can I just say, holy shit, you are almost as good as him singing that song."

"Far from it," he quietly replies, not liking the attention on him. For the first time ever, I see the tiniest bit of vulnerability wash over Rem's face, only lasting a split second before he laughs it off, and I know the moment is gone, and I don't want to embarrass him any further.

Not wanting him to feel awkward, I quickly jump up off my stool. "Can I do anything to help?" My body is full of nervous energy which seems to happen whenever I'm around Rem and it's just the two of us. I need to be moving rather than sitting here.

"You can grab the cutlery and glasses for us. Thanks, that would be great. Dinner isn't anything flash, just a quick pesto chicken pasta, and there is a bottle of white wine chilling in the fridge."

Rem might think it's just a quick dinner, but any meal that someone else cooks for you is as good as being taken out for dinner. Not having to do the preparation yourself and just having it placed in front of you is always so nice. Besides, just the smell of it is making me salivate and realize how hungry I actually am.

I spread everything on the counter and pour the wine as Rem places a plate in front of me. We both relax into our seats and start eating. As much as today was stressful for Rem in a funny way, it has been a definite turning point for us both.

The rest of the night we just chatted about nothing really. Finding out about each other's families, lives before the upheaval of this week, and before we knew it, we had been talking and laughing until past midnight.

"Oh God, I need to get to bed. Blaise will be up before I know it, and I want to spend some time with him one on one tomorrow, starting on some basic English words." Standing from where we are still sitting at the kitchen counter, Rem reaches out and tenderly grabs my wrist before I can move too far. The look in his eyes isn't what I wish it would be. I know it's all in my head and only one-sided, so I'm ignoring the feeling of sexual tension between us that is zinging up my arm from his touch.

"Thanks, El, I really enjoyed dinner and just getting to know you. It's been rocky, but I couldn't do this without you. I want you to know I appreciate you being here. I'm used to living on my own, so to sit and enjoy a meal and some laughs at the end of the day was nice." Why can he be a total asshole one minute and make my heart melt the next?

"Thank you, I totally get it. I enjoyed the company too, and the food was yummy, thank you for cooking. My turn tomorrow night."

Rem releases my wrist and stands too. He looks as tired as I feel.

"About tomorrow… I know I said I would be on leave for a while, but Flynn's little sex tape has given me a problem that needs to get solved quickly. If you're okay with it, I'd really like to head into the office in the morning. Hopefully not all day but just to get a handle on it, and to wrap my hands around his throat for being so freaking stupid." The way Rem rolls his eyes at me has me giggling a little.

"Of course. I'll be fine, and we both need to find our feet in this new role, so tomorrow sounds like as good a day as any. Will I see you in the morning before you leave?" I don't know why I even asked that, but eating a meal with Rem is starting to become one of my favorite pastimes.

"Yes, I won't go in super early so I can see Blaise before I leave." It's only been a few days, but that little boy has already buried himself in Rem's heart.

"Okay. I'm off to bed, good night." I walk away this time before he can see how much his soft side makes me swoon over him.

"Night," I hear him say behind me as I make my getaway, thinking about what tomorrow will now bring, being my first day as a nanny on my own.

Really, it will be just like a normal day for me, but the truth is, it's the part of me that is already thinking about how much I will miss having Rem around that I am trying to put a lid on.

REMINGTON

"I know we have been over this, but seriously Flynn, what the hell were you thinking!" Standing in Nic's office, I'm staring him down, but I know it's having no effect on him. It's like I'm his father standing here, about to give him a lecture. Which makes absolutely no sense with him being older than me, but if you count age in maturity, then I'm old enough to be his damn grandfather.

"She was hot. We were having a drink at the bar, it became fun and flirty, and when she offered a night, I took the chance. Nothing different that any of you would have done in the same circumstances." He huffs a bit at having to explain himself.

"Yeah, maybe so, but not with one our biggest competitors' daughters, for fuck's sake." I shake my head at him, but he's just smirking back. "Okay, well, I hope it was a good fuck because now we need to clean up your mess."

"What's the worst that can happen? People get to see these buns of steel pounding into her as I gave her the best night of her life," Flynn remarks as he turns and slaps his ass cheek, punctuating his point.

"What is wrong with you!" Forrest growls at him. "How are we even brothers, seriously." He's standing to the side of Nic's desk with his feet spread slightly, shoulders back, arms crossed, and all the body language that tells me he is pissed and trying to hold off from punching his brother. "Do you think Mum and Dad really want to see you plastered all over the tabloids and across the internet having sex with someone? Imagine them at the local pub having to cop that every time they go in for lunch. Start thinking about someone else for a change. Surprisingly this is not just all about you. And what about Felisha? How do you think she is feeling right now knowing that her naked body is about to be exposed to the world—assuming she had nothing to do with it, which I'm not entirely convinced of, but still, I'll give her the benefit of the doubt."

Flynn's about to open his mouth to reply to his brother, but Nic doesn't give him a chance.

"Enough!" He's sitting in his chair, arms on the armrests and looking like he is the king on his throne. In a way he is, but we won't let him know that.

"I don't want to hear this crap. Rem, where are we up to with it?" All heads turn to look at me, and just like that, we are back to being four businessmen who are trying to solve a problem.

"Ian is on it, and Broderick touched down from Australia this morning. When I spoke to him, he said give him twenty-four hours and he will have it sorted. And we are not to pay any money to this bitch. So, we sit tight while my team sorts this. If she reaches out again, then we will send back an email, stalling. I'm about to meet with Felisha, her father, and the head of their security team to try to stop them from reacting. We need to portray a united front. I know their security guy, and I'm sure he will be on the same page as me. Paying them money will never guarantee that the video won't be posted anyway. We need ammunition against this woman so her blackmail actually has no power, and instead she is the one who needs to watch her back. Everyone has a past, and if there are any secrets in her closet, Broderick will find them."

Flynn falls back on the couch in his normal spot, with his head back against the leather. He lets out a sigh that tells me he finally understands the gravity of it now.

"I'm sorry, guys. I didn't know." He runs his hand through his hair, staring at the ceiling, which I think is so he doesn't have to look any of us in the face.

"We know, Flynn," Nic says, "and I'd be more pissed if you did. You were trapped and had no control on the outcome. Let the team handle it, and you just lie low until it's sorted." Nic is calmer than I would be if my company name was about to dragged through the mud. Although Flynn had nothing to do with the video being filmed, I still expected Nic to be ready to tear shreds off us all. Because we don't know what angle they are going to spin this story, and no matter if it is fake news, people still believe what they read. So I just need to make sure it doesn't make it that far.

"Better still, Flynn, call Felisha and invite her for dinner so you can talk. And before you say you don't want to talk to her, if she is out with you, then she is not off doing something dumb and making this situation worse." I can see the wheels in Nic's head turning like he has an idea.

"Just don't fuck her!" Forrest mumbles under his breath.

"You think I'm that stupid?" Flynn throws his arms in the air at his brother's comment, and all of us look at each other and burst out laughing.

We are all replying at the same time.

"Yep," Nic answers calmly

"Absolutely!" Forrest is the loudest.

"Totally." I think of all the times he has let his dick lead him astray. The seriousness of the moment is broken, and the plans are ready to be put in motion.

After we all get over giving it to Flynn, I know I need to get moving.

"Right, I'm out of here. I need to get over to Kentwall's office and try to soothe the old man down, and then I'm heading home to work from there."

"I am sorry you have had to come into the office because of me instead of being with Blaise." Flynn looks at me with guilt for pulling me away from home.

"It's fine, I'm sure Elouise has it all under control." Walking toward him as he stands, I hold my hand out and slap it against his and take him in a bro hug. "Besides, it's what we do. We have each other's backs."

Flynn just nods at me, and with that, I give a chin lift to both Nic and Forrest and leave the office. All I can think about is how El and Blaise are and how much I've missed them this morning. Which is a shock to me because I'm not used to having anyone to think about. But today, it has felt so different to have my work brain invaded by the thoughts of my home life. I'm going to need to learn how to shut that out because I can't be thinking about them when I'm trying to keep everyone around me safe.

Compartmentalizing at its best.

Pulling into the driveway, I have been away longer than I was expecting after the meeting with the Kentwalls didn't quite go to plan. Felisha wasn't anything like I expected, but her old man sure was. Full of chest puffing and raised voice trying to intimidate me, which of course didn't work one bit.

Whereas Felisha was polite, strong willed, and not prepared to let anyone walk over the top of her. Much to her father's disgust, she is in agreeance with us that she doesn't want to pay this person. She wants them strung up by their toenails and made to pay for invading her privacy.

Her team is reviewing all the security footage from the past few weeks, trying to work out how the camera was planted without them knowing. Of course, if we can find who it was and have proof, then she wants the police involved. But none of us want to report anything yet and for there to be any leak to the media that the video exists. That just gives the woman who has it more power, and the price will increase dramatically.

Before I walked into the office with them, I was certain that Felisha had something to do with this and it was some scheme to tarnish our branding. But within five minutes of being in the room with her, I know she didn't do it. Her body language was on the defense, and the way she stood up to her father was impressive. He is known in the industry for being an old-fashioned hardhead. Don't get me wrong, Nic is stubborn as hell, and that's what makes him so successful, but Ewan Kentwall is so tunnel-visioned with his thought process, it works against him when he won't listen to other opinions. He is in his late sixties, having Felisha later in life from his third marriage, so that the two of them are not on the same page.

Their head of security, Sandon Bock, I can't quite get a read on yet. I thought we would be coming at this from the same angle, but I have a feeling what he wants to do, as opposed to what he is being ordered to do by old man Kentwall, are two different things. But I guess money talks. In the end, I finally got them to agree with Felisha and me, allowing us to investigate this before we all react.

Opening the front door just after four pm, I hear Blaise's little laugh coming from the living room, which brings an instant smile to my face. I could get used to having someone to come home to each day.

Slipping off my shoes at the door is something I love to do as soon as I get home, and I walk toward the voices.

"Fucccckkkkkk!" I scream as the piercing pain radiates up through the ball of my foot. Hopping a few steps, I turn to see what I trod on, and straight away I take back my thought of coming home to people in my house being great. Apparently, I have just been initiated into being a parent by standing on a piece of Lego in socked feet. Holy shit, that fucking hurts.

Then through her laughing, I hear El call out to me. "Watch the language, one pound in the swear jar." And then she continues to laugh at me. I'll give her a damn swear jar. That is going to be the least of the problems if I keep coming home to Lego on the floor in the doorway. It might be a simple but effective security measure, but I think I'll take my very expensive, high-tech computer security system over the pain of the Lego barrier.

I compose myself even though my foot is still throbbing from the little sucker that is smaller than my big toe.

The moment I step into the lounge, Blaise is up off the floor where he was playing with El and runs for me. He leaps into my arms and hugs me tightly. He is making it hard to still be annoyed at my pain.

"*Bonjour, Blaise*," I say as I squeeze him tightly and shake him from side to side, bringing out a giggle in him.

"Hello, Papa." He looks at me after carefully getting out his first word of English he has ever spoken to me. The excitement on his face waiting for my reaction makes me smile with so much joy for him.

"Well, hello, Blaise, my clever boy." I repeat his words back to him so he knows I understood him. His face lights up and he is already squirming that he wants to get down.

Looking at El, I can see that she is beaming that he has learned something today.

"Wait, there's more," she blurts out as Blaise runs back across the room, grabbing a car and holding it up.

"Car, Papa." He drops it back to the floor, and then he has his favorite truck. "Truck, Papa." Then he gives it to El before he reaches for another toy. "Ball." He continues to point to a few more things, proudly rattling off the correct English for it in his proudest four-year-old voice he can muster. When he gets to the end of the words he has learned, he starts clapping for himself, which has both El and me joining in and clapping his big achievement.

"I'm so proud of you, Blaise." I take both his hands and hold them above his head and slap my hands on to them, cheering him and teaching him how to show excitement. El jumps up off the floor and gives him the double high five too, which has him cheering again and jumping up and down on the spot.

All my dramas of the day seem to disappear from my thoughts at the innocence of the little boy in front of me who mastered a dozen English words today, with of course a very broad French accent.

His attention is quickly diverted to the television that is on, and the Australian kids show Bluey comes on. I had never heard of it before, but El insisted it's a great show and all her kids at school love it. The theme song has him dancing in front of the television, and the excitement of Dad being home is now gone.

"Can I get you a drink or anything to eat?" Elouise is at my side, still beaming at the happiness that has rubbed off from Blaise.

"I should be getting you a glass of champagne to celebrate your first day of being an amazing teacher." Placing my hand on her lower back, I direct her toward the kitchen.

"What, I wasn't amazing all the other days I have been a teacher before I landed on your doorstep?" she digs at me as I step past her and head toward the wine fridge.

"But you weren't *my* teacher, so I'm just celebrating you being mine." I'm popping the cork on the bottle when the words start repeating in my head.

Looking up, her face tells me that I need to fix this. I start trying to clarify what I meant.

"You know, mine as in my employee, the person who is working for me and looking after Blaise, the nanny, no, I mean my friend… Oh fuck it, you know what I meant." Handing her the glass, we stand there looking into each other's eyes until the laughter starts falling from El's lips, and I breathe a sigh of relief, laughing with her. Clinking our glasses together, we toast the beginning of her journey with Blaise and my relief at being able to communicate freely with my son.

A few sips later and El as usual is the one who is good at breaking the silence.

"How did your meetings go today? Do you think you will be able to stop the world from having to vomit up their meal seeing Flynn naked and having sex?" She leans her backside against the counter near the window and the afternoon sunlight surrounds her silhouette, softening her features and reminding me no matter how hard I try I can't deny her beauty and how much I am attracted to her.

"Strange is the best way I can describe it. But one thing is for sure, there is something not right about this whole thing, and I can't seem to put my finger on what it is. And that makes me twitchy, and I hate the feeling of…" My mind wanders back to Felisha and the way she reacted today.

"Feeling of what?" El asks.

"The unknown." It's the only word that can describe it.

Chapter Nine

ELOUISE

The last few days has seen everything start to fall into a nice routine. Blaise and I work on words in the morning, and then we spend the afternoon playing. Today I want to take him out of the house and get him used to being with me on his own out in the car and around other people.

We have planned to meet Tori at the park near The Darby Hotel's head office and have a late lunchtime picnic. I was going to drive, but Rem has insisted that I use the driver he has assigned for me whenever I go anywhere. His reasoning is so I can concentrate on Blaise and not have to worry about traffic, parking, or Blaise getting upset or confused if things don't go to plan.

For someone who told me he never planned on having kids, he sure is an overprotective father already and one that I think is going to drive me crazy. Not that I can say anything, because he calls the shots here, and it's early days.

We have packed some cold meats, cheeses, bread, and of course, a salad full of greenery for the bride-to-be who is supposed to be watching her weight. Hidden inside the basket is a little chocolate treat for Blaise, and it's not really him I'm hiding it from but Tori who is a champion at sniffing out chocolate from miles around.

"Okay, we are almost here," I translate to Blaise whose face has been glued to the window since we left the house. Luckily, the car seat has him high enough he can see out.

I haven't heard from Tori since I messaged her that we were on our way, but she is probably in a meeting or busy. I'm used to her crazy schedule. To be honest, I haven't really noticed it before now, because during the day, I'm too busy in the classroom to even think about talking to Tori.

Art, our driver who I'm sure is more than a driver if Rem has anything to do with it, pulls the car up to the side of the road next to Regent's Park. Already I can see Blaise getting excited at being able to get out and run around in the open space. It must be such a huge adjustment for him to come from a home where he spent his days running over the mountain with absolutely no restrictions. Even at Rem's house there is a garden, but still, it is nothing like he's used to. So, the park is the first time he has seen a large open green area since he arrived in London. One that he is about to be allowed to put his feet on and run off all his energy, and for a four-year-old boy, that sounds like heaven.

I try to explain to him before I open the door that he must stay with me and where I can see him and is not to go with anyone else except for me, Tori, and Art, who I'm guessing is our bodyguard. I don't want to scare Blaise, but he needs to understand that this part of the world is different from what he knows.

Taking his hand, we leave the car and start walking to the southern end of Regent's Park, Marylebone Green. It's the part of the park where I saw in my internet search that there is a wonderland of play equipment, just perfect for what we are after. So, I arranged to meet Tori there. The backpack is my makeshift picnic basket, because of course, Rem doesn't own one. But to be honest, the backpack keeps my hands free to deal with Blaise easily.

Already the noise of the other kids has him skipping toward them and almost pulling my arm out of its socket, while I'm trying to keep up with him. Finding a safe spot where I can see him and again having a quiet talk to him about our rules, I let him run off onto the playground equipment and join in with the other kids. Being school holidays, it is probably busier than normal here, and some of the kids are older than Blaise, but he seems to be coping quite well. I don't know who he used to see and play with, and I plan on bringing that conversation into our play time. I don't want to be constantly trying to drag information out of him. I want our relationship to build and for me to be a safe person for him, someone he trusts, and not the person who is only ever being annoying.

"Elouise," Blaise yells to me in his adorable accent, waving from the top of the slide and waiting until he has my attention so he can slide down. Grabbing my phone, I video as he lets go and squeals with delight. I can't stop smiling as he races around to the stairs to line up again.

I need to talk to Rem about getting some play equipment at home. With the amount of energy that Blaise has, I think a trampoline would be perfect. Because let's be honest, who doesn't love to bounce? Maybe we can get one big enough that it will hold my weight too. There's a reason I'm a teacher; it gives me the opportunity to become a kid for a small part of every day.

"Oh wow, he is loving that." Tori's voice from behind me has me jumping a little, as I was so focused on Blaise and not game to take my eyes off him.

"I doubt he has ever had a slide or maybe even seen one. He is loving life right now. Plus, the more energy he uses, then there is a higher chance I'll be able to get him to sit still long enough to eat something and tonight's bedtime will be easy."

Tori sits beside me, and we look like chalk and cheese. Her in her Jimmy Choo heels, black business pants, with a yellow fitted shirt under her black jacket. Hair pulled back in a tight bun, her face looks like she just stepped off a model shoot with her impeccable makeup. And here I am looking like a parent of a four-year-old, even though I'm not. Jeans, trainers, a white t-shirt with a yellow smiley face on it, and a navy sweater that is hanging on my back with the arms tied together on my chest. Comfy and practical is going to be my way of life for the next year. If I was at school, I could dress up a little more, but to spend the day with a four-year-old, it's just not practical.

"I'd love to see where he lived one day. Maybe when he is a little older, we can all go on a little trip to see his home. Of course, only if it wouldn't be triggering for him."

Leaning back on the seat now, Tori makes herself comfortable, crossing her legs, and her phone is sitting on her lap. Even though it's on silent, it is constantly vibrating. I would hate that, but I know it's part of the business world.

"Just ignore my phone. Nic and Rem know where I am, and the rest of them can just damn well wait." Closing her eyes, she lets the sun fall on her face like she hasn't been able to sit in the fresh air for days.

"Don't get sunburnt, that won't be a good look in a wedding dress," I say, watching her sunning herself.

"Like my skin isn't going to burn red like a tomato the moment we land in Australia anyway. Last time we were there, oh my God, it was so hot. It's like Nic's skin was immune to it, but I just looked like my skin was as dry as the Sahara Desert after the sun sucked all the moisture from it. And that was in their winter."

"You really are a drama queen, aren't you." I watch Blaise trying to talk to another child on the pretend pirate ship bridge. I'm curious to see how he goes, not knowing what the other little boy is saying.

"That's what amazes me about kids," I say, and the change of subject has Tori opening her eyes and sitting up to find out what I'm talking about. "They don't even speak the same language, yet they are making friends to play together. So cute."

"Why can't adults be the same? If it's that simple for them, surely, we can all manage it."

Reaching across, I squeeze Tori's hand and smile at her. "Now you know why I love to work with kids. Everything in their world is just that simple." I'm so happy that Blaise is playing, and the smile on his face is so bright, telling me he is having the best time.

Before I can say another word to Tori, my phone starts ringing in my hand. It's an unknown number which normally I would ignore, but with so many changes happening in my life at the moment, I know I need to answer it.

"Hello, Elouise speaking." Tapping Tori, I point at Blaise, to which she gives me a thumbs-up, understanding that I need her to watch him while I take this call. I love that we can communicate without words, that's how close we are.

"Elouise, it's Dr. Drew Keats, I hope I'm not interrupting anything?" I'm confused about why he is calling me, but then my brain starts panicking that something serious came up on the tests that he did on Blaise.

"Is everything okay?" My voice has a quaver of panic that has Tori looking at me with worry too.

"Oh, sorry, yes, there are no problems at all. I'm just calling to book in those extra tests that we needed done so we can monitor Blaise's heart murmur. Do you have a moment so I can give you some dates and times?"

"Yes, sure, I just thought it would have been your secretary calling me, so I was a bit worried."

"I had a few minutes, so I just thought I would touch base and see how Blaise is settling in and how you are finding your new job." In the back of my head, already I'm thinking the doctor never calls to book in tests, this call is more than that.

"Oh, thank you, yes, we are both doing fine. He is starting to learn a few words and catching on very quickly. We haven't had any problems. He is eating and sleeping well, so fingers crossed that just continues."

"And how are you finding working for Mr. Elders? Is he treating you well?" Why is he asking about me?

"Yes, he is, it's a great job. Sorry, I'm at the park watching Blaise. Is there any chance you can just either text or email me the details of the appointments and I'll make sure we are there?" I roll my eyes at Tori because I need to shut this down before he gets any idea about taking the conversation to a place that I'm not interested in.

"Of course, sorry, I don't want you distracted from watching him. I'll send it through now, and we will see you soon. Have a good day, Elouise."

"Thank you, you too, Dr. Keats." Pushing the end button on the call, I can't help the groan falling from my lips.

Refocusing, I check that Blaise is exactly where he should be. He's still standing on the tower shaped like the front of a pirate ship that's attached to the bridge, now with another little girl and boy joining in their game.

"What was that all about?" Tori is already laughing, and I know full well that she could hear Dr. Keats on the other side of the call. She has expert hearing and doesn't want to miss out on any gossip.

"Dr. McHottie seemed more interested in me than Blaise. I mean, what doctor calls to book in your appointments? Aren't they normally busy helping sick people?" I flop back in the seat with exasperation.

"Wait, how hot is this doctor and why is this the first time I'm hearing about it? Spill it, woman!" She is instantly sitting up straight and turned toward me.

How can I tell her the whole story, including the way Rem reacted to the doctor flirting in the appointment? Telling her part of the story gives the exact reaction I was expecting from her.

"Lou, why aren't you playing up to him? You said he's hot, successful, obviously likes kids as much as you do, and is into you! Far out, here I am telling you we need to find you a man and there is one landing in your lap. Get on that, girl!" No matter how high-class the world Tori is in now, she will always be my Tori, the one I love. Straight to the point, no beating around the bush.

"You are crazy. It's so not appropriate to be hitting on my client's doctor. Plus, now is not the right time. I need to devote all my time to Blaise until he is more settled into his new life," I say, waving to Blaise who is calling to me to watch him go down the slide.

"Bitch, that's crap. You don't have to put your life on hold for Rem and Blaise. It's a job, but you are still entitled to a private life. What if this guy is the love of your life and you let him get away? You will never know unless you put yourself out there. I'm coming to that next appointment with you. I'll have you on a date with Dr. McHottie before you know it." She slaps her hand on my knee, and we both start laughing.

"You are so not coming with me. That would be a disaster and we both know it." Standing from my chair, I wave for Blaise to come over so we can find a spot to put the blanket out and have something to eat.

"You're no fun. But don't you worry, I will find a way to get you on that date." Her wicked grin has me worried, but I've got to let it go as Blaise comes running toward me and hugs me around the waist. He is obviously having a lot of fun, and that is my main priority right now.

"This conversation isn't over, Lou," she whispers to me and then takes Blaise's hand, and the two of them walk off to find a spot to eat. He has already taken to Tori even though they can't communicate. She has that big-energy personality that he gravitates to, which is great for both of us.

But for now, I just need to change the subject with her and concentrate on feeding both of them so she can get back to work, and we can play a bit longer before we head home.

However, all I can think of during lunch are the words that Tori just said:

"*What if this guy is the love of your life and you let him get away? You will never know unless you put yourself out there.*"

She thinks she is talking about Drew, but all I can picture is Rem, and I wonder if he is the man that I've let get away.

It's too late now, though, because I have already shut the door on that possibility. And thrown away the key.

REMINGTON

"He did what!" I scream down the phone in my office.

"Mr. Kentwall felt it was the best option. He gave you all extra time, but nothing was solved, so he solved it all for you. He asked me to pass on to Mr. Darby that he now owes him for keeping his name out of the tabloids." Sandon Bock sounds like a robot as he rattles off the speech that he had probably rehearsed before he called me. His boss told him what to say, and it's obvious that he doesn't agree, but he has no choice.

"We don't owe him shit! We didn't ask him to do that. How can he guarantee that the footage is completely destroyed, and this person is not going to come back for more money or sell it to the tabloids anyway? All he's done is fucked us all over. So, you can go tell him this from me, that if his daughter ends up on the front page of the papers and all over the internet, naked and exposed, then he only has himself to blame. I'm sure Felisha will agree. Pigheaded old man. Thanks for nothing, Bock, let's hope there is no need for us to work together again."

I don't even give him time to say anything. I'm so furious that I slam my phone down on my desk so hard that it should have a smashed screen, but luckily it survives again.

Picking it back up, I send out the message to the guys, including Broderick who is working in the office today.

Rem: My office now!

I grab the stress ball on my desk and squeeze it so hard I'm surprised it doesn't ooze fluid all over my desk.

Hearing their voices coming down the hall, I know they understood my message wasn't negotiable.

Nic is first through the door. "Talk to me, what's happening?" There is the tone of the boss but also a controlled man ready to take on the next problem. The only time I have ever seen him truly unraveled was when Tori left him. Again, another reason that I know I don't need a woman in my life. They have a habit of leaving even the strongest man on his knees without trying.

"The old prick paid them off and had the hide to send a message that you owe him now."

The look of fury on Nic's face is exactly how I feel. For both reasons of Kentwall paying them off, which now gives the video footage a value and acknowledgment that it's Flynn and Felisha. But even more so, for telling Nic he owed him.

"Fucking idiot," Forrest declares.

"Felisha is going to kill him." Flynn looks stunned at this information.

The silence is deafening until Nic's words fill my office, not from the volume he is saying them but the tone that has us all knowing how angry he is. "Felisha will be the least of his problems. Old man Kentwall wants to come at me, then he better be prepared for a fight, because I don't owe him a goddamn thing. We don't stop investigating this, get to the bottom of it!" He is now staring at me with such power that I know he is not going to let this go.

"Steady on there, son. I'm not explaining to your mother I've had to bail you out of jail for the second time. You leave this to Rem and me." Broderick was already a father figure to Nic, but since he started seeing Sally, Nic's mother, he has taken that role very seriously.

"Agreed. I'm on it." Even if he hadn't told me to, there was no way I was letting this go. Flynn is my friend, and I'll never stop protecting him, even if he doesn't ask for it.

With that, Nic turns and leaves my office without another word spoken. Forrest is close after him, but Flynn closes the door behind them and stands there looking at me.

"I don't want all the bullshit. Tell me how it is. Should I be worried this is still going to be released?" His body language tells me he is worried about this more than his bravado lets him share with me.

"Yes." There is no need to sugarcoat it.

"That's what I thought. Tell me what to do." Finally, he understands the gravity of the situation. Especially now that Kentwall is placing conditions on Nic.

"Keep doing what we told you. Stay friends with Felisha but don't overstep. We need to know what's going on over there while we get to the bottom of this."

"We are watching a woman we think is the influencer the message came from, but to be honest, I don't think she is sophisticated enough to pull this off. Regardless, the team isn't discounting her just yet. So as Rem said, do what he tells you." Broderick is always stern in the way he speaks when it comes to work.

"Ughh, understood." Turning back toward the door, he stops as he places his hand on the door handle. "Nic has always been there for me. I don't ever want my actions to hurt him or this company."

He can't look at me when he is so vulnerable.

"I know, and I feel the same. I won't let you down." Already my mind is racing with things that I need to talk to Broderick about.

"You never do. Thanks, Rem." With that he pulls the door open and is gone.

In all the years I've known Flynn, I don't think I have ever seen him this serious and not trying to use comedy to laugh something off.

Seeing him acting like this just heightens my stress levels, because I'm not only trying to protect him, but now, I have to make sure Nic doesn't do something stupid either. My gut tells me that we are okay for now and I've got time, but how long, that is the question.

Sitting at my desk and working through my emails is the best thing for me. Concentrating on things I can deal with immediately. Distraction from the main problem. The next email is one from the company that I used when I went diving with sharks. It's another adventure that I had been thinking about ever since they sent out a promotional email on it. Ziplining in Cancun in North America. My cursor is hovering over the book-now button. If things weren't so crazy around here right now, I'd already have this on my schedule and paid for.

But to be honest, it's usually at the time I feel the instability around me, whether it's work or my personal life, that always has me thinking about an adrenaline rush that I need to feel better. I don't know why, but they do go hand in hand. It's like a reset for me when I'm so scared out of my head that all I can do is think about surviving what I'm doing in the moment, so it silences everything else in my head. And when it's over, the relief and happiness I feel makes me forget all the negativity around me, and instead I enjoy the adrenaline rush that was pulsating through my body. I take control of my mindset, and I'm ready to go again.

The silence of my office is broken as the door bursts open, and the whirlwind that is Tori comes barreling into my room.

"Okay, we are on operation get Lou a man, and you are going to help me." She drops into the seat on the other side of my desk and waits for me to react.

"I'm busy, Tori." I don't even look up at her because I don't want her to see my irritation at what she just said.

"No shit, Flynn has everyone around here busy and agitated. But this won't take long. I need to know who this pediatrician is so I can make sure he is at our next function and Lou won't be able to ignore him. He is trying to get her to notice him, and she is disregarding him because she thinks she needs to concentrate on Blaise and working for you. But I told her she still gets to live a life, and I know you will agree."

The hairs on the back of my neck are standing on end, and I can feel the touchiness at everything she is prattling at me. How the fuck is he getting her to notice him and why does she need a man? She has Blaise and me, and that's all she needs right now.

"Not interested, Tori. She is her own person. If she isn't pursuing him, then that's her choice, not yours." Typing a reply to an email, I hope it will give Tori the hint I don't want to have this conversation with her.

"But that's the problem, she thinks he's good-looking and has all these excellent reasons he is a perfect match, but she is just using you and Blaise as an excuse because she is too scared to put herself out there. Don't be an ass and help me."

Standing up, I glare at her. "Tori, I don't have time for this childish matchmaking. If she wants him, she will do something about it. Now I have a meeting I need to get to. See you later." I walk away, leaving her with her mouth wide open and questioning my outburst, but I don't really care.

I'm too busy storming through the building to a meeting that I don't have just to get her out of my office and to stop talking about how hung up on Dr. Deadshit Elouise is.

In the ride down the elevator, I make the call for the only thing that will get me through today.

"I need a session now. I'm on my way." I hang up because I know that is all I need to say.

This shouldn't be riling me up as much as it is, but I'd be kidding myself if I didn't acknowledge that deep down, I don't want to share her with anyone else in any capacity at the moment.

Playing happy pretend family has been nice this week. Our friendship is getting stronger by the day, and Blaise is already doing amazing with his learning. I've even managed to get a few French words to use with him too, because I don't want him to think he has to lose his language and culture at all. Apparently, my pronunciation sucks, but hey, at least I'm trying. And having Elouise there giving me someone to talk to at night has been kind of nice for a change.

Yet Tori's words that Elouise thinks Dr. Deadshit is good-looking and would make a good catch is grating on me more than it should. She is not my girlfriend, and nor will she ever be. It can't happen, especially with Flynn's infatuation with her, and also, he is relying on me to be there for him right now. If he was to find out that I had slept with Elouise behind his back, then he would lose all trust in me, and that would kill me. If I'm honest, though, as much as that upsets me about Flynn, Elouise looking at the doctor with some interest in him upsets me more.

I need to work this out of my system and get on with the job at hand—helping Flynn get this video buried for good and not having it hanging over his head.

Arriving at the rooms, I walk in, and Cherie is there ready to greet me.

"Good afternoon, Remington. Second room on the right." Just hearing her voice is calming, and she hasn't even touched me yet.

Storming past her and into the room, I'm already stripping down before she joins me. I need this, otherwise I'm about to do something that I know I'll regret. There is a reason Elouise is in the friend zone, and I need to get control of my head to keep her there.

Being back at the office for a few hours, I know I've done as much as I can today, and I promised Blaise I would be home to see him each day before he went to bed. In the future that won't always be possible, but when we are still in such early stages, I want to keep my word and make sure he knows he is loved and wanted in my home. It's his home now too.

I'm later than I wanted to be, and the message just came through from Elouise that she is about to take him upstairs to start the bedtime routine of getting into bed and reading a few stories to him in French. She reads simple English books to him during the day, but at night I like the idea of him still getting that joy of floating off into the land of make-believe as he sleeps. My mum used to read to us, although I found it difficult to keep still, but she did it anyway, and it's a memory of feeling loved every night to finish the day.

I park the car and come through the front door, kicking off my shoes, and I head up the stairs two steps at a time. I can hear Blaise chatting away to her as he picks his books. I have to say, although I know nothing about education in children, to me he seems like he is bright and all the years up in the mountains have not put him behind in anything.

"Papa." His little feet carry him across the carpet at speed as he launches himself into my arms. It has become his new thing, not afraid to show me his affection when I get home, and deep down, I love that hug as soon as I arrive. Today it hits right where I need it.

"Hello, Blaise, how was your play at the park?" Giving Elouise a strained smile, she translates to him, and between the two of them, they tell me about their day.

"Okay, *bonne nuit*, enjoy your stories. Papa needs to go downstairs." Leaning down, I kiss him on the forehead as I tuck him into bed. Stepping back to leave the room, he smiles up at me.

"Good night, Papa," he proudly replies, and already his eyes are looking heavy. I'm sure the park wore him out, and Elouise will be lucky to get through one book.

I need to keep busy, so I head straight into my office as I reach downstairs. I'll just tell Elouise to order takeout for us both once she comes down. My guilt over the way I have reacted to Tori's little revelation is making me uncomfortable with having a nice casual night chatting over dinner and a glass of wine with Elouise.

Diving back into my emails because they never go away is the best option for me. All my staff send reports constantly that I don't necessarily need to read, but they are important to have things documented for if I do need them, but today, these reports are a good distraction.

Hearing her footsteps on the stairs, I brace myself to mask my guilt at my jealous rage today after Tori's visit.

"Hey, you okay? You look like you've had a rough day or got bad news on something." Her sweet voice is enough to set me off, and I don't know why.

"Yep, shit day. Did you get a call from Blaise's doctor today?" I can't even look up at her, my eyes glued to the screen.

"Ah yes, how did you know?" She walks into the room a little closer, with hesitation in her voice.

"What did he want?" My tone is now completely different to the one I was using with Blaise upstairs.

"To give me dates and times." Even though I know what she means, it's enough to get my head whipping up to look her straight in the eye.

"For Blaise or for you?"

And the moment she twigs why I am in a bad mood, she stands tall and bites back, "Both of us. What's it to you?" She is ready to take me on, and I'm here for it tonight.

"Nothing, but if you want to go fuck him, do it in your own time, and don't you dare see him with Blaise unless it's a medical appointment." Fuck, what did I say that for?

The gasp of air she sucks in tells me it's time to leave.

"What. The actual. Fuck. You asshole! How dare you speak to me like that. And for your information, if I want to fuck him, it's none of your business either!" She turns to storm out of the room, which is probably a good thing, but I can't let her have the last word.

"Whatever, and by the way, I have booked a zipline trip to North America in two weeks' time. I will be away for ten days. So, you will be on your own."

Instead of her just ignoring me like I was hoping and leaving my study, she freezes in the doorway.

"You have got to be joking. You are a father now, you can't go off and do dangerous shit like that anymore. Blaise already lost one parent, don't make him lose another." Her words are like a hot poker being jabbed into my restless body, igniting my anger that has been under the surface for weeks.

"I didn't ask to be a father!" Standing, I hear the words that I have been wanting to scream out since all this was dumped in my lap.

She just shakes her head, disappointment written all over her face. "And Blaise didn't ask to have a dad who's an asshole, yet here we are."

She leaves me standing here wanting to scream more, but all I feel is remorse for saying such a hurtful thing about my son.

Maybe I do need to book that trip to try to get this under control and reset my stupid brain. That's two huge mistakes I've made today, and now I have to work out how to fix this.

Why did Tori have to tell me about Elouise and drag up the feelings for her that I thought I had buried when we slid nicely into the friend zone?

This is not how you act with a friend, you idiot.

Hearing the cupboard slam in the kitchen, I know I have created a storm that is about to explode. This conversation is far from over tonight.

So, batten down the hatches, the second wave will be coming shortly.

Before I even have time to move too far toward the kitchen, I hear her feet stomping down the hallway, and she reappears in front of me. Inches from my body, I can feel the heat radiating from her.

"Why can't you admit you hate that someone else wants me and do something about this thing between us."

And there is the detonation I can't ignore.

Grabbing her face, I pull her to me as I slam my lips on hers.

I'm not holding back now, and she better be ready for everything I've been burying deep down inside me.

Chapter Ten

ELOUISE

What right has he got to be angry at me and obviously jealous!

How did he even know that Drew called me today?

Of course, Tori!

I'm going to kill her. She obviously said something to him that has him acting like an idiot. He can be shitty with me all he likes, but putting his life in danger because of it and hurting Blaise is unacceptable.

I'm staring into the cupboard that I don't even know why I opened. I can't let him get away with being gutless. Growling, I slam the door. I need to tell him to man up!

I stomp back into his office, and the moment I see him, I see red! I blurt out what I can't keep to myself anymore. "Why can't you admit you hate that someone else wants me and do something about this thing between us." I know it's hypocritical because I was the one who told him we have to be friends, but it's been boiling inside me, and his comments just fueled my fire. I couldn't hold it any longer.

What I wasn't expecting was for him to slam his lips onto mine without a word to deny it.

Oh God, how I've missed his lips.

They have a roughness to them, not all perfect and smooth but like what I hear them talk about what a real manly guy is like, and it's got my lips tingling all over. His urgency to have me tells me what I already knew. We are fighting something that I'm not sure we will be able to stop from happening.

His hands are so tight, holding my head in just the right position. I can't breathe, but I don't want to stop. Any minute he is going to pull away, and it will all be over again. My gut's churning with emotions, and I'm already dripping wet from the frenzy that's thrumming through my body. I need to hold on for as long as I can. I wrap my arms around to his back and cling to him like I'm about to fall. Just like I knew he would, Rem starts to pull away.

No, no, no, no, please don't stop.

The panic is obviously written all over my face when looks at me. My mouth is open and I'm panting like he has just kissed every bit of air out of me.

"Don't worry, I'm just beginning." That deep rasp in his voice has the electricity rushing through my body, and I feel like I'm back in that place of euphoria I was at Christmas.

Enveloping me in his arms, he kisses me roughly, this time claiming my mouth with his tongue.

There is no holding back now, and I'm all in too.

I want this more than I let myself believe, but now that it's happening, I'm not letting my conscience get involved. This is lust-driven, and it's what we both need. He walks me backward until the back of my legs hit his desk.

Our lips separating, I can't tell if he is looking at me with desire or annoyance that I have put him in this position.

"You keep telling me no, yet you pushed us to this point. This is your last chance to stop it."

I shake my head quickly. In my head I'm screaming, "Don't stop!"

"Use your words, El, tell me what you want." I love hearing him call me that. It's something special just between us. I know what I want, but part of me is scared to ask for it.

My voice all breathy, I say, "Touch me… please, Rem, touch me." A shiver runs through my body as his fingers find their way to my jeans button.

"Is that all you want, to be touched?" He nuzzles into my neck and kisses me behind my ear as he whispers to me.

The zipper on my jeans is pulled down, and he runs his fingers along the top of my panties. I can't keep from shuddering as he starts to slide under the elastic and down my bare skin.

"Words, El," he growls, nipping at my neck at the same time his finger skims across my clit and slides down the front of my folds.

"Fuck." I'm groaning without control of what I'm saying.

"Are you telling me it feels good… or are you asking me to fuck you on my desk?" Lifting his head, he looks deep into my soul with his dark eyes.

"Both!" I grit my teeth as he continues to rub up and down over my clit, and every time he touches it, my body fires with the most intense sensation. "All of it, I want it all."

The wicked smile that appears on his face tells me whatever I'm about to get is going to be good.

"Push your jeans and panties down." His demanding voice has me moving quickly, but I'm desperate to feel him too. My hands jump to his trousers, and the faster his finger works me over, I can't help but keep moaning. It makes me want his trousers on the floor, and his cock, that I can already feel is rock hard, in my hands right now.

"Don't touch my cock." His gruffness makes me stop dead and look up to his face above me. "I'm hanging on by a thread, and I'm not ready for this to be over." Without warning, he thrusts his finger deep inside me, and he pushes his thumb hard down on my engorged clit. Curling his finger, he has me falling forward into him as my orgasm is building hard. I'm shamelessly riding his hand, and I couldn't stop even if I wanted to.

"That's it, let me take away that ache… because you ache for me at night, don't you, El. Show me how much you want me."

I can't hold on any longer. I shudder all over his hand as my body explodes, knowing he's right. The ache is so deep that I don't how to get rid of it.

But before he lets my body come down from my huge high of indulgence, he spins me on his desk and pushes my face down into the dark timber.

The loud slap of his hand landing on my ass echoes along with my noisy gasp. No one has ever slapped me on the ass before, and if you'd asked me before if I wanted it, I would've said absolutely not.

But instead, it just makes my pussy wetter than it already was, and I'm craving another one.

"That's what naughty vixens who tempt me get." His fingers are back working over my entrance and dragging the moisture all over my pussy. "Oh, you liked that, didn't you. You are so wet. Just like my cock that's leaking from seeing my red handprint on your pale and supple ass."

I can feel my body chasing his hand as it withdraws from me.

His hard cock is lying in the crack of my ass as he leans over my body to whisper in my ear again. "Keep quiet because we don't want my son to hear me fucking his nanny on my desk, do we. You scream, I stop."

And without warning, he is upright, and his cock slams all the way inside me. The surprise and the sting of his size has me about to scream, but instead, all he can hear is a whimper as I almost draw blood on my bottom lip from biting so hard into it.

"Take it, El." His hands are on my hips, gripping me so hard I'm sure I will have fingerprint marks tomorrow. Pounding into me hard over and over again, all I can think is that I never want this to end. *Use me to take away the frustration you feel, Rem, because I feel the same.*

It's what we both need.

Not sweet lovemaking but a good hard fuck to release everything we have both been fighting.

"You drive me fucking crazy!" His mumble of exasperation is loud enough to be heard over the noise of our skin slapping against each other, hard!

The position he has me pushed onto his desk has his cock hitting all the way to my core, and the pressure of the corner of the desk right on my clit is enough to make me want him to keep pounding me as hard as he can. I'm gripping the desk with every bit of strength I have, making sure that I'm not flying over the table from the force of him hitting me from behind.

I can't hold my body off as his cock hits me in the most tantalizing way, and before I can even say a word, I'm coming hard, but it doesn't stop Rem. If anything, he steps it up a notch and lets me take everything he needs to let go of. Finally, his orgasm rips through him, and he grunts as he empties inside me. I can still feel his cock, deep down, pulsating inside me.

My muscles now soft, I mold to the desk. I could stay here for the rest of the night, exposed to the world but feeling oh so satisfied.

My top is shoved halfway up my body, and Rem presses his lips softly on my back, his hands caressing my side. It feels so different than the way he kissed me a moment ago. It spreads a warmth through me I wasn't expecting but makes me feel so treasured.

The only noise that can be heard in the room is our breathing coming back under control, but it's broken by a sigh from Rem that makes me nervous because his touch is gone, and I feel him pulling out from inside me.

That empty feeling is already in my gut, and I don't know what I'm about to encounter when I stand and face him. Not even giving me a chance to clean myself up, Rem has dropped down to my feet and pulls my jeans back up, covering me, which is my sign to move, without him even saying it.

Slowly pushing myself back up to standing and buttoning my jeans, I pull my shirt back down and have the disgusting feeling of Rem's come running out of me. By the time I turn around he is already dressed and just looks at me like he is unsure what to say.

The feeling of the come reminds me. "Shit, I just realized we didn't use protection." The look on his face is the beginning of him panicking which I need to stop from happening. "But don't worry, it's the wrong time in my cycle for anything to be a problem." Watching Rem start to calm a little, I'm not sure he is actually paying attention to what I said anyway.

"I trust you, and I'm sorry," Rem says to me quietly. But in my head, I know that I'm not sorry. That was so amazing, and that's all I want to think about.

This super-confident man seems to lose the certainty when we are in the same room.

Taking a step toward him, I touch his hand, and it's like it jolts him back into the room.

"We need to talk." Back now is his calm soft tone that I've seen him use with Blaise too.

He's right, but I don't want to admit it. Talking is going to lead to pushing this back into the closet, and although I know that's what needs to happen, I'm desperate to tell him how I feel. Not just this insane lust that we both obviously share, but there is something more. I don't know what, but I just wish I could explore it.

But at my core, I feel like he is about to remind me that we can't be doing this, and I will have to agree.

Taking me by the hand, he leads me to the couch, sitting, and then pulls me into his lap which takes me off guard and is the last thing I expected.

"Rem!" I let out a little screech as I land on top of him.

"What, you didn't think I was going to fuck you and then send you on your way, did you?" Laughing, he wraps his arms around me and kisses me so sweetly on the lips. Nothing like we have kissed before.

The kind of kiss I didn't think I wanted, but oh, how it makes my heart ache with longing for more of this.

Putting my hand up and wrapping it in the hair on the back of his head, I sense him leaning more into the kiss. This is not where I saw this going, but my whole body is so on board for more of this. He rubs up and down my back, and I'm just melting into him the more he does it.

My brain is racing like crazy.

I want this, but I can't have this. There are too many reasons why. All of them flash though my head one after the other.

Hurting Blaise, Flynn, Tori and her friends, working together, Rem and his fears, not that I know what they are, but I can tell he has them. Lastly, because I always put everyone else first, my heart. I know I am already too invested, and if I take this any further then I will be free falling, and that will just end in disaster and heartbreak.

This time, it's me that's reluctantly pulling away from the kiss. I need time to get the words in my head right before I try to articulate my fears.

I lay my head on his shoulder and just breathe him in. His hand is still rubbing my back, and for a moment, I just relish the feeling of contentment that being in his arms gives me. I could stay here forever, but it's just not in the cards for us.

"Rem, we can't do this." I can't even look up into his eyes when I say the words that feel like a knife's point poking into my chest. Not quite piercing my heart but just enough that I start to feel the pain that I know will only get worse if I let it.

His deep sigh tells me that he realizes it too. "I know, but we have to work out how to ignore it." The slight laugh tells me that he isn't sure it's possible, and neither am I, but we have to try.

The laugh is enough to break the seriousness of my emotions, and I sit up so I'm still close but not nuzzled into him like a girlfriend would be, and I'm far from that.

"I know it isn't fair, but I think we both agree there are too many reasons why we can't be together." Starting the conversation is what I do, it seems to be a pattern with us both.

"Agreed, but it doesn't mean I don't want you…" He runs his hand through his curls that are now damp from exertion. "Ughhh, this is so fucked."

"Really, you use that word to describe this thing between us." I can't help but start to giggle, even when we are trying to be serious.

"You're the one with the dirty mind, young lady. If I was describing what we just did, I would have used a lot more adjectives, I can assure you." The hand that was in his hair drops and rests on my thigh.

"Like what?" I can't help but wonder.

"Amazing, spine-tingling, breathtaking, hot as fuck, I know the perfect one… orgasmic!" To which we both start laughing, but deep in my bones, I feel a sense of peace that it's not just me feeling that this could be much more that a quick fuck to relieve some of the sexual tension between us. There is something real beneath the surface.

"Okay, moving on and back to the real world." Looking at him, I can see determination in him.

"Don't you ever doubt how real that was, El… I mean it."

My hand moves involuntarily to his cheek, and my thumb traces across his lips that are a part of his body I wish I could get more of. "I know, I truly do." I finally drop my hand to take away the temptation to start something again.

"There are just too many roadblocks." We both nod in agreement with his words.

"Flynn." The word comes from both of us simultaneously.

"He would kill me," Rem says with a smirk on his face, knowing too well that he could beat him in a fight any day of the week. Something I would never want to happen, especially because of me.

"Tori would kill me for breaking up the wolf pack, and I couldn't bear losing Tori either." I exhale with exasperation.

"Wolf pack, hey?" He's looking at me with his head tilted.

"Yeah, can't you see it? Nic is the alpha wolf, the leader or boss of the pack. Flynn and Forrest are the middle pack, the advisor's beta/deltas depending on the situation, and you are the omega of the pack."

"What the hell is the omega wolf?" Rem asks, intrigued by all the names.

"The one in the group who is always on the lookout for danger, the protector of the pack." Which is Rem all over. Without the others knowing sometimes how much he is circling them and putting his own life aside to make sure they are safe in theirs.

"Makes sense, but in this house, know that I'm the alpha, beta, delta, and omega wolf, and no other man will ever step into any of those roles where Blaise and you are concerned, El." There is almost a growl in his voice when he is referring to me.

I want to believe it, but I know I don't have the right to hold that place with him. I can't say that right now though, so instead I throw up a left-field question that I know will make him laugh.

"Where do you think Tori fits into the pack?" I smile at the thought of it.

"Is there an alpha woman who has the alpha male's balls in her hands and who runs the whole pack, with the rest of them all bowing down to her and just saying yes ma'am? Because I feel like that is the truth of this group, not that I would ever say that out loud, and never to Tori or Nic."

"I think you might be right there. And it would be safer if you kept those comments to yourself, for sure."

Even though we are breaking the tension, he still leans down and kisses me on the top of the head.

"There is so much knowledge in that beautiful head of yours, isn't there." Rem watches my reaction.

"Pfft, yes, but it's all useless." The reality is that the knowledge comes from liking to read about social behavior, and that reading feeds my yearning to study psychology. So many of the traits in children fascinate me, where they came from, is it environmental or hereditary. I just wish I could read Rem a little better and know what makes him the way he is.

"Don't do that, put yourself down. I've heard you do it before, and I don't like it. You are an amazingly talented and beautiful woman. It's about time you start believing it. Is there a man I need to teach a lesson to, that makes you be so down on yourself?" This man's loyalty knows no bounds.

"Steady on, Rambo, unless you want to go back in time and find a group of twelve-year-old girls who made me feel worthless then I wouldn't be too worried." I shock myself with the memories that are flooding into me that I must have buried a long time ago. I haven't thought about that stage in my life for a very long time, and obviously how harming it was on my self-confidence. God, that's not something I want to talk about now.

"Let me fire up the time machine I keep through that secret door over there." He points to the closet door that I'm sure has nothing behind it except files and random crap like most office cupboards do.

"Let's go." I pretend to stand up, only to have his strong arms pulling me back to exactly where he wants me and a place I'm loving being right now.

"We have gotten off track here." I need to get us back on track because we can't walk out of this room tonight without finally putting this to bed. Well, let's not talk about the two of us and a bed, but instead, sorting out how we are going to get through this.

"Your fault with all your wolf pack knowledge." I can feel his body tensing a little under me, and I know neither of us want to talk about this, but it's time.

"Yes, well, now I'm bringing up the hard things. It's obvious we have a thing for each other, and we have both agreed we can't pursue it. What just happened on the desk can't happen again."

"Right, so next time we can try the kitchen counter?" he mumbles to himself.

"Rem, be serious." I slap my hand on his chest right above his heart by accident, and his big hand quickly lands on top of it, pressing my hand even tighter against his heart. He's not saying anything but just looking at me and speaking to me without words to tell me how torn he is.

"One year…" The way he is looking at me has me frozen, and I feel like I can't breathe. "Can we put it on hold for one year? See where both our lives are then. You won't be working for me anymore."

I wish that was our only problem, but there is a small glimmer of hope in his words.

Taking in what he's saying, I just don't think he has really thought about this. "It won't work, Rem. Remember what you told me." As much as it hurts, I have to protect my heart. "You don't do relationships."

The look of disappointment registers on his face, and a small whisper escapes him that makes me want to cry for both of us. "But you're the first woman in a long time who has made me think about trying again."

Oh, Rem, what happened in your life, why are you so closed off? I wish I could dig deeper but that will only pull us further down into the vortex that we are both trying to fight from falling into.

I just let us both sit in that moment of silence until he could get through the feelings that he is battling against.

Sitting up straighter and readjusting me on his lap, I can tell the walls are back up, and he is about to say what he needs to and then shut this off.

"No restrictions, we live our lives, but in a year's time, if we are both still single, will you agree to let me take you on a date? Start this properly. Out in the open, to hell with all the reasons not to." Rem is serious, and the look of hope for my answer has me unable to say no to him like I probably should.

Instead, the only answer I can give him is one that I have lived my adult life by.

"If it's meant to be, it will happen." I pull my hand out from under his on his chest. I need to move away from him. Attempting to stand up, sadly this time he lets me.

"Oh, it's meant to be, my little vixen, because no woman has ever made me come so freaking hard in my life. And I don't intend to miss out on feeling that again."

"Rem, stop it! Boundaries, we need them." I cross my arms to let him know I'm serious.

"Okay, list them, but I get to veto the ones I don't like." He lays his arms along the back of the couch like he has all the control, and the reality is that he probably does.

Then I start listing them off the top of my head. "No sex! In any form." Why is he smiling at me?

"No kissing."

"Mm-hm," is all he replies while I continue.

"No flirting, because you are an expert at it."

He pretends to gasp and holds his chest like he is saying "who me?"

"You let me do my job and don't give me any special treatment."

"What makes you think I would?" The smirk on his face tells me he knows full well that the two hundred thousand pounds that is now sitting in my bank account blows that answer out of the water.

"I'm not even bothering to answer that. And you will get on with your job and working out how to fit Blaise into your work/life balance."

"Easy." Rem is so smug with these answers.

"Always put Blaise first, before me and before yourself."

"A given." Not that I'm sure he understands what that really means yet.

"Treat me like your friend, and let's get to know each other, no expectations, just two housemates who are friends. I repeat, friends, do you hear that? Repeat after me."

"Friends, or friends with…" He thinks he is hilarious.

"Don't you dare say that word."

"What word, El? Friends with… a working relationship." He smiles in satisfaction at being such a smartass.

"We both know that's not what you were about to say, and let me assure you, that word is off the table. I told you, that's not me."

"Mm-hm." I hate when he doesn't answer properly, because I know he is just saying it to make me happy when in fact he is ignoring what I said.

This will be the hardest one for him to accept, but it is non-negotiable. Getting ready for the reaction, I take a deep breath and start with the extra confidence I'm pulling to the surface to stand my ground.

"We can date if we choose to." I know full well I won't, but I need to make sure he has the opportunity.

"No, strike it off." There is no casual tone in his voice. It's blunt and to the point and forceful. Just like I expected.

"I won't back down on this one. This is one of the most important ones. There is no way you can go twelve months without sex, I'm not stupid. That thing in your pants is a beast that will need release, and don't try to deny it. You need to be able to have your normal one-night stands or find a woman who satisfies you."

My words are irritating him as he stands slowly but with purpose and goes toe to toe with me in a few steps. He drops his face so close to mine that our lips are almost touching, and I can feel his breath as he replies, "Just watch me, baby. But thanks for the compliment."

My legs almost collapse beneath me, and if I didn't know before that statement that I was in trouble with this man, he just confirmed it… loud and clear.

I have never met such a sexual man that is so possessive of me, even though he can't have me.

"Rem, please, you have to accept, we aren't together."

Oh God, my whole body is reacting to him being so close.

"Keep telling yourself that, El. In the meantime, I'll be getting off with my hand every night with you in the room next to me, while you are doing the same. And don't keep quiet… I want to hear you cry out my name."

He smashes his lips onto mine and takes what he wants before he pulls away smiling and leaves me standing in a puddle in the middle of his office.

Oh. My. God!

I'm in trouble.

Big trouble, but I'm so here for it!

Chapter Eleven

REMINGTON

I knew telling Mum and Dad about Blaise was going to be intense, but I didn't expect them to just turn up on my doorstep the next day.

Even if I wanted to spend time alone with Elouise, which probably wasn't a good idea at the moment, it wasn't possible anyway with my parents staying in my house too. Mum is constantly walking around with tears in her eyes from the happiness she feels at smothering another grandchild, and how overjoyed she was that I'm a father when I've been telling her for years it was never going to happen. But the main reason is, of course, Blaise's cuteness, who just looks so much like me at that age. She has been cooking up a storm, and thank God tonight is their last night here. Nic invited us all out to the farm for the afternoon and dinner so Blaise could see the animals and run around with my dad.

Before Nic became filthy rich, inheriting his family's hotel chain, he and Flynn were pretty impressive chefs in Australia. They both love to get back into the kitchen every so often, and we all get to sit back and enjoy them in their element. With my parents here, we've also been able to relax, keeping the conversation light and not talking or worrying about work.

Blaise is now fast asleep on the couch in the sunroom while we are all out the back in the outdoor entertainment area, sitting around the fire pit and enjoying some very nice red wine. Nic's wine cellar is impressive and of course full of great Australian wines that he loves to tell the story of where they were produced. Mum and Dad are looking tired as I glance at them, and I know it's time to get them home.

Glancing across the fire, I can see Elouise in the red-and-yellow glow, deep in a conversation with Tori. The moment I start really watching her intently, she looks toward me like a magnet and just smiles softly, before turning her head back to focus on Tori.

We have managed to slip into a good place. But it doesn't stop me from feeling that intense longing; I don't know where it's come from, it's all new to me.

I have never felt like this about a woman before.

But maybe it's because I can't have her. The age-old saying of you always want what you can't have.

It's become the Elouise effect, desiring what I can't have.

Mum's voice next to me breaks my distraction.

"Yes, and now we just have to find him a wife and a mother for Blaise." Her voice is loud enough when she gets excited about something that everyone pauses their conversations, and all eyes are on me.

But there is just one set of beautiful warm brown eyes that I care about, and they seem to be looking straight into my soul with the same question that I lie in bed and think about each night.

Is she that person?

Before I can even say a word, my mother is already answering her own statement that she was telling Nic, which turned into a conversation with the whole group.

"But all I have heard from him for years is that he doesn't do relationships and will never marry. He seems to think that being single and having a smorgasbord of women parading through his bed is a far better option. Maybe watching you and Tori will give him some ideas." My mother is completely oblivious to the way Elouise's shoulders sag, and the warmth in her eyes disappears the moment Mum reiterated every fear in Elouise's head.

"Heidi, stop harping on Remington about this. I think his life is full enough right now to be worrying about looking for a soulmate. Don't they say that when you aren't looking for something, it will fall into your lap?" My dad's deep voice from across the circle gets her attention.

"Oh, like I did. Seriously, Warwick, I had to chase you down and almost smack you in the forehead before you decided to ask me out on a date. You men are oblivious to what's in front of you." Mum laughs at her own joke, but Tori and Elouise are now joining in too.

"Sounds a lot like being dragged along kicking and screaming to me." Dad rolls his eyes but then winks at her as he takes the last sip of the wine in his glass.

This is what their marriage is like. Constantly laughing at each other but with so much love underlying the joking.

Needing to break this conversation that is directed at me, I start standing.

"On that note, I think it's time I get these oldies home and tucked into bed, along with their grandson."

"Can't we sit a little longer and sort out your love life? Surely Tori and Elouise have friends they could introduce you to. They are good girls who seem like the settling-down types, so we just need to find a girl like them." Yep, Mum has had one too many wines now. Time to get her out of here.

Before I can say a word, my damn so-called friends are all joining in.

"I'm not sure Victoria is the best example of a good girl." Nic smirks at Tori across the fire and lifts his glass in the air to her.

"Be careful, Nicholas, you don't want to start an argument." She lifts her glass in return.

Christ, I need to get my parents out of here.

"Yes, Rem, let's find you a good little girl." Flynn is almost convulsing trying to hold in his laughter.

"You wouldn't know a good girl if she bit you on the nose,"

Forrest throws back at Flynn, and we all know that he looks for the opposite. He likes naughty women, and I don't need to say any more.

"Lies, Elouise is my kind of good girl…" Flynn starts to say, but I jump in before I let him finish this sentence.

"Let's move, we're leaving." Leaving the group out the back and striding straight inside, I message my driver who brought my parents out here in a hired car so it wasn't too squished in my car with Blaise's car seat. Not even waiting for them, I pick up Blaise who is in such a dead sleep he doesn't even murmur, just snuggles into my chest, and I know no matter what, I'll always have him.

But even that doesn't calm the fury that is running around my body hearing how much Flynn wants her. How she is his type of woman.

Bullshit.

She's not!

Not even close to what he needs. He would be the worst kind of man for her.

The word *mine* is floating in the back of my head, but I won't let it come to the front of my thoughts because I'm not allowed to think it or feel it. Instead, it just makes me want to take them all home and leave for the rest of the night to take out my frustration. To call Cherie and see her now. I don't want to have to go back to my frequent visits with her, I thought I was past this. That my life was different, but just like Elouise said, there's no way I'm going to be able to get through this year without something.

Settling Blaise in the car, his head falls slowly to the side, he lets out a little sigh, and then is back in a deep sleep. Backing out of the car door space, I feel a hand on my forearm, and I know she can tell that what was said bothered me. Looking over my shoulder, the look of pity on her face is not what I need right now.

"Rem," she whispers, but I don't want it from her.

"Don't, just don't." Pulling my arm away and closing the door, I pull the mask on that I seem to be getting too good at wearing and walk back over to the group. Not showing that I just want to get out of here, I'm busy thanking the guys for the beautiful food, wine, and evening. Everyone says their goodbyes, but the one person besides Elouise that is giving me a strange look is Tori. I need to continue to push through as if I'm not so pissed off that I just want to hit something.

"Thank you, all you lovely people, we will see you soon when we come for our next visit," Mum calls out from the car door as Dad closes it for her. The wine is catching up with her, and I think all we will hear from her tonight will be her atrociously loud snoring, which is made worse when she drinks.

Once Elouise and I are in the Range Rover and driving down the long gravel drive of Nic's estate to get back onto the main road, she slips her hand over the console and just lays it on my thigh.

No words are spoken, and I want to tell her to take it away, but I just can't.

The warmth that I can feel even through my jeans is calming. My heart that is beating so strong and fiercely is now trying to match the slower consistent stroking of her thumb back and forth on my leg. It's like she knows the rhythm that I need to see through the testosterone fog that is bubbling in my body.

Why can't I control this? I know I can't have her, and she told me I can't touch her, yet here she is putting herself in a situation she doesn't want just because she can see straight through me.

Vulnerability is not a quality I possess, and yet her body language is begging me to lay my feelings all out for her. I can't do that when I don't know what they are.

This is why I can't do relationships.

I'm fucked up, and there is nothing that can change that.

Believe me, I've tried, and the only thing that gets close to it is jumping off some cliff and feeling the wind rush around me at the possibility I might die or to spend time with Cherie, and that's the least healthy option of the two. And that's saying something when there's a strong possibility I could die in the first option.

If I was alone in the car, my speed would have been faster, but with precious cargo, I won't do anything that will risk either of them.

The trip was long, but finally pulling into the driveway, I

hadn't realized until she lifted her hand that Elouise had been touching me all this time. Looking across at her now, I just see concern.

I'm not ready to talk about it, so jumping out of the car, I head around to get Blaise out, when my father also starts slowly gliding my sleepy mother out of their car. The drive obviously put her to sleep, and I'm thankful that I don't have to continue the conversation with her tonight. By the morning, she will be too busy with Blaise, and I will step into the background again.

Carrying Blaise straight upstairs to his bedroom, Elouise follows me, but I shoo her away. He can just sleep in his clothes tonight, because I don't want to disturb his peaceful sleep that he seems to be enjoying. Just pulling off his shoes and socks, I drag the blanket over him and lean down, and I kiss him on the forehead like I do every night.

Thank goodness I have put Mum and Dad in the bedroom downstairs because of Dad's bad knee that he tries to hide from us all. It's old rugby injuries that are catching up with him as he ages, but he will never admit it.

After checking on them and saying good night to Dad as he is about to help Mum into bed, I close the door behind them and head toward the front door. Placing my hand on the doorknob to open it to leave again, my brain stops me from turning it.

I'm angry, frustrated, and worked up, but none of that is with Elouise. I should at least tell her I'm leaving again and that I will be back later.

Stomping up the stairs, I'm now standing outside her room, but what do I tell her? I can't tell her where I'm going because that's just fucked up. Besides, I can't bear being witness to the disappointment she will have in me and another reason for her to put on her never-ending list why she can't be with me.

Tapping not overly loudly on the door because I don't want to wake Blaise, I hear her movement coming from the other side of the room. The door opens and reveals her standing there looking flushed.

"Rem, come in." Her voice is breathy, and it's then I notice she is holding the shirt that she had on tonight, the two sides scrunched together in her hands because her buttons are undone.

I can't help my eyes from dropping to her nipples that are hard and pushing against her shirt.

This woman is going to be the death of me.

She's standing here in front of me with no bra on, and the longer I stay here, the more her cheeks pink up nicely. I know that if I slid my hand into her pants, she'd be wet, and I shouldn't even be thinking about her nice bare pussy, but I can't stop my brain from going there.

"No. I'm leaving. Be back later." Because if I stand here any longer then I'm going to do the very thing she forbid me to do in those stupid boundaries she set me.

Moving to leave, her hand is on my arm, pulling me into the room, with the door closing behind me. She isn't strong enough to push me around, but catching me off guard and the zing of electricity that hit me as soon as she touched me, she has me almost falling into her room.

Righting myself as she tries to catch me, both her hands have let go of her shirt and now her cleavage is on full show and the shirt is just barely hanging over the nipples, but it doesn't matter. It's enough for my cock that is already hard to let me know he wants in on this.

"Talk to me, Rem. You look like you are about to explode."

If only she knew how close, I really am. I know I'm better not saying anything.

"Flynn was just joking, he knows..." El steps closer to me, and it forces me back against the wall.

His name is all I need to hear to stop me from holding my thoughts in any longer.

I wrap my arm tightly around her back and drag her against my body.

"He can't have you…" My teeth are grinding together. "And you tell me I can't have you either. But don't expect me to be happy about sitting back and watching him think he can."

I grasp my other hand tightly around her neck and kiss her like I need to remind her who she belongs to.

Her rules say I can't claim her, but I just fucking did. Enough to let her know I'm not giving up and I'll wait the year I promised her, but she better be prepared to live with an arrogant asshole who will remind her every chance I get.

She's mine whether she is ready to tell the world that or not.

I push her away and take in how she looks, so ready to be fucked. But doing what I promised her, I walk away.

"I'll be back later. Good night."

Walking to the door, I turn to take one last look of her pale peachy skin and cheeks that are on fire with lust, her big brown eyes that are open so wide, and her lips that bear evidence that I have just been there.

Yeah, I'll be dreaming of that tonight.

But first I need to deal with my emotions, and the only one who can deal with me when I'm like this is Cherie. I better be ready to pay her double to be demanding a session on such short notice tonight.

The drive is short, and I walk into reception where Jordana is on the desk, all dressed up for the night, with a face full of heavy makeup and bright red lipstick, which I'm sure she's about to put around some guy's cock.

"Remington, she told me you were coming in. You don't want me to join you?" Her voice irritates me every time she opens her mouth.

"No!" Storming down the corridor to our usual room, I open the door to see her sitting on the couch waiting as Jordana yells at me down the corridor that it's my loss, but I'm not even listening as I close the door.

I know she is pissed at me for calling her out tonight, but she'll forgive me by the time we're finished.

"Strip off." Her voice does the same thing to me every time. It's like a hypnotic chant on my body that makes me just do as she says.

Dropping my clothes and leaving just my boxers on, I pull up the gym shorts I always have in my car, and she throws me my gloves.

I walk over toward the mats that are my safe space, and before I have time to even get prepared, she has my legs out from under me and I'm flat out on my back with her standing above me, smirking, gloves raised and ready for my retaliation.

If anyone knew what we did here, that I spar with a woman, they would be appalled that I deliberately hit her.

But it's not like that!

This woman is a friend, and she is far tougher than I am and takes great pleasure in beating me and getting paid to do it. Cherie is an ex-street fighter from her youth, and when she pulled herself out of the drug-addicted family she was living with, she put herself through college to train in mental health and anger management. For years I didn't know how to manage my temperament besides seeking out adrenaline-fueled activities. Until one night I met her in a gym, and she tried to correct my boxing technique. A few of the guys I was with started clowning around and making fun of her.

Daring them to put their money where their mouth was, she challenged them in the ring. Before we knew it, she had all three of them on their asses on the mat, and she was still ready to go against me.

I'm not stupid enough to deny when someone is better than me.

We went out for drinks afterward and talked about life in general, and not once was there any chemistry or spark between us. She told me about a program she wanted to get off the ground with kids, where she teaches them to defend themselves, get the raging hormones under control, and talk to them at the same time. Helping them get off their chests whatever had them so pumped up and angry.

I was at a point that I needed some help, and I just wasn't prepared to admit it. So, we struck up a deal that I would be her first client, and I would pay her to spar with me and to try to teach me ways to control my mind.

I was seeing her twice a week in the beginning, we boxed, along with a combination of other martial arts techniques, while she had me talking or should I say yelling out my problems. It takes a lot of skill to try to defend your body and your mind at the same time. So, while your brain is busy protecting your body, Cherie beats down the walls on everything else you need to let loose.

"What are you crying like a baby about tonight? This is twice in one week," she throws at me while we are dancing around each other on the mat.

"Just fucking hit me," I yell at her, because tonight I feel like shit, and I need to feel pain. The whole drive here I couldn't stop thinking about El and how she is turning me inside out, and my friend Flynn who I am being the lowest of friends to.

"Got it, it's still the girl." She swings a right jab, and I manage to duck under it.

"And then some." I grunt as she lands one in my ribs, being distracted over the vision of El that is back in my head. She laughs as I groan from the next hit.

"Sounds like we are in for a long session. Hope you aren't planning on walking out of here until you get it out. I'm not seeing you again this week, so start fucking talking."

Annoyed at the reminder that I have let myself fall back into this position that I'm here at all, I land one in her ribcage this time, but she doesn't even flinch, because after years of doing this, she now wears body armor.

I'm the only stupid one that wants to feel the pain in all its glory.

I don't even know where to start, but she helps me out with one sentence that opens the flood gates. "Did you fuck her again?"

And there it is. Sexual frustration mixed with anger is not a good combination I've learned, and all the words start falling from my lips.

She's right, tonight is going to be a long night, and if I'm still walking by the end of it, it will be a miracle.

But at least I'll wake up tomorrow and be able to handle living in my home with the woman who has my balls in a knot and my heart betraying the rules I set in stone years ago.

It has taken a while, and my body paid the penalty, but I have finally been able to move past wanting to fuck El against every wall in my house.

Looking at the date on my computer screen, I can't believe it's been two months since Elouise moved in and Blaise became part of my life.

So much for taking it easy and everybody settling into a new routine. First there was Flynn's sex tape problem, which I haven't let go of yet and am still having Broderick investigate.

Like Broderick's first thought, this influencer woman doesn't seem to connect to the actual emails, and the background checks he has done, in his secret unconventional ways, show that the claims she has made about having the tape just don't add up. It sounds like she might just be a pawn in someone else's game.

And then on top of that, there was the attempted security breach on our booking system which we stopped, but it was the most sophisticated hacker that has tried so far. But what I'm worrying about now is that there seems to be a few little problems at each of our hotels. I can't put my finger on it yet, but something is looming, and I don't know what or where it's coming from.

That's the part I hate the most.

Tomorrow I'm due to fly out to Edinburgh to check out a castle that is for sale. Nic has his heart set on owning a castle to run as a boutique luxury hotel. He and Forrest have done all the financial due diligence, but they need me to scope out the actual spot from a security point of view. What it would entail to have it up to our standard and if it's even possible in such an old building that has just been run as an Airbnb for the last ten years. It is protected under national heritage laws, which our legal department is all over, along with Tori who will be looking at the remodel design. But for me, it's as simple as figuring out if I can integrate a modern system into such an old structure without making it look ugly and ruining the whole ambience of staying in a castle. Scotland is full of castles, and it's part of the attraction, but I know Nic will want his to stand out amongst the rest as the most prestigious.

Tori suggested I take Elouise and Blaise with me for a couple of days so they can spend some time with me. Reminding her that I'll be working fell on deaf ears, and she okayed it with Nic that I take a few days off after scouting the property. She has booked the property for us to stay in for four days, and as much as I was annoyed because she did it without me knowing, Elouise and Blaise are so excited. It will be his first trip on a plane, and using the company jet, I'm sure it's going to be a hell of a first flight.

Blaise and Elouise have been working hard, and his English is to the point where I can talk to him in broken sentences, and it's awesome. I've even managed to look after him on my own at night a couple of times now, so Elouise could have a girls' night with Tori.

Besides the craziness of work, El and me have managed to slip into a routine of sorts, and the friendship she asked for is easy to do. Mainly because we don't see each other that much. Even when I get home early enough to have dinner with them and read a story to Blaise, I then need to head into my office to continue working. Weekends we have been trying to visit and do things with the guys, so Blaise feels comfortable with them all. They are his family now too. Even Nic's mother Sally has visited a few times and has taken on a second-grandmother role. She doesn't seem to have any problems with the language barrier. I guess it's just the motherly instincts.

But all in all, things are progressing well, and I think Elouise is right that it needed to be this way.

I don't like it, but I have to admit it's working.

Plus, I get the side benefit of getting to know her without the added pressure of trying to impress her constantly. She sees me in my own home and being myself. And to be honest, if we ever have a chance of this thing becoming more, then she will know exactly what she is getting herself into, and so will I.

It's probably not the most appealing time of year to head north to Scotland, as the weather is getting colder and the days shorter, but when these opportunities present themselves, you need to jump on them before they disappear.

I've been staring at the building specs for the castle for a while, and although these tell me a lot, I really need to see the physical building to make a better judgment call. Drawings are one thing, and videos are great, but I'm a visual person, so I need to be there in person.

My phone vibrating on my desk has me looking away from the screen which is a welcome relief for a minute. The concentration is intense because I don't want to miss anything.

> Elouise: Blaise is running a temp, I think he is coming down with a cold.

> Rem: Have you called the doctor?

> Elouise: It's a cold, Rem, it's nothing serious.

> Rem: And you know this how?

The next thing I know, the door to my office opens and Tori pokes her head around the corner. I wave her in but then hold a finger up as I'm waiting for the response. My heart is beating a little harder thinking about Blaise being sick. I know this is the first of many times I will have the worry of a sick son, but still, I'm not prepared for how to manage this. Should I insist she takes him to get checked out or should I just trust what she is saying?

I could call my mother to check, but it's not worth the grief it would cause me of having her land on my doorstep for the next two weeks and bringing every old home remedy that she inflicted on us growing up and pouring it down Blaise's throat too. I'd prefer to work this out on my own.

The next message tells me what I was expecting her to say.

> Elouise: Years of experience of snotty-nosed little kids. Stress less.

> Elouise: But I don't think flying or the cold air of Scotland is a good idea. I'll stay home with him.

"What's wrong, Rem, you look worried, is everything alright?" Tori can tell I'm stressed just by looking at me.

"Blaise is coming down with a cold, so Edinburgh is off the table. Do you think I should call a doctor?" In my head, I'm working out what I will reply to Elouise, but before I get a chance, I look up as I hear Tori start speaking.

"Hey, babe, how sick is he?" Phone to her ear, I'm annoyed at her for calling and even more frustrated because I can't hear the reply.

"What's she saying!" I growl at Tori.

Rolling her eyes at me, she takes the phone from her ear and hits the speaker so I can hear too.

"Can you repeat that for the grumpy bear who is sitting at his desk throwing daggers at me but also sweating bullets that his baby is sick?" Tori's sarcasm is not funny right now.

"Hey, Rem, he's fine, no need to panic. It's just a little sniffle, but I don't want to risk taking him away. Plus, we want him to enjoy his first trip." Her voice is what I needed to hear. She sounds like everything is under control.

"Great, I'll call Sally, and she will be happy to look after him for a few days so you two can go as planned and enjoy some time away from the child. You deserve a break, Lou, and you can sightsee while Rem is working." Tori starts texting on her phone while we are still on the call.

"Wait, what? Tori, stop right now. I'm not making Sally look after my sick son." I stand because I feel like I've been pushed to the side on this decision about my own son.

"She said she would love to. She'll be over tonight with Broderick, and they will stay for a few days." Tori is just speaking to us like we are part of the staff.

"Tori, I can't leave him. It's my job to take care of Blaise," Elouise shouts down the phone at her. And I know why.

She too is feeling the panic of the two of us alone for a few days and what will happen. Well, even if she isn't thinking it, I sure am.

This is going to be a disaster, I can just tell.

"You don't want to disappoint Sally now, do you? She is already so excited." As Tori is looking at me with a stupid smirk on her face, my phone vibrates in my hand with a message from Sally.

Far out, how can I get out of this now? She is already packing her bag.

"My son, my house, my nanny, Tori," I say, letting her know I'm not happy about her stepping into my life.

"Whatever, and you're welcome." Taking me off speaker, she walks back out of my office before I even have time to continue this conversation.

This is going to be hell, and I'm already trying to think of how I can get out of it, while at the same time, an email from Nic appears on my screen about the negotiations for the castle and how he needs my answer from up there tomorrow ASAP.

I'm screwed.

Looks like I'm taking Elouise to a castle and then locking myself in the dungeon.

It'll be safer for both of us.

Chapter Twelve

ELOUISE

"*Why are you protesting so much?*"

Tori's voice keeps repeating in my head as I'm sitting on the jet trying to read a book while watching Rem engrossed in his computer, working.

It's not like I could tell her.

I hate keeping secrets from her, but this one would blow apart the group, and I'm not going to be responsible for that.

Rem hardly spoke to me last night, spending all his time with Blaise until bedtime and then continued lying with him for a while after he fell asleep. As much as I was freaking out about the trip on the inside, watching him with Blaise, stretched out on the bed, arm wrapped around him and protecting him from a sickness that he had no control over, it had my ovaries exploding. My heart skipped a beat at what a great father he is.

His back was turned to me because he was just intent on watching Blaise sleep. I know I shouldn't have been standing there watching him, but it was like I was in a trance, and I couldn't move.

My body reacted to the sight of his broad shoulders, that then chisel down in the perfect way to his waist. His shirt pulled tightly against his arm as it was outstretched over the top of Blaise's body, which meant the muscles on his back were showing, and I just wanted to feel them under my hands again.

That's the problem when you've had something, then you know exactly what you are missing.

And I'm missing that body!

So much so, that just like most nights I spend in my bed, I closed my eyes, sliding my hand over both my breasts and pussy while thinking back to him taking what he wanted from my body as he had me pinned down on his desk. I loved his strength and control over my body and then the tenderness and truth he shared with me afterward. He truly is a paradox of emotions, and I think that's what pulls me to him.

Rem is nothing like the man I ever imagined I would be with. Not that I'm with him now, but that doesn't take the want or need away from me to have him in my life more than as my boss and friend.

I want this man to totally consume me but be man enough to let me live my life as I choose to. I don't want a man to tell me what to do, but it didn't take much to learn that I want him to show me what I want in a man. I can see that Rem wants to protect with every bone in his body, it's in his nature, and it's not something he can turn off. And along with loyalty that he takes very seriously, this gives him strength to be who he is. But it also leaves a chink in his armor when he is conflicted on where to lay his loyalty.

Should it be to Blaise, and then who comes second? His friends, me, or the person who he sadly puts last, himself. He has forgotten that his own happiness is important too.

It's like looking in the mirror for me as I'm thinking this, because I know it's one of my worst traits that I put myself last. I'm a people pleaser. Always have been, and it's why Tori and I work so well in our friendship. She comes up with some plan, and I carry it out to please her. I think you would find the same trait in most teachers in the world. We want to help and please people, it's who we are.

A bump of turbulence has me grasping the arm on my seat as I look straight to Rem for reassurance. I haven't told him how uncomfortable I am flying, but I think he has worked it out.

"Just breathe, it's all good." That calming tone is like liquid gold in my head.

"Mm-hm." Looking back down at my Kindle, I reread the same sentence that I think I have read at least seven times and still haven't moved past it.

It's probably part of the problem, that I'm all up in my head thinking about Rem when I'm reading the line in the book that says, "*Your body is so passionate and all I want is to worship you with every part of my soul, while I fuck you senseless,*" and I want that too. With the man sitting across from me that is oblivious to how I can't turn off the way my body responds to him.

I told him we couldn't act on any feelings, that friendship is all that is possible. But to be honest, I wasn't expecting him to listen.

Damn it, he also has respect as one of his important qualities.

I shouldn't be thinking about this, I should be coming up with plans on how I am going to stay away from him for the next four days. It's easy at home with Blaise around, but now I have to navigate this and stay true to my words. I saw what it did to him the night Flynn's words rocked him. I don't want to push him back to that point again.

One of the awesome things about a private jet is you have Wi-Fi. Dropping my Kindle to my lap, I search on my phone for things to do in Edinburgh. Oh, look, the Harry Potter train trip. It would be amazing to see that and be able to share it with my kids at school. It's three hours away. Excellent, a day trip on my own so he can work. Ticked off one day, now to fill the rest.

Before I get to do much more searching, the captain announces we are heading in to land, and I need to switch off the Wi-Fi. Oh well, it's back to trying to read this book. Or maybe I should save this scene for tonight when I can guarantee I will need relief, although it's not been a problem lately to find my own inspiration.

I can tell Rem is in work mode, the way he is speaking to the crew on the plane, the driver that dropped off the car and castle keys to us at the airport, and even to me. It's short, straight to the point, like I hear him on the phone in his office. He delivers instructions and expects them to be followed. They are clear and concise, and I can't imagine what happens when people don't listen. I giggle a little on the inside because truth be known, I've already seen what happens when I push him. But I'm sure that's a different story.

As the noise of the car's turn signal echoes through the silence inside the car, I gasp at the sight before me.

"Oh, Rem." We drive between big stone pillars. The beautiful large wrought-iron gates look like they have been here for hundreds of years, and the excitement has my body tingling so much I just can't contain it.

Without hesitation, I grasp his forearm in the driver's seat next to me in the car.

Finally, for the first time in days, he laughs lightly at me. I'm the woman whose face is almost plastered to the window, taking in everything around me. It's like the dreams I had as a little girl. Being a princess, living in a castle, having the most handsome prince by my side, and living the most magical life. I doubt boys have the same dream growing up, but then I've never asked.

"Did you ever dream of living in a castle as a prince when you grew up?" I quickly look across at him for his reaction.

"I wouldn't fit the role of a prince. I'd be more the knight in shining armor protecting the castle or the hunter providing the food." He smiles at the little girl I'm sure he can see inside me that is about to live out her fantasy for the next few days.

"Oh, I can so see you as all three in one person. The protector, the provider, and the seducer." I smack myself on the forehead metaphorically inside my head because that wasn't something I meant to say out loud.

I'm about to pull my hand off his arm where I latched onto him in surprise, but instead, I instantly grasp harder as we come out of the tree-lined driveway and the castle appears in all its glory in front of my eyes.

The old gray stone is so tastefully weathered, and you can see how well it has withstood time. The main part of the castle is taller, standing three stories high, giving that majestic feel, with the four circular towers standing tall on each corner of the building. The rest of the castle is two stories high, making it look like such a prestigious home. The tall trees towering over the castle look incredible and frame the building perfectly.

Tori has told me a little about its history and that the current owners started a restoration project twenty years ago but ran out of money. They have both since passed away, and the children don't want anything to do with it, being a money pit, and are keen to get it sold so they don't have to manage it. The part of the building that is livable they were leasing out for short stays, and the rest is closed off, just sadly deteriorating. Nic has organized with the owners to be able to access the whole castle so Rem can see what condition it's in and make his recommendations back to Nic.

This will be their most difficult and expensive acquisition since Nic took over the family business, but he is so adamant he wants this castle to add to the huge property portfolio he already owns. Must be nice to have the wealth to see something and decide you want it. I know there is more to it than that, but still, who gets to buy a castle!

The car comes to a stop in front of the entrance, and all I can do once I'm out of the car is stand and look up in awe at what is before me. I know Rem is moving around me, but I can't look away. I'm thinking of all the people over the centuries that have stood here in the same place and been so intrigued about what is behind these ancient stone walls. I need to know more about this place.

The hand on the arch in my back sends a rush of feelings through me that has the hairs on my body standing up. Rem touching me in this moment has me jolting out of my thoughts. There is something about a man's hand on that part of your back that is so sensual. I don't know why, but it is. It's not like it's a sexual place but more than that.

The sensation of "*I've got you*" or showing the rest of the world, "*this woman is mine and off limits.*" Either way, they are both things that I can't be thinking that Rem means when he touches me like this.

It's a longing that I've told myself from the beginning I'm not allowed to feel when it comes to him.

"Your castle awaits you, my queen," Rem says beside me, and I have to say it's the worst Scottish accent I have ever heard before, as he waves his other free hand in front of me, gesturing me to move toward the door.

"Oh, I have graduated from a princess to becoming the queen, how noble of you." I step away from him to stop the warmth that was almost burning his handprint on my back with the heat he is conjuring up in me.

I move toward the large old solid door that Rem opens with the quintessential skeleton key that you'd imagine from early last century.

"They may as well have just left the door open," Rem grumbles, not surprisingly unhappy with the lack of security here.

"Maybe the men in Scotland are too busy trying to keep their kilts down in a breeze to be breaking into castles. They are protecting their crown jewels." I try so hard not to let the laughter out as he glares at me.

"What? I thought that was pretty funny…" I'm still waiting for his answer, but from the look on his face, his sense of humor is not with him today. "Or not." I shrug and walk past him and into the foyer at the entrance of the castle.

It's not like I was picturing, with a big entryway and some grand staircase that takes you to the upper levels. Instead, it has a small receiving area, and then there is a staircase to the right heading upstairs. The houses and castles of the centuries past that we see in all the historical romance movies are usually based in London where grandeur was a status symbol. Here in Scotland the castles where probably more practical; smaller rooms are easier to heat in the colder months, and maybe they were more worried about hunting trips than the big balls that the English seemed to attend constantly. To be honest, I don't know much about the Scottish history, and what I'm thinking in my head is actually a load of crap I'm making up, but it will give me something to concentrate on learning over the next few days.

"Don't move from here until I've done a quick sweep of the

place. Sit on that chair and don't even think about following me. Yell loudly if you need me."

Rem places our suitcases down in the foyer. I can tell he is torn about leaving me on my own or taking me with him into unknown danger.

I mean, seriously, it's just an old place that nobody cares about. It's not like there are some drug dealers or the Scottish mafia operating out of the upstairs rooms. Is that even a thing? Mafia in Scotland? I really need to put a lid on my overactive imagination.

I can hear him stomping around upstairs, going from room to room, making sure it's safe. Although it's probably not necessary, it's kind of sexy.

I wonder how fast I could get him back down those stairs by screaming his name out nice and loudly. It would be funny to see, but also pretty mean too. Knowing my luck, he would fall from running so fast and break his leg or something on the steps, and then I would feel like an idiot. It's a prank that Tori and I would definitely pull on each other, but in these circumstances, it's probably not that funny.

If there's one thing I've learned about Rem it is that he takes his protection of me seriously, and I love how that feels, so I need to respect that.

Looking around me, I feel so out of my depth. This is not my style, to be whisked off for some trip on a private jet and staying with Rem who won't let me pay for a thing. That in itself has been hard to get used to the last few months. It's still a shock to see my bank account constantly growing from week to week, because I'm not spending a single penny. Because when I'm not with Rem, I'm out somewhere with Tori, and she won't let me pay for anything either.

Part of me is a little pissed off that they won't let me stand on my own two feet. Before money came into Tori's life, we did just fine as two women who were making their way in the world, sharing the bills and buying each other little treats as we went along. But now with Nic's fortune that seems to have dragged us all into the wealth bubble, I feel like everyone looks at me as the poor person in the group that they all need to look after.

I mean, I appreciate the love that comes with that, but it still makes me feel like I don't fit in this circle. And I know it's only me that looks at myself like that, and they would be annoyed if they knew how it made me feel, but it's who I am. I don't ever want to have to rely on anyone.

My mum raised me to be an independent woman, and as much as I have three brothers who think I need them, she taught me to show them I didn't. Forging my own way in this world is what I want and what I need.

It's beautiful to be loved and protected but not smothered by either.

Thankfully my family knows my boundaries and respects them. I just need to get my friends to understand the same boundaries.

I watch Rem come back down the staircase and hear every step creak with his weight and the age of the timber. I'm guessing there would be no sneaking out at night as a teenager living in this house. Not even saying a word, he walks past me and in and out of the downstairs rooms now too. Walking back toward me, he looks satisfied with himself.

"All clear, you can start to explore now," he says as he is replying to something on his phone and stands back for me to walk past him.

He truly is preoccupied today.

I start wandering into the first room on the right side of the hallway and am transported back in time to the period of the décor. There is color everywhere. A large sitting room with multiple single and double seats with carved wooden legs and tapestry cloth on the seat and back. There's a mixture of glass and wood coffee and side tables which I can picture many pots and cups of tea being served on and enjoyed by guests. A window seat with a padded cushion on the seat and two floral pillows on each end standing against the wall. I can picture myself curling up there with a good book, a cup of tea, and the open fire crackling away; it's very tempting. The dreams of any reader.

The walls are pear green, and the floor is carpeted in an old-looking patterned carpet, a navy color with different flowers all over it. Very old-worldly, but it suits the room.

"Well, it looks like someone vomited color in here." Rem's voice behind me startles me, and I let out a little squeak.

"Stop it. I'm sure the owners were trying to stay traditional to an earlier era. Just because you are a man who doesn't like any fuss in his decorating, that doesn't mean you can't appreciate other people's work," I say, while thinking to myself that although this might be in period with the early years of the castle, I'm not sure they hit the mark with it. He has a point, but I won't admit that to him.

"Well, if Nic buys this, then I can't wait to see Tori let loose. I'm sure she can't do any worse than this," Rem says, stepping level with me, and I can't help but turn and give him a friendly slap on the arm for his comments.

"I'll tell her that you think her design skills are just one level up from shit. I'm sure she will love to hear that." I walk back out of the room as I hear him laughing behind me, knowing full well that would be like waving a red flag to a bull for Tori. She might just kill him for that comment. He's only just earned enough brownie points to be off the bottom of the shit pile with her after the way he acted when he wanted to hire me. Luckily for him, Flynn is always doing something stupid which keeps him on the bottom of the rankings of who is the most annoying.

"Let's go check out the bedrooms upstairs," I comment as we head toward the stairs. I hear him groan behind me because both of us are thinking the same thing, I'm sure. Let's pick ones that are as far as possible away from each other. No point risking temptation when there are thirty different rooms to pick from. Admittedly, most of them are inhabitable, but I'd even consider one of those at this point.

I shouldn't have expected anything less when I hear Rem's phone ringing with the ring tone that he has just for Nic. He would have known what time we were due to arrive, and he is being impatient as always. It's corny but the words from "Down Under," by Men at Work come out of the phone and echo off the stone walls, announcing it's Nic calling. Can't say I'm disappointed I missed it, but apparently Nic did an atrocious rendition of this song at karaoke the night the boys landed their first big hotel purchase together. I can't picture that from Nic, but it's amazing what people will do after way too many drinks.

Nic hates that all the boys have their ring tone set at that, and they keep promising to change it, but so far, he hasn't won on that one.

"Seriously, I've been here five minutes, and you are already calling me." Rem already sounds frustrated, but I can see by the look on his face that he understands the pressure that Nic is under and how important it is for his boss.

Deciding to leave them to it, I start up the steep stairs. They aren't fancy, and I'm sure that once it becomes a Darby Hotel, it's one of the first things that Tori will be changing. There is something about a grand staircase that gives you a feeling that opulence and luxury await you at the top. And that's exactly the feeling that Nic will want his guests to experience upon their arrival.

I just want to take the chance to peek around the rooms and see what it's like before I drag my bag up here. Besides, the fact that as soon as I started to walk toward my bag, Rem scowled at me, and I could tell what he was trying to say to me with just one look: "*Don't you dare touch that.*"

The rooms are similar sizes, but all decorated differently. I know nothing about styling and décor, but even I can tell that this will not be up to Darby Hotel standards.

The last door I step through at the end of the hallway is to a room filled with dark wood panels halfway up the walls, navy embossed wallpaper, and a beautiful big wooden four-poster bed as the star attraction in the room. It is set against the wall opposite two windows that look out toward the large trees behind the castle. Of all the rooms I've seen on this level, this is the one I would pick to stay in. It feels warm, inviting and the sort of old-world luxury I can imagine would be set for the man of the house. It's masculine yet still has a softness to it in the way it is accessorized.

On the wall to the side of the bed there is a large painting of a man standing behind a woman seated on a chair. He is dressed in a suit while she is dressed in a full-length dress, long sleeves, and neckline buttoned all the way up to her neck. The only indication that they are together is his hand resting on her shoulder in a possessive way. But both their faces are stoic and wiped of any emotion. In fact, he looks surly and like he is grumpy at having to stand here and pose for the piece of art.

What was it with the artists of the late seventeen hundreds, early eighteen hundreds that I'm guessing this is from. Surely it would have been a better painting if they were smiling, or she was looking up at him with love and adoration.

That look that says it all without saying a word. Where you can't breathe when they are near, yet your body can't help but be drawn closer to them. It's an expression showing that once you have found that person that the universe kept just for you, you become whole. They fulfill your needs with every part of them. I feel a shiver pass through my body, and I can't focus on what it is, my arms instinctively wrapping around my body, holding tight as my mind is fixated on these two in the painting.

Did he love her?

Was it an arranged marriage like many of them were back then?

Or was he just an alphahole like a few rich men I know—actually, one in particular that I left downstairs about to get into a heated argument with his boss for hounding him as soon as we arrived. There are many times that Rem gets all broody and withdraws into his office at home. I can never tell if it's about work or something else. Some nights after dinner he disappears to what I assume is a gym because he comes home all sweaty and retreats to shower and bed for the night. I mean, I don't doubt he's tired after his workout, because any man who looks like he does, packed with solid muscle, must go hard. Toned so perfectly that his chest looks like it's been chiseled by a sculptor to be admired by all.

Oh my God, what is wrong with me?

Why have I gone from looking at an old piece of art where you can barely see a piece of skin to fantasizing about Rem's body and sending me into a heightened state of arousal that I definitely don't need to be feeling right now. Especially when I'm about to be sleeping in a castle with this man for the next three nights, all on our own.

Hearing his footsteps coming toward the room, that same shiver runs through my body again, and I know I need to get out of here and make myself busy doing something… yes, something other than what my brain is thinking about in a very detailed way.

Meeting Rem in the hallway, I can see he is in work mode already. His call with Nic has him focused on why we're here.

"Sorry about that. Anyone would think the arrogant boss man is going to die if he doesn't get this castle. Probably lucky he didn't grow up with money, because chances are he would have been a spoilt rich kid, demanding what he wanted." He's holding my suitcase he has brought upstairs with him.

"Dare you to tell him that to his face." I laugh at the reaction he would get.

"I just did but not in so many words. Did you pick a room?"

I can't think straight because all I'm thinking about now are the abs that are under that navy shirt that is the perfect cut to hug him in all the right places.

So much for erasing that thought from my mind.

"Um, yes, the navy one at the end of the hall will be fine." Rem passes me like he is on a mission just to get rid of my bag and jump into whatever he needs to do.

Before I even have time to move from where I'm standing, he is back and muttering about how he will take the first room at the top of the stairs, the one that looks like a unicorn farted a rainbow in it. I try not to laugh, but one thing I know for sure is that I think it's an excellent choice because it's as far away from me as possible. He probably thinks it's perfect because no one can get past him to get to me, always on guard.

Following him down the hall, he comes back up the stairs with his bag as I reach the top. Standing aside to let him pass, he comes back down the stairs behind me so quickly.

"I'm sorry, Elouise, I need to get to work. Would you like to take the car and head into town and take a look around, maybe grab us some food for an afternoon snack? Check out if there is a restaurant for dinner, and I promise to be finished by then so I can report to Nic and get him off my back." Rem holds out the keys of the Audi that we picked up at the airport.

"Oh wow, I'm trusted to drive now that I don't have the precious cargo of Blaise in the car." I take the keys out of his hand before he changes his mind. I haven't driven a car since I moved in with Rem, having my own driver assigned. There has been no need, well, in his eyes anyway.

"Don't push it, El, you are just as precious to me as he is. Now be careful on the roads, you don't know them, and it will be getting dark soon." He's got his arms crossed and a stern look on his face to make sure I'm listening to him.

"Okay, Dad, I think I will be fine. There's this thing called GPS that will keep me from getting lost and lights to help me see the road in the dark." I knew as soon as I opened my mouth, I was poking the bear that was already agitated.

Covering the three steps that were between us, Rem is so close that as I step back a little to give me space, my back hits the wall, and his face is so near as he leans into me to make sure I hear this.

"I might be older than you, but I will never be your daddy. Because a daddy shouldn't be picturing you naked and tied to that four-poster bed of yours while he does some really… dirty… things… to you." Before I can process what he just said, Rem is already stepping back from me, about to walk away.

I gulp down air to try to keep breathing while my body just wants to slide down the wall into a puddle on the ground. But I can't let him think he can say shit like that when we agreed no flirting. To be honest, that was way more than flirting; he was telling me straight out he wants to fuck me on that bed, and I can't let that happen.

"That might be your kink, but it's not mine." Instead, I just add fuel to the fire.

"Oh, do tell then, El, what are your kinks?" He's about to step closer to me, but before he can, I panic and scurry off toward the front door.

"Not something that you need to know. I'm leaving." I wave over my shoulder as my feet carry me as fast as they can to the car. My cheeks are pink from embarrassment because I don't even know that I have any kinks. Before Rem turned up in my life, I was a missionary girl, and that was the only kind of sex I'd had. But that night when he bent me over his desk was something I could definitely get used to.

Driving into town, my mind is running wild with all the visions I'm imagining of being tied to that bed while Rem ravages my body. I couldn't get out of there quick enough to stop him from seeing how turned on I was. Maybe I need to visit one of the old shops here and see if they sell the old-fashioned chastity belt that I can put on and throw away the key until I get back to London. Because right now that's the only thing I can think of that is going to keep our no-sex pact intact while we're here. But then again, knowing Rem, he would just find a way to bust through it. I have a feeling that he is the kind of man that when he wants something, nothing will stop him. Not in a bad way, but in a strong sexual way that makes my knees weak and my underwear wet.

If only Blaise were here. He is the perfect wet blanket on any sparks that start flying between Rem and me. Sally has sent us a few messages already with pictures of Blaise happily playing with Broderick. You can tell he has a cold with his little puffy eyes but looks fine and isn't missing us at all. If only Tori knew that by getting Sally to babysit, what a predicament she's put both Rem and me in.

What a mess my life is.

I should be living the dream, being paid a gazillion pounds to spend all day with one adorable little boy, being driven around by a chauffeur and given all the luxuries of Rem's home and lifestyle. But instead, I'm on the edge of this feeling of not knowing if I should jump, and if I do, when should I take the plunge. Or should I take my most obvious and sensible option of moving away from the edge of the cliff, or better still, turning and running away.

Pulling into a parking spot, I feel like I just need to walk for a few minutes and get some crisp cold Scottish air into my lungs. Clear my head of everything… well, not everything, just him. The broody English man that keeps invading my thoughts.

My calm head lasts all of an hour when my phone vibrates in my pocket with a message.

Rem: I need you back here now!

Rem: You are never going to believe what I've just found.

My mind of course jumps to the worst conclusion.

Elouise: If it's a dead body then I'll see you in London.

Because there is no way I'm paid enough money to cope with something like that.

Rem: It's not. Just get your ass back here now.

No matter how hard I try, I just can't seem to get away from him. But in saying that, Rem is not one to be a drama queen like Tori, so for him to want me back at the castle, I know he is freaking out about something.

Elouise: On my way, but it better be worth it.

Rem: Hmmm, I'll let you be the judge of that...

Great, now I'm curious and anxious at the same time.

But either way, I'm going back inside those four walls that are not nearly far enough away from my biggest problem in life but also my greatest desire.

Chapter Thirteen

REMINGTON

I don't know how to be around Elouise without a buffer.

I'm a strong man, and when I put my mind to something, I can be stubborn as all hell. But that also goes for when I want something, I don't walk away from it either. Or more correctly, her!

I want her, badly, and it's getting harder to stay away from her the more I get to know the real El.

My first impression of her was a shy woman that lacked a little confidence when in a situation where she felt out of her depth, like when she first walks into a society event with hundreds of people she doesn't know. The snobby rich society women look at her like she doesn't belong, but sure enough, she proves them wrong as soon as she opens her beautiful mouth and speaks with intelligence and kindness. But when it was just us as a group, her beautiful personality truly started to shine, and she actually has a spark inside that she needs to show the world more. I see it every time she is with Blaise, and I can imagine it's the same when she is with her class at school, but I do feel she lets it dim a little when she is in unfamiliar territory. I'm just glad I'm no longer in her unfamiliar territory.

My restraint in all areas of my life is top notch, but for some reason, she weakens my strength in ways that I have never struggled before.

I need to snap out of this Elouise trance and do what I need to for Nic, or more simply put, just do my job.

At least she has left me here on my own for a while, and I can concentrate on checking out this place. Not that I was that keen on her heading into the village on her own, but I need to remember that she is a grown woman who survived this world perfectly fine without me. Not a concept I want to accept, but for now I have no choice.

Taking my time, I move from room to room taking photos and checking on structure. All the rooms that have been restored are actually in good shape. They look terrible aesthetically, but the building is in a good condition and a solid base for Tori to make it all look better with her design magic.

At the end of the smaller corridor that leads off the main hallway on the ground floor is the doorway that was installed to separate the house from the area that's not been touched yet with restoration. I'm not sure what I'm walking into, but one thing I'm sure of, it will be dark, dirty, and probably smell like something died in here.

Finding the right key, the door creaks open, and I doubt it's been opened in a very long time. The previous owner's children don't live around here and had left the keys with the booking agent for me. Using the flashlight I packed in case I needed it, I start looking into rooms that are like the others on this floor, just in poor condition. Some are bigger than others. The bigger ones could be used as reception or conference rooms, or perhaps luxury rooms with ensuite bathrooms built into them. Not my problem to worry about, but even with my limited styling ability I can see potential. I can also see the ability to get technology and security measures installed without it encroaching on the historical nature of the building.

At the end of the hallway, the last door leads me into a huge commercial-sized kitchen that looks like it could easily be adapted to run the hotel's catering needs. I know Tori is keen to host weddings here, and it would be the perfect location for that charming classical feel, along with great options for wedding photos. I can't help it that my hobby of photography is always in my thoughts when looking at something. But the electrical fittings here might need a fair bit of work to get it up to standard for modern appliances and the voltage drain it would take on the power circuits.

I jot more notes into my phone that we will need a rewire, which we already assumed anyway but know from past experience is hugely expensive. There is no way a building this old will have safe wiring, let alone be able to cope with the power needed for today's technological needs.

Taking more photos with my phone, I get to the last door on the right of the big thick wooden back door of the building. The door is stuck but nothing a small shove with my shoulder can't fix, and it opens to complete darkness and my flashlight shows steps leading down into what I assume is the cellar, or should it be called a dungeon in a castle?

I smile to myself at what I thought the moment I knew I was heading here with El. This was where I figured it would be safer for me to sleep, but there is no way in hell I would be game to spend one more minute down here than I need to. I have no idea what would have happened here over the life of the castle, but I don't think I want to know.

Thank God we will be paying contractors to come and clean it out and do the work we need here. But what I can see is that the ceiling is high enough for us to be able to use the space to run wires and cabling that will be needed upstairs and have it hidden from sight. And knowing Nic and Flynn, this will make a perfect wine cellar for them, cold and damp, or as they would say, a perfect wine storing temperature. One of the things with many of the older buildings we have across Europe is that they usually have an underground space of some sort that has been converted to a wine cellar by the previous owner or us once we purchase it. With the clientele we attract to our hotels, they have money, and they like luxury. With that, they expect good food and high-priced, good-quality wines.

Most of the rooms down here are just bare stone brick walls that have either a door in it, most of which are broken, or a few still have iron bars. Obviously at some time in history they were used for not great reasons. The last door at the back of the room is locked, but a piece of it has fallen, leaving a small hole in the door large enough that I can see inside.

"Holy shit." The surprised whisper falls from my mouth, jaw open, while I blink to see if it is what I think it is.

Out of the whole building, this room is probably the most modern and in the newest condition. I need to get inside the room and check this out.

I methodically go through the keys on the key ring, but none of them work in this lock. Maybe the key is hidden somewhere here. I start to feel around the bricks to see if there is one of those secret spots like you see in the movies, but everything feels solid and there is no chance that anything is a false brick.

I know this isn't our building yet, and I shouldn't be doing any damage, but if I know Nic like I think I do, this is already a done deal. He wants to give his soon-to-be wife a castle, so that's what he will be doing. Besides, one damaged door won't matter, and if it does, I'll pay to fix it myself.

The hole in the door is at the top of the panel in the center. Pushing hard with the bottom part of my palm, it starts to crack down a little farther. The harder I push, the lower the crack goes, until finally more of the wood breaks away and crashes into the room. A gap opens up, big enough I can get my arm in and down to the back of the handle, and I unlock it from the inside. As I pull my arm back through, the jagged edge catches my shirt and the cotton tears, and I can feel a sharp pain down the side of my bicep.

"For fuck's sake." Losing my patience with trying to do this gently, I pull my arm out as I feel warm blood start trickling down my arm.

Taking my shirt off, I turn it inside out to the clean part and wrap it around my arm to stop it from bleeding any more and to keep it as clean as I can. Who knows what germs are down in this dark place. Finally, I open the door to the room that has me so intrigued. Panning the flashlight around, I find the light switch, but when I flick it on and off, nothing happens. The wiring has probably been chewed through by rats since the room hasn't been used for a while.

The moment I step into the room, my suspicions are confirmed. But there is way more than I need to see.

"I suppose age doesn't matter these days." I look around the room at the photos that are framed and hanging proudly on the deep-maroon-colored walls. I assume they are of the old couple who owned the castle before they both died and left it to their children. This room could very well be the reason the kids didn't want anything to do with the property, and I can't blame them. Not sure I would want to see my parents in that light either; knowing they have sex and seeing what sort of sex are two very different things.

In the corner is what looks like a St Andrews' cross, and beside it is a spanking bench. Another apparatus I'm not sure about looks as if it is used to suspend a person from the ceiling. There's a rack along the wall that contains multiple whips, paddles, and floggers, and to the side is a large bed with straps attached to the headboard. And lastly, in the center of the room, is a swing that looks like it would give the perfect position to have a fucking good time with your partner, literally.

Holy shit, this is a lot, and they have obviously knocked down a few walls to combine a few of the rooms to make this one big room when they set it up.

Grabbing my phone from my pocket, I can't get a signal, so I take the photos I need to send to the guys but just make sure the photos on the wall aren't in them; they're not my pictures to share. As I walk back upstairs, my arm starts to hurt more, and I know I should get El back here to take a look at me, but I don't want to scare her. So, I just message her with part of the reason I need her here. Someone needs to be my witness.

Because no one is going to believe me that this old castle contains a modern sex room in its basement. With naked photos of a few perhaps fifty-year-old naked people in various sexual positions on the walls and one of the same couple later in life in their seventies. A selfie where they have a black fluffy blanket draped over them in bed, naked from the shoulders up, and she is lying on his shoulder, looking lovingly up into his eyes and he into hers. It is framed and placed on a table in the corner of the room with a candle next to it. I mean, as someone who loves the art of photography, they are tasteful and artistically done but just not what I was expecting, that's for sure.

I head back into the main part of the building and find the small kitchen that is on the ground level in the restored part of the castle, checking all the cupboards for a medical kit. But there is nothing in sight except for a few cans of tomatoes and some dry pasta, a box of tea bags, and some sugar packets, and weirdly, a bottle of oil with no label on it. My mind goes to places it shouldn't for what that oil is used for in this house, but surely it wouldn't be in the kitchen.

I can't remember how long ago Nic said that the owners died except for the fact that they died within four months of each other. Bizarre but in a way cute, I guess. Tori went on and on in the meeting about how romantic it was, but seriously, how can you find romance in death? I'm guessing it must be a woman thing, because listening to Tori and El talk, they can find romance in anything they put their minds to.

Deciding I'm better to just wait for El to deal with my arm, I start taking a walk around the outside of the building and check out the gardens. It has been let go, but besides the atrocious decorating and that room downstairs in the dungeon, the old place is growing on me. Not that I have anything against sex rooms or clubs, but it's just not my thing.

I spend my life protecting people and especially the ones I care for. I can't think of anything harder for me than to hurt them in any way, even if they enjoyed it. It's just not in my nature. And that is my biggest conflict with what I do with Cherie.

Suddenly flashes of El on the Saint Andrew's cross downstairs make the hairs on the back of my neck stand on end. There is a difference between playing with her and tying her to the bed so I can pull the most intense orgasms from her and binding her to the cross to whip her.

To each their own, I say.

It does make me laugh that here in Scotland where their flag is the Saint Andrew's cross, these Scottish people have taken their love of their country to a new level.

My arm is now throbbing, and if I had clean hands and the right first-aid supplies, I would have fixed it by now, but instead, I'm pacing the front room of the house waiting for the car to appear from the tree-lined entrance. Finally, I hear the crunch of tires in the gravel coming up the driveway, faster than I would like. She needs to drive more carefully, I don't want anything happening to her. I've not been getting my body beaten by Cherie to work off my frustration of having to stay away from Elouise for twelve months only to have her taken from me before we even start. I think I'm going to need an Academy Award at the end of this for the performance of a lifetime. I've been fooling everyone including myself that I'm not falling for Elouise.

The car comes to a halt in front of me, and El jumps out of the car, racing around to where I'm standing.

"And that's why I got you a driver." My frustration of waiting for her bubbles over at the way she came to a screeching stop.

"Rem, what the hell did you do to your arm?" Her hands are on me, and she's looking at me like I'm dying when it's just a flesh wound, the blood making it look worse than it is. "Wait, what did you just say about my driving?" It's like her hearing just caught up with her brain reacting to what she was seeing.

"Nothing," I grunt at her, not wanting to get into an argument right now.

"Hmmm." She rolls her eyes at me. "Now start talking, what did you do?"

"I'm fine, just a little cut that I need you to clean up and dress if you have anything we can use. I couldn't do it because my hands are dirty, and I can't find anything to sterilize them from God knows what old germs I have touched today in this building."

I might not be telling the truth about how big the cut is with the way my arm is aching now. Either I sliced it deeper than I thought or there is a piece of wood from the jagged door still in the cut. Whichever it is, I'll just get El to fix it and we can get on with the day. There is no way I'm spending time in the hospital waiting for hours for them to look at me like some pathetic wimp who needs one single stitch or just one of those bandages that are shaped like a butterfly.

"Let's get inside and see what I can find in my little first-aid kit in my suitcase." She places her arm around my waist. "Do you need help, are you feeling dizzy or anything?"

"I'm not useless. It's just a scratch. Walk," I bark, pointing in the direction of the door. I know I'm being a bit sterner than I need to be, but I don't want to be treated like one of her kids.

Glaring at me, she turns and heads inside by herself, without another word to me. As we both enter the foyer, she just points to the first chair inside the sitting room and looks at me. "Sit." And with that, she takes the stairs two at a time.

"It's just a fucking scratch," I yell up the stairs but still find my feet are moving toward the sitting room, and my ass is planted on the seat by the time she comes into the room again. Just like she told me to.

"Then why are you acting like such a growly bear, if it's nothing?" Unzipping the little black square bag, she flips it open and lays it in my lap, positioning herself on my left side next to my hurt arm.

"Damn, woman, should I be worried about why you have a fully stocked hospital-grade first-aid kit with you? Are you that clumsy you constantly need all this shit?"

"I ought to punch you right now for that insult, but I don't want to hurt you anywhere else. And who is the clumsy one here, hmm? For your information, it was packed for Blaise before I knew he wouldn't be here. Now shut up while I fix this." She starts to unwrap my shirt off my bicep, and the funny thing is that even though she is looking at my arm, her eyes keep going to the side to look at my bare chest. I'd actually forgotten that I was without a shirt because I was preoccupied with her. The way she frustrates me and makes my blood run hot at the same time.

"Doubt a punch from you would hurt me." But it wasn't the punch I should've been worried about. "Fuckkk, watch it." I grit my teeth as she rips off the shirt without an inch of care.

"Suck it up, tough guy," she snaps back at me while she is looks at the wound and rips open the little sterile wipe sachet. I have to clench my fist as she continues to wipe it with the alcohol wipe because it stings like a bastard.

"I beg to differ that it's a small scratch, Rem." I'm sure that is her teacher voice that she is scolding me with.

The look on her face tells me she isn't happy with me, and the rough way she is tending to my arm is showing me the same thing.

"You still haven't told me how you did it." The fresh and not-so-gentle wiping of the cut has it now bleeding again. "And I'd really be happier if we went to the hospital to check if you need stitches. Pass me that gauze." She points to a packet in her Mary Poppins first-aid bag.

"You wouldn't believe me if I told you, and not a chance. No hospital. Just patch it up," I growl as she presses down on the gauze to stop the blood again and places some adhesive tape over the top of it.

"When was your last tetanus shot?" she snaps at me.

"Two years ago. I'll be fine." That's one thing I'm good at, remembering details.

"Fine." She steps back from my arm. "You're a stubborn ass, aren't you." Collecting the kit off my lap and placing it on a table nearby, she picks up my shirt off the ground and throws it at my chest as I stand.

"If it's taken you this long to work that out, I'd call that a slow learner." I'm finally feeling a little less off kilter now that the cut is sorted and El is back by my side. I hated suggesting she head into the village alone, but I can't keep her attached to my side twenty-four seven while we are here. I have work to do, and she would kill me if I even tried it.

"Don't even try to joke about this. Why are you trying to be the big tough guy? What if you get an infection? Or blood poisoning? Hmmm?" She's got her hands on her hips as she is still mad at me and trying to chastise me for not getting it looked at.

"You know how cute you look when you do that?" I take a step toward her, but she is already stepping backwards to get away from me.

"No, no, no. You don't get to say that." And I can see I'm already breaking the anger in her, and there is that spark in her eyes that she gets when we are dipping our toes into the murky water of what is between us.

"Why not, I'm just stating the truth." I take a bigger step this time.

"Because we have a rule. No flirting, and you've already broken it today. Twice!" Trying to appear strong, I can tell she weakens the moment she makes the mistake of reaching forward and poking her finger into my chest to make her point.

"Third time's the charm, they say." My forearm comes down on the top of hers, because I don't want to place my dirty hands on her. It causes her hand to be flattened onto my abs and pulls her toward me. As she falls against my body, I whisper in her ear, "Were you remembering what my skin feels like while you were eye-fucking me a moment ago?"

The way her breath hitches is the best noise I've heard all day. But I'm not stopping at that. "Because I remember every inch of yours, the seductive feel, the tantalizing smell, and the taste I can't ever forget on my tongue." Her breathing is loud and rapid. But I know I have to pull back and leave her in that state of breathlessness, just thinking about what she is missing out on. Because there is no way that I'm letting her even find space in that beautiful brain of hers to think about another man when she is still fantasizing about me.

I slide my lips to her cheek and kiss her softly. "Thanks for being my nurse." Then I release her hand and step away from her.

Oh yes, she looks just how I like to see her. Flushed and in the place where she can't think rationally. It will only last a few moments, but I'll take every little bit I can get.

Time to give her a bit of her own medicine.

"Now, you sit and don't move." I manage to guide her into the nearby chair without actually touching her with my filthy hands. "I'm just going to wash my hands and grab a clean shirt."

Her mouth opens but nothing comes out. She's forgotten she was angry at me, so my job is done.

Knowing I don't have long and that she will be moving from that seat within minutes, I race into my room and drag my toiletries out of my bag, finding my soap and not just washing but scrubbing my hands within an inch of their lives to remove every germ that's on there. I don't want to touch Elouise unless I'm clean, and the way things are going, it'll be a miracle if I can manage to keep my hands to myself while we're here.

Pulling another long-sleeve shirt from my bag as I'm racing back out of the room, I can hear her talking to herself downstairs.

Slowing at the top of the stairs before she can hear or see me, I can't quite hear what she is mumbling. One thing I learned very early on when I went into security is how to walk so quietly that no one knows you're there. Stealthily moving down a few steps, her words become clearer.

"It's all Tori's fault. Should've stayed home. Four days with that dirty-talking, muscly sex on a stick without crumbling. Stick to the stupid rules. Fuck, why do I always have to be the good girl? Why can't I be the slutty nanny who jumps into bed with the boss at her first opportunity? It'd be easier if I wasn't always trying to do the right thing for everyone else but me. No one knows how bad I want him. Can't tell Tori, no one to talk to, no one to tell me I'm crazy and to stay away from him. It's not right. Blaise needs him, he needs his friends and his job. Flynn and Nic would kill him. Tori caught in the middle, and I'd be left on the outside on my own because I made everyone choose. And deep down, I know no one would choose me." Her voice cracks a little, and my heart breaks for the position I have put her in and how little she thinks of herself because of me.

I just want to walk in there and take her into my arms and tell her that I will choose her every damn time.

Fuck, doesn't she understand I've already chosen her?

Since that first night, I haven't slept with another woman. No one has even come close. The guys don't know that and neither does Elouise, but I haven't been able to shake that ache she left me with that night in Rome.

She's right, I am an asshole! For making her feel like that. I need to fix this.

Stomping down the stairs with footsteps loud enough to wake the dead so she knows I'm coming, I walk into the room, and she's looking out the window with her back to me. I can tell she's wiping a few stray tears that have escaped as she was beating herself up about our insane connection that is getting stronger the longer we're together. Not rushing her, I stay where I am and just change the subject to random conversation.

"I haven't had time to really walk all the property, but I think the gardens look like they are more tastefully done than the décor in here." Her hand drops back down to her side which is a good sign. "I mean, it doesn't look like someone threw a bucket of seeds in the wind and let anything grow where it fell, like the randomness they have done with the amount of color in this castle." I watch her shoulders bounce a little, and by the tiny laugh that comes from her, I know we are in a safe territory… for now.

"You really hate the decorating here, don't you?" Turning and facing me, I can see she is smiling, and that is what I was aiming for.

"There is nothing good about it. Come on, you have to agree. I mean, the only bit of class and style in decoration is the room downstairs, and that's just weird." Shit, I had forgotten the reason I even messaged her to come back. If anything is going to take her mind off us, then it will be this.

"What room?" Her confusion is apparent as she starts to walk back across the room toward me. "Is that why you messaged me, or was that a bullshit message because you didn't want to panic me?"

"Me, worry about you? Not a chance." I laugh when she tilts her head to the side like I'm speaking another language.

"So, what's with this room that is so different?"

"Yeah, different is probably a good word to use. Come with me and I'll show you." I hold out my hand to take hers as if I am showing her the way, but the truth is that I just want to center both of us. And it's the only thing I can think of without overstepping the line I should never have crossed today.

It's a funny thing I have with El, where silence is okay between us. There's no need to fill the air around us with mindless chatter as we make our way through the castle and down into the dungeon. Her hand in mine starts to squeeze a little tighter as we descend into the darkness, so I give her a little squeeze back, letting her know that she is safe with me.

Stopping just before the open door, I shine the flashlight at the ceiling, so we have dim light to be able to see each other.

"You know that movie where he stands outside the locked door and says, '*I want to show you my playroom*'? Well, it's not mine, but check out this playroom." I laugh at the surprise on her face.

"Holy shit, Rem, are you serious? I know they had sex rooms back hundreds of years ago too, but I can't believe it's still here after all this time." And I don't know why but part of me loves the naivety of Elouise sometimes and the intrigue at her hidden knowledge of random things. She is a reader, and I'm sure she takes in every word she devours on the page.

"Yes, but this is not from back then. Turns out this castle was owned by a couple of old kinky lovers. Just don't touch the door, it bites, so I learnt earlier." I look to where the scratch on my arm is, and it registers with her what I mean.

"Can I say I'm glad it was just the door that bit you in the room?" Her little giggle has me laughing too.

"You and me both. Shall we?" Walking through the door, I pull her behind me.

There is silence as I watch her eyes open wide and slowly move around the room, taking in the photos as well.

"Oh… my… God." Her free hand comes up and covers her mouth. Then it drops a little as she points at the photo of the woman naked and tied up in ropes, but with an expression of pure joy at the man I assume is her husband cupping her face in his hand while kissing the top of her head. I still see what I saw the first time I looked at it. The angle of the shot is artistic and captures exactly what the photographer was aiming for, which was probably her husband who staged the shot.

It's the look of pure and raw love between two people.

"She doesn't look like it hurts," El whispers.

"No, she looks like she is in what I imagine is her perfect position. A safe place of his love."

We both stand for a few moments, staring at the picture. Until Elouise's words break the silence.

"Is that why you think it's the best room in the house...? Do you like all this?" Even in the dim light, I can see the fear in her eyes.

Stepping closer to her, I release her hand and tilt her chin up toward me so I have her full attention. "No, beautiful, but all I wish for is that one day..." I stop to take a deep breath. "I will be your safe place to feel that loved."

"I think I have the same wish," she says in the softest and sweetest whisper that falls from her lips.

I just want to take her in my arms and kiss her until she understands how much I want that now, but I can't.

It fucking sucks, but I have already stepped over the line too many times today, so being the gentleman she needs me to be, I step back and take her hand again.

"We need to get out of here so I can breathe," I grumble as I start pulling her by the hand toward the stairs to the kitchen.

"That makes two of us," she agrees with me.

Then her whisper echoes off the thick rock walls of the dungeon. "Ten months and counting. Who are we kidding!"

I give it ten days if she's lucky.

Chapter Fourteen

ELOUISE

Settling my head down on the pillow, I'm glad the bed is at least comfy, because I doubt I'm getting much sleep tonight. It's hard to rest when the brain is thinking so hard.

My mind has been reeling since this afternoon, from what we saw down in the dungeon and then the hot-and-cold vibes that Rem is giving me.

I can't work him out today.

One minute he has me to the point I can't breathe, with his smooth seductive words, and the next he is treating me like I'm a dear friend that has known him for years. Moments of touch, with his body so close to mine that I feel like we are sharing the same breath of air, and then he is so standoffish that I start to think I've done something wrong. It's happened before, but it's usually flipping from home life to work mode, and I can understand that one, because it's from a world where I'm in it to the world that he must give every ounce of his attention, and there is no gap for me.

After we moved past me playing nursemaid, and he sent emails to the guys with all his thoughts on the castle so far, we headed out into the gardens and went for a walk around the grounds. I can see how this would be the perfect place to set up a classy countryside wedding venue and accommodation. The open fields are bordered by tall established trees that look like they have been here for a long time. It will make a picturesque background for photos. I know that Rem has plenty of hidden things about him that I don't know yet, but still, I did find out that all the photos in his home are ones he took on his travels. Watching him today and talking about the different perspectives on the beauty we were seeing and how it would make the perfect shot, it was then I realized how much he enjoys it.

The more I get to know him, the more I see that he has a creative soft side to him. The photos he takes are artistic and I appreciate them, but his singing is something I truly love. Every time I hear it I turn to mush, and the shivers running through my body are uncontrollable.

Dinner in the village at the pub was just what we needed to get back to the way we were before we left home—friends who enjoy each other's company, laughing over a meal and a pint of beer. It's not my favorite drink, but there was something about being in this quaint little stone building with a thatched roof. The bar area was small and dark with dim lighting that set the mood, along with the open wood fire that was burning. Although the weather today wasn't too bad, the late afternoon brought rain and wind which has a chill in it, and it made the gentle warmth from the fire delightful. We sat in the corner on two wooden chairs tucked nicely under a tabletop that is sitting on an old beer barrel. We couldn't help but relax and let the tension of the day slip away.

It made tonight easier to say good night and retreat into my bedroom to shower and settle into bed. I've tried to read like I normally do to get to sleep, but it was purely a waste of time. My mind is so perplexed on where I'm at with Rem. And the longer I lie here in the dark with just the sound of the wind and rain lashing on the window, I think of all the things I would tell my best friend if I could just talk to her. When she battled her feelings for Nic, I was there for her. But this time, I'm the lucky one who gets to battle the world of forbidden lust and attraction all on my own.

I mean, would she be able to keep it a secret if I confided in her? Not that I would want to put her in that position with Nic, but let's be honest, she was my friend before she was Nic's fiancé. Why does he get to trump me?

I giggle to myself when I answer my own question. The monster orgasms she told me about. Yep, that will do it every time. From personal experience of what that really means now, I totally get it.

Although I'm tucked nicely under the heavy bedding, that cold feeling that passed through me earlier today in this room is happening to me again. Causing a whole-body shiver that makes me uncomfortable and a little freaked out. There is something not right with it. Why would I feel cold when I'm warm in bed? And it's not an overall sensation. Instead, it starts in my chest and moves through my body to my toes. At the same time, the floor creaks, and I hear the soft noise of the chair in the corner of the room dragging on the carpet.

Oh my God, that beer must have my mind running away with itself tonight. I'm hearing and feeling things that aren't there.

Just close your eyes and go to sleep, you idiot.

Finally, the storm starts to fade, and the peace of night settles over me. My body relaxes, and I can feel sleep coming to claim me.

All I'm begging is that I don't have another dream of Remington like most other nights. I need to douse that flame before it gets any bigger tomorrow.

As the real world slips away and sleep overtakes me, I'm immediately brought back into the here and now with a thud next to my bed and the weird cold feeling running wild through my body. My eyes instantly fly open as wide as a possum as I sit bolt upright in the bed and look at the painting that has fallen off the wall onto the floor next to the chair which has definitely moved position.

I'm done.

My feet land on the floor and I'm running out of this room and down the hallway, screaming Rem's name as I burst into his room.

"El!" He's out of bed and to me before I even make it across the room, wrapping me in his arms, and I hold on so tight. "Talk to me." His demanding voice is calm but reassures me that whatever it is, I'm safe.

My breathing is erratic, and I try to take a few deep breaths before I can even explain, but he decides not to wait for me and starts to ask me questions.

"Are you hurt?" He tries to pull back to look at me, but I won't let him. I just pull him tighter to me, shaking my head sideways to confirm I'm not.

"Is there someone in the castle?"

How do I answer that without sounding like a lunatic?

Looking up at him, it's then I realize that his room isn't completely dark. The door to the bathroom is slightly ajar to let a faint amount of light in.

The concern in his eyes has me melting into him further.

"Maybe?" It slips from me in the faintest voice like a child.

"What the fuck does that mean?" His patience with me starts to wane as he drags me toward the bed where I see him reach for his gun on the table beside the bed.

"Shit, no, not a real person!" I yell at him.

"Elouise, explain now!" He pushes distance between us and grabs my jaw with his free hand, crouching slightly and staring at me hard.

Gulping, I blurt out my fear. "Ghost. In my room. It's haunted and the painting fell, the chair moved, and the spirit is fucking with my body." And with strength I didn't know I even had, I break free from his hold and move into his body again, wrapping myself around him like a koala bear.

While I'm still as tense as steel, his body starts to soften under me. He places his gun back on the table, and before I can say another word, he steps to the side of the bed and lays both of us down, pulling the blankets over the top and running his hands up and down my back.

"I know you're scared, but you know ghosts aren't real, right?" And now he is back talking in that calming smooth tone that makes my heart slow and my brain kick in to think rationally.

harder into Rem's hand as he continues to take my breath and every last part of my resolve to stop this from happening.

"Ohhh, yes." I can't hold back as he pinches my nipple and pulls it at the same moment his hand slides under the elastic of my shorts. And the moment one of his fingers finds the top of my pussy, I start trembling with anticipation.

"You think you need me, but I think it's more than that. Isn't it, El?" His damn finger is now purposefully touching me on either side of my clit, teasing me but not giving me what I'm desperate for.

"Rem, please." I'm begging now, and I can tell by the change in his breathing that he likes it.

"Answer the question, El." His hot breath is on my neck again, and he gives me the faintest kisses, again holding back because he loves seeing me so aroused and hanging on his every move.

Shaking my head, I refuse to give him the satisfaction.

"I don't believe you, beautiful." He moves his hand away from my breast and walks his fingers down my stomach and pulls my shirt up tantalizingly slowly. "I can read you and your body, babe, and I know the answer… but I want… to hear… you say it." His whole hand is cupping my pussy, and I can't help but buck against it, trying to get some relief.

"What you need is to feel safe and protected… but what you want is…?"

Knowing I'm almost about to lose it completely, he has me right where he wants me.

"Say it." His filthy whisper in my ear breaks every resolve I was trying to hang on to.

"You!" I scream. "I want you…" The moment the words leave my lips, he pushes hard on my clit and slips another finger instantly inside me. His large hand is now ravaging my bare breast, and the roughness of his skin on mine is like heaven.

But it's the deep guttural growl next to my ear and the words that make me fly over the edge of my orgasm that has been hovering at the surface.

"Fuck the rules, you're mine, and I don't fucking care who knows it." He sinks his teeth into the base of my neck as it curves at my shoulder, and the pain feels intense and euphoric as he continues sucking my skin.

My mouth is open, and I want to scream, but not a sound escapes as all rational thought is taken by the wave of my orgasm. Small convulsions keep my pussy chasing his hand, wanting more, but the sensitivity is like needles on my skin.

Rem slowly strokes my body, and as I come down from my initial high, I can feel his hardened cock pushing against my ass. But he isn't rushing me for more; instead, it's me that is ravenous for his body. It's the spell he weaves over me whenever we come together. I can't get enough of whatever he wants to offer me.

Reaching behind me, I push my hand between our bodies and clamp down on his cock. He lets out a moan of how much he wants my hands on him. As he starts to roll my body, he releases me so I can see his face and the creases in his forehead. Biting down on his bottom lip, he is obviously trying to stop this from being over too soon.

"Naked now!" He pulls my hand away from his cock and is up off the bed, leaving me feeling the absence of his body heat around me.

Before I move, his boxer shorts hit the floor, and his naked ass is disappearing into the bathroom. The extra light into the room with the door now fully open is harsh on the eyes, but the sight of him striding back toward me, his penis hard and bouncing off his stomach is enough to have me quickly pushing my sleep shorts down, sitting up, and pulling off the shirt that was already halfway up my chest anyway, throwing it onto the floor.

Moving to the end of the bed, he rips the condom packet with his teeth and quickly rolls it down his cock that is obviously sensitive from being so turned on. I see him wince at his own touch, the veins protruding and the head ready with pre-come already leaking.

Now with more light in the room, I can see the power of my man standing before me.

I'm not even going to correct the statement. He's mine, and I'm not sure I can let him go after this.

I don't know what tomorrow will bring, but tonight, I'm letting myself be his El, and he is my Rem.

I can't take any more foreplay, I just want the same thing Rem does. To be joined together with nothing between us.

"I have dreamed of seeing your face the next time I fucked you. Seeing you take my cock and what my body's doing to you. The bliss and pleasure that you've been craving. I'm the one giving them to you, making you feel so fucking good that you won't be able to walk away from me, no matter what." Rem's words do things to me I never imagined, because it's true. When he touches me it's like he suffocates my logical brain, and all I can think of is him and nothing else.

He kneels on the bed between my legs, not waiting any longer as he drags me down the bed closer to him. He grabs me by my hips and lifts my ass off the bed.

"You have the most gorgeous body." And as I'm reeling from his words, the first thrust of his cock has me screaming out in sheer unbridled passion.

"Yessss!"

Rem is not holding back. He pounds into me over and over again as the lower part of my body is suspended in the air, the muscles on his arms bulging from holding me up just where he wants me. The arch in my back gives him the perfect angle to hit deep inside me, and it feels so raw and primal. This is all about Rem letting go of everything we have both been trying to bury.

The passion that no matter how hard we try just isn't going away, but instead, it's growing in ferocity by the minute.

I want to make it so good for him, but I can't hold back anymore.

"Rem, I'm going to come, fuck, I'm going to come…" And I'm almost scared to let the orgasm take over my body because it feels like it's building to a height I've never reached before. Like I'm about to have my body torn apart by this magnificent man.

"Do it. Let me ruin you!" His voice bounces off the walls as he roars at me, and my eyes try to close as the immense explosions of sensation erupting all through my body, but I fight to keep them open.

Because the look of Rem losing complete control while fucking me through this orgasm is a picture I never want to forget.

It's etched into my soul to remember the day I knew there was no going back.

I'm Rem's!

Every single cell belongs to him.

His body stills and shudders as he comes so hard inside me. I watch his face finally show the inner peace he just found, the tense lines from earlier all softening and the sparkle in his deep brown eyes telling me the same thing that I already know.

There is no going back from this, he won. I stepped over the lines we drew. In all honesty, we both jumped feet first into hell, and although I'm petrified of the repercussions, it never felt righter than it does right now.

As he slowly lowers my body back to the bed, I feel like a porcelain doll. Treasured and delicate but totally fulfilled with the affection he shows me.

Leaning over me, he softly kisses my lips. "Amazing." And as he pulls back a little, he's just shaking his head and laughing a little at me.

"What?" I ask, confused.

"You gave us ten months, I gave us ten days, and we were lucky to last ten hours." Rem is still laughing as he stands up from the bed and walks toward the bathroom to clean up.

"And now I'm giving you ten minutes before we do it all again." The hunger in his eyes tells me how serious he is, but I can't help but laugh at him out loud.

"You think you only need ten minutes, old man?"

That stops him dead in his tracks, and as he turns toward me again, I can see that his cock is already getting hard again. "Oh, I don't even need five, but I was trying to give you a chance to breathe. But if you're going to be like that, buckle up, baby, because I'm going to show you just how good my stamina is." Turning back away from me, his perfect firm ass disappears into the bathroom, and all I can do is sink into the pillow and look up at the ceiling. Every thought of the ghost in my room is totally gone. Now all I'm thinking about is how fast Rem can get another condom on and get his hot body back on top of mine and have me screaming away any demons that have the hide to think they can take up residence in this room with us.

The next few hours are filled with joining our two bodies in more ways that I knew existed, and I know that no matter what happens between Rem and me, he has totally ruined me. I can never feel like this with another man. I know that deep in my soul, he has locked up my heart and thrown away the key.

I'm not at a place I can share that with him, but there is no denying it.

I've fallen for Remington Elders, and there is no going back.

The sex is out of this world, but lying here after our long sexfest is just as beautiful. Snuggling in his arms is a new thing, and the other times before now have been just about getting each other off. Now we let the enormity of what we have done settle between us. Rem wanted to take me to the shower, but I just wanted to stay here, with him, in a post-orgasmic daze.

But the longer we lie here in silence, the more I know I need to say what needs to be said.

"We need to talk about what just happened." I lift my head off his shoulder and roll my body so my forearm is on his chest and I'm looking at him.

"No, we don't. The fucking said everything we were trying to say." That calm and controlled look tells me he isn't worried about where we are heading from here.

"Rem, I'm serious, we need to talk about this. What we just did."

"Can't it wait until tomorrow? Sleep sounds so much more appealing." His hand moves to my cheek. "Don't stress about it. We both know there is no going back after tonight, but how we make that work sounds like a tomorrow problem. Agreed?" Lifting his head, he kisses my forehead so softly.

"Now sleep, woman, this old man needs to recharge before he eats you for breakfast." He pulls me back into his side, and I relax my head onto his shoulder again. I can't do anything but agree. I don't have the energy to argue or even think clearly. Except for repeating his words in my head. Maybe I should have accepted the shower if he plans on going down on me again in the morning.

This man is insatiable, and surprisingly, I'm learning so am I, when I feel the moisture between my legs at the thought of his beard there again.

The sound of running water from the bathroom has me starting to come out of the sleep coma I must have fallen into last night. Before opening my eyes, I reach across to feel the bed next to me, and the sheets are still warm, so I know that it's not been long since Rem got up.

Mmmm, a hot shower sounds delightful. Opening my eyes, I stretch my body out on the bed. I throw back the covers and feel muscles in my stretch that I didn't even know I had.

I quickly tiptoe on bare feet, naked, to the bathroom before Rem has time to know I'm awake. Standing in front of the shower, I admire the strong Adonis of a body that is before me. He's leaning his arm against the tiled wall, and every muscle in his back is tensed, showing me how all his fitness nights have brought perfection.

I thought I was quiet, but I forget that he has this extra sense that none of us seem to have.

"I can feel you watching me, but let me assure you, touching is so much more fun than watching." His morning voice is so hot, thick and gravelly, like he is just getting himself together for the day.

"Oh, I know how good touching that body is, I don't need convincing." Opening the door, I take one step in as he turns to face me, and before I even have time to close the door behind me, I'm in his arms with my back against the tiles and my legs wrapped around his waist. The hot stream of water runs over both of us from the showerhead on the ceiling.

I don't even have time to worry about my morning breath as Rem kisses me like it's been forever since he had his lips on mine.

We come up for breath, our foreheads touching.

"Good morning, beautiful." And all the fears I have start to raise their head again. "No, no, we aren't worrying. We are showering. I'm washing you and praising your body. Then I'm eating my breakfast and feeding you yours, before I clean you again."

Trying to open my mouth to say something, his finger lands on my lips.

"Shh, just relax and enjoy the early morning." And his cock that is already hard rocks into my pussy, pulling a groan from both of us. Just grinding over me is enough to set me on fire again. Without a condom, we continue writhing on each other, and it's so erotic to get off without the penetration.

"Now that's more like it." He starts kissing me hard as my legs drop to the floor, and he continues to make my body his until I'm orgasming again so hard that I can't stand. I end up on my knees with his cock down my throat.

All I can think about is how I could handle this sort of breakfast every morning, even though that's not reality, but it's nice to dream.

Finally stepping out of the shower, Rem wraps me up in a large, fluffy cream towel and pulls one around his waist too. He brings his hands back on top of the towel and rubs over me to keep me warm and dry me.

"Turn for me." He directs me to face toward the large mirror on the wall in a large gold gilded frame.

Looking into the mirror, all the air leaves my lungs when I see my neck, and the raging fear and panic comes racing to my brain.

"Remington, what did you do!" I yell without even one bit of control.

My hand jumps to my mouth in shock, my eyes almost out of their sockets as I stare at the large, dark mark that is obviously from him.

"I told you last night, I don't care who knows you're mine. I was marking what's mine." I can see the arousal in his eyes, inspecting his work.

I glare at him like I'm about to tear him apart, but his doesn't seem to care.

"What are you, sixteen? Seriously, how the fuck do I explain a hickey to Tori and the rest of them!" My rage boils over, and I storm into the bedroom to get dressed and get as far away from him as I can before I do or say something I'll regret.

Until I'm standing in the middle of the room remembering that my clothes are in the room with the ghosts, and there is no way I want to put my shorts from last night back on. They were wet, and I'm too angry to think of how that happened right now.

Storming to his suitcase that is open on the luggage rack in the corner, I rummage through it until I find a clean pair of track pants and a shirt and start to put them on.

"Mmm, you look sexy as fuck in my clothes." His voice makes me turn and look at him casually leaning against the doorjamb of the bathroom, still in just a towel and checking me out from top to bottom.

"Really?" I throw my hands in the air. "That's all you can say?"

"Yep." His smirk pushes me over the edge, and I storm out of the room.

I don't know where I'm storming to, but as long as it's away from him, that's all that matters.

And as I reach the small kitchen downstairs, my brain is now back onto the terrifying thought of how I'm going to get through this. Do I have enough makeup to cover what has to be the hickey of all hickeys?

If I had to give it a score, it would be a ten out of ten.

Point made, Remington!

Chapter Fifteen

REMINGTON

Okay, maybe not my smartest move. It was in the heat of the moment, and I was feeling possessive.

Pulling a pair of black jeans on and grabbing a button-up shirt, I head downstairs to find El who is totally pissed at me, and I need to fix that.

Not the way I wanted this morning to go, but here we are, and instead of the cool, calm talk we needed to have, in its place there is about to be an argument, and I need to defuse that quickly. And the only way to do that is to apologize, even if I don't regret it one bit.

I can hear her in the kitchen, and it's not like she is being quiet, trying to hide. The banging of things onto the kitchen counter tells me that although she is pissed, she's still hungry. I can work with that.

Walking in while she has a big kitchen knife in her hand is probably not the safest, but I continue with my hands in the air, surrendering.

"I'm sorry, El. I don't want you to be upset." I stand just out of knife reach but close enough that I can almost touch her.

"Upset?! What the fuck, Rem! How am I going to explain this to Tori? You know nothing gets past her, and she's like a dog with a bone if she thinks something is going on. She will keep at me until I crack." Her anger subsides, and the fear is starting to make her voice tremble a little.

Stepping closer, I take the knife from her hand which she never meant to use as a weapon, it was just in the air while she talks with her hands. With it now on the counter, I pull her into my arms which at first, she resists, but it doesn't last long, the moment I start whispering into her ear how sorry I am and asking what I can do to make it up to her. I know money doesn't fix everything, but if I need to go and buy the whole of Harrods out of every bottle of cover-up she needs to conceal it and twenty different scarves, then I'll do it. Not that I want to hide it. The possessive man inside me did it for a reason, but I know when I have to back down too.

"It's not supposed to be like this." Her little voice is muffled in my chest and sounds like she is on the verge of tears.

Releasing her from my hold, I pick her up and place her on the kitchen counter, pushing her legs apart and stepping in between them, taking her face in my hands.

"Like what, baby?" I ask, trying to keep her from falling over the edge.

"A mess. When you fall for someone, it's supposed to be all sunshine, hearts, and roses, not fear, secrets, and hickeys." The moment her brain catches up with what she just said, I can see the embarrassment as her cheeks start flushing.

"Who are you falling for, El?" I tease, trying to lighten the moment, when on the inside I'm puffing my chest out in victory.

"Not a vampire, that's for sure." She playfully slaps my chest. It's not much, but there is a small hint of a smile on her face.

"That's a shame, because I read that they are good with their mouths, very talented in sucking and the use of their tongue too." I lean toward her with a quick peck on her lips and look back into her eyes.

"You're an idiot, you know that, right?"

"So I've been told. Now let's talk and clear up a few things." She nods, signaling she's listening.

"Firstly, just so we are clear, I'm falling for you too, and I'm done waiting." I want to tell her the truth, that falling is the wrong word. I fell a long time ago, but she is already unsteady, and I don't want to frighten her. But instead, what I said brings back that calming smile I made disappear earlier.

"Secondly, I don't care how we do this, but I want to be with you. It's torture having you so close, yet I can't touch you."

"But what about Tori and Flynn, and God, I don't want to confuse Blaise." The mention of my son as one of her greatest concerns just makes me more attracted to her.

"I know, baby, but more importantly, what about you, what do you want? Be honest with me and more importantly yourself." Her words that I overheard yesterday in her moment of panic downstairs in the sitting room come back to me now. She feels like she always puts everyone's happiness before her own.

Her hesitation is evident, but I don't want to rush her.

But the way she sits up taller with her shoulders pulling back slightly sets my body on fire. She's ready to stand up and take what she wants.

"You, I want to be with you." Her voice is strong and solid, with determination that she is going to get what she wants.

"Then let's work out how we make sure we both get what we want." Dropping my hands and wrapping her back in my arms, I relish the feel of her against my body, knowing that I don't have to back away again.

"To be happy?" she asks, looking up at me.

"Yeah, baby, to be happy and thoroughly fucked, same-same in my eyes." Our bodies move in unison as we laugh.

"New rule, though, no more love bites, Rem." Then her eyes drop down slightly as she finishes her thought. "Well, in places that can be seen, I mean."

"Oh, beautiful, be careful what you wish for, or I'll be branding you with my mouth all over those luscious tits of yours and your ass cheeks that look like a tasty peach."

"Christ, Rem, you always have to take it to the next-level dirty."

"And you love every dirty word that comes out my mouth, so stop complaining." I slide my hand under my shirt that is hanging loosely on her and feel the warmth of her skin on her stomach. My fingers gently stroking over her belly button piercing that I love, I just let it sink in that she is giving me her body, and I will be able to touch her like this whenever she wants me to. "Maybe I should find one of those hidden spots now to leave my mark."

She pushes down on the top of my hand on her stomach.

"Too soon, Rem, too soon. How about I feed you breakfast... actual food before you get any ideas, and then we can work this out." This time it's El taking my face in her hands and kissing me like she has been wanting to do for months. Oh, I think I'm going to enjoy this new El who is ready to take what she deserves.

"So, we agree to keep it between us for a while. And you promise not to break this rule if I climb into your bed every night." Her words sound like heaven to me. El in my bed every night. For that I think I can keep my hands off her during the day while others are around. Well, most of the time anyway, but I'm not saying that out loud.

"Agreed. Now, are you going to make me do one of those secret handshakes?" I hold my hand out to her and watch her roll her eyes at me.

"Some days I think it's easier to deal with Blaise than it is listening to your comments." Standing from her seat at the kitchen table, she starts to clear away the dishes. "Now go and work while I clean up and find some clothes to change into."

"I kind of like you in mine." I shrug at her as she bursts out laughing.

"You only like me in these because they are easy access to my body, admit it."

"Valid point, El, I like your way of thinking." I stand from my seat, and she quickly turns back around from the sink to look at me and puts her hand up to signal stop.

"Don't even think about it. Go, work, remember? Before both our phones start blowing up, checking in to make sure we are still alive because they haven't heard from you." As she shoos me out of the room, I know she's right. I still have a few things to sort out, plus I need to review my daily update emails from all the hotels.

"And so it begins, already the fun is stopping." I laugh as I retreat toward the door.

I'm almost out of the room when her timid voice calls me. "Um, Rem?"

"Yes, baby, I will put your suitcase in my room so the ghosts can't watch you undress."

"Asshole," she yells from behind me as I'm partway down the hallway. "But thank you."

"That's what boyfriends do," is what I whisper under my breath as I'm climbing the stairs.

She might not be ready to hear it, but the word sounds perfect in my mind.

With all my emails sorted, it's time to send the message to the group chat about the room we found in the dungeon. They won't believe me unless I send pictures, so maybe I'll start with that.

Just pictures, no words, and then I sit back and wait for the reaction.

> Forrest: Didn't picture you'd be into that, but okay.

> Nic: Why are you sending this to us?

> Flynn: Hell yeah, Rem is getting his freak on in Scotland.

I should answer them, but I love leaving them hanging for a moment.

Flynn: Wait, you didn't take Elouise there, did you?

What the hell, Flynn! You might think she's yours, but that doesn't mean you have the right to be so protective of her. My muscles are tightening with agitation, but then I have a thought—if it was Tori, I would be just as protective of a friend as he is being with Elouise. My fingers hover over the phone, and I stop myself from replying so I don't say something that gives away how I feel about her. As I calm down a little, the messages keep popping up on my screen, and I can't help but smile at how much my silence is pissing them off.

Nic: Rem? Tell me you didn't do that!

Flynn: Don't make me come up there and beat the shit out of you.

Forrest: For once I agree with my brother.

Okay, time to put them out of their misery. My fingers now dance over the screen as I reply.

Rem: Wow, nice to know what you all think of me!

Nic: Start talking and then we will stop thinking anything bad. Now, where is that?

Rem: In your damn castle's dungeon, idiot. Happy now?

Rem: Surely you can all see how dark and dirty it is, and I'm not talking about sex!

I shake my head at how little they really looked at the pictures, missing the details of the low-level lighting and the rock walls behind it.

Flynn: We are buying a sex castle!! This is gold!

Nic: What the fuck, you're kidding me!

Forrest: Oh, this is so good. Can't wait to hear Nic explain that one to Tori.

Flynn: Happy wedding, sweetheart. I bought you a sex-dungeon castle as a present to celebrate. Surprise!

Nic: Fuck off, Flynn

Nic: Rem, tell me what's going on.

Rem: Well, if you would all shut up for a minute, I would.

Flynn: A bit testy there, Rem, feeling a little frustrated...

Rem: Not a bit, nothing to be frustrated over.

If only he knew what I was doing last night, then he wouldn't be accusing me of having an inch of sexual frustration in me. Because to be honest, my cock and I are feeling fully satisfied this morning.

Rem: Back to the sex room. It's in the back of the dungeon and looks like it's been set up by the owners and looks modern and taken care of. Just dusty and now has a broken door, where I gained entry.

Nic: What makes you think it was the owners, besides the obvious in that it's their property?

Rem: There are photographs on the wall of a couple, and it looks like it was their personal haven. The same couple are in a single photo on a table with a candle. My guess is whichever one died first, the other one was living in the memories in the room. Although weird, still romantic... I guess. I'm no good at that sort of shit.

Flynn: Wait, what? Photos, holy shit. That's ballsy. How pornographic are we talking? Show me.

Forrest: Don't you even think about sending them to him, Rem!

Rem: Give me some credit. What is with you all today, doubting me. I'm the most respectful out of all of you.

Flynn: Debatable.

Rem: That's rich, coming from you.

Nic: Rem, I'll call you shortly. About to walk into a meeting. We need to talk.

Nic: Flynn, those photos will never see the light of day. You of all people with a sex tape out there should get the whole privacy aspect.

Nic: Forrest, what happened to your brother when he was younger, was he dropped on his head? I swear, sometimes I wonder where his brain is at!

Flynn: Why do these messages always end up with someone saying shit about me!

He's right, but I can't really think too much about Flynn's feelings right now. Especially when I know I'm the one who is walking all over them with the woman in the next room.

Nic: I'm not even answering that. Now everyone back to work. Do whatever the fuck I pay you all to do.

Rem: On it.

Forrest: Been working this whole time.

Flynn: My brother, the kiss-ass.

And as per usual Nic's boss comment ends the text messages, and we all get back to our day. I do often wonder though how Flynn really feels about all the shit we put on him. He is the jokester in our group, but nobody likes to be made fun of all the time. Maybe I should be paying more attention to what is said, or man up and talk to him face to face.

Perhaps just not right at the moment when I'm skating on thin ice. Oh man, these next few months are going to be hard, but on the other hand, totally worth it.

If I had my way, I'd throw out in the open now about El and I being together and let the chips fall where they may. But she is too frightened, and I respect that. So, we will do it her way until I believe it's time to start doing it my way.

Checking on Elouise, I find her now sitting tucked up in the window seat of the room I have been working out of. I love that she is close by but happy to leave me to work while she reads. I'm up and down from my computer, leaving to check things in different rooms as I create my master document that Nic will be working off when he approves the due diligence for the purchase.

Really, there's no doubt on Nic buying this castle. From the moment he set his eyes on the property advertisement, he wanted it badly.

My phone rings on the desk, and I put my ear pods in so I can still talk to Nic without El hearing what he is saying. Just in case he starts talking about her, I don't want her to feel awkward. But also, he wouldn't be impressed that he was on speaker with her in the room. He loves her like a sister and trusts her, but business is business, and he is very protective of his empire.

"Nic, I'm almost finished the report. Should be ready in the next hour." El looks up at me with a smile and then goes back at her book, readjusting her sitting position and already tuning me out.

"Thanks, Rem. I'm guessing from your messages yesterday that there is nothing glaringly obvious to stop me from buying it?" As he pauses, I can tell he is doing two things at once. It's the way he works, at full speed, until he clicks off for the day and then he stops momentarily to relax. Makes me think marrying someone who is in the business is not such a good idea, but they seem to make it work and still have down time away from the job. "Of course, except for the obvious that this is going to cost me a crap load of money to renovate and get to the standard I expect from a Darby Hotel."

"You said it, so I don't have to. No more than you were already prepared to spend." I laugh at him groaning at my comment.

"Remind me in six months' time why I thought this purchase was a good idea." Nic laughs.

"I won't need to remind you, because the reason will be standing next you wearing a gold wedding band and answering to Mrs. Darby. Tell me I'm wrong." I laugh along with him.

"Okay, smartass, that's enough from you. She drives me crazy, but I want to give her the world, you know what I mean?" I know he is just saying it as a matter of fact and not really expecting me to answer, but it slips out before I realize.

"Yeah, buddy, I do. Money means nothing unless you have someone to spoil with it." I look across at the beautiful woman oblivious to what I'm saying. The sun is streaming through the window and highlighting her rich brown hair with hints of gold that she has pulled off her face with a clip, but the rest is softly falling down her back. She's wearing a soft cream wool sweater and blue jeans with a pair of socks on her feet, and her tan knee-length boots are on the floor beside her.

"I suppose you do now that Blaise is in your life." I want to correct Nic and tell him it's so much more, but I just can't, and it's already eating me up inside.

My job is all about trust, and I'm breaking that important thing with everyone around me, the people who rely on me to keep them safe. Which is both stupid and dangerous, I know. I'm giving this a couple of weeks and then I'll be revisiting it with El and reinforcing to her how important it is that we let everybody know and that I'm sure they will all get over it. After all, we are grown adults, and it's none of their business who we are with.

Our conversation continues as we talk specifics and then get onto other issues at different hotels too. An hour has gone past and El hasn't complained once or even given me a sigh or daggered look. She understands how important my work is and has seen first-hand how this company works. I could almost say she is part of the company, now that she is around so much. I'm sure Nic would hire her tomorrow to keep Tori happy, but her skills and dreams don't involve the corporate world.

Just when I think Nic is winding up the conversation, his random side question throws me a little.

"How's Elouise? Are you keeping her safe and happy?"

And all these words come flying into my head. *Sure, happily sated in my bed, safe from everyone except me, and that's probably who she should be protected from.* But of course, I can't use any one of them, but instead just answer with the generic response.

"Yeah, of course I am, she's doing just fine." And she is, so I'm not lying.

"Good to hear. Tori just said she didn't hear from her this morning, so wanted me to check on her." His voice starts to fade, so I know his mind has already moved on to the next thing he needs to do.

"Yeah, reception isn't great. I'll let her know to give her a call or something." I'm trying to be vague, and in my mind, I think it's just that she is probably avoiding Tori because she has something to hide. It actually surprises me how she has managed to keep it from Tori for this long. After we slept together that night in Rome eight months ago, I thought the cat would be out of the bag, because girls talk and these two are so close.

"Great, something else I'll have to fix when I buy it." Nic's grumbling now, and I know it's time to end the call.

"We all know how much the patrons complain when the Wi-Fi isn't up to their standard. Some of them should learn to just switch off for a while, it's invigorating." I don't get to do it often, but when I'm off on a trip to do something insanely dangerous, it's usually in a remote area and I'm out of reach to the rest of the world. It's heaven for a few days.

"Maybe so, but it's not what they want, so we need to make sure we are giving them a gold-star stay. Anyway, I have to run, I have a ton of work to do. Let me know when the report is finished. And thanks for being so quick and thorough, as always. I would be lost without you, buddy."

"Will do, and it's no problem. Just doing my job and keeping everything under control." Well, sort of. In my work life anyway. Let's just leave it at that.

Getting straight into finishing the report so I don't have to leave El to sit around being bored all day, I enter the last piece of information and write the email to Nic, Flynn, and Forrest. I cc Tori in on it, because while it's information she doesn't directly need, we always want her to be involved in the big decisions happening in what will shortly be her company too when she and Nic marry. After making a quick call to Nic again to explain a few things, I'm finally done, for now.

Hanging up on the phone call, I sit back and take in the pretty picture in front of me. I could get used to this, El relaxing while I work away, making her life easier. Thoughts of Blaise then drift in too. He loves Elouise, and she's right in that we don't want to confuse him too soon. He is used to her being in the house and knows her as his nanny and teacher but changing that to a stepmum is a huge step.

Alarm bells go off in my head at the word stepmum. What am I even thinking about? This is not how I mapped out my life. I wasn't going to have any children, never wanted to settle down. Now I'm here looking at the woman who has completely taken every bit of control of my world from me, just by being herself.

I didn't ask for Blaise to come screaming into my life and turning everything upside down, but he did, and I couldn't love him more if I tried. He has brought so much fun into my house, and it finally feels like a home, in all its mess and noise. But I can never thank him enough for being the catalyst to bring Elouise into both our lives. I would have sat back and just longed for her from a distance, never saying a thing and watching her find some stuffy guy to step in and date her.

Another teacher that would marry her and give her a mediocre life, while I continued to be out there jumping off cliffs without a harness because I'm emotionally inept. I don't even know why I can't get past my lack of ability to be involved in a long-term adult relationship. I'm a grown man and should be able to move forward after such an awful experience, but for some reason I'm stuck. And for years after my only relationship that I really thought might have been something, I haven't even wanted to try to pursue a woman.

But then Elouise pushed her way into my world that night in Rome, and even after agreeing it was nothing, she had already gotten under my skin, and I couldn't stop thinking about her. I tried so hard to keep it in the friend zone, but once I was at my most vulnerable the night Blaise arrived, there was no holding back the feelings that had been simmering silently inside me.

Still, I didn't believe I was right for her because I couldn't give her anything in return, until that night in my office where we couldn't hold back any longer. But I wasn't going to let my heart get involved, thinking if I took her from behind and didn't look her in the eyes while I fucked her that it could be just another one-night stand. Until the moment I slid inside her and I knew it was game over. Elouise had already charmed me with her intellect and witty sense of humor that I was seeing more freely the more I spent time with her, but the moment our bodies touched again, I knew she was it.

No woman has ever ignited me the way she does, and for the first time, I am thinking about wanting more.

I might not have been given the choice about being a father, and I'm trying to learn on the run. With Elouise, she is a choice I am making to find happiness and explore the emotional connection that is so strong between us. And although I think we should tell everyone else, part of me is happy with the time it's going to give me to make sure I can stand up and be the man that she deserves. Financially I can provide for her, but it's the emotional side where I need to push myself to make sure I'm not the selfish single man I have been for the last thirty-six years of my life.

"Why are you looking at me like that?" Elouise's soft voice breaks me from my inner thoughts, startling me a bit.

"Like what?" I stand from the desk and close my laptop, sliding it into my bag.

"Like you are trying to figure out how to solve world peace or something as big as that. Is there a problem at the office?" She swings her legs around in front of her and lets them touch the floor in front of the window seat, closing her book and setting it beside her.

"Nothing like that, just enjoying the beauty in front of me." I walk toward her and run my hand over her head and down her softly falling hair. "How about we head out and do some sightseeing for the rest of the day? I don't want you heading home and the only thing you saw is a pub in a little Scottish village and a rundown castle." Taking her hand in mine, I pull her up off the seat.

"Don't forget the sex dungeon, because I know I won't." Both of us laugh as she bends down to put her boots back on, and I grab my work bag to hide it out of sight upstairs. Although I have high security passwords on it and everything is stored on a server, not this computer, I'm still not taking any chances.

Taking El under my arm, we walk out to the car. I can feel the vibration of her phone in her jacket pocket that I'm carrying for her.

"Have you spoken to Tori today?" I ask, just remembering the message that Nic asked me to pass on a few hours ago.

"No," is all she replies as we reach the car.

Opening the door and settling her in the passenger seat, I pass her the coat and smile at her. "Well, I suggest you do, because Nic already mentioned that she was worried that she hadn't heard from you this morning." Closing the door, I walk around to the driver's side, and as I'm sliding into the leather seat of the Audi, I can't help myself. "She's probably just found out about the sex room and is worried I have you tied up and I'm doing naughty things to you."

"Stop it, Rem, don't make me laugh. You know why I haven't called her. I'm terrible at lying."

Laying my hand on the center console, she places hers in mine for comfort.

"I've got you, babe. FaceTime her while we are driving and she won't be game to ask you anything too bad while I'm with you, surely."

I start the engine and have just turned the car down through the tree-lined driveway as I hear El's phone connect and Tori's voice screaming into the phone. "Lou! Why haven't you been answering my messages!" And there it is, the firecracker that is Tori.

"Good day to you too." El turns the camera toward me. "Say hello to Rem."

"Hi, Tori. God, you two make me laugh the way you talk to each other." I look sideways and give her a wave before El turns the phone back toward herself.

"Shut up, Rem. Right, now both of you need to tell me what the hell is going on in my castle." I can't tell if she is frustrated with El or nervous about the purchase of the property being in jeopardy.

"*Our* castle." And that is when I hear Nic's deep voice in the background.

"Hey, boss," I call out and chuckle at Tori who is now telling him to butt out.

"Semantics, Nicholas. Anyway, start talking, you two, and why wasn't I the first to know?" Tori continues, and I can hear Nic groaning beside her.

And before El can answer, I throw my answer out there. "Because we were both busy last night, fucking for hours and testing out your sex castle for you."

The look on El's face is sheer panic and she instantly turns the phone toward me so neither Tori or Nic are able to see how red her face is and how much she is about to kill me.

"Yeah, right, now stop being an asshole and tell me all about it." I doubt she means for me to tell her about the sex because Tori totally missed how serious my statement was, but Nic's face appearing behind her does not look so easily fooled.

Why I said that I don't know, but I think part of it is that deep down inside, hiding this feels wrong, and I don't want what we are sharing to be a dirty secret.

Or maybe it's the part of me that I can never turn off. Trying to be in control of everything, including the uncontrollable.

Chapter Sixteen

ELOUISE

I'm sitting on the plane heading home from four of the most unexpected but incredible days. I still can't help but think back to Rem just blurting out to Tori that we had sex. Thankfully, she didn't even think that was at all possible and dismissed it as him joking with her.

I was so mad with him that it took me a good hour or so to calm down, but as per usual, he started sweet-talking me, or was it dirty talk, I can't remember, because they tend to be the same most of the time. Both of them turn me into mush and have me falling under his spell.

Regardless, after that hiccup, the next couple days were sheer heaven. Not a soul knew us up in Scotland, so we could do and say what we liked the whole time and not have to be careful about who could hear or see us. It was the first real feeling of new love. Not that we are using the L word, but you can tell it's simmering just under the surface. Because it's not like we've just met, and these feelings have been building for a while. My head and heart feel so light, but sadly, all good things must come to an end.

It's so hard leaving it behind and coming back to the reality of home.

Although I can't wait to see Blaise and get one of my adorable little-boy hugs. We have been FaceTiming him several times a day, and he is feeling much better and I'm sure is being spoiled rotten by Sally. Lord help Nic and Tori when they have children. I think that will be the final factor that will have Sally moving to London permanently and just visiting Australia for holidays. She is trying to juggle living in both places now, but as she gets older, I don't think the long-haul flights will be so easy. Not that I would know, I've never done it, the wedding flight will be the first. Although I'm not sure flying on a private jet really gives any of us a right to complain.

Rem is already in work mode and engrossed in his computer, but this time, instead of sitting across the cabin from him, I'm so close that every so often his hand slips onto my thigh and either gives it a light squeeze or just runs up and down my leg a few times, letting me know he is still there and not ignoring me, checking that I'm okay.

It's one of the things I love about the way we connect. Words aren't needed. Touch is everything.

His smile when I look across almost makes me melt into the rich leather seat. I know what I want and what we have agreed on, but I'm not sure how well I'm going to be able to pull this off. The wall I had built between us has fallen and is just dust on the ground, but that means I don't have anything to hide behind when he looks at me like this and other people are around. And even if he tries, I don't know that he'll be able to stop looking at me like he's about to devour me the moment we are alone. It makes my skin sizzle, and I'm sure my face gives away that I feel the same.

We need to work hard at this, otherwise our worlds will be blowing up before we know it. And I can't let that happen!

Without making it obvious, I know I need to avoid Tori and the others, and social occasions are certainly off the list for the next few weeks anyway. It will give me time to get better at just being the nanny and not the woman who is falling hopelessly in love with her boss.

As we start our descent, I close my eyes and pray to whoever will listen, please let me keep this man who makes my heart sing and that everything will turn out okay.

Looking back now over the last few weeks, life has been amazing in our little bubble at home. Blaise is too young to understand the body language between Rem and me, and thank goodness he is a heavy sleeper. Because as much as we try to keep quiet, it's not easy when you have a man pounding you into his bed every night like it's going to be our last time together. Or how Rem takes great pleasure in trying to break the record of how many times he can make me orgasm. My appetite has increased significantly since we got home from Scotland, and not just for the food that I need to keep up my energy.

We have managed to make it work so that if Tori is coming over, then Rem is at work, out with the guys, or even just gone for a run. That way it makes it easier for me, and for him too really, not to react to each other while she is here. But tonight is going to be a huge challenge. Tori just messaged to say she and Nic are on their way over and they're bringing pizza for all of us, and the guys are coming too. Something about a big football match that is on tonight that they want to watch and decided it was time to get Blaise into learning about the game.

I don't care one bit about football, or any sport really, but what I do care about is how the hell I'm going to get through a whole night of a testosterone-fueled sport, alcohol-fueled best friend, and an excitable little four-year-old who absolutely loves all his dad's buddies being here.

Especially since he's been finding it far easier to understand them and communicate in some English that he is learning so quickly.

Working with him every day and watching Rem being so patient with him, giving him all the encouragement with his new words, has been so gratifying. I don't know why Rem had been so against being a father, because in my eyes, he is becoming a great one. He's still learning French in his spare time, which he doesn't really have much of, and then it makes me laugh seeing Blaise being the patient one with Rem as he tries to speak to either of us in French.

The major benefit to his whole learning experience is the preschool I found is a dual-language preschool. So not only do they teach English, but they teach in French too. He is learning to become bilingual, but more importantly, he is making friends who understand him too, gaining great social skills that are important before he starts school next year.

I told Rem over the phone that first day I took Blaise to preschool that I need to give him some of the money back because I now get two days a week where I have several hours in the middle of the day on my own. Of course, he refused, which resulted in a heated argument between us and me hanging up on him after telling him I'm not a charity case. But before I even had time to calm down from the phone call, he was loudly coming through the front door, up the stairs, and pinning me against the wall in the bedroom where I was tidying up some clothes. He kissed every objection about the money out of me until I understood that no girlfriend of his is ever to feel like a charity case.

What that day did teach us, though, was that we had two days a week with no little ears or eyes in the house, and the sexting started the moment Rem left the house in the morning, telling me what he had planned for the day and that I needed to be ready.

One morning, as I arrived home from dropping off Blaise, there was a package on the front doorstep. A plain black box with a gold ribbon. A white rose slipped under the bow and a card that read:

To the woman who spins my world and calms my soul xx

Hurrying inside and rushing up to our bedroom, because no, I haven't slept in the guest room since we came home from Scotland, I gently pulled the ribbon, and the bow slid free from the box. Opening it up, I found gold tissue paper and a note on a card.

you a massage, and finish the night off with some of that mind-blowing fucking you speak of." And Rem's lips are on mine as he finishes his last word, kissing me until I can't think of anything more than how he tastes and the tickle of his beard on my mouth.

Breaking apart and gasping for air, I look at his smile and it warms me fully.

"I've got you, El, trust me." Placing his forehead on mine, we stay in the silence for a few moments before I reply with the only answer I have.

"Always."

Before we can talk any further, there are little feet running from the lounge. His show must have finished, and he is looking for me.

"Blaise," Rem calls out, and the feet change direction in the hallway where he was heading for the kitchen, and he is now running toward the study, calling out excitedly.

"Papa! Papa's home!" Blaise barrels into the room and wraps his arms around Rem where I had quickly stepped back from before he came in.

"Hey, buddy. How was your play at the park?" Rem bends down to be at the same level as Blaise. It always makes me smile, because it's the little things that mean the world to a child.

"It was fun, and Patrice's *maman nous a donné sucettes*." Both Rem and I starting to laugh because it's when he is excited that he falls back into his French.

Before he even has to ask, I explain to Rem that he means lollipops.

"Well, aren't you a lucky boy." Rem picks him up and walks toward the door, looking over his shoulder at me and waiting for me to follow him. Although I'd much rather lock myself in this room, I walk behind him, knowing shortly I'm going to be in a world of crazy.

With his words circling inside my head, I take a deep breath, stand up straighter, and pull my shoulders back as I hear him telling Blaise that everyone is coming for pizza. The scream that comes out of such a little boy is deafening. I can do this. I just need to keep myself busy being the perfect hostess. Leaving the boys and heading into the kitchen, I start preparing for the arrival of a lot of food, because Nic always over-caters, and a house full of noisy people.

No surprise that they all arrived at the same time and that the guys were starving. So, there was no time for much talking until we were all stuffed with way too much pizza, and the television is now on football. Now I understand the significance to them all wanting to watch it. It's not just any game but England is playing Australia, and of course it's everyone against Nic, although Flynn is sitting on the fence with his loyalties, claiming he is now partly Australian after living there for so long. I'm not sure how that works, but of course Flynn always makes up his own rules in life.

Australia has just evened up the score, so it is two all, and Blaise doesn't care whose side he is on, he just gets excited because it's fun to him. Thank goodness the clock has just ticked over to the end of the first half, and the room is settling down while everyone uses the time to use the bathroom, get another drink, or check their phones. They all tell me they switch off from work to relax, but the truth is they do as much as they can, but I'm learning a business this big never sleeps.

Preparing a tray of desserts that Flynn turned up with, I carry them into the lounge, bending down so Blaise can pick something before the vultures all descend. Because apparently, no matter how full you are, there is always room for dessert.

Just as I'm standing, Tori who is curled up on the couch next to Nic starts talking to me.

"Oh yeah, Lou, I forgot to ask you, mainly because I've hardly seen you, did you organize that babysitter for Blaise for that charity event on Friday night that we all are booked in for?" My stomach does a flip at the thought of being at a big event, while on the inside, I feel so anxious around the people who are usually the ones who calm me at these events. But I know there is no getting out of it.

"I did. Miss Larissa from Blaise's school is going to be here. She does babysitting, trying to earn a bit of extra cash, which is perfect for us as he knows her, and we are comfortable with leaving him alone with her." Carrying the tray, I move around the room to

Forrest who takes his time picking. He's always the cautious one in the room and can't be rushed.

"Yay!" Tori squeals a little too excitedly, and my *"oh no, what is Tori up to"* radar fires up. "I have invited a plus-one for you for the night. It's about time you get out and start dating. I mean, Rem can't keep you locked up here forever." By now I'm standing in front of Rem with the desserts, and the sheer panic of her words has me overbalancing, dropping the front of the tray, and the sweets start sliding off into his lap at the same time he pushes off the arms of his chair and stands up, looking like someone just picked a fight with him.

There are cakes everywhere! I'm standing here so flustered that I don't know what to say, and Rem pulls the tray from my hands. I can see the rage in his eyes, but he instantly pulls on that work face I have seen before where he appears calm.

"Sorry," is all I can say, and to everyone else it looks like I'm apologizing to him for dropping the cakes on him, but we both know it's so much more.

Sorry I've put us in this situation. Sorry I'm not strong enough to speak up for what I want, but most of all, sorry that I'm going to have to go through with this, otherwise Tori is going to start pushing me about why I'm refusing.

"I would've been her plus-one if she needs a date. I'd be the perfect gentleman." Flynn thinks he is being funny, but it only makes it worse.

"Victoria, stop trying to be a matchmaker. Elouise is a grown woman who doesn't need your help." Nic takes the wine glass out of her hand, knowing that nobody needs a drunk Tori here tonight.

"Oh, shush you. This is what best friends do for each other. Isn't that right, Lou. It's a girl thing, and I just want her to be happy like I am. Well, most of the time anyway. You drive me crazy most days, but the benefits are worth it." Tori is oblivious to me standing still, looking so stunned, and she continues on her reasoning. "And Flynn, we have all told you that Lou is not interested. I don't know when you are going to get it through your thick head."

"How can she not be interested in this hotness? I mean, I'm a perfect catch," Flynn replies, while Forrest is groaning beside his brother.

Still, I haven't said a word, but Rem's deep voice echoes in the room.

"Not happening!" The anger in him makes me jump a little. "She doesn't need a date."

I can feel the burn of his stare deeply, right into my core. He's angry and feels unable to control this, and that's my fault.

"Don't be an asshole, Rem. You might be her boss, but you don't control her love life. Actually, we have you to thank for this date. I tracked down Blaise's pediatrician, Dr. Keats, the one who hit on Lou. He was more than happy to take a ticket at our table and support the Children's Cancer Foundation. He was wanting to go but didn't have a table to sit at so was glad to have company."

"So, is he just at our table, you didn't actually tell him it's a date with Elouise?" Forrest asks. I can always rely on him to see things simply.

"Oh, of course, I'm not that crazy. Lou would kill me if I had done that. But if they are sitting next to each other, I can't be held accountable. It would be rude to ignore the man all night, and I mean, he is scorching hot." Not for the first time in my life I just want to scream at Tori to shut the hell up and stop the word vomit. Her pushy personality paired with a little too much damn alcohol strikes again.

"Watch it, woman." Nic is scowling at her for the comment about Dr. Keats's looks.

"He'll sit next to me." Rem places the tray of now ruined desserts that everyone has forgotten about on the side table.

"Not a chance, he's not interested in fu… um, fudging you." She looks toward Blaise, remembering he is in the room and what she was about to say.

"Tori!" Finally, I find my voice, and it's not to stick up for myself but to protect Blaise. "Little ears."

"I know, I know, I'm sorry. Anyway, it's already sorted, he is coming, and we need to find time to shop this week to find you an uber-sexy dress that will have him drooling over you all night."

"I suppose it's just one night, one dinner…" I try to answer her to defuse the situation, knowing full well that I won't need a dress, because I intend on faking sickness that night.

But my sentence is interrupted by Rem's phone ringing, and all the guys are reaching for theirs too, with notifications starting to signal out loudly across the room like crazy.

"Talk to me," is all Rem says to whoever is on the phone, knowing with all the phones going at once that something big is happening.

"Fuck!" Flynn says with anger.

"I knew this would happen, stupid old prick." Nic stands quickly, and it seems all concern about a small child in the room has gone out the window.

"Oh, this isn't good." Forrest is looking at Flynn with sadness, and my mind starts catching up on what I think has happened.

Rem is already leaving the room, and the guys are up and following him toward the study. I assume it's to get to a computer and take this conversation to a more private place.

"Holy shit, this is bad." Tori holds her phone up to me, showing the Google alerts on Flynn and his sex tape.

My heart sinks for him and the woman he was with. How can someone be so cruel as to invade their privacy and then use it for personal profit?

"Can they stop it?" I ask Tori quietly, but I already know the answer. Once something hits the internet, it has been screenshot so many times that it will never go away. It's there for life, no matter how hard you try to have it taken down.

"Not now. All we can do is start damage control and hope it doesn't blow back too hard on Darby Hotels, or Flynn. At the end of the day, Nic will always put his friends before money, and Flynn will be his number one priority here."

I sink down onto the couch next to my best friend, and no matter how much I want to kill her right now, I pull her into a hug, knowing she is going to need it. It's going to be tough few weeks, maybe months, in front of them all.

"Well, that put a sour note on a fun night, didn't it?" Tori lays her head on my shoulder, and I can't help but laugh out loud.

"That is an understatement." We both giggle together, her thinking it's just about Flynn, but for me, the whole night went exactly like I was imagining it would. Like a massive shit show.

It's then I look across and spot Blaise sitting next to the side table, with chocolate on his fingers and all over his mouth. Oblivious to what is going on, he's just happily devouring the desserts and watching the football that has started again. Lord knows how many of the mangled messes he has eaten, but I have a feeling I'm in for a hell of a night trying to get him to sleep with that much sugar in him.

Why can't life be simple? I thought I wanted a change, something exciting, on those long days in the classroom with my kids that were climbing the walls and weren't listening to one thing I was saying.

Tonight, I would take that complete chaos over the stress and anxiety I have brought on myself. They always say be careful what you wish for, and now I understand.

Lying in bed, the house is so eerily quiet. The guys left for the office hours ago, and I haven't heard a thing from them, and I don't know what I'm supposed to do.

After Tori left, it took me a while to calm Blaise down, and in the end, I went through our normal routine of giving him a bath, reading books in bed, and then just sitting with him until he finally closed his eyes and started to slow his breathing down. I mean, there is nothing wrong with two baths a night, and to be honest, with the amount of chocolate on him, it was probably a good idea.

It's one in the morning, and I can't keep my eyes open any longer waiting for Rem. We need to talk, and I know now is not the time, but I just need to make sure he understands that it won't matter if I'm sitting next to another guy. Rem is still the only man I want. The one

I want to cuddle up to at night, listening to him whisper dirty things in my ear and letting him leave his mark on me so I'm reminded every time I look in the mirror who I belong to. Just because no one else knows that, as long as he does, then we can get through anything.

I keep telling myself it will be okay, that once I feel his body crawl in against me when he gets home, I'll wake, and we'll talk then.

But waking up to my alarm and a cold bed beside me, I know he hasn't been home. My logical brain tries to tell me it's because he is working to protect Flynn, but my emotional brain is convinced it's because he's avoiding me.

But it's morning, and I don't have time to sort out my ridiculous head of crazy thoughts. I need to get Blaise up and ready for preschool. I hate being late, and it's important to teach him the etiquette of turning up to places on time.

Continuing through our morning routine, Blaise isn't even concerned that Rem isn't here. Although he tries to have breakfast with us most mornings, there have been plenty of times that he has left early for a meeting or to sort out some problem somewhere. We even had a few days where he had to go to Paris to one of the hotels, and I still remember him coming home so proud of himself and how he got to use his new French-speaking skill. I tried not to laugh, picturing the staff in the hotel and the contractors he was working with, pretending that he was speaking perfectly, when the reality is that he was probably saying sentences that made no sense, but they managed to fill in the blanks to get the idea of what he meant. I mean, no one wants to tell the boss he is wrong.

Ready to leave, I pick up Blaise's little Bluey backpack off the kitchen counter and hand it to him as he starts running to the front door. I hear it open.

"Rem," I whisper to myself. Thank God. But the moment I walk into the hallway from the kitchen toward the two of them hugging, Rem looks up at me and his face is stone cold. Not an emotion to be seen, and now I know I'm in trouble.

I need to fix this.

"Hey." As I walk slowly toward them, he stands up from his crouched position with Blaise. "Can we talk quickly?"

"You'll be late, and I need to shower. We'll talk later." Without even touching me, he leans down, kisses Blaise on the top of his head, says goodbye, and walks straight past me up the stairs.

Standing there watching him go, Blaise takes my hand and pulls me toward the door to go to the car. He loves preschool day.

But by the time I get back to the house, Rem is standing next to the driver's door of his Porsche, his gym bag in his hand, and he just looks at me as I get out of the car.

"I thought we were going to talk," I asked, but he stares at me with that same cold look from before.

"I can't do this now, I need to see Cherie." And his words are final, not giving me a chance to reply.

Getting into his car, he drives out the gates, the tires screeching as he takes off down the road like I've never seen him do before.

"Who the fuck is Cherie!" And for the first time since last night, I'm not feeling weak.

My adrenaline is rushing, and I climb back into the car with my driver, Art.

"Don't give me any bullshit. Follow him, and don't say a fucking word to him or let him see us. He wants to be an asshole, then it's about time he meets my inner bitch too!"

Not a word was uttered as Art drove the Range Rover down the street quicker than usual. At least Art takes his job seriously, being my driver and personal security, which I hope means that his loyalty is with me first and the asshole in the black Porsche second.

Now to find out who this woman is!

Chapter Seventeen

REMINGTON

All night her words kept going around in my head.

At a time when I should be able to completely shut all thoughts out of my head and just be focused on the problem at hand, and instead, all I keep thinking about is her agreeing to a date with another man.

Her words repeating over and over, *"I suppose it's just one night, one dinner…"*

This stupid little charade of hers has to stop. I'm not letting another man touch what's mine or even think he has a possibility of it.

And if El thinks I'm letting her anywhere near Dr. Dropkick, then she can think again. From the first moment I met him, I knew he had a thing for her, and while I wasn't in a place to make a stance then, I sure as shit am now.

I'm sitting in my office on my third strong coffee for the night. I'm pissed as hell at the situation we are all in now, scrambling to stop Flynn from being dragged down by a video that is already viral. Before I even made it to my office, I paid Ewan Kentwall a little visit and told him what I thought of him and his useless security team. His reaction to me was not what I wanted. In fact, there was no reaction at all. I was waiting for a screaming match or one of the guys he surrounds himself with to take a swing at me, because although I don't like to fight like that, I was ready to release hell's fury on someone.

All I could do was continue working all night, and even if it wasn't on the Flynn saga, I found things that needed my attention at other hotels. I woke staff up with pointless calls at a ridiculous time of night, but I couldn't give a fuck. I'm up, so they can be too. It's part of the job you take on when you get involved in security. Especially in a business that runs twenty-four hours a day, three hundred and sixty-five days of the year. But all that has done is left me alone in the office after I sent the others home to get some sleep, because there is nothing they can do now. It's my responsibility to fix this, and although I can't stop that video from being out there forever, I'll be damned if I don't find the real fucker who uploaded it and make them pay, big time.

Broderick found the influencer who was paid a measly two thousand pounds to send the emails to both Flynn and Felisha from her account. She claims she never had the file in the first place, and the bank account listed for the blackmail money is some anonymous offshore bank account. She swears she didn't upload it, and she has no idea who it was that contacted her. Through all the tracing Broderick and my team did, it just sent them in circles which just pissed me off more. But that doesn't mean I'm giving up.

So now I'm sitting on my couch in my office at seven am after my team has managed to get as many sites to take the video down as we can and have the PR department preparing a statement to be released this morning. We need to be on the front foot with this and drive the narrative. I've had no sleep, and I just want to go home, but I know it's not a good idea. I can't face Elouise yet.

There is something I need to do first. Well, two things in fact, but the first is to take a session with Cherie to calm the adrenaline that is coursing through my body. Nothing good is going to come from seeing El while I'm this ramped up. I'll say things I don't want to and act in a way I shouldn't, to El or in front of Blaise.

Going home and sleeping is probably the smartest option, but I know I won't be able to do that either. Picking up my phone, I call Flynn to check in on him. As much as he is a thorn in my side, it's not his fault, nor does he even know that now. And regardless of him having a thing for the woman who he doesn't know is my girlfriend, he is also my friend and one I will protect no matter what. No woman will come between my friendship or the vow I took when I accepted Nic's job. To protect all of us, it's my job and my life's mission.

"Hey," he says as he answers my call. His voice is not like I've ever heard from Flynn before.

This has really hit him hard. All the bravado and cockiness he displays on a daily basis is gone, and on the other end of my call is the rawness of a man who is feeling vulnerable.

"Hey, buddy, how are you doing? Get any sleep?" Looking out the window across from me, I know while London is waking up, this is going to hit the papers and is about to get worse before it gets any better.

"I don't know, maybe, I couldn't tell you. I feel like I have just stared at my ceiling for a few hours, but there may have been a few naps in there. To be honest, I'm pretty numb right now." And that is the voice of a broken man. We need to fix this. We can't let him fall into the bottomless pit that is the repercussions of social media and the internet.

"Have you spoken to Felisha? Is she doing okay?" Because I know her father didn't appear to be give a shit when I was there. I hope to hell that it was his poker face when he felt backed against a wall, otherwise he is an even bigger dick than I thought he was.

"Not good. Shattered, actually. We are meeting up this morning."

"I don't think that is a good idea, Flynn. Today you both need to just lie low at home, don't leave your apartments, and avoid all chance of the media getting hold of you." I'm waiting for Flynn to tell me to fuck off, but instead, the words I hear confirm what I was thinking.

"Yeah, okay, whatever you think is best." Flynn is defeated. The world is completely off kilter because this is not normal. He should be yelling, objecting, and telling me he's a grown man and will do what he likes.

I need to call Nic and get him over there. I don't have time to look after him, and Nic knows him far better than all of us. He knows how to handle him.

"Alright, I'm going to let you try to get some more sleep. I have things I need to do. But like we told you last night, don't answer the phone unless it is one of us. Don't answer the door, and let the doorman downstairs deal with anyone who tries to get into the building. We have posted extra security on the door to help them, so there is no way some sleazy reporter can pay off the doorman to sneak in. We both know everyone has a price, and whoever this was will regret not asking for more, because no amount of money is going to be worth the hellfire about to hit them when I find them. And I will find them!" No matter how exhausted I am or how the rage I feel is coming up and boiling just below the surface again.

"Rem?"

"Yeah."

"Thanks, and I'm sorry. And for what's it worth, I know I joked about this happening, but I didn't think it ever would. I'm sorry you have to clean up my shit. You are a good friend." This poor man is in the worst moment of his life, and he has no idea he has just made me feel like the lowest man on this planet. How can I be a good friend to him when I'm fucking the woman he has been infatuated with since the moment she walked in the door with Tori?

If I didn't feel like I wanted to explode before, then I do now.

"I've got you, Flynn. You don't have to apologize for anything. The person who took that video does, and they will be on their knees in front of you and Felisha when they do. Talk later." Hanging up and laying my head back on the couch, I throw my phone down next to me and let out the biggest sigh.

I need to fix this.

All of it!

I didn't quite time it right when I finally went home, and as soon as I saw El, I knew I made the right decision not wanting to talk to her yet. The hug from Blaise felt amazing, but I knew if I touched El I wouldn't leave, and that wouldn't be good for either of us. So instead, I left her standing in front of the house thinking I'm the biggest asshole after the way I spoke to her.

Pulling up out the front of Cherie's studio in the Porsche is not ideal because it's not in a good neighborhood, but that's why it's here. She is trying to make a difference with the kids who need her, and the reality is they come from the worst areas and live hard lives. Normally I bring the Range Rover which isn't a whole lot better, but the kids are likely to think it's an undercover cop car and leave it alone. The Porsche just screams wealth.

Getting out, I grab the bag off the front seat that I brought with me from home when I quickly threw some gym gear in it. My other bag is still in the back of the Range Rover because I haven't needed to see Cherie since we got back from Scotland. My energy is being used in a far more enjoyable way than getting challenged in a boxing ring.

Standing on the pavement and looking back at the car, I push the lock and alarm system. I walk toward the door, but something doesn't feel right. I hate that feeling because I'm normally right. Not seeing anything as I look around, it's probably just the lack of sleep and being the most wrung out I have been in a very long time. My senses are off, and I just need to get back in control.

"I thought I'd finally got rid of you." Cherie laughs at me as I pull the gloves on.

"Don't want to hear it. Don't hold back." Shaking out my arms, I try and loosen them up.

"That shit doesn't fly with me, big guy. Get your fists up and start talking." The first jab hits me in the ribs just under where I had my arms up. My concentration is off, and I've got a reaction speed worse than Blaise. "Fuck, you haven't been this useless since you first started with me years ago. Fucking hit me, or did she take your balls too when she screwed you over?"

The explosion I have been holding in since last night erupts at the words she just threw at me. "Don't talk about her like that!"

Thump, duck, cross, duck, and this time she connects with me.

"Who, the girl you're regretting letting in?" The more she yells at me, I'm struggling to hold it together.

"No! I didn't let her in, she just pushed open the door, and I couldn't stop her."

Shit, that jab into the gut takes the wind from my lungs.

"So now it's not worth it because the bitch has screwed you over. Is that it?"

"Not… a… bitch!" I grab her in a hold while I try to get my breath back. "She's a precious jewel that I need to protect from people who want to steal her."

Cherie ducks out of my hold on her and pushes me, trying to get me moving again.

"Why would they steal her?" Cherie calls as she stumbles backward from a few punches from me.

And I feel like I'm releasing a burning flame from my heart. "Because they don't fucking know she's mine!" I can't hold back. Letting go of everything inside me, I unleash hellfire on Cherie.

Punch, punch, punch, punch. Repeatedly, and she just stands there letting me go until I'm slowing enough, then she whips her leg out around mine. I find myself on the mat on my back, looking up at one of the only people in this world who I've given every piece of me to, and she has taken good care of it.

"God damn it, she's mine." My voice a little less aggressive, just sucking in the air I need to even be able to get up.

Standing there just waiting me out, Cherie holds her hand out to help me up, but my stubborn ass won't accept it. I need to pull myself out of this crazy mess, and it starts now.

"Okay, asshole, do it yourself." She steps back from me, allowing me room but not walking away from me on the mat. "Now we are getting somewhere."

I position my feet in the stance to balance myself because I know we aren't finished.

"Now, what are you going to do about it?" Cherie starts pushing me again, a few jabs into the air that this time I manage to dodge.

"Don't know. The timing is fucked up." I'm moving quicker on my feet now, the more I start talking.

"Why?" It's all she needs to reply, and it all starts pouring out. Everything with El and the Flynn problem that has just complicated everything. I keep going, and she doesn't let up on me until I physically can't do anything more. With the last kickboxing move she landed on me that has me face down on the mat, Cherie has her elbow in the middle of my back, and I tap out.

After I strip off my gloves and towel down my body from the sweat that is running after such an intense workout, I drop into the seat across from where Cherie is sitting drinking her water.

"Well, that exorcized some demons, didn't it?" She laughs at me rolling my eyes at her.

"Too bad I'm still in the same situation I was when I arrived." I gulp down water that my body desperately needs to replace what I just lost in sweat.

"That's where you are wrong, and you know it," she says, pointing her finger at me with a serious look.

Letting it sink in, she continues, "If you had tried to speak to Elouise before you came to me, it would have ended badly for you both. And if you found this internet scum, you would have beaten them within an inch of their life—if they were lucky. Instead, you can leave here and now go to her, talk rationally, and tell her how it made you feel to think of her even pretending to be with another man, just to keep some stupid secret."

I drop my head into my hands in exhaustion. That workout would have drained me on a normal day, but without any sleep, I can feel the fatigue hitting harder than normal.

"And as for Flynn, when you find the fucker responsible for this, give me a call. I'll happily have your back as you take them down like they need to be. But more importantly, send Flynn to me. I'll make sure he doesn't end up falling further than he already has. He might think this will break him, but I can show him that he's got strength he didn't know he had. Just like you did, and we both know that letting out your fears and anger in a controlled environment is far better than being a ticking time bomb, just waiting for someone to light that fuse."

Chuckling out loud, I sit back up. "Not sure I could see Flynn in the ring with anyone, let alone you."

"What do you mean with me, what's that supposed to mean?" Cherie sits forward in her chair, getting ready to give me a mouthful of retort for whatever I'm about to reply.

"Only that he'd be shit scared of you, and I'm not sure the counselling session would work too well if he can't talk from fear or in between the blubbering because you have hurt him."

I'm picturing my friend, who is so bold and cocky but who's never been into boxing, facing off against a woman who does this all day every day and never even looks like she breaks much of a sweat.

She smiles at me like a Cheshire cat. "All the more reason to get him in here, I'll make a man out of him."

"Oh, don't get me wrong, he's all man, and there are hundreds of women who can testify to that. He's tall and built, but I just have a feeling behind the manly persona is a big softie."

"You know I need to meet him now, right? Regardless of if it's in here or not. Make it happen, Rem. He sounds intriguing, and I bet I could get him to agree after one meeting to take me on in the ring." She loves a challenge, and Flynn must sound like one to her.

It must be the delirium from lack of sleep or the few beatings to the head I just had every time I hit the floor. "Do you own a dress?" I ask before I think this through.

"Fuck off, asshole, of course I own a dress. I don't wear this all the time," she says, waving her hand in front of herself. "Damn, I might not be rich like you, but I still have some class." She huffs like I have insulted her.

"I didn't mean that how it sounded, I meant a glam dress, or evening dress I think they call it," I say, trying to dig myself out of the hole and not really succeeding.

"Oh, so you aren't talking about the mesh one that just covers my ass, and you can see my nipples through the holes. A different one than that?" She throws her gloves at me to make her point.

"Okay, got it, you own an evening gown, then have it on and be ready at seven pm on Friday night. I'll have my driver pick you up, and you can be my plus-one for the dinner. And if you can behave, I'll sit you next to Flynn and watch you crash and burn. I'll bet fifty quid he will never box you on this mat."

Reaching out with my hand, she is quick to take it and shake on it.

"Challenge accepted. I'll message you my address. But can I just say I'm not sure me being your plus-one is a great idea."

In my head, I probably agree with her, but it's too late now. Because part of me can't wait to see two of the cockiest people I know meet up, and it may be just what Flynn needs right now. A distraction from all the crap that is around him.

By the time I reach my car, which is still sitting perfectly fine on the street where I left it, I hadn't noticed how long I had been here. Two hours is a long time to be offline when we are in the biggest crisis for the company since Nic was falsely accused of drug possession in Rome. At least we had his innocence on our side in that one, but this is clearly Flynn and Felisha, and there is no getting out of that. He just needs to own it and hope like hell someone does something even more stupid in the next few days and his hairy white ass on camera becomes old news.

I sit in my car for another forty-five minutes answering messages, emails, and checking on how bad the media reports are, until finally, I'm on the road. Instead of going home, there is one more place I need to visit.

"Rem, I wasn't expecting you." Nic's tired tone hits me as he stands in front of the apartment door.

"Yeah, sorry, I knew you were at home by the tracking for your phone." Something I have had on all our devices since the beginning but have very rarely looked at them. But I needed to be able to talk to Nic on his own and away from the office.

"Must be serious for you to track me. And if it's anything worse than last night's drama, I'm not sure I want to hear it today."

Walking in his bare feet back to the large lounge that looks over the London skyline, I can tell he is trying to relax amid the chaos.

"Yeah, it is, but nothing like last night, although it does have to do with Flynn." And the sound of his friend's name leaving my lips has him stopping dead in his tracks and turning back to me, with tight lips and a look that tells me I need to start talking now. We might all be friends, but there is a special bond between Nic and Flynn that comes from years of friendship before we even knew them.

There is no easy way to say this, and I'm sick of holding it in any longer.

"Elouise and I are together and have been since Scotland. But if I'm being honest, I first slept with her on Christmas night in Rome."

"Fuck, Rem, I fucking knew it." Clasping his hands, he reaches up to the top of his head. The annoyed sigh coming out of his mouth tells me he's not happy. "Why? I told you all she was off limits! Fuckkk!" he yells loudly in the air to nobody and turns away from me, walking to the window, and I can see his fists down by his side, clenched so tight, and the muscles in his shoulders and neck are now tense.

But as much as I'm trying to tread lightly, I'm not about to sit back and not stand up for myself or Elouise.

"Yeah, maybe so, but we are grown adults, Nic, who you don't get to tell who they can be with. If I had told you Tori was off limits for any reason, would that have stopped you?"

He's silent for a few seconds, and thankfully his shoulders drop slightly. He turns back toward me, but he is still pissed. Now I just need to find out if it's with me or the situation I've just dumped in his lap.

"Not a chance, and you know it." I can see the lines on his forehead are tight, and he is staring so intently that it's like he is trying to read my soul. "Do you love her?"

"Yes." And it's as simple as that. I might not have told her, but in the center of my heart I know without a doubt that she is the only woman I have wanted to have more with, to be more, and can see me making a life with.

"Then sit down, we need to talk." And although I can tell he still wants to kill me, he won't, and I can trust that he will help me find a way through all this.

"Actually, fuck, what time it is? I need a beer, and if I'm drinking, so are you!" Storming toward his kitchen, he returns with two cold beers, passing me one and clinking his on mine.

"Here's to the women who complicate life and drive us insane, and we wouldn't have it any other way."

I can't help letting a deep laugh escape me. "I'll drink to that." I take a long, deep mouthful of a beer that hits just right.

Nic has a few sips and has just been staring at me, and I can tell he's thinking his plan of attack through before he finally starts the conversation.

"You can't tell Flynn, not yet." The protective friend already makes sure he lays down the ground rules.

"Obviously. He's worse than I thought. Did you go over and see him?"

"Yeah, but don't get off topic. So why now, of all times, why did you choose to tell me now?"

And that's the ten-million-dollar question, isn't it. I could make up some bullshit reason, but that's not why I'm here. It's time for the truth.

"Two reasons." I take another gulp of beer, swallowing it and then taking a deep breath.

"I hated lying to you, but Elouise was scared of telling everyone, because of Flynn, our strong friendship group, Tori warning every one of us to stay away from her and forbidding Elouise to be with any one of us. And of course, she worried about what it would mean for the business if something went wrong. Plus, we didn't want to confuse Blaise; he is only little and has had so much change, we didn't want him to get even more attached to her than he is and then she walks away. Fat chance I would let her, but she didn't know that then."

"Christ, women are complex thinkers. Seriously, that's a lot, and it's only the first reason. What's the second?"

I feel my adrenaline starting to rise again. "I'm a jealous fucker!"

I admit it more aggressively than I should have and grasp my beer bottle tighter in my hand.

I leave the words just hanging in the air until Nic starts laughing a deep belly laugh. Putting his beer down on the coffee table in front of him, he continues to laugh.

"Victoria's matchmaking," he gets out between chuckles.

Not that I can see the funny side of it, I'm sure to him this is just a daily occurrence of the stupid shit his soon-to-be wife does.

"No way in hell Dr. Dipshit is getting anywhere near El, mark my words. If he even gets close to touching her on Friday night, then you will be bailing me out of jail for assault." Standing, I walk to the window, just trying to calm my annoyance down again. Every time that guy's name is mentioned it's like something explodes in my brain.

"Take it from me, jail food sucks, and the steel seats are cold on your ass, so let's avoid that if we can."

"Don't worry, I just plan on tying El to our bed and not giving her a reason to leave all night, and then the crisis will be averted. That work for you?" I need to lighten the situation up like Nic is trying to.

"Okay, firstly, El, is it?" The smirk on his face finally tells me this is all going to be okay, well, for now anyway.

"Yeah, that's mine, and no, you can't call her that." I know it's just a name, but a part of my personality that hasn't really reared its head before now is that I don't like to share.

"Noted. And secondly, don't tell me shit like that. If you are with someone who has become like my little sister, never ever utter a word about your sex life with her, not even a hint. Got it?" He is a little more serious this time.

And it's my turn to laugh at him, especially when Tori is the queen of oversharing their sex life or insinuating things we don't want to know.

"Noted."

My mind moves to what we need to sort out. "But now that you know…"

Nic cuts me off. "I already knew, or suspected and prayed like hell I was wrong. Not because I don't approve, because fuck, I do, and I love you both. But just because it's messy and you know how much I hate messy. Christ, I'm about to marry messy, and she's enough for one man to cope with in life. And how Victoria hasn't worked it out yet is surprising, but lucky for you both. Now continue." He waves his hand in the air at me to keep talking.

"Understood. So now that you know, you can't tell anyone, and especially not Tori, not yet."

"See? Fucking messy, I told you." He rolls his eyes at me.

"There is no way Flynn can take another hit right now, and there is also no way Tori can keep a secret, and let me assure you, you don't want her to try. I'm watching it eat away at El, and not being able to talk to Tori is almost killing her. Those girls are so close, and she has never kept anything from her, so I can't imagine it's going to go down well when she does finally tell her. To be honest, I'm surprised she hasn't suspected something yet too."

"One word—wedding! She is trying so hard to find out what I have planned that she is missing the normal things that would trigger her nosy nature. You're lucky, buddy."

"So, we need to keep it between us, and I'm not telling El you know either. But I respect you too much to keep it from you any longer."

"I appreciate it, Rem. That's why you are one of my guys. I trust you with my life. Nothing says respect more than that. Got it?"

"Yeah, boss, got it." I try to keep my face blank but can't when he reacts straight away.

"Don't you start that shit! That's Flynn's department to piss me off."

"Speaking of Flynn, what are going to do with him?"

"Protect him as much as we can, that's all we can do besides the obvious. Oh, and find that fucker and destroy them like they are trying to destroy us."

You can see the moment both our brains click back into work mode by the body language, sitting up straighter on the couch, both getting ready to move and get on with the day.

We both stand and make our way toward the elevator like an unspoken end to our meeting.

But before I leave, there are two more things I need to say.

"I haven't told her I love her yet."

"Then don't leave it until it's too late," Nic replies, talking from experience.

I nod to him before I drop the next thing on him. Pushing the call button for the elevators, the doors open in front of me.

As I step in, I give him the last piece of information I need to share. "Oh yeah, and I'm also bringing a plus-one on Friday night. And if anyone can fix Flynn, it's my friend Cherie, you just wait till you meet her. Talk later." The doors start closing, and his eyes tell me what he is thinking before he starts saying it.

"See? Fucking messy. I hate you, asshole!"

And I don't know why, but that brings me a little joy for the day. Because it feels normal to piss off one of my friends.

Lord knows we could do with some normal today.

Now to go home and face the next problem.

Chapter Eighteen

ELOUISE

I'm sitting in the back of the car as we slowly drive down the street where Rem parked, and all I see is the back of him disappearing through a black door with nothing on it. The windows on the building are painted black, and I can't see anything to tell me what is inside.

My first thought is to ask Art if he knows what that business is, but I don't know if I really want the answer. It doesn't look how I imagined a gym looking.

Next door to it is another similar-looking building. One single door, windows that are covered up, and a sign above the door that isn't huge but enough you can read it. It just says in red writing *Strip Club,* and that's it. Which to me screams that it really isn't, because they aren't really advertising it well. My gut feeling is that it's probably a brothel, which even though they are illegal, still exist in lots of back streets like this.

I can't be here anymore and need to leave before I overthink it. I can't see Rem being the kind of man to visit a brothel, but then again, how much do I really know about him? Sure, I know about his family, friends, his work life, but do I know anything about his past? He traveled, and of course that led him to become a father when he always said he never wanted to be. But I don't know why he didn't want kids or why at thirty-six he has never had a serious relationship. The only thing I know for sure is that inside that seedy-looking building is a woman whose name is Cherie and that I know nothing about. Who she is or what she is. My mind is racing, and I'm so confused.

"Take me home please, Art." Looking back at me with compassion in his eyes, he doesn't say a word, just nods and then accelerates away.

Small little tears escape down my cheeks as the reality of the last twenty-four hours hits me.

This is why I didn't think it was a good idea, Rem and me. There is too much at stake, and the first bump in the road is now derailing us far quicker than I expected. I truly don't even know what happened after Tori started on the date thing, except that rage was consuming Rem, and he was having trouble holding it back. I always knew I would struggle with my emotions, but I figured he would be better at keeping calm than I was. Clearly, I was mistaken, because if the phone call hadn't come when it did, then I don't know how it would have ended up.

But with all that, I still didn't deserve the cold shoulder I got this morning. Then for him to leave me standing there, obviously upset, to go to another woman for whatever reason, and have the hide to tell me that's what he was doing, has me feeling like I want to vomit.

I rest my head against the window, feeling so lost.

This is the time where you run to a friend to vent about the man in your life, and she either tells you that you are being dramatic, or you both devise a plan to make him pay for being a dick. But that's my problem. I have done this to myself by keeping the whole relationship a secret from my best friend.

Walking into the house feels cold and different. Like all of a sudden, I don't belong here. That I have been living a life that wasn't really mine to live. If Rem and I were truly meant to be together then this wouldn't be so hard. We would have been able to date and spend time with friends, feeling their support of us becoming something. Maybe it's a sign from the universe that this isn't meant to be. That I don't belong in this world of wealth and high-powered people. The simple life of a teacher in a suburban school, living in my tiny home, is sounding more appealing every minute.

I really should be doing some housework, which always annoys Rem because he pays people to clean for him, but it makes me feel useful when I am home on my own. But instead, I'm just sitting in the chair out in the sunroom. This is one of my favorite rooms in the house, well, besides the bedroom, but that's not for the décor, I can assure you. There are big comfortable couches that are a dark rust color. The cushions are ones that your body sinks into, and every couch has a throw over the back of it. The glass along the back wall of the house lets the light in, and you almost feel like you are sitting outside in the garden but with the comfort and warmth of inside. The room is full of potted plants and even a couple I have planted with Blaise whose eyes lit up at getting his hands dirty. He has left a life on the land and been placed in the middle of a city, full of big buildings, traffic, and millions of people. I know it's important to keep him connected to the land whenever we can. Nic and Tori's farm is great for that, and I could see in the look that Rem had last time we were there that he is thinking about a farm of his own down the track.

But knowing him and his adrenaline-junkie world, it would probably be full of dirt bike racetracks, obstacle courses, and other dangerous things he could find. A place that both he and Blaise would love and I would be freaking out like crazy that one of them would get hurt as soon as they step out the back door of the house.

I stop the dream from going any further in my head because I don't know if I would even be there. I desperately want to be, but it's still such an unknown.

For all my fears, and the things I don't know about Rem yet, there is one thing that has become abundantly clear to me last night. I love this man, and I don't want to lose him. I've felt such a connection from that first night but was dismissing it because I knew nothing could come of it. Yet life has a funny way of playing the game, and now I'm snuggled down into a couch in his home, wrapped in his blanket that smells like him, fearing that even though I managed to have him as mine, it's about to be ripped away from me.

I don't know how long I've been sitting here feeling sorry for myself when my phone starts buzzing next to me. Snatching it so quick from on the couch beside me, I almost drop it on the floor but catch it last minute and swipe the screen before it stops ringing, even though I can't see who it is with my fumbling. I'm desperately hoping it's Rem, but the voice that comes through the speaker isn't him, and although I wouldn't have called her, hearing Tori on the other end of this call is a comforting relief from going insane inside my head.

"Lou, just checking in. How you are today?" She sounds less chirpy than usual, but that's to be expected.

"Hi, hun, yeah, fine." I'm not, but I can't say that.

"Great, then you are one less person I need to be worrying about. I'm trying to hold down the fort in here today, and three out of four of the guys are missing in action from the office. I mean, I get it. Nic is trying to focus and is working from home. Flynn, well, nobody expects to see him for a few days, and Rem is probably out doing some ninja shit tracking down the scum who has put us all in this position." I can hear the worry in her voice for the men who have all become her family. "At least Forrest is here, and between the two of us we are handling the media shit storm as best as we can with the PR team. One thing my fiancée does well is hire staff who are awesome at their jobs. Rohan, our head of PR, has been amazing and worth every bit of whatever he is being paid. Hell, he deserves a bonus after this one. The way he is spinning this has Flynn sounding like a saint in the public eye, and you and I both know he is more like the devil in disguise when it comes to women."

"Speaking of Flynn, how is he? Have you spoken to him?" My heart really feels for him. Nobody wants their naked body or private business shared with anyone, let alone the whole world.

"No, Nic told me to leave him alone, because apparently, I can be annoying and never know when to shut up. Can you believe that? How fucking rude, even if he has a point."

Even as shitty as I feel, I can't help giggling at that comment. It's so spot-on, but it's why we all love her.

"Yeah, yeah, you are both so funny… not!" Tori stops to let me get my laughing under control. "Anyway, I haven't, but Nic has seen him and is keeping an eye on him. He's tough, he'll bounce back and probably come out of this lapping up his newfound popularity, you know what he's like."

"He might be strong, but this a pretty big thing, and it's not going away anytime soon." Thinking of how I would feel if it was me, I doubt I would ever leave my home again.

"True, but you don't get this far in such a high-profile role without growing tough skin. He'll shake it off, I guarantee it."

And that's the part of this life I don't think I would ever manage to accept. Once you become so successful, then you become public property whether you like it or not. Tori has taken to it like a fish to water, but she already had the strong character before she met Nic. He just helped her to gain the confidence to use it.

Me, on the other hand, I'm nothing like Tori. Where she springs out of the box throwing her hands in the air and cheering to anyone who will listen, I'd be the opposite and slowly peeking my head over the top of the box, making sure no one is looking, then I'd stand up, climb straight over the edge of the box, and get to the side of the room and just blend in with all the other people, hoping like hell nobody noticed me.

"You're probably right. Is there anything I can do to help?" I know the answer will be no, but it's what you do, you offer anyway.

"The guys have this under control as much as they can, so no, but what you can do for me is give me a distraction. We need to sort out what you are wearing to the event on Friday. We only have three days, and you need to be looking super sexy so we can lure this guy in."

Without restraint, I groan loudly into the phone. "Tori. This is a really, really bad idea."

"Oh, shut up, this is the best idea I've had in ages. Plus, it's a safe space, you know, with all of us there. If you think he's a dickhead or boring as hell, you can just give me the sign and I'll have a fake girl moment, and we can leave him with the guys to deal with."

"The last thing the guys need right now is dealing with my stupid fake date." I squeeze my eyes shut, knowing I just said the wrong thing. I haven't had enough sleep to be talking to Tori with a filter on.

"Bitch, there's nothing fake about this date. He's smoldering hot, and you are perfectly single and ready to mingle. It's a perfect scenario. Now stop pretending you aren't ready to find love. I can tell you it's the best place to be, and I won't give up until you are as happy as I am. That's what best friends do, we have each other's backs."

How the hell do I get out of this? I'm just going to have to play along and then pull the sick card on the night of and stay locked in my bedroom at home because I'm stuck pretending to be running to the toilet.

"I know I've said this millions of times over the years, but why do I let you talk me into these stupid things?"

"Yay! I knew you would see it my way. And I believe the answer is that I bully you into doing things that then turn out to be spectacular. So tomorrow, when Blaise goes back to preschool, I'll meet you in town and we will get a dress and shoes. Oh, and some racy lingerie. Yes!" I can hear her clapping her hand down on the table with excitement.

"No. Stop right there. A dress and that's it. I won't be needing anything like that. It's a dinner and that's it."

I sit up straight in the seat and the blanket slides off me onto the floor as I'm battling to pull Tori back from going for a full-blown Elouise makeover that she's been nagging me to do for months.

"Mm-hmm, whatever you say. You are aware that I know all your measurements, right?" Her giggle tells me I'm trying to row up the river without a paddle.

"You are ridiculous. You can buy what you like, but you can't make me wear it. I'm going to be wearing my big white granny undies and a full big bra with not one piece of lace or color on it."

"Why are you being like this? Come on, let me help you, and I guarantee you will walk out of the charity auction Friday night with first prize. And just think, when you are married and having kids, you won't need to worry when they get sick. Daddy can get up in the middle of the night when they are puking everywhere. It's a win-win situation."

"Seriously, Tori, have you been drinking today?" No matter what, she still makes me laugh.

"No, you should know this is what happens when they give me too much coffee. I should stick to the tea I love, but they figured I needed some energy to get through the day. I'm sure they are regretting that decision now." Both of us laugh together because I've seen what too much caffeine or alcohol does to Tori. One makes her hyperactive and the other gives us crazy Tori, the one we need to look after before she gets herself into trouble. Thank God that's now Nic's problem, not mine.

"Oh, shit, I have to go, Nic's trying to call me. Talk later, and don't you dare think about backing out of this. I'll drag you there kicking and screaming if I have to. Bye."

Sitting in silence with the phone still in my hand, I can't help but laugh. Picturing Tori here, me in my old gym pants and my favorite big baggy sweater, with the pocket at the front and a hood I hide inside if I want to just take a moment to myself. Tori trying to lift me onto her shoulder and carry me out of here, dressed like that, and not caring as long as she gets me to the stupid dinner.

Looking at my watch, I have another hour before I'm due to pick up Blaise, and I should probably eat something. I skipped breakfast this morning, and it's past lunchtime. I just couldn't stomach anything and wasn't at all hungry, but now I'm starting to feel like I need something to fuel me to get through an afternoon and night with an energetic four-year-old.

Standing and then dragging my feet toward the kitchen, I hear the front gate opening and the sound of the Porsche pulling up to the front of the house.

My body is frozen still from anxiety. I don't know if I should continue to the kitchen so I'm busy doing something or run to the room that is supposed to be my bedroom and hide, but before I can get my legs to move, the decision is taken out of my hands. The front door swings open, and standing there looking at me is Rem. Instead of bursting into tears, which was my first thought the moment I heard his car, the anger from this morning comes roaring to the surface, and I walk toward him with purpose, yelling at him.

"Who the fuck is Cherie and why were you visiting her in a brothel!" I ram my hand into his chest with the full force of the emotions I'm feeling right now.

"Whoa. What the fuck are you talking about!" Rem has my hand in his and pushes me away from him. Slamming the front door behind him, he drops his bag on the floor.

"Bedroom now! We need to talk!" His voice is annoyingly calm but still firm.

"Bedroom? Not a chance. I'm not talking in there. You can start explaining yourself right here, right now." I stand my ground, well, I try to, until he grabs my hand and starts pulling me into the living room. He pushes me down into one of the couches and sits down next to me. He grabs my legs and spins me to the side so we are facing each other and there is no hiding.

"Fine, we start talking here, but I will be finishing this conversation in the bedroom with you naked and forgetting whatever it is you are pissed at me for. Because I can assure you that whatever you think you know or saw, it is the furthest it can possibly be from me visiting a brothel." How the hell does he do that? Curb his emotions enough that he speaks clearly, states his point, but makes sure you understand he isn't happy with you. I can't seem to manage the same as the screaming comes from my lips again.

"I had no idea what was happening, then you turn up here, looking like shit which, I get from the night you must have had, but then you treat me like crap, refuse to talk to me, and take off like a lunatic in the car, telling me you are going to see some woman I have never heard of."

The lines on his forehead are tight, his lips in a straight line, but he holds his tongue, waiting for me to get it all out.

"That's not normal, you have never treated me like that, ever! I was pissed, *so* pissed, and decided if you wanted to act like an asshole then I'd follow you and show you what it's like. Everyone thinks I'm this meek and mild teacher, well, guess what. You back me into a corner, and I'll come at you like the biggest bitch. I'm not weak, I have more strength than any of you realize. But then I saw you walk into that brothel, and my heart broke into a million pieces. How could you?" Leaning forward, I thump him in the chest again. "What does she have that I don't? You promised me that it was just us, only us."

The anger is being overtaken now by tears, and I can't breathe.

"I was ready to fight for you… but in that one moment you threw us away, and I don't know what to do with that."

My vision is blurred from the tears, but I don't need perfect vision to see how furious Rem is with all I'm saying.

Trying to fill my lungs with air is difficult, but Rem looks like he is breathing like a freight train, and the nagging thought that has been plaguing me all day finally falls from my lips.

"Is that where you have been all the times you left the house, at odd times of night and whenever things got awkward? Instead of dealing with it, you just run to some trashy whore to make it all better?" And now the sob that I've been holding in all day comes out, and I can't control it. All I want is for him to tell me it's not true and take me in his arms, but instead, he just stands slowly, taking a step backward, putting distance between us.

The only sound in the room is me crying, and then Rem takes a deep breath and starts speaking.

"You know me. Think about it deep down, who I truly am. I can't even find words to talk to you now. I'll pick up Blaise and drop him back here so you don't have to go out. That should give you time to pull yourself together. I'll stay at the hotel for a few nights. I need space to process all that."

He walks away from me for the second time today and still hasn't told me a thing.

"What the hell? I haven't done anything wrong, and yet you are treating me like I'm the problem. Is this what you do when it gets hard, run away? Back to her!" Jumping up from the couch, I follow him to the door. I'm getting sick of only seeing the back of him.

Rem stops with his hand on the front door handle, about to open it. Not even bothering to turn and look at me, his words have no emotion and cut me like a knife. "That's the irony of all this, Elouise. For the first time, I don't need to go back to Cherie. The only person that I thought I needed was you… but now I'm not so sure."

Opening the door, he starts stepping out, and I'm not letting him have the last say.

"Fine, fuck off then. Don't come back until you are ready to apologize and talk about it. Or go stay with your whore but don't bother ever coming back home if you do. You won't be welcome!"

The voice I hear from him now is one I don't like and full of sarcasm but not a piece of humor. "Like you can throw me out of my own house." He spins and glares at me like there is not one ounce of love left in his body for me.

"Watch me, asshole!" Slamming the door as hard as I can, I gasp for air, dropping to my knees and sobbing uncontrollably.

Curling myself into a ball on the floor, I just repeat to myself over and over. "No, no, no, no." This can't be happening. I thought I loved him, but now I don't know who that man was.

I'm still lying there long after the tears have stopped because there is no more water left. The alarm on my phone starts ringing from my pocket. It's the one I set so I'm never late to pick up Blaise, only apparently today I'm not needed. My heart starts racing because I need to get upstairs and make sure I look normal for when Blaise gets home. There is no way I want him to panic that anything is wrong. There have been a few times where he gets anxious about Rem if he is late when he says he will be home for dinner or he can't see me watching him in the park. He was young to lose his mum in the way he did, so it's completely normal he is still clingy at times.

Standing in front of the mirror and taking one look at myself is the shock I need to make me take a deep breath, pull my shoulders back, and push aside the anguish for the moment. I have a little boy who needs me. And no man gets to make me feel like that. The longer I stand giving myself the pep talk, there is a nagging feeling in my gut that something just doesn't add up. Rem didn't deny he's been with Cherie, but the way he spoke to me was like I was the disappointment. It doesn't make sense, and a man like that would just own it if he had been caught out. He doesn't owe me anything. After all, I'm just his nanny, and he could have just told me to leave for speaking to him like that. The timing would have been difficult with the Flynn saga, but he would have sorted it. Instead, he left me in his house, the one he has told me how much it has now become a home since Blaise and I arrived. But more importantly, he left Blaise, his son, the little boy who has stolen his heart, here with me and didn't seem one bit worried about it, giving both of us space to process this mess.

Nothing makes sense, and I know what I need to do.

I am going to regret it, I already know that, but I can't do this on my own anymore.

I splash my face with some cold water, drying my eyes and putting on a bit of light makeup to cover the dark circles and puffy eyes from Blaise. That little boy is so gentle and in tune with others that if I don't glam up a bit, he will be asking questions.

Then I push the button on my phone and call in the cavalry, knowing that she'll be happy to charge in with all guns blazing.

"Hi, sorry to bother you when I know you are so busy, but can you come over tonight? I need to chat."

"You okay?" And that is why I love my friend. No matter what is happening in her life, she is always worrying about others.

"Yeah, sort of. Just need a girls' night, it's been a while."

"Girls' night. Fuck, yeah, that's exactly what I need too," Tori yells into the phone. "What time, and I'll bring the food, wine, and is it a full-fare girls' night that requires copious amounts of chocolate?"

"Is that even a question? How long have you known me? It's in the by-laws of girls' night that there must be chocolate for every meeting. Geez, you move on to caviar and champagne and forget where you came from." As much as my heart is so heavy, my stomach rolling and the tightness in my chest feeling like an elephant is sitting on it, Tori can still make me laugh.

"My apologies, I'll make up for that and bring your favorite dinner. A roast from the pub on Georgian Street. With extra pumpkin and lots of gravy." Both of us giggle at the ridiculousness of our conversation, but it's made me feel stronger knowing I just need to get through this afternoon, put Blaise to bed, and then I can finally let my walls fall.

The chocolate is for me, but I know I'm going to need it to calm Tori down once I drop this bombshell on her.

The next hour was awful when Rem walked Blaise to the door, greeted me with a nod, and then left while I stood there just trying to get a read on him. My brain is trying to fathom what the hell happened today and who the man is, that no matter what I'm feeling, I still love deeply and am not ready to let go. Until he stands and looks me in the eye, admitting that he screwed a hooker and has been cheating on me this whole time, I can't walk away from him. There has to be more to this that I'm just not seeing and for some reason he's not telling me.

Blaise was full of conversation about his day and a new little boy, Jules, who started at the preschool in his class today. I know children his age can pick up a language quickly, but it truly has surprised me the speed his English has come along. I never knew his mother, but of course his father is a very intelligent man, except not when it comes to women and relationships it seems.

Thankfully, because he had such a big day at preschool, Blaise was out like a light at seven o'clock, and by the time Tori came through the door at seven-thirty with her arms full of dinner, alcohol, and chocolate, I was so hungry because I still hadn't eaten. I have to say it was the best-tasting roast I have had for a long time. Everyone has a list of comfort foods, and a roast beef dinner is at the top for me. My mum's will always be number one, but this one runs a close second.

Clearing up from dinner, Tori pours us both a big glass of red wine, grabs the bag that's overflowing with Maltesers, Orange Twirls, which are my favorite, and Kit Kats, with of course several different-flavored blocks of Cadbury. This woman is on to me that something is going on, because there is about a week's worth in this bag.

My heart is pounding, and for the last forty-five minutes, I have been trying to work out how to start this conversation, but as I take a deep breath and am about to open my mouth and start, Tori looks at me with a wicked grin.

"Right, now what the fuck is going on between you and Remington?" There is no anger, just her straight-shooting voice.

My mouth drops open wider, and all I can manage to say is, "How did…"

"Never mind, and yes, you're in trouble, but we will work that out later. Right now, I just want to know, who fucked it up and how are we going to fix it?"

Falling into her arms, I thank the universe for the day Tori walked into my life.

My tears are falling and I'm laughing at the same time. "Of course, you knew. I'm so stupid."

"Well, who else would have put that huge hickey on your neck in Scotland that you tried so hard to hide? I doubt it was the horny ghost you told me about."

I love my best friend, full stop, end of story.

Chapter Nineteen

REMINGTON

I should be in my hotel room away from people who know me and see me as their boss. Especially with all the media interest in us now, but I can't seem to settle tonight. I'm on to my second straight scotch, and although it's top-shelf, it just doesn't feel smooth like it should.

It's definitely not the scotch, but it's my mood that's souring the good alcohol.

I just want to make the feeling that it's happening all over again go away by having a drink, but that's stupid really. My life is full of problems I can't get control over, which should have me in the office and yelling at people, trying to get action on solving them. I hate with a passion that I've left the two most important people in my life alone, and the only thing I'm doing is sitting here in a bar on my own. Trying to stop my brain from thinking about anything at all.

What the fuck is wrong with me?

Even worse, I'm hovering my finger over the closed security camera app on my phone, considering opening it, just to see her for a quick minute and to make sure they are both safe. But the last shred of my manhood holds me back from spying on her and feeling like a stalker.

I know the security detail I have watching the house will keep them safe, but that is not much comfort when I know it should really be me.

The reason I'm here is because I want so desperately for her to trust that I am still the man she thought I was before this morning. So, in turn, I need to be that man and show trust in her too and believe that she is strong and taking care of both of them.

I've left them before when I've traveled for work, but this is different. When I'm away, normally Blaise and El are video chatting with me whenever we can. And late at night, El and I have sat and talked about our days and ended up with me watching her erotically get herself off and come hard under my instructions, which was so fucking sexy. I blew my load without hardly any work needed from my own hand.

So where did this all go so wrong?

I have done everything I could to show her who I am, or so I thought. The night she let me take her for the first time in Scotland, I felt hope between us. It's why when we both agreed the next morning to continue what we started, there was no going back, we were meant to be together. I breathed a sigh of relief that I had finally found the woman who was made for me. I know I'm not wrong about that, but today, she threw me with her accusations.

Sure, there are things I haven't told her, that I haven't told my buddies either, but there was still time to share more of myself as we continued to get to know each other. I doubt I've seen all there is to know about her either, but I was working on learning all the parts she was ready to show me. Isn't that what a relationship is, learning, living, and loving each other every day, through all the changes and challenges? Sharing, caring, and accepting each other for who you are?

That's what hurt.

I thought she knew who I was, but when she accused me today of cheating on her and visiting a brothel, I saw red.

Then, I did what I've learned to do, which is walk away, calming my brain before I speak and ruin everything that I was working so hard to save. I thought I had already done that successfully this morning and was coming home to be able to talk freely to El. Obviously not, so here I am drinking, feeling lonely and trying to figure out my next move.

I'm angry and hurt, but I assume all relationships go through periods like this. Before my first scotch I was ready to walk away and tell her it's over. I wasn't prepared to go through being accused again of being the whole problem in the breakdown between two people. It feels like a lifetime ago, but the only time I thought I had found a woman I wanted to be with for more than one night, she stripped me bare of all my money and emotions. The fights between us that happened night after night for over a week were horrendous and relentless, until I couldn't handle it any longer, and I walked away from her and moved on to another city. Only to find out, after I had moved three different times to new cities looking for work and was working in a bar, that one of the kitchen hands turned out to be the guy she was sleeping with at the same time as me. He was the man she was running off to when she would storm out each night after she screamed at me.

I'm too old to worry about labels, but she was gaslighting me, and I had no idea.

I took it hard, and the months of lead-up to when we finally split took their toll on me. The way I coped going forward was by numbing the emotion of love and taking the prospect of it happening again totally out of the equation. If I didn't ever get serious with anyone again, I couldn't get hurt like I did back then, and until now, it's worked.

The only difference between then and now is that I have just had the epiphany that I didn't want to fight to save the relationship with my ex, Shannon. Although I was hurt badly by her, and I didn't think it could be any worse than that, I know that if I can't be with El, then life wouldn't be worth living. Shannon was never my person.

But this time, I will give every bone in my body to find the place where Elouise and I can be together, happy, at total peace and madly in love. Elouise is my forever person. It's as simple as that, and I need to fix this.

I stand from the stool and lift my chin to tonight's barman, Gus, knowing he will settle my tab onto my charge card that Nic never lets us pay anyway. Walking toward the elevator, I know what I need to do, and if it doesn't work then I'll try again, because I am not giving up until my life is in complete control again.

And the only way that will happen is with El right beside me, helping raise Blaise the best way we know how.

I won't give in until I have what I want.

If I'm honest with myself, it's more than want, it's what I *need.*

Elouise is mine, and it's about time I tell her and the rest of the world.

ELOUISE

"I can't believe you did a strip tease in Rome. Holy shit, Lou, and you say I'm uncontrollable when I'm drunk." Tori is still trying to get through all the sordid details that I've told her over too much chocolate but luckily not too much wine. Well, we aren't at the point we can't walk, but everything seems to hurt a little less now. But we need to stay sober with Blaise in our care.

"That's the problem, isn't it. I'm the good little girl. Fuck that! Sometimes it's so good to be bad." My mind keeps going to thoughts it shouldn't be right now. I remind myself I should still be angry with him.

"Amen, sister. But can I just say you have the shittiest timing to finally tell me your big dirty secret? I'm still mad you didn't think I would understand, but part of me does get it. We both know I'm hopeless and suffer from word vomititis. Yes, yes, I know vomititis isn't a word, but it should be, just for me and my rambling. Anyway, I suck at secrets and all that, but this is big for you. Like, super huge, and you needed me, and I wasn't there for you like you were for me when everything was happening with Nicholas. I couldn't have gotten through it all without you." Tori takes both my hands in hers and tries to be serious for a moment.

"I know you don't believe this, but you are the strongest woman I know, and the last few months have proven that. I just wish you could see yourself like the rest of the world sees you. And I know you don't want to hear it, but Rem, the way he looks at you even when he is trying not to, that man loves you. To the point that he walked away from you today when you made some pretty big accusations, and then he messaged me telling me that you needed me. He was hurting, but still, he was thinking about you and making sure you were okay."

"Wait, he messaged you?" My brain starts short circuiting.

"Why do you think I called you back after you called me to talk for the second time today with some lame excuse about checking if you wanted gravy on your roast? Surely you knew I'd already know that answer. Look, he didn't say why, but I knew it was about him. Christ, I already knew that the moment I spoke to you this morning the first time. I just can't believe what you are saying is true, so we need to find out what is going on so we can then get on with having cute double dates and planning another wedding."

I groan at her words, already thinking how badly I'm going to regret telling her everything.

"Can we not go all Tori on this? We aren't even together right now." The sadness sinks into my gut again at spending another night alone in his bed.

"Oh, that's just geographically, but there is no way you two aren't together. There is no way the heat in this exact room last night when I brought up the date with Dr. Hottie is going away anytime soon. That man would chain you to him if he could, rather than let another man touch you." Tori laughs at herself.

"Hang on, let's rewind a little. If you knew we were together, why did you set up this date with Drew?"

"Seriously, Lou, sometimes you are so naïve. I knew if I pushed you both hard enough something would have to give and either Rem would explode last night and blurt it out to everyone, or I would force your hand to tell me to back off. But we both know Flynn's naked ass put an end to that but only for the time being. But it could still work in a different way." The look of mischief in her eyes tells me I'm in trouble, and once again, I won't be able to say no to her.

Flopping my head back on the back of the couch, I sigh into the air. "I should be worried, shouldn't I?" I pull my hands from hers and place them over my eyes, spreading my fingers and peeking through at her.

Tori pretends to be shocked. "Whatever do you mean, Lou? You know I've got this all under control."

"Lies, all lies, but tell me your plan anyway so I can hit the anxiety button even harder. If I wasn't already going to have trouble sleeping tonight, then what you say next I'm sure will push me to the point of insomnia anyway." Sitting back up, I get ready for whatever crazy scheme she has conjured up.

"I wasn't joking about the dress for Friday and all the accessories." Raising her eyebrows up and down, she looks ridiculous, but it makes me smile.

"There is no way Rem will go to the dinner on Friday night after what I said. Plus, I don't think that's the place to have our big heart-to-heart talk, do you?" I already know she will have an answer for any question I throw at her.

"Pfft, don't you worry about that. I'll get him there. Your job is to turn up and look hot as fuck, and no matter what you said today, he won't be able to resist you." And then her second thought pops into her head. "Oh, and don't worry about Flynn, I'll sort that too—well, not the sex tape, but the you-and-him problem. I can fix that one easily."

"Crap, yes, Flynn, I don't want him hurt, especially now when he is already in a shit place. Like I have already said before, this sounds like a terrible plan. What, you think just because I look good, he is going to forgive me? But that doesn't necessarily mean I want to forgive him!" I stand up and pace a little.

"What a load of bollocks. Stand still, look me in the eye, and tell me you truly believe that Rem has been cheating on you with a hooker. Really! Come on, you can't honestly believe that." Standing in front of me, she pushes me to say what is on my mind like only Tori can.

"Alright!" I throw my hands in the air in exasperation. "No, I don't think Cherie is a hooker, but who the hell is she and why didn't he just tell me when I asked, well, possibly yelled?"

"Right, I don't know the answer to that except to say he is a stupid butthead, and when I sort this shit out between you two, I will tell him how much of a dick he is and how he is going to pay big time for hurting you."

Wrapping Tori in my arms, I take comfort from her craziness which sounds ridiculous, but it's what feels normal. If Tori was all soft, comforting, and crying with me then I would know this is way worse than I already think it is and that the world was about to end.

"This burns coming out my mouth, but I'm saying it anyway—I trust you," I admit, taking a deep breath. "I love him and need him back here where he belongs. I need your help to make that happen."

Before I can take much more of this touching moment, Tori pushes me away. Dancing around the room, she sings the words, "Lou trusts me and wants my help. Life is good. Lou trusts me and wants my help. Life is awesome. I'm the queen of fixing shit." And that is when I know she's reached her quota of alcohol. Time to message her driver to pick her up.

As she is standing at the front door and leaving for the night, I put my arms around her.

"Thank you. Love you, and I couldn't get through this without you." Tears are welling in my eyes as she starts giggling.

"Finally, the woman realizes she can't go through life without me. So, if you ever keep anything from me again, I will kill you! Or maybe not that extreme, but you know, do something drastic, like putting a spell on you so you can't eat chocolate ever again. Yes, that would be worse than death, I reckon." She laughs at herself, which is a common occurrence for Tori, but instead of leaving me on the doorstep in tears, she walks down the steps, waving to me over her shoulder.

"My work here is done. Get some sleep. Tomorrow, we start

operation find that Cherie bitch and have Rem on his knees begging to get you back on Friday night. No one messes with us!" The driver closes the door on the car, and I walk inside laughing harder that I thought was possible with how bad today had been.

Locking the door, I tidy up our mess and hide the chocolate before I have a crazy child in the morning finding it and getting high on sugar. As I set the alarm on my way up to bed, the house feels so empty.

Checking in on Blaise, I see he hasn't even moved from where he fell asleep as I was reading the first book at bedtime. I bend down and kiss his forehead, leaving him to enjoy his happy dreams, not knowing there is turmoil all around him.

Finally settling down in Rem's bed, his scent wraps around me, bringing me both comfort and sadness. Although I understand after talking to Tori that I trust Rem, it doesn't stop me from needing to know more. If we are to have a real relationship and one that will stand the test of time, any secrets we have need to be revealed, and that takes total honesty from both of us.

I can't say what I need to say over a message, but I need him to know that there is still hope.

Lifting my phone and before I regret it, I type out three simple words.

Elouise: I miss you.

The dots on the screen dance, telling me he is replying, then stop, then dance again, then stop. My heart is beating fiercely, waiting for the words to appear, but then nothing.

My tears dropping onto his pillow, I pray to whoever will listen, *Please, bring him home.*

I don't how long it's been, but exhaustion finally pulls me to close my eyes, but the moment they do, my phone chimes, and I open them with such speed, I see a reply from Rem that makes me cry harder.

Rem: I know. Sleep.

What does that even mean? And once again, sleep has slipped away, and I curl into a ball, trying to overanalyze three little words.

When I have turned so many scenarios over in my head, finally the only thing I tell myself is that I need to get up tomorrow and do what Tori said.

Fight for my man, and more importantly, I need to fight for myself and what I need.

Which is answers and Rem.

In that order!

REMINGTON

Last night was tough, and all I wanted to do this morning was book a session with Cherie, but I know that's not healthy. I need to learn how to cope with emotional turmoil on my own if I'm ever going to be able to stand up and be in a relationship with Elouise.

Last night, I was trying to rationalize everything in my head, but no matter what she said or did, I still kept coming back to the same conclusion.

I love her.

We all make mistakes, and Christ, I've made many in my life too.

But to get through this, we need to sort through her fear of never being good enough for me and my past trauma of a relationship that scared me.

Pulling my jacket on, phone in my pocket, I'm picking up my wallet when the banging on my door has me reacting by reaching for my gun from the holster under my jacket.

Before I make it to the door to check the peephole, I hear Tori's voice. "Hope you are decent because I'm coming in." Luckily, I was, because the door lock opens, and she's halfway into the room as I drop the hand from my gun.

"Tori, what the fuck? Do you know how dangerous it is to barge into the room of an armed man? Who the hell gave you access to my room key?" My mood was already bad, but this has got my blood boiling, and I have no patience for whatever she is about to unload on me.

If it had been one of the guys who burst in here like that, they would be getting a lot more of a mouthful of colorful language than what I just said.

"Do you forget who I am?" She stands there with her right hand on her hip and her left hand in the air, waving her engagement finger at me. "Boss man's fiancée. Plus, I have very good persuasive skills. You should know that by now."

"Is that the same as saying you can be a pain in the ass?" I'm not in the mood to try to be diplomatic this morning.

"Whatever. Now let's get to work, there are things that need to be sorted." She makes herself at home at the small table in the room. I could have booked a suite, but what for? It's not like I want to be entertaining here or am on holidays. I just needed a bed and a place to shower. That's it.

"Why here? We have a big fancy office building that Nic pays for us to work in. So, tell me, what the fuck is going on and why are you really here?" In the back of my mind, I'm thinking Nic could have warned me that Tori was on her way here ready to ambush me about something. I would bet money it's about El, and although I greatly want to know everything that was discussed last night, it would be a really bad idea to enter into this conversation with Tori.

"God, you really are an asshole sometimes." She frowns at me, waiting for me to react, but I don't.

"Fine, okay, here it is. I'm here because there was no way you were coming into the office today, and I know you will ignore my phone calls. So, in point form, this is your morning brief. Lou and Blaise were fine last night. Flynn is coming into the office at some stage today, so it looks like business as usual. Tomorrow night we will all be attending the charity dinner as per schedule. You will need to be there to protect Flynn, so do not even try to back out of this. And before you ask, yes, Lou will be there. You will be nice and polite. Do you understand!" By the time she is finished, she stands in front of me, hands on hips and not about to take any crap from me.

"Since when do I take orders from you, Tori? I'm head of security here. I make the decisions on making sure Flynn is protected, not you or anyone else. Has he even agreed to this, being paraded around like everything is normal in the world for him? Because clearly, it's not, and if you've spoken to him, you will know he is vulnerable."

"I've already been to see Flynn. He agrees that he should be out there operating as normal so the media have less to talk about. If he is doing boring things, like work, charity events, and so on, then someone will become far more entertaining, and the focus will shift quickly. That is what the PR department have told him, and they report to the big boss man too. Just like the rest of us." Picking up her bag, she starts to walk toward the door to leave, when she turns to have her final say, which is normal.

"So, if you want to talk like work colleagues, just do your job, Rem, and find out who did this to Flynn. Do it quickly and make sure you are there to protect him and the rest of us Friday night." Hesitating a little, the tone of her voice drops to a softer tone. "But if you want the advice of a friend, be at the dinner on Friday night. I promise it will be worth your while."

Opening the door, all I can hear is her mumbling as she walks out of the room. "Fucking useless men. Why do I have to clean up their messes…" Her voice disappears as the door slams shut.

What did she even mean?

Why would I want to go and watch El pretending to be happy and talking to some guy? Was it El's idea to make me jealous and come home?

There are so many questions that I don't even have the time or mental space to work through right now. These two were just the beginning. Because Tori's words hit hard in my gut. She's right, I need to find out once and for all who set up the cameras and then leaked it to the internet even after they were paid.

Pushing aside my own issues, I do what I do best. I compartmentalize.

Grabbing my things, I'm out the door and calling my second-in-charge to meet me at the office, but first I need to speak to Felisha Kentwall, just me and her, one on one, so we can get to the bottom of this. She might be as innocent as Flynn, but something has triggered this attack on the two of them. I need to work it out. Just getting past her damn security team will be the issue. But I love a good challenge, and today I need a distraction, so this is what I intend to throw myself into. And I'm not stopping until I work it out. By then I might have my head on straight and I can arrange to meet with Elouise so we can talk this out. I know it's important, and she should be taking priority over work, but it's just not possible right now and she knows it.

The time for talking was yesterday, and she wrecked that, so now unfortunately she will have to wait until I'm ready.

I'm in control now. I'm not taking orders from either one of the women who think they have me all worked out.

They're wrong.

On my terms, they will find out who the real me is.

ELOUISE

"I don't wear red. It's too loud for me." I'm standing in the dressing room, in shock at the way I look in the mirror.

Tori is behind me with the most wicked grin on her face. "Loud is the best way to make a statement. Look at me, there's a reason I'm a redhead; I like to be heard." Neither of us can deny that.

"Yes, but that's you. I'm just the woman who likes to go unnoticed in a room. Come and go, and it's a good night if no one knew I was there."

I spent most of our nights out in a group just admiring Remington from a distance and wincing every time he spoke to another woman on their own. And there were plenty. He wasn't as obvious as Flynn, but the single ladies in the room noticed him and made sure they got their chance with him.

"True. But this time we want every man in that room to notice you, well, except my man, but we want the rest wondering who this goddess is in the red dress."

"I don't want every man in the room looking at me, otherwise I'll be as red as this dress." I sigh at the thought of being on show. "I just want one man to look at me and to be unable to look away until we get through this."

"Oh, that's guaranteed." Tori checks her phone, and I know I can't take up any more of her time. She's working, and just because she is engaged to the owner doesn't mean it's acceptable to just take time during the day to go dress shopping with your friend.

I take one last glance at myself, and this time, really looking at myself, I can see what Tori means. I do look good, and if I want to make an impression and show Rem that I'm a confident, strong woman, then I have to take a step out of my comfort zone. Because I want him to want to tell me what is going on and who Cherie is. To know that I can handle anything that he needs to share about his life. I don't want him keeping secrets to protect me.

"Okay, let's get this one." I bite my lip with trepidation at what will happen tomorrow night, but I know I'm in too deep now and I just have to run with Tori's plan, hoping that one day I will be telling my grandchildren about what wild thing she talked me into doing. Correction, my and Rem's grandchildren.

"Right, now let's move on to the underwear." Tori takes my arm as I'm exiting the dressing room, but I stop her walking and stand my ground in front of her.

"No! You're going back to work, and I'm going to choose my own lingerie. I want this to be something just between Rem and me. You understand, don't you?" I hope that she won't be offended that I want to do this on my own.

"Totally." Leaning forward, she kisses me on the cheek as she backs away from me, smiling. "Make sure it's something so seductive that his body heats up so hot that nothing will hold him back and you won't be wearing them for long."

"I think I've got the brief, now go." I shoo her and turn away from her, and she leaves in the opposite direction. Then I head to the underwear section of the store.

Of course, all this might be a waste of time, if we talk and he can't get past what I accused him of or his explanation of his actions doesn't satisfy me. I feel like we are dancing around a box that we suspect may have some explosive material inside. And it could all be sorted out simply, except no one is ready to open the lid to find out.

Why are relationships so complicated?

Walking through all the racks, I know I could wear nothing underneath that dress, it's so tight it holds everything in place. Knowing I had been walking around all night completely bare, now that would shock Rem completely, in the best possible way. But I know how much he enjoys unwrapping me. I already have a drawer full of the gifts he has purchased for our midday dates, but nothing red.

It's time to up the ante and watch him enjoy his present. Me.

That's if he still wants me.

After everything, please let him still want me!

Chapter Twenty

REMINGTON

The last few days have been horrendous.

Not seeing Elouise or Blaise has been like being starved of oxygen and not being able to breathe but having to push through anyway.

My private life is a mess, but at least my work life is under my control again. The meeting with Felisha was interesting to say the least. She is emotionally devastated but is still a strong kickass woman. I have a newfound respect for her, and way more than what I have toward her father. After speaking to her, I met her personal assistant, who is also her best friend and seems to be the only one who truly cares for Felisha or has her back.

I have also learned that under all the cockiness that Flynn portrays, he is a strong man who won't walk away from a fight. Giving himself just the one day to wallow in his self-pity, he then turned up to the office the next day, giving a perfect press conference then working the rest of the day like normal. Then today, he was in early, and I'm about to walk into a meeting with him, Nic, and Forrest about the castle purchase. Tori isn't in the office today, and I'm a bit relieved about that. I've managed to avoid her since our run-in at the hotel. I care deeply for her, but I know that she is the only person who will push me on anything Elouise, and I'm not prepared to discuss things with her just yet. It's between El and me, and until we see each other and talk, then the topic is off the table with Tori.

Walking through the door into Nic's office, I'm the last to arrive.

"Who pissed in your porridge this morning?" Flynn looks up at me from his favorite seat on the couch in the office, as if nothing has happened in the last few days, chirpy as hell and ready to give me shit.

Trying to cut him some slack, I don't reply as harshly as I feel. "This is my normal face when I see you." Taking my seat near the desk, I give Nic and Forrest a normal chin lift.

"Well, good morning to you too, asshole." Nic's reply hits home. Why is everyone calling me an asshole lately? I mean, I couldn't give a fuck, but it's bugging me. Have I been worse the way I've been treating everyone? I mean, El has good reason to say it, but everybody else has been labeling me with it too.

"Morning," I mumble and let Nic take over the meeting. Once he starts talking, then we all take on the seriousness that is needed in a business meeting.

An hour has passed, and the lawyers have been instructed that we are ready to take possession of the castle next week. Nic and Tori will fly up to collect the keys and have the locks changed and stay a night or two.

I haven't bothered to remind him of the important fact that he is buying a haunted castle. Not that I'll admit it, but I think El was right. I experienced a few weird things myself, like doors closing and noises in the middle of the night. The second night we were there and at the same pub in the village, El asked one of the old locals about it, and he told her a story he'd heard when growing up. That there was a woman who owned the castle back in the 1800s who was living in sin with a man her family didn't approve of. Then mysteriously they were both found dead in their bed one morning by the servants. Word was the family did it, but nothing was ever made of it. Just swept under the carpet, so to speak. El is convinced it was probably the woman in the painting who was so unhappy that she was about to be married to a grumpy man, because she had found true love with someone else. The shit women will make up to find romance in anything.

I also want to tell Nic it's too late, I've already christened the castle with El, but I don't think that's a good idea. I should have probably thanked the ghosts for pushing her into my bed, although it was inevitable to happen before we left the castle anyway. Nothing could have stopped the pull between us to be together. I quickly push the thoughts of El to the side before I lose my concentration on work.

Finally, we finish up and move on to the other topic of Flynn.

"Rem, where are we at?" Nic looks at me, almost pleading silently that I have some news.

"We are getting close, I can feel it. After talking to Felisha and her friend, I learned there is unrest in their company, and my gut feeling says the video came from someone on the inside of her dad's empire. That information is not to leave this room. I must say, I was doubtful of her at first, but I do think she is on our side with this and has been fighting her own fight trying to get to the bottom of it too. And for some reason, she actually thinks Flynn is a gentleman the way he has handled this whole thing, supporting her. Do I need to ask how you have been supporting her when we told you to stay away from her?" Looking at Flynn across the room, he gives me nothing except a smile that tells me I can sing for an answer.

"Anyway, when we get close enough, we will leak it to the press that we know who it is and see if we can flush them out, but we just aren't quite there yet. I'm not letting it go now, though. I made that mistake last time, and it's not happening again."

"Thanks, Rem." Nic drops his pen down on the desk and sits back in his chair, looking at me the way my father would when he knew I'd done something stupid and he was waiting for me to own up.

He can either read minds or he's just thinking about the same thing I've already decided on.

Finding courage, I start talking. "I need to say a few things to you all about something personal, before we go."

I gulp down the air that seems to be thick in the room now and stuck in my throat as Flynn sits forward on the couch, rubbing his hands together.

"Oh good, time to talk about someone else's dramas for a change. Let's have it." And Flynn is just making me feel worse.

Forrest just rolls his eyes at his brother. "I'm sure you should have been a woman. You love gossip more than the trashy websites that are writing everything about you." He leans closer to me, giving me a slap on the back. "What's going on, buddy?"

I know that no matter what happens in the next few minutes, I am going to feel better with everything being out in the open.

"I have something to say, and just let me get it out before you react. I'll keep it as simple as I can." The fun expression on Flynn's face now fades as he sees how uncomfortable I look.

"Long before I met you guys, I started seeing a counsellor of sorts who helped me work through when my head is scrambled, or my overactive brain needed release. But I haven't ever shared this because it's a little unconventional, and I don't know why I care, but I know some people will look at me and think less of me for it."

"Nothing wrong with therapy, man." I wish Flynn would stop being nice to me.

Nic looks at me and nods to keep going.

"You might change your mind when I tell you my therapy is that I box and kickbox the hell out of a woman who is a trained psychologist and counsels me while we spar." I feel like the air is getting sucked out of the room, and that's not even the worst thing I need to tell them.

"Wait, what?" Forrest looks confused, and I get it.

"Cherie is an extremely talented, competitive fighter who grew up street fighting and turned her life into something more by helping people who need a way to release their problems in a way that works for them. I can tell you now, she would take any one of you on and have you pinned on the mat before you even threw your first punch." Now I can feel my words coming out quicker as I try to justify myself.

"You hit a woman?" Flynn is trying to process what I just said.

"And that's the part that I struggled the most with in the beginning. It goes against every bone in my body, but Cherie made me see that it's not done in a form of violence toward her, and that I don't want to hurt her in any way. She uses her body as a tool to help people, and it's her choice. She wears body padding now, but in the beginning she didn't, and it fucked with me, but I couldn't stop going back for how great I felt after the sessions. And I can assure you the only one with bruises at the end of the session is me. I've never won against her, even after all these years."

The room is silent for a few moments until Nic finally speaks up, and I've never been more thankful for that man as I am right now.

"We all do what we have to in life to get through. I know you, Rem, and I trust you would never hurt a woman… ever. It's not our place to judge you or your life choices. I don't give a shit what you are doing, and to me, that's a better outlet than turning to drugs or alcohol."

"Thanks," is all I can say, and I'm struggling to even look at the other two, but I know I need to own this. Turning back to them, I try to pull my shoulders back and appear strong, but it proves harder than I thought.

"I don't get it, but I kind of want to meet her. Anyone who can beat the warrior man here, the one that protects us, must be some kickass woman." I knew it. Flynn can't help himself, and women in general fascinate him. But he has no idea what he is walking into, meeting Cherie. She's nothing like the little London socialite women he seems to collect along the way. She would eat them for breakfast.

Deciding that I'm not going to tell him that tonight he will get his wish, I need to get the next secret out before I lose my courage.

"There is something else, and I'm not sure you will take it as easily, but this one I don't care what you think, say, or want to do about it. It's the only thing I would ever say is important enough to me that I will walk away from this job and all of you if it becomes a problem between us. I didn't truly understand that until just now, but to be the best man to protect you, I need to put myself first which will make me a stronger person to be there for all of you."

"Fuck, what is going on!" Forrest is now getting concerned. "We have each other's backs no matter what, and you know that, so what the hell have you done?"

I take a deep breath and slowly breathe it out. "Elouise and I have been together ever since Scotland, and although there has been some drama between us the last few days, I intend to marry this woman one day soon if she'll have me. Flynn, I didn't ask for this to happen, and I'm sorry. I know you like her, but I couldn't stop it. She's mine, and I knew it the moment she asked me to kiss her in Rome. I would never step in front of you, but she has been clear from the beginning she isn't interested in you."

"Bastard!" Flynn jumps out of his seat and moves toward me.

"Hit me. I deserve it," I demand, standing and not moving away. I keep my arms lowered and wait for a fist to connect. Flynn's arm is up and moving, but from the corner of my eye, I see Forrest is moving from his seat and grabs Flynn's arm.

Wrapping him up, he holds him back. "You hit him, so help me God, I will end you, little brother." Forrest's deep voice fills the room with the force he intends Flynn to understand. A voice I have never heard from Forrest. "She doesn't want you, she never did. Back off, dickhead."

"Me, why the fuck do I have to back off? He's been fucking Lou behind my back this whole time and didn't say a word. That's a dog act. And she's not the innocent woman I thought she was either. You don't treat a friend like that. What, I suppose you both laughed at me every time I openly flirted with her? Wow, way to make me look like an idiot!" Flynn struggles out of Forrest's hold and shakes himself, trying to tame his temper. Running his hands through his hair, he walks away toward the window, which is probably safer for both of us.

"Watch your mouth. You can say what you like about me, but

don't you dare disrespect El. She doesn't deserve it." He knows full well I will take him if he ever says a bad word about her.

"El, oh how fucking cute!" he huffs, and this time I'm moving toward him. This time it's me that Forrest steps in front of, placing his hand on my chest.

"Enough!" Nic's loud stern voice bellows through the room. "Sit the fuck down and listen." He glares at both of us like he won't take no for an answer.

Knocking Forrest's hand off my chest, I step backward and sit in my chair but don't get comfortable. I'm on the edge of it, ready for the next time Flynn wants to take me on. There is no holding back now. I meant what I said.

For the first time in my life, I will fight for a relationship and the woman I love. There are no ifs, and, or buts.

We are like two bulldogs on the opposite side of a fence, knowing we can't move but growling and snarling at each other.

"This is exactly why Rem didn't tell you, because he knew it would hurt you." Nic looks at Flynn, making sure he has his full attention. "One day, Flynn, you will understand he had no choice on being with Lou. When she's the one, nothing can stand between you, nothing! Not even a best friend. Now suck it up because it's not changing, and I'm not losing any of you." Before Flynn could open his mouth to reply, Nic has already turned to face me and starts again. When Nic speaks like this, you all shut up and listen.

"And you," he says, pointing his finger at me. "Like I told you, fucking messy. Don't keep fucking secrets from us. We might not like what you have to say, but the sooner we know, the sooner we get past it and move forward. That goes for you two as well," he adds, glaring at Flynn and Forrest. "I didn't choose my friends at random. I trust the three of you with my life, hell, with Victoria's life, and I don't do that easily. We are one unit, and nothing like this is going to change that. So, work it out now and bury it. If that means you two need some gloves and a boxing ring, then find it now. Beat the shit out of each other, get up, kiss and make up, and then get the fuck over it. We don't have time for stupid shit right now. And if nothing tells you more how much Rem thinks of you, Flynn, the morning after we were all graced with your ass all over our news feed, Rem and Lou had a pretty big argument. He should have been home sorting that out with his woman, but instead, he has been here working, trying to fix this for you. His friend. The one whose back he always said he would have, and he has every single time. If their relationship doesn't survive now, just know that is because he put you before himself."

"Didn't have to," Flynn mumbles under his breath.

"No, he didn't, but he did it anyway." No one is speaking now, and Nic's words are sinking in with all of us.

"If I fuck this up, that's on me. Just like this, I let secrets come between us. I should have trusted her with my fears, but instead, it has led her to lose her trust in me. And that feels like a knife slicing open my heart, so damn painful. Take it from me, there will be no more secrets with anyone. This is who I am, laying it all out, even when it's hard to do." The aggression that was raging through my body is subsiding slightly, and I just hope they can forgive and accept the real me.

Again, the silence is deafening, and I just want to run from the room, but that's not what I've chosen to do. I'm standing up and owning every part of my life.

Flynn huffs. "The last thing I will say on this matter is that if she wasn't going to be with me, then at least she's with someone I trust to take care of her. So, whatever the hell you've done, fix it, asshole. Seriously! Because if you let her go, then I will knock you out like you will deserve." He almost growls his words at me.

"Understood… and I just want you to know we both tried so hard to resist this. But that's a story for another day." I'm almost pleading with him to forgive me. I know when the dust settles on all this, and it will, that Flynn will find El's list of demands funny. It just might take a while.

A few more words from Nic and he tells both Forrest and me to leave, and I don't hesitate to get out as quickly as I can. Forrest is right behind me. And all I can think of is that El is going to kill me for telling the boys without her knowing. Another battle to fight when we speak.

Walking down the corridor, I can tell Forrest wants to say something, but he just doesn't know if he should. Not hesitating, I walk into his office in front of him, waiting for him to pass me and then closing the door.

"It's now or never, man." I look at him and wait.

"He's a handful, but my brother is a good man. He will get past this and be happy for you. This last week has just been a lot." Forrest is always so calm, and you don't get much from him, but when he speaks, it's direct and no waffling like Flynn.

"I know." And I do. That's why I didn't want to say anything, but I couldn't keep it to myself any longer. It was eating me up inside, and I knew when I woke up this morning it was time.

"One last thing. She's a lucky woman, but you're an even luckier man. Treat her like she deserves to be treated and there will never be another harsh word spoken from us." He gives me that stern almost fatherly look.

"I promise, Forrest. With everything I am, I will protect her and love her until the day I die, and then some." When he turns his back to me and walks to his desk, I know it's time to go.

We all need space this afternoon to process before we sit down at a table with three hundred odd people all putting us under a microscope while we pretend that not a thing is wrong with any of us.

Nic keeps reminding me how messy I am. Well, bring on the messy!

"Holy shit, you weren't kidding, you own a dress. I don't just mean that it's in your possession, but you know how to *own* a dress." I'm standing next to the town car I hired for tonight to pick up Cherie. I wasn't letting her find her own way there or walk into a room full of people she didn't know without a friendly face.

"Oh, shut up. Surely you didn't think I live my life in workout gear. I truly worry about you sometimes." I can tell she is trying to use the confidence she has in the gym to dismiss the compliment I gave her.

"Shall we?" I motion for her to hop into the car so I can close the door and head to the function.

Walking around to get in the other side, my stomach twists again like it's been doing all day. Three times I almost made it to my car to drive home and talk to El before tonight, but I have a feeling there is more at play than just what I want. Especially if Tori is involved. I couldn't help myself and checked the tracker on Tori's phone. It has shown her at my house all day, so there is something going on.

"Tell me about this Flynn guy. Does he know about me?" Cherie blurts out in a hurry, and I can tell the nerves are starting to kick in for her.

"I finally told them this morning who you are to me," I say, looking at her across the seat from me.

"Wow, that's huge, Rem. How did that feel?" I love how she asked how it affected me, not what they said. I may never box with her again, but I know she will always be there for me as a friend. Because that is what she is. She stopped being just my therapist years ago.

"At first like I was exorcising a demon, you know, the one I carry about hitting a woman, but once it was out, it was quite cathartic."

Her face lights up with a smile of pride that she has in me, that finally after all the years of talking about it, I have finally done it. "I guess we are getting to the end of our sessions. You won't need me anymore now that you have Elouise. She will be your sounding board, and good luck to her I say." She laughs at me, trying to hide the sadness that we are both feeling.

"I think you're right, but instead, I want you in my life, actually *our* life, as a dear friend. You will love El, and once she gets over that you aren't my hooker, then I'm sure you two will become great friends."

"What the actual fuck, Remington! Explain. Now!" She's not laughing, and there's panic, fear, anger, confusion, and every other emotion written all over her face as I start telling her what has happened over the last few days.

"You didn't think all that might have been handy to know before I dressed up and got in a car with you tonight to face a scorned woman and her best friend? Damn it, Rem, I'm tough, but that is like putting raw meat in front of a couple of hungry bears. There's no hiding from that frenzy." She rolls her eyes at me, and I can see she would love to hit me right now and actually mean to hurt me.

"I've seen you stand up against far worse. You'll be fine."

"You don't get it, do you. When I'm in my fight gear, I know how to face anything. But you stripped me bare and got me in this glittery thing that gives me no protection against any of this." And all of a sudden, I feel terrible. I didn't think of that. To me, Cherie is hard as steel, and I've never seen her any different. But she's right, it's always been in the safety of her environment. Not like this.

"Shit, sorry. You can say no, and we will turn this car around now and take you home." I would never expect her to do anything that would upset her.

"Fuck no! But you owe me, big guy. Just remember that, and one day I will come calling to collect, and you won't be able to say no." And there she is, the fighter I know her to be. Shield up and ready to go into battle.

"Let's get your woman back, and in the meantime, I'm about to hand a few men their asses when they least expect it. Tonight might be the most interesting night of my life to date, and that's saying something."

"Damn, what have I done now?"

Both of us laughing, I didn't realize that the trip is over, and we are pulling up in front of the building where the function is being held. Cherie managed to take my mind off everything, even if only for a moment.

"You've given me a challenge, and you know how I love to win. So, buckle up, buddy."

Christ, I've created a monster.

Okay, let's do this. Let's get my girl. Because my body is aching just knowing she is almost near.

ELOUISE

"I don't know about this, Tori." I'm standing with my eyes closed as she walks me toward the mirror, not letting me look at myself until now.

It's been three hours here of a procession of people Tori organized to come to the house. First a massage which was divine, then hairdressers, makeup artists, and me trying not to freak out every five minutes. Blaise took it all in his stride mainly due to Sally being here to spend the day with him, which Tori of course had arranged without telling me.

The babysitter arrived fifteen minutes ago, and after settling her in with Blaise and giving her the rundown of the house, I'm now dressed and ready to see what I look like.

I have felt sick all day and wouldn't have eaten anything if it wasn't for Tori making me, and now, I'm even regretting that, because it feels like it's about to come back up.

"Okay, take a deep breath and then open your eyes," Tori whispers in my ear from behind me, and I'm almost too scared to do it.

But slowly, I raise my eyelids and don't recognize the woman before me.

"Stunning. Just absolutely gorgeous." I can hear the emotion in her voice as I'm still trying to come to terms with the makeover she has done on me.

"I can't believe it," I whisper to myself, my hands moving over my mouth in shock.

"I can. You never believed me when I told you how beautiful you were, even in your shabbiest clothes. But now maybe you will see what we all see, dressed up in a gown that leaves nothing to doubt. Time for the world to see the true queen you are."

Feeling water welling in my eyes, I quickly fan myself because I can't ruin the makeup now after all the effort that went into me looking like this.

"Don't make me cry." I turn and look at my best friend who has always believed in me.

"Okay, then I'll tell you the truth, you look like shit tonight, bitch." Tori's words have the exact effect she was hoping for. I can't help but laugh at the posh-looking redhead standing in front of me telling me how awful I look. My Tori is a woman of many talents.

Pulling the laughter back, I turn and take one last look in the mirror before I take my clutch from the bed and stand next to Tori, holding my arm out for her to take.

"Shall we?" Smiling at each other, we link arms and head downstairs to say good night to Blaise before we leave.

Walking into the lounge, Blaise looks up from coloring, and for the first time today, he stops talking and just stares at us. He's so stunned that his English words are lost and all he can say to me in French is, "*Tu es si jolie, Elouise. Papa t'aimera,*" in his sweetest voice.

I crouch down to him as he comes to give me a cuddle, but he hesitates to touch me. Reaching for him, I wrap him in my arms and whisper in his ear, "*Je l'espère, chérie. Je t'aime, Blaise, et merci.*" To have him tell me that his Papa will love me hit me so raw. I wanted to promise to bring Papa home with me, but I know enough that you never promise a child something unless you know one hundred percent that you can deliver.

As we start walking to the front door, Tori asks me what Blaise said.

"He just said we both looked pretty." I leave it at that. I want to keep that special moment for just Blaise and me.

Opening the front door, Nic is standing waiting for us, and he just smiles at me as he leans in to kiss his fiancé. I never doubted for a minute he would be here to escort us. There is no way he would let Tori go on her own, or me for that matter. Tori promised she wouldn't tell Nic, but either she couldn't help herself, which I expected, or Rem has told him, because the way he is looking at me right now, it's obvious he knows everything.

In a way, that gives me a little comfort because he isn't telling me not to do this.

"Good evening, beautiful ladies. I will be the envy of every man in the room with you both on my arm." His deep Australian accent sounds so smooth as he tries to woo his soon-to-be wife. He puts out both his arms for us to each take one to be helped down the few steps.

"Pfft, not likely. Lou doesn't need a man to walk her into the room. She is going to stride in there like she owns the place and claim her man," Tori blurts out as I almost throw up in my mouth.

"We all know that's not going to happen, but nice try, Tori," I say, sliding into the back of the limousine and on to the opposite seat so Tori and Nic can sit together, I feel so out of place, even if I do look the part.

"Don't you dare retreat into that shell of yours just yet. This is your Cinderella moment, and you better live it to its fullest." Tori is waving her finger at me like crazy, trying to make her point.

"Great, so if I can't sort Rem out by midnight, then I'm turning back into my usual pumpkin-looking self." I roll my eyes at her.

Nic grins. "It's almost seven pm, and I think if you make it to nine pm still clothed after Rem takes one look at you in that dress, then you'll be doing well. I don't think the midnight pumpkin hour will be a problem for you, Lou." His subtle wink confirms what I need to know.

Nic absolutely knows everything.

I don't know how I managed to walk from the car into the building, smiling at every person who greets us like I don't have a care in the world. I tried to keep my head down as we walked past the wall of photographers and flashes blasting us. At other events I've been to there were some, but nothing like tonight, and I know it has a lot to do with Flynn. There was extra security greeting us at the car, and I know that would have been Rem's doing, making sure we were safely ushered through the madness.

But now it's time, and as I take my first step into the room, Tori leans toward me with the biggest smile, mouthing the words to me, "Go get your man."

It's like the whole world is standing still as I look across the ballroom and see Rem in his perfectly tailored tuxedo. More than ever, he takes my breath away.

Until the moment I see him lean down and talk into the ear of a woman that is standing very close to him.

Both of them laugh and smile, sharing what looks like to be an intimate moment.

She is gorgeous, blonde, and everything I'm not.

Suddenly I can't breathe, and it's not from his hot looks this time. And it's not a figure of speech either, I literally can't seem to get any oxygen into my lungs.

The moment he turns and our eyes meet, the room gets darker, and all I see is him running toward me as I start to fall.

No, this can't be happening.

It's not how my Cinderella moment was supposed to go.

This is not how everyone was supposed to notice me, but there's not a thing I can do to stop it.

Don't worry, Flynn, I'm about to become the next viral video on the internet of a woman making a fool of herself, to knock you off the most-streamed views.

I suppose you call that karma.

Chapter Twenty-One

REMINGTON

The moment we walk into the ballroom, I can feel the sweat running down my back. My eyes scan the room as I do every time I enter one, especially an event as big as this. I knew that there would be plenty of people wanting to get that photo of Flynn to share with friends or waiting for him to do something newsworthy.

There is only one official event photographer allowed in the room, but with cameras in every phone in the room, nobody is safe from the gossip anymore.

Cherie leans closer to tell me, "If this was a real date, I would say you were really trying to impress me. This place is very glamorous."

"Oh, this couldn't be further from a date if we tried. Didn't I mention I brought you here as my secret bodyguard? Just in case either Flynn or El want to murder me tonight. And both of those scenarios are in the cards, let me assure you." Both of us laugh as we make our way across the room to where Forrest is standing at our table, but there's no sign of Flynn. I know he's here because his security detail messaged me to say that they had safely gotten him into the building without too much difficulty. Lots of photos, but thankfully, he managed to keep his mouth shut, and that is a miracle.

"Evening." Forrest first looks at me sternly, raising his eyebrows in a signal of what the hell is going on, not expecting for me to be here with a woman that isn't Elouise. But his manners get the better of him, and he turns to look at Cherie but is speaking to both of us.

"Hey, buddy. Forrest Taylor, this is my friend, Cherie Knight."

It takes a second and then realization dawns on him who she is. "As in Cherie from this morning's talk. That Cherie?" He's confused but at least doesn't look so pissed off with me now.

"I see my reputation has preceded me. Hello, Forrest." Cherie holds out her hand to shake his.

"You could say that." He laughs a little as he shakes her hand. "I just wasn't expecting to meet you so soon."

I shake my head. "No time like the present. Get it all out on the table in one day. Because as much as Nic keeps telling me it's messy, I fucking hate messy." I put my hand on Forrest's shoulder, thanking him for not making Cherie feel uncomfortable.

"I'll drink to that." Lifting two empty glasses off the table and reaching for the champagne bottle, Forrest pours us each a glass, and the three of us make a toast for less mess in our lives after tonight.

I spot Flynn across the room talking to a group of businessmen and women that I recognize as the staff from the external law firm we use. He is laughing and looks relaxed, which is a good start. Like we all knew he would, he has bounced back and is ignoring the whole thing, publicly that is, but it's behind closed doors I worry about him.

Leaning down, I whisper into Cherie's ear, "That guy over there to your left, the one in the middle of the crowd, owning the conversation, is Flynn. The king of attention. Think you can break him?"

Both of us chuckle as she answers, "Never met a man I couldn't break. Challenge accepted." As the words leave Cherie's mouth, I can feel eyes on me, and my body is on alert.

Elouise is in the room, I can sense it.

Turning to look toward the door, it feels like my heart has stopped beating.

Fuck me!

My lady in red.

A strapless dress is tightly fitted over every curve of her breasts and hips, all the way down her body until halfway down her thighs. The hem of the dress is curved on the front, lowering as it wraps around to the back of the dress. Sparkling netting is softly gathered and falls all the way to the floor from that seam. I try so hard to kickstart my heart, but the only part of my body I can feel moving is my cock that is now hard as rock and reminding me what I have been missing.

Our eyes meet, and I feel her anxiety rising rapidly from here, but something isn't right. Even with all the makeup, I can tell the color is draining from her face, and the anxiety is turning to fear as her body starts to sway slightly.

Shit.

My legs are moving on instinct because I know this is about to end badly.

Shoving people to the side as I'm trying to get to her, I can see her starting to faint and falling toward the ground. It's happening in slow motion, and it's like there isn't a sound in the room I can hear.

Nic and Tori have their backs to her, greeting the organizers who have been positioned just inside the doors all night.

There is no mistaking my heart beating now as my legs power me across the floor. I lunge to just get my hand under her head before it hits the floor, rolling her toward me so that she partially lands on me. I don't wait to check she is okay, just push to my feet and sweep her into my arms. I'm out the door as I hear the commotion erupt behind me. Tori is screaming Lou's name, and Nic holds her back, yelling to me he'll find help.

I don't need it! I just need some privacy.

One of my men is by my side as I stride from the room, and he points me to a room down the corridor. Pushing the door open, he hits the light switch for me and then closes the door behind him, and I know he will position himself right outside the door.

Then there is a voice of someone who is arguing with him, but I can't pay attention. I'm too busy laying El down on a couch. This is the room they must use for a wedding party to wait in before they enter their reception dinner. There are long counters and mirrors with strips of lights above them on the wall and plenty of comfortable seats around.

"El, wake up, baby, you need to wake up." She is clammy and still so pale. I need to find water or something, but I'm not leaving her. I'm never leaving her again. This is all my fault. Why was I so stupid? I should never have walked away. I should've just told her the truth that day.

"I'm sorry. I'm so sorry." I can't help it, I give her what she needs, my touch. Just like she calms my soul, I know I calm hers too. Being apart has turned the world upside down for both of us. Leaning down, I kiss her lips so softly, just willing her to open her eyes for me.

Her eyelids start to flutter a little, her body moving slightly.

The faintest whisper comes from her lips. "Rem…"

My hands are on either side of her face as those beautiful brown eyes start to focus on me properly. "I'm here, El, I'm right here. I'm not leaving." My thumb strokes her cheek, and I can see the color returning a little as she wakes up.

Kissing her forehead gently, I pull back to look her in the eyes again, when the door opens, and all I hear behind me is a voice still arguing with my guy on the door.

"I told you I'm a doctor, she needs to be checked, and they know me."

And then Tori's voice comes booming into the room. "If you want to keep your job, then I suggest you move aside."

I know my man won't move unless I tell him to--or one other person whose voice is then calmly speaking in the corridor. Nic.

"It's fine. We just need a moment. Thanks, Darren." Of course, Nic knows his name. He remembers every one of his staff. He has never mentioned it, but I know his memory is almost as good as mine, and that's saying something when I have a photographic memory.

Dr. Keats then comes storming into the room, and I swear if he touches her, I don't know if I'll be able to hold back from putting him on his ass.

I stand and place my body between them. "Stop right there." The tone of my voice tells him I'm not joking.

"Move, Rem, and let Drew check her out," Tori yells at me, but I haven't moved and neither has he.

"Not happening. I'm taking care of my girlfriend." I cross my arms over my chest and feel her hand touching my leg ever so gently.

Even when she is half out of it, El is still trying to be the calm in my storm.

"Good for you. Now move, so both my girlfriend, who is also a doctor, and I can check on Elouise and make sure it's just a simple fainting spell. You're lucky she keeps some supplies in her car." Drew stands up in front of me, not backing down, as a woman I've never seen before, dressed in her evening dress, comes into the room carrying a doctor's bag.

"Girlfriend?" I growl, looking at Tori who shrugs sheepishly at me.

"Well, it worked. Someone had to push you to stand up and tell the world you were together."

Nic looks down at Tori, and I can tell he wants to kill her as much as I do right now.

"We will be discussing this later," I say, glaring at Tori and stepping to the side but only enough that I'm now at the side of the couch and leaning over, holding on to El's hand.

"Oh God, did you think I was here for Elouise? Damn, Remington, I knew from that first meeting she was off limits. The way you looked at her and spoke to me, it was a clear message of back the fuck off. It was obvious she was never just your nanny. Still, I called her when you weren't around to make sure, but it was obvious she had no interest in me. Christ, you were at every appointment after that initial one, even though you said you wouldn't be, and didn't move more than a foot away from her. And I'm thankful because then I met Paulini soon after." Who is already on her knees next to El and talking to her in hushed tones.

"I'm so confused." El is looking up to me from the couch.

"You and me both, baby, you and me both."

Everyone then just remains silent while Paulini and Drew check over El who is now sitting up and sipping some water slowly.

The last few days are streaming through my thoughts. It's all piecing together now.

Freaking Tori and her interference were the catalyst for all this derailing. But although I'm frustrated and still must fix this, I can't be mad at her. She's right. We needed a push, and in true Tori style, she just used the biggest bulldozer she could find.

"Elouise appears fine, perhaps just a dip in her blood sugar or a panic attack. Just needs to take it easy and perhaps see your doctor for a full checkup to be sure." Paulini stands while Drew is packing up her doctor bag and then rises to his feet and places his arm around her waist.

"Thank you both, and my apologies for the way I acted. It seems there was a misunderstanding on my part." I put my hand out to shake both of theirs, and by this stage, Tori is sitting next to her best friend, and it looks like they are arguing in whispers.

"I'll take Elouise home now so she can rest." And while both doctors are nodding at me, behind me, I hear both female voices in unison.

"No!" El sounding very determined.

"Yes!" Tori using her bossy voice, trying to make her point too.

"Good luck with that," is all I get from Drew before he leans forward and quietly in my ear tells me that she is okay to stay for the night if El feels up to it. They are here and will keep an eye on her. Then he steps away and leaves the room with Paulini.

It's then that I look at Nic who has been silently standing to the side of the commotion, and without saying a word, he knows what I need him to do.

Walking to Tori, he takes her hand, not giving her a choice to stand up.

"Time to go back to the dinner and see if we can get through the rest of the night without any more attention on us." The way he looks down at Tori, I know that is his way of warning her to be on her best behavior for the rest of the night. "Do you think you can manage that, my crazy one."

Reluctantly, she blows a kiss to Elouise and playfully slaps Nic on his chest. "Whatever do you mean?" Both of them laugh as they walk out, and Nic closes the door behind him.

The air in the room starts to feel heavy, and my mind is racing.

From behind me there is a fragile voice from the woman I love, and her question is a good place to start.

"Who is she, Rem? And why is she here?" Tears are welling in her eyes, and I don't want her to pass out on me again from feeling so anxious. I caused that panic attack, and I feel like such an idiot for letting this go this far.

Moving quickly, I sit next to her, lifting her up and placing her in my lap. I need her close and to be able to stop her from running if she panics.

"Bold of you to assume I'm ready to touch you." Trying her best to be brave, El sits up, tall and rigid.

"Stupid of you to think I can't tell that you need to be touching me as much as I need to be holding you." Kissing her cheek, I'm laughing on the inside at her trying so hard to dismiss me, yet her body is slowly softening into mine.

Not waiting any longer, I start.

"That woman out there is Cherie, a woman I should have told you about months ago, the first night you moved into my home. I knew then that there was no way I could walk away from you, and I should have been honest from the beginning."

"Yes, you should have." Turning her face, she looks me straight in the eye.

"But you have to know deep down she's not a prostitute, and I would never cheat on you, and with a hooker of all people. Come on, El, do you truly think that low of me?" There is still hurt there that she jumped to that conclusion, but we can work on that later.

"I'm sorry. It was stupid, but why couldn't you just have told me? You have to admit it looked sleazy, that place you went to. Running off whenever things got too tough emotionally between us and openly admitting you were going to see a woman I had never heard of. And then I see you walk into a building next to a strip club that is obviously far from a club and looks like I imagine a brothel would look. Then when I challenge you on it, you say nothing… and walk away." Nothing is holding back the tears now, and they run freely down her cheeks.

"Please don't cry, baby. I promise it's nothing like that." Taking the pocket square from my suit, I dab her face, trying not to ruin her makeup that she has obviously worked hard on for tonight. "I know this is going to sound crazy, but Cherie is a counsellor that I have been seeing for over ten years on and off. The way she runs her sessions with me is through us boxing together, and she makes me spill everything that is trapped inside my head while I'm busy trying to stop my body from being hurt. She is a kickass woman who has worked hard in life to get where she is and gives so much to the street kids in that area, trying to teach them a better life than drugs and street gangs. That's why the gym is located in that part of town." Before I can keep going, she starts firing questions at me.

"You box with a woman, like hit her? I know you, Rem, you could never hurt a woman. How do you cope with that? How does that even work, talking and boxing at the same time? You know, like mentally, how does it help you?" El is almost running out of breath trying to ask everything that is circling in that beautiful brain of hers.

"We have plenty of time to talk all this through, but I want to make sure you understand this. I have never slept with Cherie, never wanted to, never thought of it. I've never kissed her, and if I did, it would feel like kissing a sister. Also, I haven't slept with another woman since that night in Rome where you seduced me and stole my heart. I never told you, but I knew that night that you were meant to be mine. I just didn't know how to make that happen without both our worlds falling down around us. But the universe handed me the answer in a sweet dark-haired little boy who then made us fall in love with him."

The relief in her eyes and the way her body has now completely molded against mine, I can feel the world starting to spin in the right direction again.

"But you haven't been honest with me either," I say. "You pushing me away all the time has more to it than worrying about Blaise, Flynn, and the rest of our friends. What is holding you back from really being with me?"

She sighs, knowing she needs to tell me but still not really wanting to say it. I know the feeling; today has been so draining emotionally, baring my soul.

"A guy named Keith that I met the summer before I started college. We got quite close, and he wanted to go backpacking around the world and for me to forget about becoming a teacher. Of course, you know I'm not that adventurous and teaching was my dream, but I thought I was falling in love, so I was torn. In the end I told him I couldn't go with him, and that's when he told me that I would never amount to anything much and I should go off and live my boring life in the suburbs. That's where I obviously belong." The water in her eyes tells me it still hurts. "But after a while, I thought he was right, because I was happy in my life, so I found my place. Then the whirlwind of Nic and Tori happened, and the next thing I know, I'm in a world I don't belong in and never will. This dress might make me look like Cinderella at a ball, but at midnight, I will always turn back into the boring teacher I am meant to be. You need a woman who belongs in your world."

My heart is aching for her. She has no idea how far from the truth that is.

"Baby, you belong in all those worlds, yours and mine, and I'm going to prove it to you so you can see how amazing you truly are. Don't ever put yourself in a box like that. Because as high as you build your walls, I will always break through them." I kiss her on the forehead as I continue what I need to say.

"We hurt each other by keeping secrets, and that needs to stop. Later tonight when you are lying in my arms in our bed, totally satisfied after multiple orgasms, we have lots to talk through, but right now, there is only one important thing I need to tell you."

I lift her chin up from where her head is now burrowed into my shoulder. "I love you, El. Not just the normal love. That deep gut-wrenching kind of love where I know if I can't be with you then I can't survive." I kiss her on each cheek and then hover my lips above hers. "The forever kind of love."

Finally, I kiss her like I have been dying to do for days.

It's not soft or smooth. I wrap my hand behind her neck and press her so tightly to me that our kiss is rough and frantic, both our bodies wanting more. The moment her lips part with a slight lustful groan, my tongue delves into her, and I make sure she knows how desperate I am to have her.

What started as a sweet declaration has turned into a hot, heated, claiming kiss. One that I should have saved for later at home, but I can't hold back now.

The moment her hands are in my hair and those red-painted nails scraping on my scalp, I know there is no way we are making it out of this room without me being inside her. Just once is all I need to remind her where her home is, wrapped around me while I make her see stars.

Pulling my mouth from hers, she's gasping, but I can see the fire in her eyes, and that is enough for me.

I'm about to move her from my lap, but she has other ideas. "I love you." She slides her hands to my beard, tugging at it like she loves to do, knowing it drives me crazy. "God, it feels so good to say that. I love you so much, and I trust you. I honestly do. Now fuck me, right here, right now. I can't wait."

My hands are on her waist, ready to lift her to stand, but the moment she is halfway up, she throws her leg over my lap and straddles me on the couch. There is red tulle everywhere between us, but El knows what she wants, and she is taking it. She pushes all of the dress out of the way and pulls my zipper down, popping the button, and my cock is in her hands before I have time to say a word. She rocks her body over my cock that is about to explode at the feel of lace on my skin, and her moan is all it takes for me to erupt with a loud guttural groan and assume control.

"You want to be my bad girl, don't you." My hands find hers under the dress and push them out of the way, feeling lace covering her bare pussy. With one finger, I move it to the side, and straight away, I thrust two fingers inside her. "God, so fucking wet for me, you dirty thing. It's getting you off just thinking about riding my cock and the danger of someone walking in on us, isn't it?"

"Mhmm, yesss." She's trying to talk in her quivering voice, but every time I push down on her clit with my thumb, she bites down on her bottom lip.

Taking my cock in my other hand, I pull my fingers out. I don't give her time to take a breath as she rises above me, and I thrust up with my hips and impale her on top of me.

I want to scream out her name, but this is just between us. No one else. I will not embarrass her any more than has happened already.

"Not a word. You take me hard, take it all, and hold your screams inside." Both my hands are on her waist now and holding on tight as she rides me just like she wants.

"That's it, baby, let it all go. But you can't scream. The only release you are allowed is coming so fucking hard that I can feel it running all over my balls." God, I want her beautiful tits in my mouth, but they are strapped in tight in this temptress dress that is doing its job and driving me wild. I need to mark her. Pulling her body closer, I move my mouth to the bare skin of her shoulder, desperate to sink my teeth in.

"Don't. You. Dare," El grinds out between me pounding up into her.

"Then come so I can let go deep inside you. One way or another I'm marking you as mine, and you get to choose which way it's happening." I growl out the words like a feral animal, and it's enough to have El throwing her head back, mouth open, and the hands that were on the back of the couch are now in my hair, pulling on it hard. It's all I need, and I come so fucking hard inside her.

The moment she falls forward onto me, her head on my shoulder and my arms wrapped so tightly around her back, I can feel my heart beating a steady rhythm again. The one that tells me I have control, and now I know what I need to do to keep it in my life.

To love El with all that I am and never let anything come between us.

Simple.

Thank God there is a bathroom in here so we could both clean ourselves up and look presentable enough that no one will know that I just fucked her within an inch of her life. Well, that's what it felt like for me.

Standing at the door of the room, her hand in mine, I've never seen her look more beautiful in my life.

"You sure you're ready to do this?" I ask, giving her the last chance to let me take her home. We sat and talked for a little while before she insisted that she was going back into that ballroom, head held high and showing how strong she can be, not letting a little fainting spell hold her back. And of course, she is not leaving without meeting Cherie, because apparently, they have a lot to discuss. I should be worried, but I'm really not. I want El to ask every question she has and give Cherie the chance to show El what an awesome person she is.

"I want a second chance at my Cinderella moment, and don't you dare take that away from me. I mean, I think we can safely say I have claimed my prince, but I need to clear away a few things before I turn back into the pumpkin." I can't help but laugh as I open the door, and Darren steps to the side. I see a slight blush on her cheeks, wondering how much he heard. I can tell her he heard everything but he will never repeat it to a soul, but she doesn't need to know that.

As we walk back down the corridor, I lean down and whisper to her.

"You know that's not how the story goes, right? Cinderella is not the pumpkin, and I am far from a prince."

I missed the soft little giggle that slips from her lips.

"Yeah, but it's my story, and I get to make up the ending my way." Smiling up at me, she squeezes my hand that little bit tighter as we stop outside the ballroom doors.

Both of us simultaneously take a deep breath, standing that little bit taller and edging closer.

"I heard the word messy being thrown around to describe us." She squeezes my hand as tight as she can then pushes on the door before I can, announcing to me as she drags me through it, "Well, I love being messy with you—dirty, bad, and oh so messy." She smiles at me with fire in her eyes, and I'm thankful that my jacket is covering my pants because my cock is ready to make her messy again and again.

Seeing everyone looking at us as we head across the now fully seated room, I try to work out how quickly I can make an excuse for us to leave. I'm feeling very anti-social now.

Looking for Flynn, I find him at our table. He looks up and sees us holding hands, smiles, and goes straight back to talking to Cherie. But what really throws me is the way Forrest is seated on the other side of her, looking at her the same way that Flynn is.

Oh, the man-whisperer has them both under her spell, and I hope like hell I don't have to pull them apart later. I laugh to myself. How does the saying go? *"Not my circus, not my monkeys."*

I have enough in my life to focus my attention on. I don't need to add someone else's to it.

The moment we arrive at the table, Tori is up and wrapping El in her arms, scolding her for not going home but also glad to see her. Especially now that she has her twinkle back in her eye and the most beautifully just-fucked blush on her cheeks. Some secrets are worth keeping when it's just between us.

Cherie stands tentatively and walks around to us with a look I have never seen on her face. But my gentle girlfriend doesn't surprise me one bit when she reaches out and hugs her with pure kindness and compassion for how Cherie must be feeling. As they finally pull apart, El is smiling and has Cherie's hands in hers.

"I'm sorry for thinking the worst, please forgive me." Cherie is shaking her head, trying to tell her there is no need for this, but I know my El, and she doesn't have a mean bone in her body. She needs to make things right. "I want to thank you for taking such good care of him. He's a complex soul, and I know this is old news for you, but I'm learning now too."

"If that is the polite way of saying he is a big pain in the ass, then I agree."

Both women look at me and then burst out laughing together.

"I knew this was a mistake. One I'm going to regret for years to come, I'm sure."

I pull the chair out for El to sit next to me, but she brushes my hand aside. "You can bet on that. Now swap seats, all you guys. Cherie is with Tori and me tonight. We have a lot to discuss and to get to know our new friend. Right, ladies?"

And within seconds, Tori has the table rearranged so that Cherie is sitting between her and El. Nic sits next to Tori, and I'm on the other side of El, and next to me is Flynn with Forrest beside him. There are two empty seats which I'm guessing were for Drew and Paulini, but I can see they are sitting over on our lawyers' table now. I'll thank whoever arranged that later.

Tonight is just about my circle. The people at this table who I owe everything to.

El places her hand over mine on the table, and although I'm not sure how much affection I should show in front of Flynn just yet, he takes the worry straight from my mind.

"Just want you to know I'm happy for you. I see it now. You're her penguin."

I look at him, wondering what he means.

"You know, penguins, they mate for life. She's your penguin, Rem."

I turn to look back at El, laughing and smiling like she is right where she belongs.

"Yeah, buddy, she's my penguin."

And the warmth of that thought moves through every cell in my body.

Then, in true Flynn style, the moment is broken with his voice in my ear. "Now tell me, where the fuck did you find Cherie? She's fucking dynamite, and why have you been hiding her from us?"

Yep, this is about to get fucking messy! And I wouldn't want it any other way.

Well, maybe if I could just ask for a controlled mess, but I know I'm kidding myself. Time to learn the new normal in life. And as long as El and Blaise are right beside me, I'll take it.

Bring it on, universe.

Epilogue

2 Months Later

ELOUISE

"I'm in the office, El." Hearing Rem's voice is always a comfort when I arrive home in the middle of the day on Blaise's preschool day. It's like we get to be adults, dating without being parents of a now five-year-old little boy, after he celebrated his birthday last month.

Blaise was so excited with the little party we had for him with a few of his new preschool friends, and of course all the adults who treat him as part of their family.

After the air was cleared with Dr. Keats, things were completely normal again when we saw him for Blaise's five-year-old checkup. We were both relieved to know that the heart murmur was getting better and was barely there at all now. Drew expects that he will have outgrown it in the next year, fingers crossed.

I've just left my doctor's appointment that I had finally booked after my fainting spell quite a few weeks ago, but I kept putting off seeing the doctor because I felt fine, and life just became so busy. But

Rem and Tori kept bugging me, and in the end, Rem booked the appointment for me.

After the night of the charity dinner, my secret fascination with child psychology quickly became a passion the moment I met Cherie. I couldn't stop talking to her and learning all she could teach me about how the mind works and not just what's in the textbooks. This woman has real-world experience that is so much more valuable to me. It didn't take long before Rem was encouraging me to investigate studying to be a psychologist and gaining my qualifications, specializing in working with children. I didn't realize how much I really wanted to do this until the opportunity was put in front of me. I can still look after Blaise and study during the day, especially when he starts school next year and my days will be free.

I loved my job as a teacher, but I think I can do more for children who are in need of special care and whose families can't afford it. The day I resigned from my job, I cried tears of sadness for the end of a part of my life that brought me so much joy. But it didn't last long, when that night lying in bed with Rem, after he'd made sweet passionate love to me, he asked me if I would be the joint CEO of a charity he was setting up with Cherie. They want to expand her gym catering for youth and adults, setting it up in other cities across the UK. My job would be to run the business side with Rem, and once I'm trained and qualified, I'll jump into the counselling side with Cherie and concentrate on helping the kids when boxing isn't their thing. We can find another activity that is physical that also has the brain distracted while we work on their mental health.

It's still in the very early stages, but Nic has already given Rem a million pounds to help get it off the ground. It was an emotional day out at the farm the day he told Rem he wanted to be involved. Now that we are in the new era of our friend group, where big secrets are not allowed between any of us, Nic and Tori decided it was time to share that they anonymously organize a large charity called the ARD Foundation, which Nic took over running from his grandfather. It was set up in memory of his father and grandmother, and he said looking back, he could have benefited from something like what we are doing to help him deal with his misplaced anger at his father, so he decided he wanted to share part of that money with our new venture. It's extremely generous, and Rem couldn't speak for a few minutes, trying to take it all in.

So many changes are happening, and I'm just not sure how I'll keep up with it all.

I walk straight over to Rem in his chair that he pushed back from his desk as soon as he saw me come through the door.

He loves to have me in his lap, and if I'm honest, I enjoy being snuggled there too.

Kissing me long and lovingly, he finally lets me go and looks at me with care. "Everything go okay with the appointment?"

And that's the big question, isn't it.

Did it all go okay? The answer would be yes. Was it what I expected? That is a yes-and-no answer, just as confusing.

"El, are you okay? Why are you quiet?" Shifting in his chair, he sits us up straighter.

"I'm fine, I'm fine, no need to worry. But let's just say the visit didn't quite go as planned."

"Are you sick, what is it? Tell me!"

"You know how you told me you could handle a messy life with me?"

"Every day and twice on Sundays, but what has that got to do with anything?" I could see the wheels in his brain turning and piecing things together. "Oh shit, how messy are we talking here?" Rem's face gets a little paler.

"Like the patter of another set of tiny feet kind of messy." I finally let the happy tears start to fall that I have been holding in since the shock in the doctor's office.

Rem's head falls back onto his chair as he tries to take it all in, and then he quickly pulls back and looks at me.

"But we were always careful… Oh shit, that night at the dinner in that damn red dress. I was so desperate to have you that we didn't use protection. Fuck, we slipped up a few times, but it was the dress that did it, wasn't it?" He slaps his forehead with his hand, and I'm trying not to laugh at him. "You make me so reckless. I'm sorry, sweetheart."

"Aren't you happy?" Panic quickly starts to fill my stomach.

"No, that's not it at all. I'm just sorry I took away your choice of the timing of a baby." His hand is on my cheek, and I can't help leaning into it, finding the warmth his touch always brings to me.

"The universe has a habit of choosing things for us, so why would now be any different?" My giggle is now mixing with my tears.

"A baby." His voice is so soft and gentle. "We're having a baby. I couldn't be happier." Rem takes a few breaths while still processing our news. "I love you so much I don't know what to do with it all some days, and you have just given me the answer. Another person for me to share my heart with. Oh, El, please tell me these are happy tears." He uses his sleeve to wipe my face which is just a waste of time.

"Of course they are. And if you keep saying soppy things like that then there is going to be a waterfall of tears shortly. Welcome to pregnancy hormones. We might not have planned this little one, but I'm just so in love already. I knew I always wanted kids, and from the moment I met you, I knew I wanted them with you. I thought we would have more time, but what does it matter? We are already parents anyway, so what's one more to add to the family? A little girl maybe, with your gorgeous brown curls."

"And your big brown eyes and loving heart." He pulls me into a hug with my head now snuggled into his shoulder where I feel like I'm home.

"Or I would love another little boy like Blaise too." Saying his name makes me sit up and look at Rem. "Oh my God, Blaise is going make the best big brother." I throw my arms around the back of Rem's neck and hug him with such excitement.

Who would have thought I would be the first to have a baby between me and Tori. She is going to be happy for me, and I doubt she'll be jealous. She's out there loving her life, conquering the world, one hotel at a time, oh and a haunted castle, we can't forget that. I have no doubt she will have children, just not yet. There is time for her when she is ready.

"Shit, the wedding, I'm not going to fit into my dress. I'll have to tell Tori. She's going to kill me." Not sure a pregnant best friend was what she was counting on in her wedding photos. I did tell her we would need a cloth sac for me to wear, and now I might be right.

"You are delirious. She is going to be screaming with excitement and will just find you another dress. I can't imagine you will be that big in another three months' time. Not that I know anything about pregnancy, which sounds weird for the father of a five-year-old." I can see a little twinge of sadness in Rem's face for all the time he missed in Blaise's life, but to be honest, I'm not sure he would have been ready when he was born. His instinct would have been to just throw money at the problem and move on with life.

As sad as it is that Blaise lost his mother, the universe knew exactly the right time to bring him into our life, and I will always be grateful to Camille for the gift she gave us both that brought us together.

"Is it selfish of me to not want to tell Tori just yet? Let this special news just be ours for a little while." Slowly letting go of Rem, I sit back slightly to look at him.

"Not at all, but can I ask one thing?" he asks, a smile on his face as he places both his hands on my cheeks. "Can it only be for a few days? I don't think any of us in our circle can cope with big secrets anymore." His lips softly touching mine brings butterflies to my stomach and that tingle he gives me running through my nerves.

As he sits back smiling, I know there is more in his mind now, because that is not an "*I love you so much*" smile. It's the "*I want to bury myself inside you and I'm just deciding where I want to take you*" smile.

"We have an hour to celebrate, so move that sexy ass of yours upstairs onto our bed. I've heard pregnancy hormones make women horny. Let's test out that theory." He pushes me off his lap and onto my feet. But before I have time to start walking, he picks me up and throws me over his shoulder.

"Rem, stop, I'm too heavy," I squeal as he starts storming up the stairs like he is on a mission.

"Do you hear me complaining? Even when you are fully pregnant, I'll still carry you. That's my job, to carry the load for you."

I know he is trying to be sweet, but there is no way he will be lifting me when I weigh another nine pounds for the baby and every extra pound I put on too. He's dreaming.

"Oh God, you are going to be one of those overprotective boyfriends and fathers, aren't you. You'll treat me like glass and won't let me or the baby out of your sight." I laugh as he places me down in our bedroom, his hands on my waist and wearing the most serious look, his forehead in lines and his lips straight.

"Yes," is all he replies, looking at me and waiting for me to complain, but I can't do that to him.

"Good. I'm looking forward to feeling your love through the way you protect your family… even if it will be a bit overbearing, but I'm sure we will cope."

"Lucky. Because you know there will be no choice, right? It's who I am." Rem's hands move to my shirt and start to undo the buttons.

"I wouldn't want you any other way." I kiss him again as he continues to get me naked, and all talking ceases as he has me screaming his name and forgetting my own.

Life with Rem is precious, beautiful, and full of grand orgasms, and I wouldn't change it for the world.

3 Months Later - The Wedding

REMINGTON

Flying into Australia for the wedding was a challenge, getting everyone out of the office but more so out of the country at the same time. But what the boss, or should I say bosses want, the bosses get.

Flynn and Forrest will fly home the day after the wedding, then we've planned for the jet to come back for us so I can spend a few days relaxing in the sun with my two and a half special people. It will be the first time we have holidayed together, and I'm looking forward to a few days of turning off work. Not that I'm ever completely detached but as much as I can be, and luckily, Elouise totally understands that. Especially with the charity getting off the ground shortly and the fitting out on the new building almost complete, there are decisions that need to be made that just can't wait.

Cherie and Elouise have become so close, and when you add Tori into the mix, it's a wild time. Cherie was invited to the wedding but decided to stay and supervise the construction, while she also has some clients she didn't want to leave just yet, until we have other staff trained up to take the load off her. While my life has changed so much, it certainly has for her too.

Yesterday was a day that not only will I have imprinted on my brain, but the photos that I couldn't stop taking will be memories for us to look back at, and I already know which one I'm framing for my office at home. Sitting on the sand, camera in my hand, I watched El in her bikini that she looked amazing in, with her precious pregnant belly on show and Blaise kept coming up to her and kissing it, while she was soaking up the sun on our growing little baby. She was still hesitant to wear it, but after a few whispered words on what it does to me seeing her in it and the rewards that will come later tonight, she was parading around our villa at the resort like a runway model as I cheered her on, laughing together. I love those precious stolen moments we get. Just simple but full of love.

And now we have made it, and it's a perfect sunny day for a beach wedding, on the same beach that Nic proposed to Tori on. A place that is special to him and the memory of his dad. The music starts, and looking to the back of the crowd, I'm smiling hard at the vision in front of me. Not sure Tori and Nic ever planned on having a page boy in their wedding party, but watching Blaise walking down the aisle holding El's hand brings tears to my eyes, and I don't cry, well, rarely. Dressed in his little bone-colored shorts, a white shirt, and a brown bow tie, kicking his bare feet in the sand, he is so damn cute. Makes me proud of the boy he is growing up to be.

Escorting him is his mama El, which he asked if he could start calling her now. She has her own baby inside that is just for Blaise, well, that's what he keeps telling everyone. Between hormones and the immense happiness it brought her, El was so overwhelmed. However, she insisted he call her Mama El, not wanting to take anything away from Camille. She has the biggest heart, and I'm so grateful she has chosen to share it with us both.

Elouise on the other hand is far from cute. The bigger her belly grows, the more beautiful she looks. The olive-green dress she is wearing, that can barely contain her ever-expanding plump breasts, flows so softly over her tiny baby bump, and I just wonder how I got so lucky.

I was never going to be in a relationship, have a family, or settle down my crazy adrenaline-filled lifestyle. Yet I haven't felt the need to go on one daredevil trip since I told Elouise how much I loved her, and then she dropped the bombshell we were expecting a baby. She made me promise I wouldn't do anything to put myself in danger. I told her I couldn't guarantee that in my job, but that for the time being, I would stop purposefully picking things to do that make my blood rush. After a heated discussion, we agreed that was the rule for now, but I reserved the right to revisit it later. She doesn't want to change who I am, but I understand her fear of losing me and obviously the fear of Blaise losing another parent. Luckily, the new dirt bike I ordered for Blaise hasn't arrived yet, so I haven't had to get through that argument yet.

The week after we found out about the baby, I paid the deposit on an estate near Nic and Tori's place in the countryside. El just laughed at me, knowing full well I had been thinking about it for a while. I wasn't waiting because I want it renovated and the security system and office fully functional by the time the baby is born. We can then escape to the country to be alone and take time to find our feet as a family of four.

But I didn't promise El that I would wrap Blaise up in bubble wrap either. He's a boy and needs room to just be a healthy, adventurous terror, just like I was. My parents laughed and said it was payback for what they went through with me, much to Elouise's dismay. She proclaimed it's not fair that she has to endure the payback too.

What I love about the property is the size of the house, and there are two guest houses already built which is perfect for our large family. Both sets of parents want to be around, and with my crazy sister's kids and Elouise having so many brothers, it's perfect to have space out of the main house when they visit.

I spend the whole ceremony with my eyes just on El, watching her cry happy tears for our friends, while Blaise is sitting at her feet, playing in the sand.

Although parts of our relationship have all happened so fast, I don't want to rush marriage. I plan on putting a ring on El's finger as soon as we get home from Australia, but I want her to have a day just like this, her in the white dress of her dreams that doesn't need to be modified for our little bubba that she is keeping safe right now. But I want her to know there is no doubt I'm all in with her, and there is no other woman I want to share my life with for the rest of our days.

Love is a big emotion! One I didn't know how to navigate for most of my life. But now that I've found it, there is nothing easier than to be with the person who owns my love.

And I'm no prince, but she is my Cinderella.

The woman who is gentle, kind, and a natural beauty. She sadly couldn't see it in herself, but I've made it my life's mission to tell her every single day.

I hear the celebrant announce that Nic can kiss his bride, and everyone cheers loudly when he doesn't just kiss her gently, but so heated we are all calling for them to get a room already.

The reception has been in full swing now for over an hour, and Blaise is out on the dance floor with Tori and El, dancing his little heart out. I'm not sure who will sleep the best tonight, him or El.

Standing to the side of the dance floor with the guys, we are all just laughing about random things and enjoying being away from the hustle of our fast-paced lives.

"What the fuck is she doing here?" Flynn announces with dismay, which has the rest of us turning quickly to see Felisha Kentwall standing at the door to the room, looking a little the worse for wear and waving for Flynn to come to her.

We got close but never found the person who leaked that video, and as we suspected, it disappeared from the gossip sites as soon as there was another scandal with a married actor and his costar in the US. Yet another standard Hollywood scandal that I'm sure half the time are leaked to promote the upcoming movie.

"I'll go." My instinct already has me moving, but before I get a few steps, Flynn grabs my arm and stops me.

"No! This is my mess. Let me be the one to sort out the next chapter. Apparently, my life is not just a news story but a fucking novel with way too many plot twists for my liking." Flynn storms toward Felisha with determination.

Looking at Nic and Forrest, my fists are clenched because I don't want anything wrecking this day for my friends. "I'm giving him ten minutes and then I'm out there. I don't trust either of them not to do some dumb shit that I'm left to clean up again."

There wasn't any laughing from any of us because we all know it's more than likely true.

I'd hoped we were moving away from a messy life, but I guess not. Looks like I'll be spending the rest of my days controlling everyone else's messes. And loving every minute of it!

Because I live to control the uncontrollable.

FLYNN

Walking toward Felisha, I'm confused but also really worried about why she's here and looking like someone stole her puppy.

I don't even know if she has a puppy, but she'd look cute with one.

The closer I get, the more worried I am because I can tell she has been crying, and this woman in front of me is a tough one. She's someone I wouldn't want to pick a fight with in the boardroom, because I know there's no way she would back down.

"Felisha, what are you doing here, what's wrong?" Taking her by the hand, I lead her outside to a quiet place where the palm trees are gently blowing in the sea breeze and the moonlight is reflected softly on the water.

"I'm sorry. I'm so sorry. I didn't know what else to do. You told me where the wedding was just in case something happened, and I didn't want to give away the secret, but I just felt so lost and needed you." She can't hold her tears back now, and I can't help but pull her into my arms, letting her sob freely but also to feel safe doing it.

After she starts to pull herself together, I can't help asking her more questions. "Are you okay, are you in trouble, what can I do to help?" Fuck, I wish she would just tell me what is going on.

"I was in such shock, I just brought a ticket on a commercial flight and left because I didn't know what to do." Surprisingly, she has hardly any makeup on and just a small overnight bag at her feet.

"Shock from what? What the hell is going on?" I know it's something big, because Felisha Kentwall doesn't do commercial flights, that's what her family's private jet is for.

"It's my father. My own father was the one who filmed me with you and blackmailed Nic. He sold his own daughter's body. My body!"

Rage runs wild through my body, and I want to rip that pathetic old man's throat out.

"All to stop me from taking over the company on my fortieth birthday as planned in the articles of association that govern the way the company is run. They were put in place by my grandfather before he died, and my father hasn't been able to change them. If he couldn't stop it, then he would bury me instead." The tears start to dry up as she is looking at me. I can tell all she needs is someone on her team who has the power to help her.

I can be her strength!

And that's why she flew halfway around the world to find me, because I'm the only one who truly understands how she feels.

"The only person who is going to regret this tape ever being made is your father!" My voice is no longer full of softness and compassion for her. That's not what she needs.

She needs me to be the man she submitted to that night.

"Are you ready to fight?" I ask, putting my hands on her shoulders and standing her up straight.

"I am now!" Her beautiful eyes light up again, and I know it's game on!

Thank you for reading *The Desire*. If you enjoyed Rem and El's story and would like to know what happened behind closed doors when Rem sent El the gift of lingerie in chapter 16, there is a free bonus scene available for my newsletter subscribers.

Visit www.karendeen.com.au/bonus-content and subscribe to my newsletter to to download your FREE copy of
The Desire Bonus Scene - The Gift

Read on for a sneak peak of ***Gorgeous Gyno*** - *Book 1* of *The Chicago Boys* series.

Also by Karen Deen

The Craving

Gorgeous Gyno

Private Pilot

Naughty Neuro

Lovable Lawyer

The Chicago Boys Box Set (above 4 books in one set)

New Year's Eve with The Chicago Boys (Novella collection)

That Day

Better Day

Defining Us

Love's Wall

Love's Dance

Love's Hiding

Love's Fun

Love's Hot

Time for Love Box Set (All Love's books in one set)

Acknowledgments

This story of Remington and Elouise came to me at midnight one night, ten days after the release of The Craving. I grabbed my phone, and I couldn't get my fingers to type quick enough to take down my thoughts before I went to sleep. I knew I loved them before they knew they loved each other.

Writing is my love, my passion, and a part of my soul that once I found it has brought me so much happiness. But at times it can be difficult and really push you to places where you need to work harder to get the story written. This book was one of those, and I want to thank everyone who reminded me every day that I could do this.

To my beta readers, Lee, Di, Lisa, Christine, and Nicole. Thank you for all you do for me, the suggestions and fact checking, the cheering from the sidelines, and the love you share. You are all amazing.

To my editor Lindsay from Contagious Edits who holds my hand and guides me through the nightmare of making the story readable. One day I'm going to write a list of all the Aussie slang you have sent me a note wondering what the hell I'm talking about. It's almost a challenge every book to slip something in there for you. Couldn't do this without you, and I'm so thankful of how patient you are with me missing every deadline!

Thank you to Sarah at The Book Cover Boutique for an awesome cover as always and Wander Aguiar for a great image. And to Linda and the girls at Foreword PR & Marketing who helped me to get this book out there.

To my wonderful PA Lee who suffers in silence at all I throw at her at times, but never complains. Life is so much better with you picking up my messy pieces. Thank you from the bottom of my heart.

To my family who have been patient with me as I found my feet working as a full-time author. Not once have they questioned my dream of living this life, and I'm so blessed to have them all around me, supporting me and loving me. You are my world, and I'm so grateful every day for you all.

Most importantly to you, my fantastic readers. I can't thank you all enough for continuing to buy my books and love my stories. The joy you bring me at reading your kind reviews and the messages on how much you love my books fills my heart.

Thank you, thank you, thank you.

I hope you love Rem and El as much as I do.

Until next time, I'll see you between the pages.

Karen xx

GORGEOUS Gyno

KAREN DEEN

Chapter One

MATILDA

Today has disaster written all over it.

Five fifty-seven am and already I have three emails that have the potential to derail tonight's function. Why do people insist on being so disorganized? Truly, it's not that hard.

Have a diary, use your phone, write it down, order the stock – whatever it takes. Either way, don't fuck my order up! I shouldn't have to use my grown-up words before six am on a weekday. Seriously!

I'm standing in the shower with hot water streaming down my body. I feel like I'm about to draw blood with how hard I'm scrubbing my scalp, while I'm thinking about solutions for my problems. It's what I'm good at. Not the hair-pulling but the problem-solving in a crisis. A professional event planner has many sneaky tricks up her sleeve. I just happen to have them up my sleeve, in my pockets, and hiding in my shoes. As a last resort, I pull them out of my ass.

I need to get into the office to find a new supplier that can have nine hundred mint-green cloth serviettes delivered to the hotel by lunchtime today. You would think this is trivial in the world. However, if tonight's event is not perfect, it could be the difference between my dream penthouse apartment or the shoebox I'm living in now. I'll be damned if mint napkins are the deciding factor. Why can't Lucia just settle for white? Oh, that's right, because she is about as easy to please as a child waiting for food. No matter what you say, they complain until they get what they want. Lucia is a nice lady, I'm sure, when she's not being my client from hell.

Standing in the bathroom, foot on the side of the bath, stretching my stockings on, I sneak a glance in the mirror. I hate looking at myself. Who wants to look at their fat rolls and butt dimples. Not me! I should get rid of the mirror and then I wouldn't have to cringe every time I see it. Maybe in that penthouse I'm seeing in my future, there will be a personal trainer and chef included.

Yes! Let's put that in the picture. Need to add that to my vision board. I already have the personal driver posted up on my board—of course, he's sizzling hot. The trains and taxis got old about seven years ago. Well, maybe six years and eleven months. The first month I moved to Chicago I loved it. The hustle and bustle, such a change from the country town I grew up in. Trains running on raised platforms instead of the ground, the amount of taxis that seemed to be in the thousands compared to three that were run by the McKinnon family. Now all the extra time you lose in traffic every day is so frustrating, it's hard to make up in a busy schedule.

I slip my pencil skirt up over my hips, zip up and turn side to side. Happy with my outfit, I slide my suit jacket on, and then I do the last thing, putting on lipstick. Time to take on the world for another day. As stressful as it is and how often I will complain about things going wrong, I love my life. With a passion. Working with my best friend in our own business is the best leap of faith we took together. Leaving our childhood hometown of Williamsport, we were seeking adventure. The new beginning we both needed. It didn't quite start how I thought. Those first few months were tough. I really struggled, but I just didn't feel like I could go home anymore because the feeling of being happy there had changed thanks to my ex-boyfriend. Lucky I had Fleur to get me through that time.

Fleur and I met in preschool. She was busy setting up her toy kitchen in the classroom when I walked in. I say hers, because one of the boys tried to tell her how to arrange it and her look stopped him in his tracks. I remember thinking, he has no idea. I would set it up just how she did. It made perfect sense. I knew we were right. Well, that was what we agreed on and bonded over our PB&J sandwich. That and our OCD behavior, of being painfully pedantic. Sometimes it meant we butted heads being so similar, but not often. We have been inseparable ever since that first day.

We used to lay in the hammock in my parents' backyard while growing up. Dreaming of the adventures we were going to have together. We may as well have been sisters. Our moms always said we were joined at the hip. Which was fine until boys came into the picture. They didn't understand us wanting to spend so much time together. Of course, that changed when our hormones kicked in. Boys became important in our lives, but we never lost our closeness. We have each other's backs no matter what. Still today, she is that one person I will trust with my life is my partner in crime, my bestie.

Leaning my head on the back wall of the elevator as it descends, my mind is already running through my checklist of things I need to tackle the moment I walk into the office. That pre-event anxiety is starting to surface. It's not bad anxiety. It's the kick of adrenaline I use to get me moving. It focuses me and blocks out the rest of the world. The only thing that exists is the job I'm working on. From the moment we started up our business of planning high-end events, we have been working so hard, day and night. It feels like we haven't had time to breathe yet. The point we have been aiming for is so close we can feel it. Being shortlisted for a major contract is such a huge achievement and acknowledgement of our business. Tapping my head, I say to myself, "touch wood". So far, we've never had any disaster functions that we haven't been able to turn around to a success on the day. I put it down to the way Fleur and I work together. We have this mental connection. Not even having to talk, we know what the other is thinking and do it before the other person asks. It's just a perfect combination.

Let's hope that connection is working today.

Walking through the foyer, phone in hand, it chimes. I was in the middle of checking how close my Uber is, but the words in front of my eyes stop me dead in my tracks.

Fleur: *Tonight's guest speaker woke up vomiting – CANCELLED!!!*

"Fuck!" There is no other word needed.

I hear from behind me, "Pardon me, young lady." Shit, it's Mrs. Johnson. My old-fashioned conscience. I have no idea how she seems to pop up at the most random times. I don't even need to turn around and look at her. What confuses me is why she is in the foyer at six forty-five in the morning. When I'm eighty-two years of age, there is no way I'll be up this early.

"Sorry, Mrs. Johnson. I will drop in my dollar for the swear jar tomorrow," I mumble as I'm madly typing back to Fleur.

"See that you do, missy. Otherwise I will chase you down, and you know I'm not joking." I hear her laughing as she shuffles on her way towards the front doors. I'm sure everyone in this building is paying for her nursing home when they finally get her to move there. I don't swear that often—well, I tell myself that in my head, anyway. It just seems Mrs. Johnson manages to be around, every time I curse.

"Got to run, Mrs. Johnson. I will pop in tomorrow," I call out, heading out the front doors. Part of me feels for her. I think the swear jar is more about getting people to call in to visit her apartment. Her husband passed away six months after I moved in. He was a beautiful old man. She misses him terribly and gets quite lonely. She's been adopted by everyone in the building as our stand-in Nana whether we like it or not. Although she is still stuck in the previous century, she has a big heart and just wants to feel like she has a reason to get up every day and live her life.

My ride into work allows me to get a few emails sorted, at the same time I'm thinking on how I'm going to solve the guest speaker problem. Fleur is on the food organization for this one, and I am on everything else. It's the way we work it. Whoever is on food is rostered on for the actual event. If I can get through today, then tonight I get to relax. As much as you can relax when you are a control freak and you aren't there. We need to split the work this way, otherwise we'd never get a day or night off.

The event is for the 'End of the Cycle' program. It's a great organization that helps stop the cycle of poverty and poor education